"Emma Newman is an extraordinary new voice in SF/F."
  Paul Cornell, Hugo Award winner, and author of London
  Falling *and* Saucer Country

"Newman has created a unique blend of urban, historical,
and crime fantasy clothed in a Regency veneer."
  A Fantastical Librarian

"Emma Newman has created a reflection of Bath that
reminds one that charming is not safe. *Between Two
Thorns* shows the darkness beneath the glamour of the
social Season. Learning to be a young lady has never
seemed so dangerous."
  Mary Robinette Kowal, author of Shades of Milk and
  Honey *and* Glamour in Glass

"This novel draws you in from the very first, tempting
you with magical creatures set against present day Bath.
I tried only reading one chapter just to test the writing
style, etc but found myself, a few hours later, having
read a vast amount of the book ... It sits beautifully
within my favourite type of fantasy novel, fairy tale
within the present day."
  SF Crowsnest

"Missing people, kidnap, three wishes, charms,
deception and Grand Tours collide in a story that's
part fairytale, part fantasy, part Jane Austen, with a
sprinkling of bonkers brilliance."
  And

ALSO BY EMMA NEWMAN

The Split Worlds
Between Two Thorns
Any Other Name

Twenty Years Later
From Dark Places (*stories*)

EMMA NEWMAN

All is Fair

BOOK 3 OF
THE SPLIT WORLDS

ANGRY
ROBOT

ANGRY ROBOT
A member of the Osprey Group

Lace Market House,
54-56 High Pavement,
Nottingham,
NG1 1HW, UK

www.angryrobotbooks.com
As iron sharpens iron

An Angry Robot paperback original 2013
1

A catalogue record for this book is available
from the British Library.

ISBN: 978 0 85766 325 2
Ebook ISBN: 978 0 85766 327 6

Set in Meridien by EpubServices

Printed and bound by CPI Group (UK) Ltd, Croydon, CR0 4YY

For the one who sews as she listens

1

Fifteen hours after the Sorcerer announced it was the perfect day to take over the Agency, Max finished the preparations. He sat in the chair at the head of the table in the Agency's largest meeting room, satisfied his sweep of the area was complete. There were no indications of sorcerous magic, no residue of Fae magic picked up by the Sniffer, and the traps were laid. He looked at the gargoyle standing by the window ready to give the signal. It looked back at him, eager for something to happen in a way Max couldn't remember.

"Tell Ekstrand we're ready," he said and the gargoyle closed the curtains, counted five seconds and then opened them again.

"We wait bloody ages for him to give us something useful to do, and then he wants it all done yesterday." The gargoyle's grumble was accurate enough. Max would have preferred more time, but Ekstrand hadn't listened to his concerns.

After a few moments of peering out into the grey mists of the Nether the gargoyle said, "Acknowledged. Get the stick ready. I hope Ekstrand realises that it's his fault if this doesn't work."

Max pulled it out of the pocket of his raincoat. The rod looked like it was made of smoky quartz tipped with copper, and was covered in sorcerous formulae. As Ekstrand had instructed he twisted the top two inches forty-five degrees until the formulae glowed and then thrust it through the floorboards by his feet. It went in as easily as a pin in corkboard and disappeared out of sight, leaving only a neat round hole in the wood.

"What now?" the gargoyle asked.

"We wait."

A tremor shook the building, making the upturned glasses in the centre of the table rattle against the wood. The gargoyle gripped the stone windowsill with its claws. "He's not being subtle," it said. "Look!"

Max followed its stony gaze out the window and saw the mists turning red. Everyone else in the Agency headquarters who'd been woken by the shaking would probably take one look out of the window and–

The door banged open and a man in pyjamas burst into the room, hit the nearest chair and stumbled forwards. He recovered his balance and gripped the chair back as he looked around the room in confusion. The door closed behind him with a slam. Max recognised him as Mr Derne, the head of the Agency.

"What the bloody–" He saw Max sitting at the far side of the conference table and then the gargoyle. "Who are you? What–"

The door opened again and another man – this one pulling a dressing gown over his pyjamas – ran into the room and crashed into the first. There was a burst of swearing and exclamations when a woman and a third and fourth man arrived in the same manner.

"That's all of them," Max said to the gargoyle, which signalled with the curtains again.

The movement distracted them and the group quietened.

"What's going on?" one of the men asked.

There was the sound of shouting in the room above and someone beating on a door. The woman glanced up and then at the other men who had come into the room. She looked older than most of the puppets allowed their wives to look. It had been a while since Max had been in a room with a woman who had a few grey hairs. Max had been given the chance to carry out only a few days' surveillance, but during that time he'd heard Derne call her Matty when they were alone. Max guessed her name to be Matilda.

"We've been compromised," she said. "I ran out of my room straight into this one and I suppose you all did too. A Sorcerer has found us."

"Shit." One of the men frowned at Max. "You're an Arbiter, aren't you?"

Max nodded. "And you're the ones who run the Agency. Feel free to sit down."

None of them did. Max kept his attention on the one he'd identified as the boss. He'd recovered faster than the other men but he wasn't as calm as the woman. She was one to watch too. It wasn't clear exactly where she was in the hierarchy but she was one of the most trusted of the inner circle.

For the past week, Max had been watching three rooms, including the one they sat in, using the same scrying beetles Ekstrand had sent into the Chapter building to see what happened to those within. He would have preferred an opportunity to thoroughly brief Ekstrand before coming through but the Sorcerer had been unavailable. Petra had said it was because he was at war with the Sorcerer of Mercia, which was clearly demanding, but Max agreed with the gargoyle's appraisal: Ekstrand was actually only remotely useful one day a week. As they'd arranged outside, the gargoyle sat behind Derne to identify him for Ekstrand.

"How dare you break in?" Derne said. "How dare–"

He stopped when a burning line described a doorway in the stone wall and a Way opened out onto the Nether. Mr Ekstrand strode through, wearing his black suit, cape and top hat. As it had been when speaking with the puppet and at the Rosa party in Aquae Sulis, his face was obscured. He pointed at the group with the silver tip of his cane as the doorway returned to stone behind him. "Sit down."

They complied.

"I am the Sorcerer Guardian of Wessex and now the owner of this Agency and the information contained within its walls. Operations will continue as they always have, but I will be informed of all decisions made outside of the day-to-day running, and will veto any I disagree with."

"You will not," Derne said. "We're outside of the Heptarchy and a long way from your domain. You have no right to do this whatsoever."

Ekstrand smiled. "As you so rightly point out, you are outside of the Heptarchy and indeed outside any recognised domain. Therefore you have no protection from any third party so I can do as I please. I don't care if this upsets you and I have no interest in what you may think your rights are. You are parasites, living off the Fae's puppets, and have no moral high ground to speak of."

"And what if I refuse?"

"Mr Derne," Ekstrand sighed. "I understand that you and your employees use Fae magic here on a daily basis. I am quite certain the Fae are unaware of how you profit from this, and indeed how you profit from their own puppets without any tithe paid. It's a common courtesy you've failed to extend to them. I'm sure they would be fascinated to learn of your existence. If you have no interest in working for me then I will simply open a Way to the Royal Court in Exilium and introduce you to the King and Queen personally."

Derne opened his mouth to speak but the tallest man leaned across the table. "Better to deal with a Sorcerer than a Fae, Geoffrey."

Derne looked at Matilda who met his gaze and nodded slowly. "He's right. You need to discuss terms."

"Those are simple," Ekstrand said. "I have no interest in money so you don't have to worry about that. I just want access to all of the files on the puppets you hold here and to have any questions answered."

"For now," Derne replied.

"Yes, for now," Ekstrand nodded. "I may want more in the future but I can be certain I'll never want a share in your profits."

"It can't be that simple," the woman said.

"I've already made a slight alteration to your foundations," Ekstrand said. His words sparked an exchange of nervous glances between those sitting at the table. "I will know who goes in and out, and when. If you contact any third parties to appeal for help, I'll destroy this building and deliver you all to the Fae. So it's quite simple really."

"It could be a lot worse," the woman said to Derne.

"I could have killed you all as you slept," Ekstrand agreed. "But you'll be so much more useful alive."

Derne gave a heavy sigh. Max knew he wasn't going to argue any more but he was far from cowed. He'd expected them to be terrified and wondered why they were so ready to accept the terms. He hoped Ekstrand's "slight alterations" were enough. They needed a Chapter to keep a constant watch, not a single Arbiter and gargoyle. And there were other things that needed attention, not the least of which was the war with Mercia and the murder of most of the Sorcerers of the Heptarchy. London's corrupt Chapter was still on his mind, too.

"Now, I have a question for you," Ekstrand said. "Where are the anchors for the building?"

"You want to know why there isn't an anchor property in Mundanus," Derne replied. "It's easier to show you."

Cathy was still half asleep when the glass was brought to her lips but the pungent smell of aniseed was enough to make her groan. "What is this stuff?"

"Medicine," the nurse said. "Drink it all up now."

She obeyed, used to being given potions to ease pain and draughts to help her sleep. The ointment that had been rubbed into her hands smelt of Lord Poppy's magic and had made her retch the first time it was applied. Now the wounds in her hands left by the thorns she'd pulled from Sophia's neck were nothing more than pale red marks and they would fade over time.

She couldn't remember most of the days since the attack. She had confused memories of the mundane hospital and none whatsoever of how she got home again. Sometimes she thought she remembered Will being there but then suspected those were dreams. She knew the nurse had been using Charms to keep her sleepy – it was common practice in the Nether, when one was injured or very ill – but that morning had been the first when her head had felt clear.

Today's medicine was the most foul tasting she'd had to date and burned her throat as it went down. It made her cough, which caused the wounds in her chest to hurt, and she tried her best to stop. For a few minutes all she could do was let herself sink into the pile of pillows and catch her breath.

There was someone in the room with her; even with her eyes closed she could sense it. Hoping it was Will instead of the nurse, she opened her eyes and saw a man standing at the end of the bed. The nurse had left.

He wasn't her husband and he wasn't Fae; that was something at least. It took a moment to place him.

It was the man from the Agency she'd shocked with her determination not to be conned. "Mr Bennet?" Had he found the bug she'd planted on him for the Arbiter? But that was weeks ago.

"Mrs Reticulata-Iris," he replied, but there was something in the way he said it that made her nervous. That and the fact he was in her bedroom. A folder was tucked under his arm.

"Why… What are you doing in my room?"

"I wanted to speak with you in private."

The adrenalin was helping her now and she struggled to sit up straighter. "Surely you understand I'm not receiving visitors. If there's something urgent to discuss then talk to the Steward."

"That wouldn't be appropriate," he replied, now standing beside her. His chin was just as non-existent as before, but she didn't remember his eyes being so narrow and hate-filled.

She was dressed in only a nightgown, high enough in the neck to cover her wounds and dressings, but not substantial enough to make her feel comfortable in his presence. She pulled the sheets up higher. "Your being in this room is not appropriate. Please leave."

"Our business won't take long. A great deal has changed since we last spoke. I know all about you now."

The medicine was still burning; it felt like it was fizzing in her stomach and threatening to come back up again. "I don't know–"

He leaned over her, making her press back into the pillows. "I know about your time in Mundanus, your love affair and your betrayal of your family. I know who you called on your mobile phone before the attack, your personal bank account details and that you still keep the flat in Manchester for when you plan to escape. Everything."

Her heart was pounding so hard against her ribs Cathy feared it would open the wounds again. She tried to think of something to say, some way to wipe the sickening look from his face, but there was nothing except panic.

"I'm certain you wouldn't want Dame Iris to know of such things," Bennet said. "I know how traditional she is, and how difficult to please. A simple matter of paying me one hundred thousand of the Queen's pounds would ensure she would never know."

"You're blackmailing me?"

He smiled. "I'm proposing an exchange of money in return for a crucial service. It's not a huge amount. It is, in fact, exactly what you deducted from my original estimate of your estate costs for the year. Isn't that fortuitous? It makes it so much easier for me to explain away the amount in a revised bill and it gives you the convenience of merely having to sign this piece of paper to authorise the transfer of funds to correct an administrative error."

"If you think I'm going to—"

"I think you're going to sign, Mrs Iris," he opened the file and pulled out an invoice with an authorisation of payment. He pulled a pen from the inside of his jacket. "I think your husband's wealth makes this a trifling amount of money to pay for peace of mind and the preservation of your lifestyle. And I think the curse will stop you from telling anybody about this."

As he spoke, the burning spread up from her stomach into her chest. The medicine! He nodded and looked at the glass. "Yes. The nurse didn't know, for what it's worth. You'll never be able to seek the antidote if you can't speak or write about it and I can assure you, a generic Curse Lifter won't work against one made specifically for you. So there's only one thing to do, isn't there?"

He held out the pen and she took it, fantasising about plunging its nib into the back of his hand. She tried to promise she'd tell Will but even the act of opening her mouth to do so made her cough so hard she cried out in pain.

"Powerful, isn't it?" Bennet's smug grin made her feel murderous. "Just sign and I'll leave you to rest."

She considered bolting but she hadn't been out of bed since the attack, and she wasn't even sure she'd be able to walk out of the house. And she'd decided to stay and fight. Caving in to his demand didn't feel like the first step in her new direction. She felt weak and scared and filled with a fury she was unable to express. She couldn't even think of an insult so she clenched her teeth and signed.

He whipped the paper away into the folder and tucked it under his arm before she'd even had a chance to screw the cap back on the fountain pen.

He turned to go but paused when he reached the door. "I'll be watching you, Mrs Iris. I would think twice before you speak to anyone in Society about the way the Agency conducts its business." So he knew she'd told Margritte and Georgiana that the Agency was conning them. "I wish you a speedy recovery," he said, all fake smiles and good manners again.

I wish you a slow and terrible death, she thought, exhausted. All that remained after he left was the faint scent of aniseed and a bitter rage that burned as much as the potion.

Derne led them down the corridor. Max brought the gargoyle with them, not wanting to leave it there to chat with the Agency directors and give something away.

They passed the main entrance of the building with front doors ten feet high, made of solid oak and reinforced with iron bracers with no arcane design. There were three different locks and a reinforcing crossbar. It seemed to be designed to repel invading hordes rather than Fae or Sorcerers.

There were no paintings and the decor was functionally minimal. Stone walls, flagstone floors with a narrow carpet runner to muffle footfalls, and nothing else. Max had been inside dozens of Nether properties and was used to matching architectural features on the inside with what he knew of the anchor building. Something wasn't right about the proportions of the one he was walking through now. The windows in the main administrative room, the one in which he and the gargoyle had found the file on Miss Rainer and the rogue Rosas, had windows of Georgian proportions out of keeping with the thick medieval walls and relatively small footprint of the mundane foundations he'd found with the tracker.

The main staircase came into view, also made of stout oak. The banging and shouting from the staff trapped in their rooms echoed down the wide stairwell but less than when the building had been shaking. Max estimated there were about fifty staff that never left the building from day to day and another twenty who dealt directly with the puppets. He hadn't been able to watch all the floors, though, and there were four storeys above them which could be filled with other staff for all he knew.

Derne walked past the staircase and down the corridor of the opposite wing until he reached a heavily fortified door with a sliding panel at eye height. He knocked three times rapidly, then added a fourth knock after three seconds. The panel slid open straight away.

"Mr Derne!" A male voice on the other side of the door accompanied a pair of eyes looking through the slot. "What happened? Is everything–"

"Let me in," Derne said. "There are people with me... from outside. Switch off the secondary defences and don't attack them."

"Are you—"

"Just do it," Derne snapped.

A scraping of bolts and the tumble of several large locks filled the hallway. The door opened and Derne beckoned them through. There was a narrow staircase leading down, lit by oil lanterns at regular intervals. The guard stood in the corner, holding the door open and watching them with wide eyes as they passed.

"What are the secondary defences?" Ekstrand asked as they descended the stone steps.

Derne pointed up with his index finger without looking. "See the holes in the ceiling? Darts tipped with curare are fired out of them if a person walks down these steps in the wrong way."

"Blimey," the gargoyle whispered.

Max looked at the holes and then watched Derne more closely. He was following a pattern of placing his foot on certain parts of each step. Max put a hand on Ekstrand's shoulder to stop him. "Derne, you're still walking like the defences are active."

"Habit," Derne replied but Max sent the gargoyle ahead as a precaution. No darts were fired and he released Ekstrand's shoulder. Going down the stairs made his leg ache and he leaned more heavily on the walking stick but he eventually made it to the bottom without incident.

There was another fortified door and a similar conversation with another guard through a slot. The stone floor was less even and the walls were made of the same stones as the mundane foundations. They were in the only part of the building truly reflected in the Nether.

"Before we go in, I must ask you to be quiet. You'll need to put on a hooded cloak and move slowly." He frowned at the gargoyle. "That… thing can't come in."

"Best you stay out here and keep watch," Max said to it. He didn't want all of them to be on the other side of the doors, even though they were with Ekstrand. The Agency was using magic beyond sorcerous knowledge and there was every possibility Derne was leading them into a trap.

The gargoyle took up a position outside the door, sitting on its haunches and leaning forwards as if perched on top of a cathedral.

On the other side of the second door was a small chamber with several grey cloaks hung on a row of pegs, a table and chair for the guard, and another door, less fortified. The guard wore a holster with a semi-automatic pistol still tucked in it, something Max had never seen in the Nether. The puppets shunned modern weapons; for them anything more advanced than a flintlock was seen as uncouth. The guard held his hand a couple of inches above it.

"Don't touch that," Max said, and Ekstrand noticed the weapon.

"Or I'll extract all the water from your body," the Sorcerer added.

Whilst the threat did make the guard look nervous he didn't stand down until he had a nod from Derne. They were well trained and loyal. They had to be, for the Agency to have stayed secret for so long. Max wondered how Derne elicited such loyalty.

Derne put on one of the grey cloaks and handed another to Ekstrand. He stared at Ekstrand's top hat when the Sorcerer held it out to him and, not taking the hint, pointed at a hook on the wall. Max collected a cloak for himself and checked it inside and out before draping it around his shoulders. There was a hook-and-eye at the neck to hold it in place and a generous hood, not unlike that worn by mundane monks.

"Remember, move slowly, and once we're through that door you mustn't speak. No doubt you'll have questions. Save them for when we're back in this room."

Ekstrand gave a curt nod and all three of them put up the hoods. The third door was opened and Max saw it was thick enough to be soundproof.

They were led into a large room with a low ceiling, a space Max suspected was once the cellars – and possibly dungeons – of the former castle but with all the dividing walls removed to make one space. The air was stuffy and thick with the scent of flowers that irritated the back of Max's throat. There were thick columns of stones at intervals to bear the weight of the building above but little else Max saw made sense.

About fifty or so men and women were seated around the room, strapped into wooden chairs. They weren't straining against the bonds, rather it looked like they were being held in, as all were slumped and slack faced. The chairs were positioned in small groups around tables brightly lit from above by lanterns which left the rest of the room in shadow. On the tables were models of different parts of the building. Some featured the whole structure, others individual floors. The people strapped into the chairs were staring at the models and nothing else.

A movement drew his attention to a person on the far side of the room, dressed in the same grey robes as they'd been given, moving very slowly towards one of the men in a nearby chair. Drool was wiped from the chin of the slack-faced man who didn't seem to notice.

Ekstrand walked slowly around the room, inspecting the models and the seated people. Max saw three other people wearing robes, all tending to various needs. When he saw one lingering behind one of the chairs he too went further in and looked more closely at the nearest chair. Its high back also formed a sort of cupboard in which an IV bag was hung at the top and another bag lower down collected urine. The woman in the chair was so pale he wondered if she'd ever left the Nether since reaching adulthood.

The model on the table was a perfect replica of the exterior of the Nether building down to every detail, including slight imperfections in the individual stone blocks. Max stooped a little to try and get an idea of what the woman could see as she stared at it. When he straightened back up again he looked at the man seated opposite her. Something about his nose caught Max's eye and he seemed familiar. He was thinner, paler and his hair had been shaved off, but Max was certain it was Horatio Gallica-Rosa, the one who'd tried to pass off Lavandula's secret house as his own.

So that was what happened to the Roses.

Max had a sudden awareness of the gargoyle on the other side of the door, ready to pounce on the guard. It was time to leave. Ekstrand had seen enough too and they both headed for the door, Derne close behind the Sorcerer.

The gargoyle was staring at the guard, who was standing in front of the door and had to be pushed aside by Ekstrand. The gargoyle's teeth were bared and its head was low and shoulders high. Derne closed the door and ushered them towards the exit but the gargoyle headed for Max.

"We have to go back in there," it growled. "We have to stop this."

"Not an option," Max replied and took off the robe. "If the building collapsed or stopped existing it would kill all the people here or, at best, they'd be lost in the Nether."

A low rumbling percolated in its throat. "We can't ignore it."

"We need to go, sir," Max said to Ekstrand.

"Not yet, I have questions. Derne, those people in there, *they* are the anchors, aren't they?"

Derne nodded, his eyes darting to the gargoyle and back to the Sorcerer. "Yes. It's a form of wish magic altered for our purpose." He glanced at the gargoyle again. "They collectively wish the building into existence in the Nether, and the mundane foundations are enough to hold it in place."

"Ingenious," Ekstrand commented.

"Ingenious!" The gargoyle focused on Ekstrand. "Are you–"

"I'll take it upstairs," Max said and headed for the door. "Come on," he said to the gargoyle.

"I won't be long," Ekstrand said. "Now, tell me, how do they maintain their concentration?"

Max didn't hear the answer as he started up the stairs. The gargoyle followed him, muttering to itself all the way. When they were back in the hallway upstairs it prowled up and down as they waited for Ekstrand.

"Wait till we get back to his house," Max said when the gargoyle opened its mouth to speak. "Not here."

Max leaned against the wall. He was tired and his leg ached. His thoughts kept returning to the sight of the Gallica-Rosa in the basement. He'd only seen him briefly in the ballroom after he'd rescued the Master of Ceremonies and hadn't given any more thought to what had happened to the family other than where he could find them for interrogation.

"That code in his file must have something to do with it," the gargoyle said. "We need to ask them what it all means."

"They'll tell us now," Max replied.

"If I had a stomach I'd be throwing up," the gargoyle added. "This is–"

"Wait until we get back," Max said, and the gargoyle went back to its prowling.

Ekstrand took longer than he said he would but Max had anticipated that. He emerged from the doorway down to the basement with Derne. "That's everything for now," he said.

"Sir, there's a code in Horatio Gallica-Rosa's file," Max said. "We need to know what it means."

"Write that up, will you?" Ekstrand said to Derne. "Max will collect it soon."

Derne sucked in a deep breath through his nostrils and then nodded.

Ekstrand moved to the edge of the carpet runner and tapped on the flagstone floor with the tip of his cane. "The doors will open again in one minute. I'm leaving now but remember, I'm watching you."

"I doubt I can forget it," Derne replied.

Ekstrand opened a way into the Nether and, when they stepped through, the building was a hundred yards away. Ekstrand looked at it for a few moments and then opened a Way to the hallway of his house. The moment they were through and the Way closed behind them, the gargoyle rounded on the Sorcerer.

"So when are you going to shut the Agency down?"

"Why in the Worlds would I do that?" Ekstrand asked as he took off his hat.

"Because of the people in the basement."

"What about them?"

The gargoyle didn't answer immediately; it just stared at Ekstrand with its stone marble eyes. "You don't give a flying buttress about those poor bastards, do you?"

"Mr Ekstrand." Petra's voice cut cleanly through the gargoyle's outrage. "I've finished the last autopsy and there's something you need to know."

Max glanced at the clock. It was three in the morning and she looked exhausted. "About the Sorcerer of Essex?"

He knew Dante was the last one to be autopsied of the dead Sorcerers.

Petra nodded. "Yes, Dante. Sir, his heart was turned into stone too, just like the other Sorcerers and the people in the Bath Chapter. But Dante was different; that didn't kill him."

"I beg your pardon?" Ekstrand was now focused fully on her.

"His heart being turned to stone didn't kill him because he was already dead."

2

"This is it."

Will peered out of the taxi window at the terraced mundane house. It lacked any of the beauty and majesty of Bath's splendid architecture. He asked the driver to wait and got out. Although the prospect of enduring the terrible smell of the mundane car once again didn't appeal, it was less troublesome than having to find another in the rain. The driver nodded and parked whilst opening a packet of crisps with his teeth at the same time. That explained the beefy tang to the taxi's smell but not the odour of rotten eggs.

He walked to the gate and had a moment of doubt. Should he have brought his armed footmen? Was this a good idea at all? He frowned at the thought of being so crass. He might be Duke of Londinium now but it didn't mean he couldn't take care of a personal matter alone and in the way he saw fit.

He'd spent days at Cathy's bedside, racked with guilt about the stabbing and endlessly ruminating upon the scant information he'd been given after the attack, only to discover how much she'd been hiding from him. The man from the Agency had delivered the dossier on his wife's secret life four days earlier. It detailed a flat she rented in the dark city of Manchester – the only city in England without a single

Nether property, or so he'd been told. She'd even attended university there.

The dossier created more questions than it answered. It listed, amongst other items, the mobile phone that she'd used to call the man who saved her from the assassin. Quite how she'd struck up a relationship with a dull computer programmer from Bath wasn't forthcoming, but he had to make sure that, however it had started, it was going to stop now. He pushed the gate open.

Two of the tiles on the doorstep were cracked and there were weeds poking their way through the path. Beer cans and fast food cartons were banked against the inside of the garden wall like a snow drift made of urban decay. He pushed the doorbell, expecting nothing to happen, but it actually worked.

He waited just long enough to wonder whether anyone was in before seeing a shape move on the other side of the dappled glass in the front door. It was opened by a very mundane man, dressed in black trousers and a white shirt. He was holding a black tie in his hand and the collar of his shirt was turned up as if he were about to put the tie on. Will noted his stubble, the dark shadows beneath his eyes, the brown hair that hadn't felt a comb for a couple of days. His face was familiar but Will couldn't place where he'd seen him.

"Hello?"

"Are you Sam? Samuel Westonville?"

The mundane scratched his chin. It sounded like he was sanding wood. "Maybe. Who are you?"

"I'm Catherine's husband."

The mundane's mouth dropped open. "Oh, right. Yeah, I'm Sam. Come in. How is she?"

"Recovering," Will said, relieved that the house wasn't the hovel he expected on the inside, but the air smelt stale and there was a pile of unopened post to the side of the door. Some of the envelopes had footprints on them.

"I can offer you coffee but there's no milk. No milk that's safe to drink anyway."

"No, thank you."

Sam led him to a small living room filled with boxes. "Sorry about the mess." He tossed the tie on the arm of a chair and lifted a box off the sofa. He gestured for Will to sit down, which Will ignored.

"I won't keep you long. I wanted to know why you were in the park with my wife."

Sam scratched the back of his head and looked uncomfortable. "She… Look, there isn't anything going on between us, you do know that, don't you?"

"But why were you there when she was attacked?"

"Well, I was just passing by." He was a terrible liar.

"After she phoned you."

"Um, yeah. Look, there's nothing dodgy going on. Haven't you asked her?"

"She's barely been conscious since the attack, that's why I'm asking you."

"I met her when everyone was looking for her uncle, do you know about that? It was before she was… um, before you were married."

"Yes, I know all about that. Go on."

"She helped me get a memory back and that helped the… people looking for her uncle to find him."

Will suddenly knew where he'd seen him before. It was in the ballroom at Horatio Gallica-Rosa's failed housewarming. He was with the Sorcerer and the Arbiter. "You know the Sorcerer Guardian of Wessex?"

"Yeah, he was the one who introduced me to Cathy."

"And…"

"And… that's all," Sam said, his hand sliding down the back of his head to rub the back of his neck. "You sure you don't want a drink?"

Will wanted a glass of the best single malt at Black's, not anything that might be tucked away in a mundane's house. His jealousy about a possible affair was fading the more the mundane spoke; he was too mediocre to be a lover worthy of concern. However, the connection to the Sorcerer of Wessex was worrying. Why would Cathy maintain a friendship with this man if not to maintain a connection to the Sorcerer? And why else would she do that, other than if she was going to run away again? That was why she was in the park; that was why she still had her old flat, her bank account, her old life in Mundanus. She was still planning to go back to it. She was going to leave him.

"Why did she phone you?"

"To see if I was OK. Look, Cathy knew me and my wife were having problems–"

"You're married?"

"Was. She died."

"Oh. My condolences."

"Yeah… she was still alive when Cathy was at the park. She wanted to know if I was OK and I wasn't so she offered a friendly ear."

"So you weren't just passing by. You were at the park to meet her, in secret."

"There was nothing dodgy about it, though."

"Then why lie? Why say you were just passing?"

"Because I knew you'd think the worst, OK? Cathy wouldn't do anything with me, it's not like that between us, we're friends."

"My wife is the most important woman in Londinium." Will kept his voice calm and low. "You are nothing more than a mundane with a talent for getting yourself tangled up in things you should not. Catherine is not your friend and you will not see her again."

"Now just wait a minute." Sam's voice rose. "I saved her life! And it's not up to you to decide who is her friend or not, it's up to her."

"Perhaps I'm not making myself clear enough for your limited capabilities. Stay away from my wife."

"I don't know who the fuck you think you are, coming into my house and–"

Will felt for the scabbard of his rapier, glamoured to be invisible to mundane eyes, and drew the sword in one motion. The Charm was broken and Sam yelped at the sight of him drawing the weapon seemingly out of thin air. Will held the sword perfectly still and straight with its point pressed lightly against the mundane's throat.

"I am the Duke of Londinium, a Reticulata-Iris and the man responsible for my wife's honour. Now before you force me to be any more impolite I will leave you with a message you may better understand." He leaned forwards and increased the pressure fractionally. "Don't fuck with me or my family or I will kill you."

Margritte lifted her heavy black taffeta skirts as she ascended the staircase to her son's study. The Wesley room, made famous by one of the mundane alumnae, was one of her favourites in Lincoln College but today the memories of the times she and Bartholomew had spent there were not welcome. She had cried enough. Now it was time to do something about the crime committed against her family.

She knocked on the door and entered when called. Her eldest son was sitting on one of the leather armchairs in the centre of the room, reading. The walls were covered in dark wood panelling, exquisitely carved, the room lit by the sprites trapped in glass globes at intervals along the walls. She couldn't stop herself looking at the stone fireplace and the small marble bust on it. She remembered Bartholomew showing it to her for the first time and how they had kissed in front of it.

"I'll be with you in a moment, Mother," Alexander said.

She forced herself to breathe again after looking over at him. From behind, he looked too much like his father: his hair just the same shade of dark brown, tied back with the same small black ribbon her husband favoured. She clutched at the locket hanging over her bodice, thought of the lock of her husband's hair within and marvelled at how yet more tears were ready to come.

"I do apologise," Alexander said, positioning his bookmark carefully before getting up to come to her. "Did you manage to sleep any better?"

"Not really," she said and they kissed each other's cheeks three times in the Dutch fashion. She doubted she would ever sleep well again. How could she lie in bed alone and drift off after spending over two hundred years of nights with the man she loved curled around her? She'd have to visit the Shopkeeper soon and buy a Charm to give her some rest.

"Are you happy with your room? It's one of the best in the college. Or would you prefer another? I'm sure it can be arranged." When she didn't reply immediately he twisted one of his cufflinks. "Or do you plan to go back to Hampton Court? Father provided most generously for you in the will. You don't need to worry about a thing. I'm more than happy for you to live at Hampton even though I own it now. For as long as you wish, I have no desire to–"

"Alexander." She held up her hand and seated herself opposite him. "Darling, that's not what I want to discuss. We need to talk about the Londinium throne."

He leaned back in the chair, laced his fingers in front of him. "Is there anything to talk about?"

"Yes! We can't just ignore what happened. Your father was accused, judged, murdered and now remembered for a crime he didn't commit."

He squirmed, looking away. "I know."

"And it isn't just the fact that the throne was taken from him in such an offensive way, it's the fact that it was an Iris who took it. They destroyed our influence on the mundane royal line and then, when we finally achieve our rightful place in Society, they take power from us again."

"Father always said we needed to put that behind us."

"Your father didn't know the depths the Irises would sink to."

"But he did know what it did to my grandfather," Alexander replied, now looking at her. "He said feuds between families did nothing but tear people apart as well as Society. He knew that better than anyone."

Margritte sighed, remembering the last time she'd seen her father-in-law. He was a broken man, drunk and mostly mad, hidden away by the family before he drank himself to death. Once the Earl of Oxford, one of Queen Anne's most important politicians, destroyed along with her and her reign by the Iris curse. "Your father was a sensitive, noble and patient man. He waited over a hundred years for his time to come and then it was stolen from him in moments. Can you rest knowing your father was murdered by an Iris – nothing more than an arrogant child with his patron pulling the strings?"

Alexander took a breath to say something, reconsidered and instead reached across to pull the cord next to the fire twice. "I remember when I used to get upset about things, Father always used to remind me to look at the bigger picture."

Margritte controlled a flash of rage. "I'm not a child, Alexander."

"But there *is* a bigger picture to consider. You're speaking as though you want to take revenge–"

"Not revenge, I want to take back the throne that was stolen from your father."

"Regardless," Alexander said, "that's tantamount to war. Is that what you want?"

"I didn't march into the Court accusing a decent man of terrible things! I didn't murder him and steal his Dukedom! I didn't ask for this war but if that's what it takes to restore to us what is rightfully ours – and has been for hundreds of years – then so be it!"

Alexander paled. "Mother, you're grieving, you're not–"

"You are avoiding facing up to your responsibility."

"Which is?"

"To help me clear your father's name and take back the Dukedom."

"You want me to be Duke?"

"It's your birthright."

There was a knock at the door and Alexander called in the butler, who had tea, sandwiches and cakes ready to serve. Margritte seethed as the tea was poured. Her son had been left in his ivory tower too long.

Once the butler had left and he'd taken a rather audible gulp of tea, Alexander said, "Mother, I'm no Duke, I'm a professor and the Vice-Chancellor of Oxenford! I can't just abandon my responsibilities here. And I'm sorry, but I can't share your opinion on the way to proceed. Starting a war with the Irises would be… foolish."

"You think I'm a grief-stricken fool?"

"I think you're making decisions whilst traumatised. I couldn't possibly sanction a war with the Irises; there are many who live in Oxenford. They hold three colleges here, and, after the terrible disruption to the university caused by the fall of the Roses, I couldn't possibly see how a war would be supported by my peers or the Chancellor."

"Damn the Chancellor! He isn't one of us!"

"Mother–" Alexander made no effort to hide how appalled he was "–I cannot risk the stability of Oxenford just because you cannot manage your grief."

She stood up so quickly she knocked the tea cup onto the floor. "How dare you dismiss my loyalty to our family as a weak woman's grief. I suggest you think very carefully about where your loyalties lie."

"Where are you going?" he asked as she turned her back on him and stepped over the broken porcelain.

"To speak to the Patroon. I'm curious to see whether he thinks our family's honour is less important than the comfort of a Sorcerer and his pet academics."

3

Sam looked at the people filling the crematorium's chapel. He didn't recognise most of them. Some of the women were crying, all dressed in the same kind of corporate gear Leanne used to wear, only black. Their grieving made him aware of his own hollow detachment. He felt nothing except the sharp awareness of the man who'd killed her sitting three rows behind him. Bastard.

"I would like to speak at the funeral," Neugent had said in a letter redirected from his house in Bath to Lord Iron's vast estate in Lancashire. "I worked very closely with Leanne for several years and had the utmost respect and admiration for her."

Sam had burnt the letter and stood at the window, looking out over landscaped gardens, wondering what the fuck was happening to his life. Lord Iron had dined with him the night he arrived; they'd talked about Leanne mostly, then he'd been called away on business. "Stay, relax, grieve," Iron said as he shook his hand. "Treat this as your own house. The staff will provide everything you need. I'll be back for the funeral."

He'd watched the limousine crawl down the drive, listened to the crackle of the gravel beneath its tyres and thought of the last time he saw his wife. It was all he seemed capable of thinking about.

The funeral had been delayed by the recovery from his own injuries and by the autopsy, which gave a simple (and incorrect) conclusion: natural causes. A blood vessel had burst in her brain and then she dropped dead. The report detailed that she was slightly underweight but otherwise in good health.

Several nights in a row he dreamt of her on the underground platform. In one dream they held hands waiting for the train together. He'd woken up crying but soon sank back into the numbness that endured throughout the funeral arrangements. He'd left most of the details to her parents. His mother-in-law seemed to think the choice of flowers was far more important than he ever could. Her parents didn't seem to know about the separation, and, from the way most of the people there were looking at him, he didn't think they did either. At least she'd been discreet about it. But that was Leanne: professional to the last. She wouldn't have taken all her problems to work with her. She just left them behind in Bath.

He took care not to look at Neugent and faced forwards again, unable to stop his gaze drifting towards the coffin. Sam could still feel the pressure of it on his shoulder. He wondered if his skin would ever forget the feeling of carrying his dead wife in a heavy box. He tried to imagine her body lying inside it, cut and stitched up again. He could just as easily imagine it filled with sand or with dozens of dolls or old mobile phones. Each set of imagined contents became more fantastical; all lacked any emotional impact.

The worry that Lord Poppy would do something to wreck it all or pull him away plagued him, but he hadn't heard from him or the faerie since he delivered Cathy's painting. Perhaps Poppy had forgotten about him.

"She was so young," his mother-in-law said.

She was sat next to him and Leanne's father was sitting on the other side with an arm around her. He too was staring at the coffin. Sam realised it was the longest time he'd actually sat with Leanne's parents. He'd barely made an impression in their life. His parents were in Australia. They'd offered to come but he told them not to worry about it. They'd never liked Leanne. It would have been awkward. His mum would only have baked two dozen cakes and urged him to talk about his feelings every five minutes. He didn't have the stomach for either, nor for the way his father would have wittered on about his stamp collection to anyone he could corner.

Leanne's mother glanced at him, perhaps waiting for a response to her comment but Sam said nothing. There were no words in him.

They shared the front row with the pallbearers. Aside from him and her father they were made up of cousins and uncles, some of whom he'd never met. They weren't a close family and many of them hadn't even been to the wedding. He was sitting in a room full of strangers at his wife's funeral. As he tried to look anywhere but at the coffin he caught glimpses of people trying to point him out discreetly during whispered conversations. It made him feel like an exhibit at some grotesque circus.

The man from the crematorium started the ceremony. It was non-religious, according to Leanne's wishes, and bland. He finally stopped worrying that Poppy would find some way to interfere with it.

Then it was his turn to speak. The paper was crumpled and soft in his hand. He couldn't even remember what he'd written on it. Sam walked up to the podium, decorated with flowers lovingly chosen by another woman he didn't really know, and looked out over the congregation. Lord Iron was sitting at the back, looking straight at him. He inclined his head towards Sam. What do you want with me? Sam pushed the thought aside and looked down at the paper.

"Thank you for coming," he started. His voice was too quiet and he leaned closer to the microphone. "I'm Sam, Leanne's husband. I don't know many of you, I'm assuming you know Leanne from work. She was... very dedicated and ambitious. In many ways you could say she was the exact opposite to me." His awkward smile was reflected back at him from dozens of faces. "It didn't used to be that way. In university we were... happy." He felt a crackle in his voice and looked back down at the piece of paper but it was covered in gibberish. "Something changed. I suppose that's what happens, I think Leanne was better at growing up than I was. She became something... amazing, she had so much energy and she was fearless." People were nodding now. People who knew her better than he did. "I can't help but feel stupid when I think about her. I thought we'd have longer together, but people always do, don't they? We're all on a clock. We're all going to die. That's why we're all here – not just because of Leanne but because we know it's going to happen to us and we're scared and we want to be with other people who are scared too. Leanne should be here and I should be in that box. That's the way I see it. She had more to give."

His throat felt like it was closing up and his head began to throb. He crushed the piece of paper in his fist and left the podium. For a moment he almost left the chapel, but his mother-in-law was reaching a hand towards him, all tears and neediness. Even though it repelled him, he went to sit next to her and embraced her as Leanne's father went up to speak.

Sam didn't hear a single word he said.

••••

A knock on the door woke Cathy from dreams of the butler, Morgan, speaking to her about afternoon tea with Bennet's voice and pouring the poisonous liquid curse from the teapot. As the nurse opened the door she glanced to her bedside and saw the glass was gone, along with any outward traces of what Bennet had done. Had she dreamt it?

Will walked in and the nurse curtsied. His cheeks were pink and there were tiny drops of water caught in his hair. He smiled at her and she returned it. The Charm-addled dreams about him hadn't focused on how handsome he was. Seeing him fresh-faced and happy brought back other memories too, ones that made her heart thrum.

"My love," he said and came over to kiss her, sending the nurse scuttling into a corner to busy herself. "How are you feeling?"

"Ready to get up," she said firmly. "Have you been out riding?"

There was a moment of confusion and then he touched his hair. "Oh, yes… it's raining in Mundanus. Are you sure you're ready? It's only been three weeks."

"Nearly a month," Cathy said and pulled the covers back. "Honestly, Will, if I spend another day in here I'll go mad. I was thinking an hour or two in Mundanus would do me the world of good." She didn't want to go back to the park, but she did want to see greenery again and hear birds singing and feel fresh air on her face.

"The weather is terrible."

"And Her Grace isn't ready to leave her bed yet, if you'll forgive me for intruding," the nurse said.

Cathy frowned at her. "Her Grace"? What an odd thing to call her.

"If Cathy feels she's ready then I respect that," Will said and the nurse retreated. Cathy squeezed his hands, happy to have an ally. "I have a surprise for you." His eyes were even more beautiful when he was excited.

He helped her out of the bed which made her feel awkward and feeble. It was strange to have to think so much about moving, as if her body had got rusty inside and she had to remind it of how it used to move. As much as she didn't want to admit it, the attack had really taken it out of her. Her legs felt so heavy and when she stood the room tilted before Will wrapped an arm about her shoulders. "Are you sure you're ready to go downstairs?"

"Yes, I'm so sick of this room. How's Sophia?"

"She's fine. She's with Uncle Vincent."

The nurse helped her into a robe and slippers and Cathy shuffled out of the room, Will holding her as they walked. She remembered how gentle he was after Lord Iris had cut her wrist and the night they finally consummated the marriage. They'd hardly been together since then and she felt awkward and uncertain of herself. She could remember resolving to stay away from him once her lust had got the better of her, for fear of getting pregnant and making escape more difficult. But now that she was going to stay in the Nether and fight the system, did she still need to do that? Could he become an ally too?

The possibility of falling for her own husband was not something Cathy had anticipated and it made her nervous. She had to stay focused on what she was going to do to make Society change, and the last thing she needed was to be all lovestruck, let alone pregnant. So what if he was handsome and clever and kind? If she fell into the trap of being in love with him she'd never be able to carve out a better life for herself or anyone else.

"You're looking much better," he said as they made their way to the stairs. "The very best care was provided, both in

Mundanus and by the Agency. I'm told there won't be any long-term problems."

"It was bad, wasn't it?"

He paused to kiss her cheek again. "You almost died. If it hadn't been for the mundane doctors you wouldn't be with me now."

"Are you all right?" she asked and he smiled.

"Just glad we got through this."

She leaned against him as they walked, and felt exhausted by the time they reached the top of the stairs. She didn't say anything about Bennet for fear she'd cough and be packed off to bed again. Halfway down she noticed footfalls behind her that seemed too heavy to be the nurse. She glanced back and saw an unfamiliar man following them down a couple of paces behind. His blond hair was cropped short in a modern, mundane style, his eyes were a dull blue and his neat nose looked too small for his face.

"Who's that?"

"Someone to keep you safe."

"What, like a bodyguard?"

"Yes."

"Is that necessary?"

"Yes."

"So that man who stabbed me, he's still out there?"

"No... he's dead."

She wondered how he'd died. Did Sam do something? She jolted. Sam! Had he been hurt too? She couldn't ask Will, otherwise he'd know they'd met and it wasn't something easily explained away. The sense of the world spinning whilst she'd been tucked up in bed was becoming frightening. What else had happened? "But if he's dead–"

"You're still at risk."

"But the man attacked Sophia, it might be her they were after. I don't need a–"

"Catherine, this is not up for debate." They reached the bottom of the stairs. "I didn't protect you before, I'm not making that mistake again. There's no way Sophia was the target – no one else knows what she means to me." He stroked her cheek tenderly. "But they know how much you do."

Cathy tried hard not to lose her thoughts to the messy soup of emotions his tenderness elicited. There was no way he could love her, he was just trying to be a good husband. She was too tired to argue about the bodyguard; that would have to wait.

"Now, I don't want you to worry about a thing." Will helped her to walk again. "I've been working on something whilst you've been recovering and I think it will make you feel much better."

He guided her down the hallway, past his study and the red drawing room, to the chamber they'd originally allocated as a smaller dining room for intimate dinners. He pulled a key threaded onto a blue silk ribbon out of his pocket and unlocked the door. "This is yours," he said, placing it in the palm of her hand. "Close your eyes." She did so and he opened the door. He guided her a few steps in, instructed the bodyguard to stay outside and then closed the door. "You can look now."

The room had been transformed into a library. She turned in a full circle, taking in the shelves of books. There was a pair of high-backed leather chairs and footstools, one either side of the fireplace, each with a small table next to it. A cheval mirror stood in the corner, covered in blue silk and facing one of the bookshelves rather than into the room. She looked down at the key and then at Will. "You made a library for me?" She felt a rush of blood to her cheeks and chest. It was the thing she had wanted most as a child and the desire had never left her.

"It's yours. No one else may enter without your explicit permission."

One of the book spines caught her eye. "Hang on," she said, moving closer. "That's a Ray Bradbury and that's…" She fell silent as she scanned the shelves. "It's all science-fiction!"

"Every science-fiction novel ever published, to my knowledge. Or rather that of the expert I hired to curate the collection. Where possible I bought first editions. Some are quite rare, I'm given to understand."

"But that would be thousands of books." Cathy scanned the shelves. There wasn't enough room.

Will pulled the silk off the mirror with a dramatic flourish. "Come and look at this." He waved her over to the mirror. "Stand there."

He moved aside and pointed to a spot in front of it. Cathy looked at the mirror, expecting to see her reflection but instead she saw a bookcase stretching into a point in the distance. Confused, she reached forwards and her hand passed through where the glass should have been, her fingertips brushing against the spine of one of the books.

"The rest of the books are in there," Will said. "You can step through and walk around it like any other room. It's a simple matter to add more shelves. I wanted to keep this room cosy." He covered the mirror with the silk again.

Cathy stared at the shelves next to her. "I can't believe it."

"Do you like it?"

"Like it?" She laughed and embraced him, not caring about the twinges of pain it caused. They kissed and she felt the warmth of his hands through the robe on her back. "It's perfect," she finally said.

"I had two chairs brought in – I hope you don't mind. I was hoping you could educate me." She searched for sarcasm in his expression but there was none she could detect. "It seems only right that I devote some time to the things you're passionate about. This seemed a good place to start."

"Are you serious?"

"Absolutely. I told you it would be different from your life before. You can read whatever you like here and I won't ever tell you otherwise."

She wondered if he'd feel the same about some of the sociopolitical books on her shelves in Manchester. As the surprise and elation subsided the old fears emerged like rocks at low tide. Was it a genuine gesture of kindness, or had Will simply made the perfect birdcage for her? She didn't know whether to be suspicious or joyful that he seemed to understand her better than any man in the Nether ever had.

She gave a hesitant smile. "We have a lot to talk about, don't we?"

He nodded. "I'll ring for tea and have the fire lit. Come and see how comfortable these chairs are."

It felt good to rest. Her legs were trembling like she'd run a marathon, not just got out of bed and gone down one flight of stairs. One of the maids came and lit the fire and Cathy wondered what Miss Rainer was doing. Every time she thought of her former governess she felt sick. She couldn't abandon the most important person in her childhood to the life of a scullery maid. Then she wondered how the maid lighting the fire had come to work for the Agency. She'd been surrounded by servants practically all of her life and never once thought to ask.

Weeks of lying in bed had left her feeling disjointed and disoriented. Now she'd decided to stop running away and actually do something, she needed a plan, and allies. She needed to decide what to tell Will and how to bring it up in conversation with Margritte. Cathy was certain she and Bartholomew were progressive enough to discuss the need for change in Society. Bartholomew must have become Duke whilst she was recovering and they would be the most influential couple in Londinium. They could help her set trends and change minds. She breathed as deeply as she could. Everything was going to change now.

Morgan brought tea and gave a warm smile when he saw her. Once he'd poured the tea and left, Will sat in the chair opposite her.

"I feel terrible about what happened," he said. "I was warned. I should have protected you and Sophia."

"Who warned you?"

"Cornelius. He said Tulipa would do anything to take the throne. He was right."

"Bartholomew?" Cathy shook her head. "That doesn't sound right. You didn't accuse him, did you?"

The cup stopped halfway to Will's lips before being set back down on the saucer. He closed his eyes for a moment, the pink fading from his cheeks. "I challenged him to a duel. I killed him. And I took the throne from him."

Cathy missed the saucer as she let the cup drop and a little tea spilled onto her robe. "What?"

"I'm the Duke of Londinium. You're the Duchess, Cathy, just as Lord Iris wanted. You don't remember me telling you about that?"

"No. It's the bloody sleeping Charms… they…" She looked at him, trying to imagine him killing Bartholomew, but it had the quality of a silly film in her mind, something utterly unbelievable. Could the same man who was so kind to her, so gentle when she was in distress, be capable of killing their friend? It was as horrifying as it was frightening.

"Don't look at me like that! He sent a man to murder you."

"But that was a Rosa. There were thorns, Will, I thought I told you." She was worried she'd dreamt that.

"You did tell me, and the man *was* a Rosa, but Bartholomew sent him to kill you."

"That's ridiculous."

"That's the truth! Lord Iris and Lord Poppy supported me, I took the throne, it's done now."

Cathy focused on her tea cup, unable to look at him. How could this have happened? Bartholomew was a cultured, reasonable man. There was no way he would have done such a thing. How could Will have made such a mistake? Or was it that he wanted an easy excuse to murder the man between him and the throne? Lord Iris was terrifying; had he driven Will to such desperate measures? She swallowed the lump in her throat. She didn't want to show Will how upset she was. "What about Margritte? Has she stayed in Londinium?"

"I have no idea. I haven't convened a Court. I wanted everything to calm down. I didn't want to sit as the Duke until you were well enough to be sworn in as Duchess."

"Oh, bollocks." Cathy squeezed her eyes shut. "I'm Duchess. I really didn't think that would happen." How in the Worlds would she cope with the Court? She'd planned to persuade the Duchess of Londinium to help her change things, not *be* her! How would she be able to use the position to influence behaviour and engender social change when she couldn't even function in public?

"I'll help you. I know it's a shock. It wasn't ideal, but it was a legitimate way to take the throne."

He seemed too calm. "A legitimate… Don't you feel bad about it?"

"Of course I do! He was the first man I killed. It wasn't… I had to keep reminding myself what he did. Besides, once I was committed, there was nothing else to be done."

"Did he admit guilt?"

He looked into the fire. "No. He said he was innocent, right up to the end."

"This is awful," she whispered. "What will Margritte do now? Will her family look after her?"

"I don't know."

"The house she lived in was Bartholomew's... she'll have nothing now, unless he left it to her, I suppose. My God. I can't believe this has happened. I liked Bartholomew, I could actually have a conversation with him. And Margritte. There's no way he would have paid someone to kill me. You must have got it wrong."

"It's done now!" Will hit the arm of the chair, the anger bursting out as if she had lanced an emotional boil. "We have to move on."

An awkward silence filled the space between them. She looked at the books but the joy the library had brought her seemed such a frivolity in light of Margritte's loss. As soon as she was able to leave the house she had to find her and make sure she was provided for, although Margritte would probably hate her now.

Will set his cup down and leaned across the gap between them. "I can't do this without you, Cathy."

It was clear he didn't want to talk about the Tulipas any more and Cathy realised she had to focus on moving forwards too. Nothing was going to bring Bartholomew back and somehow she had to live with what had happened. "I'm here," she said. If she was going to stay in the Nether she needed him too. She had no idea what she was going to do about Miss Rainer and the Agency or even where to start when it came to the patriarchal hell of Society, but she did know that Will would be the best ally she could get. And despite her doubts and the shock of what he was evidently capable of, she didn't want him to struggle alone. She knew what that was like.

"There's something I wanted to discuss with you," Will began hesitantly. "I have to choose the next Marquis of Westminster. The current one has too much history with the Rosas."

Cathy dredged up one of the tedious lessons from Dame Iris on the structure of the Londinium Court. The position of Marquis was the second most powerful in the domain and was a critical component of the Duke's rule. The Marquis was supposed to keep an eye on threats from outside of the domain and keep the Duke informed as well as help defend against them. Of course, in practice most of those threats came from within the Court itself.

"You need someone loyal," Cathy said. "Someone who isn't going to use the position to undermine you."

"Quite," Will replied. "As you can imagine, there are few men I trust absolutely in Londinium." He poured them a second cup of tea. "Actually, there's an added complication. Cornelius gave me a lot of help when we first moved here, explaining who was who and how the social wheels spun here. I did tell him that if he helped me take the throne, I'd make him Marquis."

"But he doesn't have any status in Society," Cathy said. "He doesn't have any wealth of his own any more, I assume?" He shook his head. "Then you'll have to tell him the deal's off."

"I don't like breaking promises."

"Hang on, you said you took the throne from Bartholomew… he was already Duke?"

Will nodded. "I found out what he did and I went into Exilium to appeal to Lord Iris and Poppy was there too. Our patron returned me after two weeks had passed here. Bartholomew had just become Duke."

Cathy realised how truly absent she'd been since the attack. "Why did Iris do that?" she wondered out loud. "Why deny you the chance to win the throne… normally?"

Will's eyes were dark. "I've wondered that myself," he said in a low voice.

Cathy didn't want to dwell on talk of Iris and his schemes for them; it might remind Will of the pressure to have a child and she couldn't face that as well as everything else. "Well, you could argue that Cornelius didn't help you take the throne, if he makes a fuss. I'm sure he'll understand the plan has had to change. The Rosas weren't popular here and if you put a disgraced one into the position of Marquis you'll only be making it harder for yourself."

He smiled. "Listen to yourself."

"Yeah, what do I know? Do what you want to do."

"No, you misunderstand. You're giving me good advice. Like a Duchess."

"Woot," Cathy said flatly.

Will stared at her for what seemed a horribly long time. "There's something else we need to talk about." His tone was serious. "When you were–" He gripped the arm of the chair and turned a pale shade of green.

"Are you all right?" Cathy took his cup from him as he clutched his stomach.

"I'm being summoned," he said. "I have to go."

"We'll talk when you get back," Cathy said and he left her to sit amongst the books she had always wanted but was afraid to accept.

4

Max had just stretched out on the bed, found a position that alleviated the ache in his leg and closed his eyes when he felt the gargoyle's stare from the corner of his room. "Go on, ask."

"What?"

"You've been wanting to ask me something all day," Max replied.

"Why aren't we doing anything?"

"I haven't had any orders from Ekstrand."

The gargoyle clicked its stone claws on the floorboards. "We were stuck here for three weeks before he pulled his finger out and took the Agency. It might be another three months before he decides what he wants us to do next."

"And do you know what we should be doing?"

"Yes. We need to go back to London. Now Dante is dead we don't have to worry about putting his nose out of joint."

"Mr Ekstrand doesn't think it's a priority, otherwise he would have sent us. We don't know what Petra's finding even means. The Fae aren't in the habit of animating the dead. He needs time to think the implications through."

"Oh, right. I see. Sorry, it must be the stone between my ears but I thought it would be a priority to look into the corrupt Chapter that tried to kill us and let one of the bloody Fae try to murder someone in broad daylight. Stupid me."

"I haven't forgotten."

"Oh, so you just can't be arsed to go and find out what went wrong there?"

"We can't just leave."

"We so can. Ekstrand is more than a few elements short of a periodic table, he wouldn't even notice we were gone. The news about Dante is worrying, granted, but it's just another reason to look into London. If the Sorcerer of Essex was dead before the moot, who was in charge when we were shot? Is that person still there? Is he the root of the corruption? And we need to know that what happened to the Chapter hasn't happened anywhere else, or the Fae will be titting about with the innocents faster than you can say, 'Look at the pretty sparkles'. And we should find out if Cathy recovered from that attack."

"Why? We don't need her any more. We found Thorn, we know the Sorcerer of Mercia is behind everything, we're now at war. That puppet can be left to live her life as she sees fit."

The gargoyle's frustration rumbled out of its throat. "Thorn tried to kill her. Don't you care? Actually, scratch that, of course you don't. But *we* do, really, deep down."

"No, I don't," Max said.

"But she needs Ekstrand's help to escape Society. She's been clear about that all along. And we need to do that before her husband–"

"Her husband," Max interrupted, "is the Duke of Londinium now. Mr Ekstrand is never going to risk helping her escape from Lord Iris' control now she's Duchess."

"What difference does being Duchess make? She'll still want out."

"She'll be in the public eye more than ever now. You should forget about her and focus on what we need to do to stop Mercia."

"We are not going to forget her," the gargoyle replied, its stone chin jutting out.

Max turned onto his side, signalling that he'd prefer to sleep.

The gargoyle sat there sulking, then bounded across the room to Max's bedside. "We can't stay here waiting for a madman to tell us what to do next. We need to remember what we're supposed to do." It grabbed Max's arm. "It's not just following orders."

Max gripped the sheets as the rush of frustration assaulted him. His heart banged as he struggled to manage the urge to leave the house immediately and get his investigation back on track.

"Sometimes knowing how you feel is a good thing," the gargoyle whispered.

Max shrugged off the gargoyle's paw and sat up on the edge of the bed as his head cleared. The gargoyle was right; he did need to go back to London, it had been left hanging unresolved for too long now. Even though the puppet wasn't an innocent, the brazen attack was too much to ignore. "I'll ask Ekstrand for permission to pursue the London investigation again."

"No, let's just go. It's Sunday, he's shit on Sundays – he's scared of everything. On Mondays he only wants to talk about stupid stuff and eat cucumber sandwiches with Petra. Let's face it, it's going to be a week before he's even remotely decisive again and who knows what could have happened by then?"

"We can't just go without telling him."

"Yes, we can. He won't even notice. And when we report back we'll tell him he sent us in the first place. He won't remember."

Max couldn't argue with that. "We'll go and see Cathy," he said, getting onto his feet.

The gargoyle's stone features rearranged themselves into something approximating an agonised grim-ace, but Max knew it was supposed to be a smile. "Great!"

"She could still be useful to us."

"Wow, for a moment there I thought you might have actually wanted to know how she was."

"I want to know if she's well enough to help me. She's the only person we have in London, and if we're going to investigate corruption, who better to help than one of the puppets they're supposed to police?"

As if he'd been sleepwalking and had suddenly woken up, Sam found himself standing next to a table laden with a buffet, a plate in one hand and a glass of wine in the other. The room was filled with the strangers who'd been at the funeral. He watched them talking to each other and listened to the guilty pauses after they laughed.

Leanne's parents were doing what they always did: her mother was fussing over the food – even though it was all being handled by caterers – and her father was getting pissed in the corner furthest away from his wife. The room, as well as the caterers, was being paid for by Lord Iron. Sam hadn't minded; it was better than having the wake at the house.

Iron was standing next to a large bay window and Neugent was in close conference with him, appearing very earnest as Iron listened carefully. At a distance it was Neugent who looked older with his white hair and pale skin. Iron's black hair and deep brown skin made him look youthful and healthy in comparison.

Sam stared at the back of Neugent's head. How had he killed Leanne, and all the other people who worked for him? Was there any way to prove it?

He wanted to kill him.

"Sam?" A man he'd never met before held out a hand. "I'm Geoff, I worked with Leanne before she went up to the London office."

Sam dumped the plate of food on the nearest table and they shook hands. "Hello."

"I just wanted to say how sorry I am for your loss. Leanne was an amazing person."

"Yeah."

"She'll be missed."

"Yeah."

Geoff necked the rest of the wine in his glass when the conversation ran dry. Sam didn't want to talk to him – he didn't want to talk any of them – and Geoff had nothing else to say. Geoff wiggled the glass and said, "It was nice to meet you," before hurrying away to get a refill.

Sam abandoned the wine next to his plate of unwanted food and left the room. His shoes clipped on the polished marble floor. He wished he smoked so he could legitimately stand outside and take deep breaths without anyone bothering him. He didn't want anyone to give him sympathetic or pitying looks for a moment longer. He didn't want anyone to see him at all.

"Sam." Iron called his name from a doorway off the corridor just behind him.

Sam turned slowly. Was he supposed to thank him for the ostentatious arrangements?

"You can hide in here if you want."

Sam didn't need any further encouragement. The room was mostly filled by a large table, probably used for meetings. "Did you hire several rooms?" Sam asked.

"I own the hotel."

"Oh. I didn't realise that."

"It's part of a chain the company owns. You looked like you needed a break."

Sam nodded and closed the door behind him as one of Iron's security guys walked past to take a position nearby. "I'm not handling this very well."

"Nonsense. There's no need to perform for their benefit. You're free to feel what you like and do what you like."

"If only that were true." Sam flopped into one of the leather chairs and let it tip back as he stretched his legs out.

"What would you really like to do?"

"Oh, I dunno. Killing Marcus Neugent with my bare hands would be top of my list."

Iron stood near the door and said nothing for a few moments. "I think you need some time alone."

When he left, Sam let his arms drop until his fingertips brushed the floor. He shouldn't have said that about Neugent, one of Iron's employees. He imagined standing in court on trial for Neugent's murder and Iron reporting what he'd said. Sam tutted at himself. "Pillock," he whispered.

It wasn't long before there was a knock on the door. Thinking it was a member of staff, or Iron, Sam called out, "Come in."

Marcus Neugent entered and closed the door behind him. Sam sat up. Every muscle he'd just relaxed snapped taut again.

"I wanted to speak to you. I hope you don't mind."

Sam watched him sit at one of the chairs on the other side of the table. "Look, I know you wanted to speak at the funeral but it just didn't feel right."

"That's not what I wanted to talk about. And I understand. It was a family thing. I shouldn't have asked."

Sam rested his elbows on the table. "So what do you want?"

"I know you resented how much of Leanne's time was taken up with her work."

Sam kept silent. He didn't know where Neugent was going with this and he needed to stay calm.

"I wanted to explain that it wasn't anyone's fault. She was very dedicated... I didn't deliberately pull her away from home to work long hours."

"Oh, so you're saying her home life was so shit she didn't need any encouragement."

"No, not at all. I'm trying to help you realise that she loved her job and there's no reason to be angry about that."

"I'm not angry about that. I'm angry with you!"

Neugent's white eyebrows arched in surprise. "Why?"

Sam wanted to say, "Because you killed her, you fuck," but he couldn't quite get the words out. He needed proof. Even just some evidence rather than just a pattern. "Because you were always phoning up and making her work late."

"That's the nature of our line of work. I know you resented it, and now she's gone it'll be even harder."

"What do you want me to say? Thanks for ruining our marriage?"

Neugent's frown had an edge of pity to it. "No. I wanted to give you my condolences in person, without everyone watching, and I wanted to see if you're all right. I think that might have been a mistake. I'll leave you in peace."

When he stood Sam jumped to his feet. "Wait," he said without even knowing why. He reached across the table, offering his hand.

After a pause Neugent shook hands with him. Sam had an impulse to pull him off his feet and smash his head into the table but then he noticed how grey Neugent's skin was and another thought rose to the surface as he gripped his hand tighter: he's dying.

Sam had no idea how he knew this – or what he was dying of – but there was an unshakeable certainty. Neugent felt wrong in some way. He studied Neugent's skin, his eyes and the clammy palm and then another thought surfaced: he has leukaemia. But how could he know that?

Neugent was trying to break the handshake; it had lasted far longer than implicit social rules allowed. Sam released his hand, embarrassed and unsettled. "I'm sorry," he said. "You're really ill, aren't you?"

It was the first time Sam saw Neugent look anything other than composed. His mouth hung open for a second or two and he took a step back. "You should be careful around Mr Ferran."

"Mr Ferran? Oh, you mean Lord Iron."

Neugent's eyes became saucer-like. "I'm serious. Don't–"

The door opened and Iron walked in. "Oh, I'm sorry, I didn't realise you were in here, Marcus. Is everything all right?"

Neugent's face became a mask of polite confidence. "Yes, I was just giving Mr Westonville my condolences. If you'll excuse me." He gave Sam one last look and left.

"Are you all right?" Iron asked once the door had shut. Sam nodded but he didn't feel it. "Still want to kill him?"

"No," Sam replied. The acidic desire to murder him had been diminished by the knowledge that Neugent wouldn't see the year's end. There were a hundred questions he wanted to ask Iron but he needed to feel steadier before he did so. "I'm going home. I've had enough. I need to get in touch with people and... tie up loose ends."

Iron nodded. "When you're done, call me and I'll send a car. There are things we need to talk about, but now isn't the time."

Sam searched Iron's face. "Why are you doing this? Why are you so interested in me and my life? Leanne was your employee, not me."

Iron came over and rested a hand on his shoulder. "When we're back at my place we'll talk. I promise."

••••

Will adjusted his cravat and checked his hair in the mirror. When he was satisfied he was presentable he took a few moments to steady himself. He'd done everything his patron had asked of him so there was no reason to be afraid. It didn't alleviate the nerves. He took a step back, spoke Lord Iris' name three times and watched the glass ripple until Exilium came into focus.

He stepped through and walked between the trees along a familiar path lined with blue irises. The clearing came into sight with Lord Iris sitting in his usual place surrounded by the woven half-sphere of saplings. Lord Poppy stood to the right, the epitome of elegance as he held his cane slightly away from his body, its tip planted to the right of his feet. They were both dressed in the Edwardian style, Poppy with a deep red waistcoat, Iris wearing one embroidered with blue and gold irises, as he had the last time Will visited.

Both were watching his approach but he felt the pressure of Iris' stare more. Will walked through the clearing to kneel at his patron's feet, keeping his head bowed.

"William, Duke of Londinium," Lord Iris said, resting a hand on the top of his head.

"My Lord Iris," he said, then when the hand moved and a long finger lifted his chin, he looked up at his patron. "I'm here to serve."

"Good day to you, little Duke," Lord Poppy said and Will gave him a curt nod. "Tell me, how is my–" He cut himself off, glancing at Lord Iris and giving him a mischievous smile. "How is your wife?"

"Much better, Lord Poppy, thank you for your concern."

"I would dearly like to see her."

"But I won't permit it," Lord Iris cut in. "Be satisfied she is recovering, Poppy."

"Be satisfied I forgave yours for failing to protect her," Poppy fired back. Will felt an urge to duck and find cover.

"We don't need to go over this again, we've reached an accord," Iris said and looked back down at Will. "You have pleased me. You destroyed the Roses–"

"My favourite did more," Poppy interjected but Iris ignored him.

"And now we have Londinium. You've done all I have asked, and I look forward to the day you bring me news of your wife's pregnancy."

Will forced a smile. "I look forward to that day too, my Lord."

"However, Lord Poppy has been greatly distressed by the injuries inflicted upon her and so we have agreed compensation. You are to appoint Thomas Rhoeas-Papaver as the Marquis of Westminster when you convene the Court."

Will glanced at Poppy, who was smiling with satisfaction, then back at his patron. "Catherine's brother? Forgive me, my Lord, but as a resident of Aquae Sulis, Thomas has no experience of the Londinium Court, no leverage there and certainly no friendships that I'm aware of. He would bring little to the position politically."

"Are you saying the eldest son of my favourite family line has nothing to offer?" Poppy asked sharply.

"Not in entirety, Lord Poppy. I'm sure Thomas has a great deal to offer to the academic community in matters of twentieth-century warfare, but, as I far as I know, that knowledge may not be the most useful at Court."

"He's intelligent and very tall," Poppy said, chin in the air. "Both qualities will serve him admirably."

Will wanted to swear so much it would make flowers wilt but he kept his mouth shut and looked at Lord Iris, trying to convey how absurd the request was with his eyes alone. His patron looked into them with a hint of a smile that never materialised into anything substantial. "I'm sure

my wife will be very pleased to have her family close again,"
Will said, trying to voice his concern about a direct line of
communication to Lord Poppy.

Iris didn't acknowledge the subtext. "The decision is final,"
he said. "Now, if you'll excuse us, Lord Poppy, I wish to speak
to William alone."

Poppy inclined his head at Iris and gave Will a glance
before leaving. As they waited for him to go, Will struggled
to maintain his calm expression whilst under his patron's
intense stare.

"The alliance between our families in Aquae Sulis has
served us well," Lord Iris said.

"Thomas isn't a politician."

"Are you?"

Will swallowed. His throat felt dry. "I aim to do my best."

"I'm certain Thomas will, too. He will be more trustworthy than many in Londinium. No doubt his father will
press him to support you totally so as not to risk the alliance
with your father."

So that was why Iris capitulated. It was small comfort, but
a comfort nonetheless. "Was there something else you wished
to discuss with me, my Lord?"

Lord Iris' smile made Will shiver. "Oh, yes."

Cathy woke to find a blanket pulled up to her chin and the
tea cups cleared away. The fire was dying in the grate and
she felt hungry. The blanket fell away as she sat up, wincing
as the movement tugged at the wounds. She was bored of
feeling disoriented every time she woke, bored of the pain,
bored of being immobile. It was time to make plans.

She struggled to her feet, appreciating again how much
fitness she'd lost. It wasn't as if she was the sportiest of
people, but when she'd lived in Manchester she'd walked

everywhere to learn the layout of the city. She wanted a piece of paper and a pen to start ordering her thoughts and she wanted to write to Lucy. There was too much to face alone and she was certain a conversation with her sister-in-law would help. She wanted to phone Sam and see if he was all right, then remembered her phone had been in her bag when they were attacked. Would the police have it?

When she opened the door she saw nothing but the back of the huge man who'd followed them down the stairs earlier.

He turned and looked down at her. He had to be almost seven feet tall and his shoulders were wide enough to span the doorway. Instinctively she took a step back as he nodded at her. "Good afternoon, your Grace."

"You're the bodyguard…"

"Carter," he said.

"Carter, yes, hello. Is my husband back?"

Carter shook his head. "No, your Grace."

Cathy hoped Will was OK. Did Iris know she was better and think it was time to put pressure on him for siring a son? Whatever the reason, worrying wasn't going to give her any answers. "Listen, you can take the rest of the day off. I'm not planning to do anything more dangerous than writing a letter and reading some books."

He smiled. His teeth were even and white. "Only His Grace can relieve me of my duty, ma'am. I answer directly to him."

"And what exactly are his orders?"

"To escort you from place to place, to stand guard outside the room you're in and should anyone or anything pose a threat to your person, I'm to neutralise that threat immediately."

"Oh." Cathy pulled the blanket off the chair to wrap around her shoulders, suddenly cold. "Will is just overreacting. He'll get over it and you can go and do something more worthwhile. You're from the Agency?"

"Yes, ma'am, I'm one of their best. And, begging your pardon, I can think of nothing more worthwhile than protecting the Duchess of Londinium."

"Right..." Cathy marvelled at how sincere he seemed. She chewed the inside of her lip. Sneaking out to call her mundane friend was not something she wanted to be witnessed by a man in the pay of her husband who was probably spying for Bennet too. She couldn't trust any of the staff now. She wondered if she could give him the slip but it would be hard in her current state. No doubt he had something to protect himself against Charms, otherwise he'd be a poor guard. "Well, I don't want to be rude, but your being here isn't necessary."

"As I said, ma'am, that's up to the Duke. He said you might not be very enthusiastic."

"What else did he say?"

"That if you want to go into Mundanus, I'm to tell you, politely, that it isn't permitted."

"But what about Sophia? She needs to be there."

"Other provisions have been made for her. I won't inconvenience you, your Grace. It's my job to protect you. I'd like to think my being here would make you feel better."

She repressed the desire to unleash her arguments on him. He was just doing his job. It was Will she had to work on. She breathed in, reassured herself that she'd find a solution and then forced a smile. "All right then, Carter. Let's try to get along until Will realises he's being an idiot."

He raised his eyebrows.

"Are you supposed to tell him everything I say, too?"

There was the briefest pause and then he shook his head. "No, your Grace, of course not."

She smirked. "If you're going to follow me everywhere, I'd like to know a bit more about you. Come and sit down."

He didn't move and looked decidedly awkward when she looked at him expectantly. Cathy knew she was crossing a social line; asking a member of staff to come and sit with her like a guest was not the done thing. Sod convention, she thought, it does nothing but keep people miserable.

She sat down and gestured at Will's chair. "Come in, Carter, please."

He jerked forwards and closed the door after a glance down the hallway, probably to check if anyone else saw. Cathy wondered what Morgan made of it all; if Carter answered directly to Will it broke the normal hierarchy of the butler being in charge of the male household staff. Being seen to enter her company in such an informal way wouldn't help any tensions between them, but it was the perfect opportunity to learn more about the Agency.

"I never knew the Agency provided personal body-guards," Cathy said. "How long have you been one?"

"Since the age of twenty, your Grace."

"What made you decide to go into security?"

Carter looked confused. "I was assigned to that specialism, your Grace."

So he didn't choose it. "Would they retrain you in something else if you didn't want to be a security guard?"

The skin between his eyebrows pinched and a muscle worked in his jaw. After a few seconds he cleared his throat and said, "I'm very sorry, your Grace, I don't quite understand what you mean. I'm doing what I was always meant to do. What more could a person want?"

Even though his confusion fascinated and chilled her, Cathy didn't want to make him any more uncomfortable. "Indeed. How did you come to be in the Agency? If you don't mind me asking."

"Not at all." He smiled, starting to relax. "I was born there."

Cathy hadn't expected that. "There are children born at the Agency?"

"Oh, yes, your Grace."

The thought made her uncomfortable. If the Agency was willing to effectively wipe away Miss Rainer's personality, would they be capable of providing a good environment for children to grow up in? As she was trying to settle on her next question three loud knocks reverberated throughout the house. She heard one of the maids squeal and run past the room. Carter jumped to his feet. "An Arbiter."

"It's all right," Cathy said. "It's probably someone following up on the attack. There's nothing to worry about."

Carter wasn't reassured. He opened the door and looked down the hallway. Cathy could hear Morgan opening the front door but before anything was said Carter closed the library door behind him.

Cathy strained her ears but couldn't hear anything except the front door close. Then footsteps approaching the library, and Morgan's voice, which was too low for her to be able to discern individual words.

"That's not possible." She heard Carter perfectly well. "You're not on the list of approved visitors."

There was a list? There was little to distinguish between Will's desire to protect and a means to control her and it made her feel nauseous. I bet Dame Iris is on that bloody list, she thought. There was the sound of another man's voice, also too low to hear properly, then Carter again. "By order of His Grace the Duke of Londinium." Cathy shook her head. Carter was so keen to do a good job he was even willing to try and keep an Arbiter away from her. Surely he knew no one in Nether Society had the right to do that?

Morgan and the Arbiter spoke. There was a pause and then a knock on the door. Morgan entered. "Excuse me, your

Grace, but an Arbiter is here to see you. He says he needs to speak to you specifically."

Carter stepped in behind him. "I'll be present the entire time, ma'am, there's nothing to–"

"Don't be silly," she interrupted. "Show him in, Morgan. Carter, you stay outside. An Arbiter is hardly going to hurt me, is he?"

Carter's frown was quite dramatic, it couldn't be otherwise with a forehead of such size. "I'll be on the other side of this door, ma'am, if you need me–"

"I'll be sure to squeal like a helpless princess, yes, thank you."

She wasn't expecting Max, not after the last time she saw him, but she pretended to adjust her blanket to disguise any emotion she might show in front of Carter. Morgan promised tea, a staple of any visit, which would also give him a good excuse to check up on her.

Carter closed the door slowly, the shadow cast by his frown making his nose appear even smaller.

"Good afternoon," Max said in his usual monotone.

She beckoned him close and whispered, "The big man will be listening through the door, so we need to keep our voices down."

"I have a better solution." He reached into his pocket and pulled out a slender box from which he took something that looked like a hatpin and stuck it into the door's keyhole. "That will muffle our voices. May I open your window?"

"Of course."

Max left his hat on the chair and lifted the sash window. The gargoyle climbed in, landing silently on the wooden floorboards, making it seem like it wasn't really there. It came straight over to her as Max closed the window.

"How are you?" it asked in its smoker's voice. "Was it bad? You're thinner."

She looked for any signs of the anger it had expressed with claws around her throat the last time she saw it. "I'm all right. Still recovering. Yes, it was very bad."

"Sorry we were horrible to you," it said, resting its stone chin on the arm of the chair, like a dog hopeful for a pat. "We thought you'd lied to us."

She slowly reached across and stroked the top of its stone head as Max settled into the opposite chair. "All right. It's all in the past. Thanks for the file, it's been very useful."

"The last information you got to us was good," Max said. "We found Thorn. He confessed and it helped us progress our investigations, so as far as I'm concerned we're even."

"What did Thorn do?"

The gargoyle and the Arbiter exchanged a look. "You don't know?" Max asked.

"Thorn was the one who tried to kill you," the gargoyle said.

Cathy felt breathless as a memory of the knife returned with horrific detail. "But Will said it was a Rosa sent by Bartholomew. He didn't say it was Lord Thorn himself."

"He disguised himself with a Glamour," Max said. "He wanted your husband to think it was a Tulipa. It seems it worked."

Cathy realised she was shaking. "Oh, God, that's awful. I mean, it was awful already, and I knew it wasn't Bartholomew, but Will was convinced…" She had to tell him as soon as he got back. They had to tell Margritte. "Hang on, why did Lord Thorn attack me?"

"To get your husband into a lot of trouble with Iris and Poppy and thereby stop him from taking the throne."

"And probably breathing too," the gargoyle added.

"But that's not why I'm here," Max said.

She was still reeling from the news. "What about Lord Thorn? Is he still set on killing me?"

"He isn't in a position to do anything."

"The Sorcerer put him in a special box," the gargoyle added. "You don't have to worry about him. And his brother is still in Exilium. We checked."

"We understand Sam saved you from Thorn," Max said. "Have you been in contact with him?"

"He did? No one has mentioned him at all. I'm not sure they even know he was there, otherwise Will would have said something. I haven't seen him since the attack. Oh, God, do you think he's all right?"

"He survived and he's been back home since then," Max replied. "I just wanted to ask him some questions. His wife died whilst you were both in hospital, so he wasn't in a state to talk about Thorn's attack."

"Shit." Cathy shook her head. "So much has been going on. Poor Sam. He was worried about her boss, did you know about that?"

Max nodded. "That's another thing I wanted to discuss with him."

A gentle knock on the door brought the conversation to a halt. The gargoyle scampered behind the curtains and Cathy called Morgan in. The tea was arranged and Carter had a good look at her before Morgan left. She tried to look fine, but felt like all the blood in her had sunk into the floor.

"I'll pour," Max said. "You look like you need a moment."

"Will killed Bartholomew and took the throne because he thought he tried to have me killed. If he'd known it was Thorn, Bartholomew would still be alive."

The gargoyle returned and sniffed at the cake next to the teapot. "This is only half of all the shit that's been blowing up over the last few weeks, believe me."

"What else is going on?"

Max was giving the gargoyle a familiar hard stare. "Not everything is suitable for discussion here," he said as he handed her the tea.

"But you came to see me for something," Cathy said after a couple of sips. "It wasn't just to tell me about Thorn, was it?"

Max shook his head.

"I wanted to see if you were all right," the gargoyle said.

She smiled at it and tickled behind its ears, liking the way its muzzle wrinkled.

"We need your help," Max said.

"Is this where you offer me the mythical help from the Sorcerer again?"

"We can't offer that," the gargoyle said. "He doesn't know we're here." It looked at Max. "I know that was top of your 'things not to talk about with Cathy' list but there's too much going on for us to be all secretive and crap. You know it."

"I know you talk too much," Max said.

"We can't ask her to breach the Split Worlds treaty without an explanation," the gargoyle replied.

"You want me to do what?"

Max looked from the gargoyle to her. She thought she was getting used to his total lack of emotion, but it seemed odd when there was clearly disagreement between him and his... pet without any corresponding irritation or anger. Max didn't say anything for a moment, which made the gargoyle groan. "There's corruption in one of the London Chapters. They were told to ignore any breaches made by the Rosas."

"Holy crap! Really?" Cathy had been taught the Arbiters were incorruptible. It was one of the reasons the Great Families were so afraid of them.

"Yep," the gargoyle replied. "And there's something dodgy going on with the ex-Sorcerer of Essex, so we need to find the Chapter as soon as we can and look into it."

"But why isn't your Sorcerer involved?"

"He's too busy fighting a war. And he's as mad as a bag of cats if you ask me."

So there was a war amongst the Sorcerers. Cathy wondered if her uncle knew about that. Should she warn him?

"That's enough," Max said. "There's something seriously wrong in London and you're the only person in the city and in Fae-touched society we can ask to help. I can't promise Mr Ekstrand will help you if you do this for us, but–"

Cathy held up a hand. "I don't need his help any more. I've decided to stay."

"Why?" the gargoyle asked. "You were dead set on getting out." It narrowed its eyes. "You haven't fallen in love or something?" It looked at Max. "You should check her for Charms, maybe–"

"It's not that," she interrupted. "I wanted to leave because it sucks to be a woman here. But it's better to change it for everyone, than to just run away. And it's the Agency too."

"What about it?" Max asked.

Cathy feared the curse would kick in if she said anything negative about it. Was it only to stop her telling anyone about the blackmail, or speaking ill of the Agency too? Then she remembered Bennet's warning about thinking twice before saying anything about them. He wouldn't have said that if the curse prevented it. With the artefact in the keyhole, she decided to take the risk. "It's dodgy." She told them about Miss Rainer without coughing once.

"That's nothing compared to what we saw last night," the gargoyle began but Max held up a hand.

"That's off-topic," he said.

"Is it?" Cathy put her cup down. "You want me to breach the Treaty in the city of London when I'm supposed to be the Duchess of Londinium. It's a big risk – what if I'm delivered to bloody Dame Iris by the local Arbiters? Lord Iris would kill me. No, actually, he'd do something worse."

"I'll be watching," Max said. "When the Arbiter comes I'll step in and handle it."

It was still a huge risk. She'd have to do something very obvious and very public to get the immediate attention of the London Arbiters, and what if they didn't listen to Max? He was working without his Sorcerer's knowledge, after all. "I'll do it – *if* you tell me more about the Agency and get me any files I need." There were names in Miss Rainer's file she wanted to follow up, including other former students. Max was the only way she could find out more about them.

"That will be very difficult," Max said.

"Bollocks." The gargoyle put itself between her and the Arbiter. "He's just saying that to cover our arses and make out like it's something special. We can get you whatever you need to know. The files kept by the Agency are easy to get hold of now and they have one for every single person in your Nether Society."

Cathy wondered what they had in her file. She suspected Bennet had kept all of her secrets out of it, to preserve their blackmail value.

"Don't make promises we can't keep," Max said.

"And don't get in the way of something that could get us much further than we can alone," the gargoyle replied. "Cathy is our insider. She knows what it's like in their world, we don't."

"I know enough," Max said.

"We know enough to bust their asses when they step out of line, but not how the system works. And she's connected to the Fae in a way we can never be. Someone is messing everything up, not just in London but the entire Heptarchy and probably other places too, someone who knows Fae magic and sorcery. We have to collaborate if we're going to solve any of this, whether you like it or not."

Cathy sat back as the two of them stared at each other. She felt like she'd been obsessing over one messy room whilst the entire house was falling apart. Whilst she was desperate to hear about what the gargoyle and Arbiter saw that night, it wasn't the time to ask. Their relationship was strange, but then how could anything be normal when a walking, talking gargoyle was involved? Did all Arbiters have them? She didn't know what the Heptarchy was and she didn't know what the "someone" the gargoyle referred to had been doing, but one thing was clear: she had her first potential allies against the Agency.

"Listen, I know there hasn't been much trust between us," she said. "But I think the gargoyle is right. I don't know how things work for Arbiters, but I do know that Nether Society is fundamentally unjust. It's built upon suffering and I want it to change. We can help each other and I'm prepared to take a risk for you if you're prepared to help me."

Both she and the gargoyle looked at Max expectantly. "We'll try it," he said. "If your uncle can manage to work with the Sorcerer Guardian of Wessex perhaps we can manage to work together too. But if you try anything, it's all off."

"Understood," Cathy said. "Same goes if you try to screw me over. But I do want things to change, and I think the gargoyle's right."

The gargoyle grinned. "Finally. Now let's get to work."

5

Sam stripped off the black suit and the shirt and stood in his underwear until he started to shiver. He needed to shower but could only face grabbing a pair of jeans and top from the bedroom floor.

The wake was probably still dragging on but he'd stayed as long as he could. He'd said an uncomfortable goodbye to Leanne's parents and walked all the way home. His feet still throbbed from walking in the formal shoes.

He tried to remember what it was like in the house when Leanne lived there but he could only remember the arguments so he went downstairs to see whether there was any beer left.

As he walked through the hallway a flash of green made him stop before he'd reached the kitchen. He looked back at the long mirror hanging where it always had and realised sunlight was shining out of it.

"Oh, shit."

A tapping sound drew him towards it, dreading what he'd see. He'd yelled at all the people in horror movies who go to investigate a strange sound and here he was doing it himself.

The mirror looked like a window onto Exilium and Poppy's faerie was tapping on it. When it saw him it waved and his shoulders drooped.

The glass appeared to liquefy as the faerie reached a tiny hand through it to beckon him. He considered running out of the house and never coming back but his feet still moved forwards as if his body had already made the decision.

"Fuck," he said as he climbed through the surface of the mirror, feeling as if he was slowly putting his face into a pond but there was no water beyond the surface tension.

"Where have you been?" The faerie flitted about in front of him. "We couldn't find you."

"Busy," he said, wondering if the chapel had offered some sort of protection. Then he realised it was probably something to do with Lord Iron's house, seeing as his company provided a Fae-proof flat for Leanne. "What do you want?"

"Lord Poppy wants to see you. He's over there."

Sam trudged through the perfect meadow grass, irritated by the beauty of the birdsong. There were trees and poppies, like the time he'd come in with Cathy. He shoved his hands in his pockets and walked until he reached a clearing. Poppy was waiting with his cane and dozens of poppy flowers as if he had always been there and always would be.

"Ah! There you are. I've just seen my favourite's husband and I feel the need to be cheered up."

"He has that effect on me too," Sam muttered. "I'm not the best person to cheer anyone up at the moment."

"Oh?" Poppy came closer, swinging the cane ahead of him with each step. "Oh, dear, you do smell rather miserable. Has someone died?"

"Maybe."

"Someone close to you." Poppy squinted as he peered into Sam's eyes. "My, what a delightful mess you are. I have just the thing to help."

"Me or you?"

"Both of us, my little grieving one. Sit down."

"This is counting towards my debt, isn't it?"

"Oh, silly me!" Poppy snapped his fingers and the hourglass appeared. "Well, a minute here and a minute there is nothing between us."

Sam had to really stare to catch sight of the grains of sand falling. There was still so much to go. Expecting to sit on the grass, he found himself caught by poppies forming a rudimentary seat beneath him.

"I want you to draw a picture for me," Poppy said, reaching behind his back and pulling a pad of paper and a pencil from nowhere. "I have a renewed appetite for art, thanks to my little sunlit one having painted such a masterpiece. Have you seen it?"

"No. It was rolled up when I delivered it."

"Oh. Maybe you will one day, maybe you won't. I may have an exhibition and reveal it one time only." He lowered his voice. "Did she tell you what the secret is? The one she painted into it?"

Sam shook his head, glad Cathy hadn't told him. It meant he didn't have to lie. "Nope. I haven't got a clue. And I can't draw so can I go home now?"

"Everyone can draw!" Poppy dropped the paper and pencil into his lap. "Try. Take as long as you need. Well, until I tire of your struggle and find an alternative way for you to be entertaining with a pencil."

"I don't know what to draw."

"Not 'what' – who. The one who died. Yes, that's perfect. I want you to draw…" Poppy leaned down to peer into his eyes. "Her? Yes, a woman, I think. Your mother? No. Your wife!"

Sam stared down at the page, disturbed by how much Poppy could fathom from his face alone. He wanted to be anywhere else, doing anything else, but Poppy was desperate to do something awful, he knew it.

He started to draw but the face appearing on the page looked like something a six year-old would be ashamed of. He went to turn the paper over but Poppy stopped him with his cane.

"Keep going. I must see how awful this will be."

Sam's mouth was so dry he could barely swallow. The lines on the paper bore no resemblance to Leanne – they didn't even resemble a person. Poppy watched every hesitant stroke as the faerie sniggered. Sam just wanted to stick the pencil in Poppy's chest and bolt.

"It's done," he finally said, unable to make it any worse.

Poppy took the piece of paper and tipped it from one side to the other before looking at Sam. "Did your wife look like this?"

"Of course not."

"I can make you think she did." Poppy watched the horror spread across Sam's face. "No? You'd rather remember her as she was and suffer not being able to draw her?"

"Of course I bloody would!" Sam chucked the pencil across the clearing and stood up. "This isn't a fucking game! She's dead!"

Poppy's expression was that of a child at the circus: utterly enthralled by a trapeze artist. He leaned closer, reaching towards his face. "Oh…" he whispered. "It's exquisite."

Sam leaned back but Poppy's hand was too fast and he felt the gentlest brush across his cheek. Poppy pulled his hand back, a sparkling teardrop balanced perfectly on his fingertip. Sam touched his cheek and found it was wet.

Poppy lifted the drop to his mouth and tasted it with his horribly long tongue. "What a delicious creation! Grief and guilt and superbly piquant regret. You can go now. I want to enjoy this alone."

Sam didn't need any encouragement and hurried out of the clearing and towards the Way back to his house before Poppy said anything else.

Max checked there was no one on the fire escape. They were only a few feet from a busy pavement, tucked in a cramped alleyway between two huge buildings and thus far unnoticed by the innocents of London. He looked at Catherine, who was hunched in a coat and leaning against the wall. She was pale and looked tired. The gargoyle was sitting next to her, close enough to prop her back up if she needed it.

The gargoyle had said more than it should. Max took a moment to think through the reason he was there, examining each decision point for signs of her interference, or that of any of the puppets. She was happy to negotiate once they were there, but there was no way she could have steered events to force them to work together. At least, it wasn't apparent from the information at his disposal.

The gargoyle had driven it, not her. It had pressed for action, had suggested going to see her and had blurted out far too much when they were together. The gargoyle wanted this and it was a part of him. Did that mean *he* wanted this?

Impossible.

Something must have happened when the gargoyle... came into being. Something had changed it. A traumatic experience could affect the soul. It was the only explanation; he knew the puppets were untrustworthy and needed to be closely policed and his soul would know that too. Something must have warped as it became part of the stone. It wasn't the soul chain; Ekstrand had checked it.

He had to make sure the gargoyle didn't steer anything else.

"What are we waiting for?" the gargoyle asked. "I want to see this!"

It seemed excited. They were about to commit a criminal act and it showed no nervousness nor moral difficulty.

"Are you sure we have everything we need?" he asked Catherine and she nodded.

"I just need a place high up," she said. "I wouldn't be surprised if my bodyguard was watching this through a glass. Are you sure I won't get into a hell of a lot of trouble?"

"There is a risk," he replied, unable to lie. "But I am almost certain they'll be far more interested in speaking to me than in prosecuting you."

She nodded. "Because they'll want to know why you'd let me do it."

"And because they're trying to kill him," the gargoyle added. "Or at least they were the last time we saw them."

Catherine looked from the gargoyle to him. "Tell me he's joking."

"It's the truth," Max said. "But critical circumstances have changed since then. I wouldn't do this if I was sure I would be killed. I may be an Arbiter but I still have a self-preservation instinct like anyone else."

She banged her head gently against the bricks behind her and then groaned. "Let's get this over with. We've come this far and I want to see if it works. And I'm probably never going to have an opportunity to do anything like this ever again."

"It's gonna be great!" The gargoyle drummed its front paws on the ground. "Give the bag to me. Let's go!"

Catherine hooked the handle over its lower jaw and then Max led her up the fire escape. He had to take it slowly, with his walking stick hooked over his arm, and she was soon struggling too. The gargoyle made its way up by a different route, its paws too unwieldy for the narrow metal ladder struts. It leapt from corners to wall to handrail to window ledge, reaching the roof of the building first. It had already emptied the contents of the bag and was snuffling at them by the time they reached it.

"Whoa, great view," Catherine panted. "I just… need to sit for a moment."

Max did too. The majority of the roof was flat and a walkway ran around the edge. The building's facade extended above the roof line, creating a thick wall at waist height with periodic gaps perfect for spying purposes. He crouched behind it as best he could and looked down into Trafalgar Square. It was cold and the sky was a clear blue and the innocents were hurrying along the pavements as they always had. He watched tourists taking pictures of each other in front of the huge sculpted lions and people lunching together on the steps of the National Gallery. There were fewer pigeons than he remembered.

"I love it here," Catherine said. "I walked through a few times but I could never stay very long."

"When you ran away," the gargoyle said.

She nodded, thoughtful. "That first time we met," she said to Max. "Why wouldn't you give me asylum?"

"That doesn't exist for puppets," he replied. "It's never been necessary."

"Are you seriously telling me that no one from the Nether has ever wanted to get out?"

"Never."

"Doesn't that surprise you?"

He shook his head. "You people have eternal youth, power, grand houses and an easy life. If we went down there and asked any one of those people if they wanted the same, they'd accept."

"If you sold it to them like that, maybe. They wouldn't if I told them the truth. What's the point of eternal youth if all you do is sit around and do embroidery or talk about fashion or have endless dinner parties with the same people over and over? No sunshine, no wind, no rain… just endless mist."

"But they've perfected how to deal with that," Max said. He knew the Fae lost puppets to illness in the early days after the Treaty, but that hadn't happened for a long time. His Chapter Master had a theory about magic worked into their anchors by the Fae to protect them but they never got to the bottom of it. It wasn't considered a priority.

"All they've perfected in the Nether is how to control people and keep everything the way they like it," Catherine said.

"Who's 'they'?" the gargoyle asked.

"The Patroons and the bloody Fae."

"If we came back tomorrow with a thingymebob from the Sorcerer saying you could leave and never go back, would you take it?" The gargoyle was too interested in her.

Catherine sighed. "Oh, God, I'd be tempted. A few weeks ago I would have, and never looked back. Now…" She shook her head. "No. I can't. It wouldn't be right."

"We should begin," Max said, aware of the time.

"Perfect weather," Catherine said, retrieving the largest box from the pile behind them. "Will said it was raining earlier. Must've cleared up."

Max watched her tackle the modern packaging and listened to her swear like a mundane. She was different. None of the other people in the Nether he'd ever dealt with would have come up with such an unusual – and mundane – solution to the challenge.

"You're sure this will work?"

"As sure as I can be," she said as she slid the remote control helicopter from the last of the packaging. "I had a… friend when I lived in Mundanus. He had one of these. He made a payload carrier to fly M&Ms to me." She smiled to herself. "It made him happy."

As Catherine unwrapped batteries and fiddled with a reel of cotton, Max looked up at the statue of Nelson. The statue was still higher than them as the column was so tall but it was easier to see it from where they were.

"Don't worry," she said, pulling a small bundle of fabric from the inside of her coat. "It'll work. Nelson must have had a really loud voice to be heard over all that cannon fire and yelling."

"I'm not worried," he replied.

"But it won't actually be Nelson," the gargoyle said. "So what difference does it make if the real one was loud?"

"For an Arbiter's assistant you don't know much about Animation Charms," Catherine said and the gargoyle laughed. It sounded like someone scrubbing the inside of a cement mixer.

"I'm not–"

"Going to distract Catherine any further," Max cut in.

"It's nice not being called 'puppet' all the time," she said. "Do you know how this Charm works?"

Max didn't want to admit that he didn't; it wasn't a good idea to give the puppets any idea of the limits to an Arbiter's knowledge. "I know the effects."

"It's just wish magic," she said casually. "Just a narrow form of it, and weak too." She'd finished unravelling the strip of fabric and an oval phial sat in the palm of her hand. She held it up and the sunlight made the contents sparkle. In fact, there was nothing else in there except sparkling, like a pinch of glitter suspended in a trapped gust of wind. "You can only cast it on one object and it'll only behave in the way you'd expect it to. I got this for a teddy bear for a… cousin."

"Where did you get it from?"

She tapped the side of her nose. "Trade secret."

"The rules of the Treaty dictate you tell me," Max reminded her.

"Oh, come on. You say that when I'm about to create a massive breach? Surely we're off the hook here? I told you about how it works, that has to be enough."

He let it go. If she decided not to help them he couldn't force her. Even if they took the phial from her he wouldn't be able to use it and there was no way he would let the gargoyle touch it.

The gargoyle had been remarkably quiet. It was staring at the phial and grinding its stone teeth together. "Would you be able to use that on a dead body?"

"Euw!" Catherine's nose wrinkled as Max realised what the gargoyle was wondering. "That's gross. I have no idea. You can't use it on people – living people, that is – I know that. It has to be inanimate and this one can only be cast on something that looks like a person or an animal. There are more powerful ones. I heard Oliver Peonia used one to make some teaspoons dance at a garden party."

Petra told them the Sorcerer of Essex was already dead when the magic turned his heart to stone. Could it be possible that the person behind that magic had animated Dante's corpse to walk in and take his place at the table? The other Sorcerers wouldn't have noticed at first glance; Petra said his face had been covered in make-up to give him a healthy appearance. The Sorcerers weren't the most sociable of people and the others would have written off his silence as normal. Before they had a chance to find out what was going on, they were killed.

But how could that Charm have endured once past the threshold? There were wards against Fae magic. Could the person who killed Dante have found a way to mask it? It led the trail back to London. Who would know where to find Dante? Not even the other Sorcerers would know where he lived. Someone in his household? An apprentice perhaps, someone who had close access to him and also would be able to discover where the Chapters were under Dante's command. Perhaps the source of the corruption was an apprentice compromised by the Fae.

"But why?" the gargoyle asked him.

"Because garden parties in the Nether suck," Catherine replied, thinking he was asking about the spoons.

To kill the other Sorcerers, Max thought. Without the Sorcerers to run the Chapters and monitor the weak points between Mundanus and the Nether and Exilium, the Fae could work towards an escape. The puppets would be set free in Mundanus and the Fae would use them to find the best of humanity to become their playthings.

"Right, it's ready."

Catherine's announcement refocused his attention. "Do it," he said. They needed to get an Arbiter and use him to find the Chapter. Quite what he would do afterwards was uncertain, but there was absolutely nothing they could do to find a rogue apprentice without knowing where to start.

He made sure he and the gargoyle couldn't be spotted from the square, not wanting to risk being picked off at a distance. If they only saw Catherine, the Arbiter would come to them and then he would reveal his involvement.

Catherine had tied the phial to a length of cotton attached to the bottom of the helicopter's landing struts. After switching it on she very carefully used the small control box in her hands to make the craft fly upwards until the phial was hanging beneath it.

"Well, that's the first bit done," she said. "I was worried it would be too heavy. Let me just get the hang of the controls and then I'll do it."

Max watched the tiny craft fly around above the air-conditioning vents and lead lining of the flat roof. Its high-pitched whine was too quiet to be heard from the street or in the offices below. The gargoyle was as enraptured as a child by a spinning top. They'd bought it from a shop Catherine had described as a toyshop for grown-ups. Technology really had been advancing in Mundanus. The last time Max saw a toy plane it had been made of balsa wood and could only be thrown and left to the mercy of the wind.

"All right, are you really sure you want to do this?" she asked.

"Yeah! Yeah, do it!" The gargoyle cheered but she was looking at Max.

He had one last good look around and nodded. "Do it."

By manipulating two sticks under her thumbs Cathy steered the helicopter over the edge of the roof and into the air above Trafalgar Square. Max looked down at the tourists and London residents and not one of them was pointing at it. He looked around again for any sign of Arbiters or her bodyguard but there were none. The Arbiters wouldn't be far away though; it was a busy space that attracted a lot of attention and a lot of people who wouldn't be missed immediately if they disappeared. Before his Chapter had been destroyed the area around the Roman Baths and the Royal Crescent were regularly patrolled after several tourists disappeared over a summer. The puppets exploited the crowds and used Charms to attract those who were lost. Max wondered if any had been taken in recent weeks.

"Bollocks," Cathy muttered and the gargoyle's claws scraped against the ledge as it gripped it tighter. "This is hard."

Max could see the problem. It was hard to gauge the exact distance between them and the statue. The motion of the helicopter was making the phial swing back and forth so when a new approach was made it still missed.

"Let me have a go," the gargoyle said.

"No, I nearly have it," she replied, biting her lip. "I just need to practise."

She made three more attempts, swearing every time she missed and then on the fourth the phial smashed into Nelson's hat. "Yes!" Catherine yelled. "Gotcha!"

The sparkles showered over the statue as Catherine brought the helicopter back to land at her feet. As soon as it was switched off she went back to the gargoyle's side and all three of them watched closely.

Nothing happened for a few moments and then it looked like Nelson shivered. "Did you see that?" the gargoyle asked.

"It's starting to work," Cathy said and they grinned at each other.

The gargoyle seemed to be enjoying the illegal activity far too much.

"Good lord!" A loud voice boomed out from the statue and Nelson's head moved from left to right as if he'd just woken up. "What the devil am I doing up here?"

Catherine whooped with joy and the gargoyle clapped her on the back, which made her cry out in pain. As the gargoyle apologised Max watched Nelson hold out his one arm as if he were trying to steady himself, and then he crouched, just like any man would who found himself atop a plinth a hundred feet off the ground.

"How the deuce did I get up here? I say!" Nelson shouted down at the ground. "You there!" He was pointing at a man posing for a photograph beside one of the lions. "Fetch a ladder!"

Catherine's prediction was right – probably because the Charm was manifesting what she'd expected him to be – and his voice was incredibly loud. The tourist looked up and almost fell over when he saw Nelson waving his hat to get his attention.

In moments all the people around the man were looking up. In seconds almost everybody in Trafalgar Square had stopped and most were pointing at Nelson. In less than a minute over half of them were holding up their phones and pointing them at the animated statue.

"What are they doing?" Max asked.

Catherine was flushed with excitement. "They're filming him!" She clapped her hands. "It'll be on YouTube in no time!"

"On what?"

"On the internet. They're going to be talking about this on Twitter from London to Los Angeles before the day is out. This is so cool!"

Max had no idea what Twitter or YouTube were but he knew about the internet; the researchers at the Chapter used it and had mentioned it when briefing him before field trips. It was a giant library of information that anyone could access and it sounded like the events unfolding in front of them were going to be added to it. He had no idea that just anyone could enter information; he thought it was curated by librarians.

"You never said that would happen."

"What the hell did you think would happen?"

"Are their telephones taking pictures?"

"Video. Bloody hell, Mr Arbiter, you need to come into the twenty-first century. It's great here."

The gargoyle gave him a worried look. "Lots of people will see it, not just those here."

"Thousands. Maybe millions," Catherine said. "It's priceless."

Nelson was getting more and more flustered. Every time he waved his hat the spectators below cheered and waved back, only making him more irate. "Will someone please send a carriage to Admiralty House? Why is no one helping me?"

If anything was going to set off an Arbiter intervention, it was this. Max couldn't do anything about what the innocents were doing, but he could stick to the original plan. He took his binoculars from a coat pocket and peeped through a gap to scan the edges of the crowd for Arbiters. It didn't take long to spot one. Max didn't recognise him but he was still unmistakably devoid of emotion and not swept up in the roar of the crowd at all.

The London Arbiter was walking through the crowd, scanning those around him to identify the guilty puppet. He stopped and pulled a phone out of his pocket, looked at it for a moment and then appeared to take a call. The London Chapter was using mobile phones! There was a brief exchange and then he looked straight up at Catherine.

"Shit!" The gargoyle ducked lower. "They're onto us."

"That's what you wanted, isn't it?" Catherine asked. "Where is he?" She leaned out and looked for the man, who had taken his own binoculars out and was looking up at her. "Oh, I see him."

There had to be another, someone who'd seen them on the roof and tipped off the one in the square. Max looked behind them and checked the fire escape but no one was coming up yet. No one had tried to shoot him, at least. Perhaps they didn't want to risk it with the Duchess of Londinium as a witness.

Catherine waved at the Arbiter, then pointed to Nelson and gave a thumbs-up.

"What are you doing?" the gargoyle hissed.

"I wanted him to know it was us," she said. "In for a penny, in for a pound."

Max watched the Arbiter stare at them for a few moments and then press a button on his phone. Trained in the rudiments of lip reading, Max focused on the man's mouth and saw him speak Catherine's full name.

"He'll be here any minute," Max said. "We just need to wait."

"Damn, I wish I still had my iPad," Catherine said sadly. "I'd love to see how people are explaining this. And I hope you're right about me not getting into trouble. You will tell them I did it for you, won't you?"

"Yes."

The Arbiter put his phone and binoculars away, turned around and left the square at the opposite side to where they were. The person who'd tipped him off must have said he'd deal with it.

They waited. The gargoyle stayed hunkered down and seemed to have lost interest in Nelson's antics. Catherine was entertained for a little while then started to look tired again. The thrill was wearing off.

"I thought they'd be here by now," she said. "I'm getting cold. And Carter's probably bursting a blood vessel. If you weren't an Arbiter there's no way he would have let us leave and I bet he's freaking out about it."

"I thought they would be here too," Max replied. They had had ample time to secure backup, especially as they were using phones in the field. It was almost as if they didn't care. "It's like the Rosas."

"Maybe it's because I'm the Duchess," Catherine suggested. "You said the Rosas were exempt before Lady Rose fell. Maybe it's because they were the ruling family. Maybe it's a Londinium thing and no one's had a chance to tell me yet."

"No family should be exempt, regardless of their status," Max said. "I should take you home."

"But how the arse are we going to speak to them now?" the gargoyle asked. "You'd think they'd at least come and tell her off."

Max agreed. It was decidedly odd. Even if the ruling family was exempt, surely a breach of this magnitude would trigger some kind of reprimand. It was clear the corruption was still strong in Londinium, regardless of Dante's death.

"We'll think of something," he said and noticed Nelson had stopped shouting.

"Oh, it's worn off," Catherine said with disappointment.

Max looked at the statue, inanimate once more but now crouching, hat off and frozen in mid-wave. He was interested to see how that would be explained away.

6

Lord Iris laced his long fingers together and stared at Will. "Lord Tulip is upset by our recent success. The events in the throne room were rather dramatic, all told."

Will nodded, taken back to Margritte's grief and the blood on his sword. It still made him want to close his eyes and curl up somewhere dark and far away from people. But he couldn't give in to such childish urges. He was the Duke of Londinium and he had to move forwards.

"Whilst everything settles down, you must focus on Londinium." Iris leaned forwards and lowered his voice to a whisper. "The Arbiters of London will turn a blind eye to any activities north of the river initiated by you or any others of the Iris family, and will actively defend your interests should a conflict arise with another party."

It took a moment to process what he'd said. "I don't understand, my Lord. Are you saying I could cast a Charm in mundane London with no risk of punishment?"

"I'm saying exactly that. And, when you need them to, they will lie for you. Should you need to speak to one–" he pinched his fingers in the air and a piece of paper appeared between them "–go into Mundanus and use this. I assume it means something to you."

He gave the piece of paper to Will who unfolded it. A telephone number was written in blue ink. "It does, my Lord. But... I thought the Arbiters were incorruptible." As far as he knew, not even the Patroon had ever had carte blanche to do as he wished in Mundanus.

"If there is one thing that is true of all humanity, it is that everyone is corruptible, William. A fact I'm sure you will appreciate all the more once the Court reconvenes. The Dukedom will be an interesting challenge for you. I expect perfection. And a child."

Will looked down at the leaves beneath Lord Iris' shoes. He felt a certain empathy with them. "My wife almost died, my Lord. It's... delayed our schedule somewhat."

"A son within a year, William. You may leave."

Will stood and bowed. "I shall continue to strive to meet your expectations."

He left the clearing and stepped through the Way back into his study. Alone once more, he realised the implications of what he'd just been told. If the Arbiters were capable of lying, the one at the hospital could have lied to him. But if that were true, who had told that man to lie?

Sam rolled the snooker ball towards the far cushion, caught it when it rolled back and did the same again. Back and forth, the white ball left tiny tracks in the baize. There was a bar billiards table behind him, an old-fashioned pub skittle game in the corner, and pinball machines. The games room of Lord Iron's grand estate was bigger than the footprint of his own house in Bath. He felt lost there. It was like staying in a huge hotel off-season, melancholy in its emptiness. There were people maintaining the house, and a cook, but none of them treated him like a normal person. He was a guest with nothing to do except wait for Lord Iron to find a gap in his schedule for him.

He didn't really want to stay but after Poppy's latest interference he didn't want to stay at home either. He felt a tension in his chest that he tried to shut out with beer and TV in the palatial room he'd been given.

Why was he here?

"Sam, I'm sorry, the call to Buenos Aires had a terrible line. Have you eaten?"

Sam nodded.

Iron looked at the snooker balls. "Do you play?"

Sam shrugged. "I haven't for years, not properly." He sometimes played pool at the pub with Dave. It felt like he'd lived three lives since he went to work every day and went home in the evenings. "Do you play?" he asked.

Iron nodded. "When I have the time. So." He clapped his hands. "They gave you the tour of the Manchester office, I understand. What did you think of my business?"

Sam rolled the white again. It hit a red and struck out in a different direction. He didn't try to catch it. "Impressive."

Iron took off his jacket, loosened his tie and went to the rack on the wall holding the snooker cues. "Anything catch your eye?"

The only thing that had caught Sam's eye was a toy zombie on one of the desks in a huge room full of partitioned work stations. It leaped out at him as something individual in a sea of banal corporate decor. When his guide was distracted by a query he'd picked up the toy and found it was designed to be squeezed like a stress reliever. When he crushed it in his fist the zombie's eyes bulged and he'd almost laughed. Almost.

Iron struck the white with the cue and the noise startled Sam out of the memory. One of the red balls dropped into the corner net next to him. "Well, I saw a lot."

"What did you think of the office?"

He remembered how excited the man who'd given the tour had got when they reached the top floor. "This is one of the best offices in Manchester," he'd said as he opened the door. "You can see everything from up here."

"It had a good view," Sam said as Iron potted another red.

"Could you see yourself being happy there?"

Sam stuffed his hands in his pockets. Normally he would lie, out of politeness, but he didn't have it in him. "I'm not sure if I could be happy anywhere at the moment."

Iron was lining up another shot but when he heard Sam's words he straightened up and laid the cue on the baize. "It's too soon. I'm sorry."

"No, it's not that. I just... don't feel like I want to work somewhere like that. It's too..."

"Big?"

"Soulless." Sam winced. "Shit. Sorry, I know you're this amazing businessman but it's just not my scene. Leanne loved all that kind of stuff, not me."

Iron picked up his jacket. "Let's go for a walk."

Sam had walked around the estate several times since he'd arrived. He knew he had to go back to Bath again soon. Just like he had to follow up on the items in Leanne's will. There were things to pass on to friends and family, charities some of her savings were supposed to go to and a huge list of companies and mailing lists to notify about her death. Some loose ends, like her Facebook account, he simply didn't know how to tackle. And there was the sealed envelope the lawyer had given to him. His name was written on the front in her handwriting and it felt like there was a key inside. As much as he wondered what was there, he couldn't face opening it yet.

She'd insisted on life insurance years ago and he was going to get a lot of money once all the paperwork was sorted. He didn't have to rush into anything and he didn't have to worry about paying the bills. Before she died that would have been liberating. Now the freedom just felt empty.

It was sunny and cold outside, the kind of morning that autumn did best. The trees at the edges of the extensive lawn were varying shades of oranges, reds and golds. Birds were singing and Sam couldn't hear any traffic or planes. Iron set off across the grass towards the trees and Sam hurried to fall into step alongside him.

"Death is so hard," Iron said after a while. "Take as long as you need."

"At the wake you said you'd give me some answers."

"I did, didn't I. You want to know why I'm helping you?"

Sam nodded. "That bloke at the office told me that your corporation employs over a hundred and fifty thousand people worldwide and that's not counting all the subsidiary companies. I reckon, with all those employees, people die whilst working for you fairly often. And I reckon you don't invite all of the bereaved spouses to your home to grieve."

"I don't."

"So why me? What do you want?"

Iron stopped and looked back towards the house. It was a sprawling mansion with over a hundred rooms and hardly any of them lived in. "I feel guilty. I knew there was a pattern, I didn't act quickly enough and your wife died."

It sounded all too familiar to Sam. "Do you know why? What caused those deaths? It was Neugent, wasn't it?"

"He was a causal factor, I think, but it wasn't murder. He didn't actively do anything to her and it wasn't his fault."

"So how come it's not his fault if he's the cause?"

"I think it was a side-effect of her working with him."

Sam rubbed a hand over his face. He felt tired of thinking about it. He just wanted someone to tell him exactly how it happened. "Are you even certain it was like that?"

"Yes." Iron started walking again. "I've seen it before. But this time, I could help the person hurt the most by the loss. I couldn't with the others. I doubt I will again."

"So there's nothing we can do to stop it happening again?" Sam turned up the collar on his jacket. The last of the warmth from the house had left him.

"I… have some ideas but nothing has come to fruition yet. As for Neugent, I've given him a generous retirement package."

"Not that he'll have long to enjoy it." Sam realised too late that he shouldn't have said it. "I know he's ill."

"He told you?" Sam nodded. "He'll receive the best medical care. Once he realises it's terminal he'll go and live out the rest of his days on my island, I imagine."

"You have an island?"

Iron nodded. "In the Caribbean. It's very peaceful there. Would you like to go and have a few weeks in the sun? I'll make sure he doesn't go there until you're ready to leave."

Sam tried to imagine himself on a beach. "Not right now, thanks. You didn't really expect me to do anything to him, did you?"

"No," Iron replied. "I just wanted to give you a chance to work it through. Better to speak those thoughts than keep them buried. I think there's something else that would do you much more good right now."

They'd reached the treeline and Sam saw a trail he hadn't noticed from the house. His walks had taken him round the back of the house where a stream ran through the woods. The trail went on for twenty metres or so until the trees thinned and a small one-storey stone building came into view. It had a chimney with smoke puffing out of it in fat clouds.

"I think you have a great deal of potential," Iron said, heading for the cottage. "But I think it's trapped. Under grief, under depression, under a lack of self-belief. I have the feeling that you've never really strived to achieve anything. Am I right?"

Sam wanted to say no but when he tried to think of something he had really worked hard for, he couldn't.

"You've coasted and done just enough to have an average life."

"There's nothing wrong with that," Sam said.

"Not at all," Iron replied. "If you're an average man."

He led Sam to the other side of the building, which was open to the woods. There were two huge wooden doors which had been slid open revealing a forge inside. A man who looked like he was in his sixties was working a huge set of bellows, making the fire roar beneath the chimney.

"When I'm stuck, I come down here and work the metal," Iron said. "There's nothing like doing something real with your hands, making something solid that you can see and touch. I'll look after the fire," he said to the man. "You go and take a break."

Sam looked at the anvil and the rows of tools hanging, waiting to be used. He walked in as the older man left and picked up one of the huge hammers. It felt heavy and... real. More real than anything had for a long time. "So this is why they call you Lord Iron? It's a nickname?"

Iron was looking at the fire. "That's one of the reasons," he said quietly. "Now. Let's get to work."

7

Margritte tried not to listen to the sound of her son retching in the room next door. She drummed her fingertips on the table as she waited but the rhythmic tapping did nothing to block out the noise. She tried not to let the fatigue take her; there was much to do before she could go to bed, but it would all come to naught if her son didn't pull himself together.

The door opened and he came back in. His face was the same colour as his lace cuffs. He sat down next to the fire, shivering.

"Feeling better?"

He glared at her. "I haven't been able to keep a thing down since I got back from the Patroon. I can't believe what you've done, Mother."

"Did you think me utterly incapable?"

"I'd hoped you'd heed my advice and not suck the entire family into your hasty decision."

"Well, Lord Tulip and the Patroon didn't feel the same as you. Now, are you going to face up to what's ahead of us or are you going to cower over a chamber pot whilst the Patroon chooses who'll take your place?"

She felt a pulse of guilt as his brow furrowed, but, if she pandered to his weakness, events would soon overtake him.

"I can't march into Londinium and challenge the Duke. He bested father. I haven't picked up a sword for over fifty years!"

"That child bested your father because he had the backing of his patron. Now you do. And your father was unprepared. Neither of us expected the attack. The Iris boy acted alone in that Court, but you will have several families behind you."

He twisted in his chair to look at her. "Who?"

"The Wisterias, Violas and the Peonias." She smiled. "I didn't only speak to the Patroon."

"What have you done?" Alexander leaned forwards and buried his face in his hands. "That's half of the colleges dragged in."

"Those colleges wouldn't belong to those families had it not been for your grandfather, don't you forget that. They owe us a great deal. Supporting us in our time of need is the very least they can do. I know you want this to go away but life isn't just books and theory. It's family and honour too."

"And power," he said. "That's all you care about."

"The only reason you've been able to enjoy this blissful life is because of the hard work of your ancestors. You've never had to struggle with anything more difficult than a philosophical debate. It's time for you to grow up and do your duty or I'll be the first to tell the Patroon that you're not man enough to do so."

He stared at her, wide-eyed and childlike. "Can't you see what this is doing to you?" he whispered. "The monsters are making you monstrous."

She looked away from him, feeling a sting in her chest. She didn't want to tell him that she'd thought about walking away. She had sisters in Europe she could go and live with, far away from all the memories of life with Bartholomew. But every time she decided to do that she thought of William Iris sitting where Bartholomew should have been, living the life her husband should have enjoyed. There would be no peace in her until his name was cleared.

A knock at the door made both of them jump. "Are you expecting anyone?" she asked, and Alexander shook his head.

He stood. "Come in."

A young man walked in looking like he had just stepped out of Mundanus, wearing jeans and a jacket over a hooded top. He was carrying a large cardboard cup and something that smelled like the most awful food imaginable, sealed in a carton made of a material she didn't recognise. He dumped them on the table and shrugged a bag off his back.

"Chancellor!" Alexander gasped and bowed as deeply as one would to a Patroon.

"Hullo, Alex, bloody cold out there. Christ on a bike, you look like shit."

"I... I am a little unwell."

"Well, I won't shake your hand then. Is this your mum?"

"Yes, may I introduce you to Margritte Semper-Augustus Tulipa. Mother, this is the Chancellor of Oxenford, Sorcerer Guardian of Mercia, King of the mundane lands between the Severn and the Pennines, the Western sea and the river Ouse, holder of the pure Malvern springs and–"

"Just call me Rupert, Mrs T, pleasure to meet you."

For the first time in over a century, Margritte was lost for words.

"Mother," Alexander whispered.

Rupert grinned. "Not what you expected? Yeah, I'm used to that. Met many Sorcerers, have you?"

"I can't say I have, sir," she replied. "But I would expect the Chancellor of Oxenford to be more... formally attired."

"Oh, I dress up for Congregation and Council meetings. I've even worn a tie a couple of times. I know you lot expect Sorcerers to wear top hats and capes and stuff but honestly, I'd look like a wanker dressed in all that. I wore a top hat at a Halloween party last year, but only pretentious tossers wear that gear all the time."

Margritte found him hard to follow and even harder to take seriously. Was this a prank? She watched him sit down and open the strange container. The room was filled with a pungent meaty smell. Alexander covered his mouth with a handkerchief.

"You don't mind if I eat, do you? I'm starving – been running round like a blue-arsed fly all day." He looked up from the food at Margritte. "You ever had a kebab?"

She shook her head and tried her best not to look shocked as he dug his unwashed fingers into the tray and plucked out a stringy piece of meat.

"This is from the van on Broad Street. Usually I get cheesy chips from them and kebabs from the one on–" He stopped himself. "You're not going to give a shit about that, are you?" He went back to eating.

"Are you sure he's a Sorcerer?" she whispered to Alexander, who nodded from behind the silk. "I should leave you to your business," she said, standing up.

"Actually," Rupert said through a mouthful of kebab, "I'm here to see you. You don't mind if I have a chat with your mum, do you, Alex?"

"Not at all, Chancellor. See you soon, Mother." Alexander rushed from the room and Margritte was left with the sound of a pig eating at a trough.

"Sit down, Maggie. Do you mind if I call you that?"

She bristled as she sat back down. "No one calls me Maggie."

"Great. Maggie it is. Sure you don't want to try this? It's really good."

"No, thank you."

She took the opportunity to get used to his savage behaviour as he wolfed down the mundane food. Surely it was an act to throw her off balance? No one as powerful as the Sorcerer of Mercia was rumoured to be could have such abominable manners. He even put Freddy Viola to shame. He wanted her to think he was a stupid, uncouth mundane when he was in fact a powerful man with the power to destroy them all on a whim. You won't fool me, she thought.

He looked young, not much older than she did, and she had hardly spent any of her adult life in Mundanus. He seemed very relaxed about popping out of the Nether for food, suggesting he wasn't concerned about ageing as she would be. As far as she knew he'd been the Sorcerer for hundreds of years; certainly Bartholomew's father had talked about a Rupert. Had he mastered youth as part of his sorcerous arts? He wasn't unattractive; at least he would polish up well after a shave and a haircut.

He licked his fingers, guzzled down the contents of the cup and then belched as loudly as a braying donkey. Slapping his stomach he slouched back in the chair and grinned. His lips were shining with grease and a sliver of meat was stuck between his front teeth. "That's better. I heard about what happened, by the way. I'm sorry you lost your husband."

"I didn't misplace him," she replied. "He was murdered."

"Right. Yeah." He opened his bag and pulled something out which at first glance looked like a book. He lifted its cover and tucked it underneath, revealing a slab of black glass. Margritte clenched her teeth. It was the first sorcerous artefact she'd ever seen.

He pressed its side and it lit up like an incredibly powerful scrying glass. It was looking into a forest at night, but there were arcane symbols arranged in rows on top of the image.

He tapped one and the scene changed into a grid of boxes containing text and different background colours.

"I bet you've never seen one of these before," he said, tilting it to show her more. "Good battery life, killer display. Sucks I can't get the internet in the Nether but I'm working on that. I just got this zombie game and it's so addictive."

She had no idea what he was talking about but didn't want to look too enchanted by it. He was only showing off.

"Is this why you wanted to see me? To show me your artefact?"

He sniggered. "Oh, you guys, you're priceless. No. You see this?" He waved a finger over the grid. "It shows when we have Convocation, Hebdomadal and sub-committee meetings, the monthly piss-up and all the other stuff that keeps the university ticking over. You see all the red? That shows when people – important people like your son, for instance – have sent apologies in advance for not being able to attend." He swiped a finger across the glass and the grid moved in the same direction. There were a lot of red squares. "The thing is, all the messages came in over the last two days. So I think to myself, what the fuck is going on? So I go and have a chat with these people and the same name keeps coming up again and again. Margritte. Semper-Augustus. Tulipa." He slapped the cover back over the artefact and tossed it onto his bag. "You don't normally live here, I know, so I thought I'd explain why this is a pain in the arse. It's Michaelmas Term. There are Freshers fucking up left, right and centre, new bright young things to scope out, and the university is running at full steam. I don't appreciate it when most of my college heads decide they have to take time off en masse, especially when the death of the Roses has shafted us good and proper. *Comprende*?"

It took Margritte a moment to filter out what she could from his horrendous speech. "Chancellor–"

"Rupert, please."

She smiled. "Rupert. I'm sorry this has inconvenienced you but I'm sure you can understand that these are extraordinary circumstances. My husband was wrongfully accused and murdered in the Londinium Court. My family needs to take action and to do so I only require a few old friends from Oxenford for a couple of weeks at the very most."

"Alex sent me a note saying he might be leaving."

"Might? I told him to resign. He will be taking the throne of Londinium and won't have time for college duties."

Rupert scratched his chin. "Oh, will he? He didn't look so happy just now."

"He's struggling to adjust, but he will."

"Look, Maggie, I'm pretty fucking impressed by you. I want to lay that out on the table because, between you and me, if anyone else tried to pull this off I'd make a pocket realm just for them and a pack of hungry wolves. I understand that your family is upset–"

"Not just my family. Lord Tulip himself."

"Now I couldn't give a flying fuck what Lord Tulip is upset about. What I do give a fuck about is my university and your antics are screwing with it. I don't want to force my people to choose between their duties here and whatever debts they have to you, but if I have to, I will."

Margritte smiled. She would be willing to bet her jewels that he'd already applied that pressure and lost. "It seems we have a problem, then," she said. "Do you have a solution?"

"I do actually." He grinned again. The sliver of meat was still lodged in place. "You're pissed off that there's this Iris lad on the throne instead of your husband, right?"

"That's part of it," she replied coolly.

"So I propose this. You tell your friends here they don't have to run off to Londinium on some crusade. Instead, you write to your old friends back home in the big smoke and invite them to come to Oxenford. There are several colleges here that could do with some trustworthy family friends to look after them and I'm sure you're capable of identifying which of your Londinium allies would be willing to join us here."

"That would solve *your* problem. What about mine?"

"Well, that's the beauty of it." Rupert dug a fingernail in between his teeth, frowned at what he winkled out and then put it back in his mouth. "The new Duke, unpopular already, starts losing the best people from his Court."

"And their tithes," Margritte said.

"That too. 'Holy shit!' he says, and issues a formal apology to you and your family, begging people to come back. Then his patron sees what a royal mess of it he's made and drags him off to Exilium for a life of slavery."

"Leaving Alexander to take the throne," Margritte finished.

Rupert frowned. "Well, we'll cross that bridge when we come to it. So, we got a deal? You don't fuck up Michaelmas Term for me and I give your old friends a whole lot more power and influence than they'll ever have in Londinium, plus you get to screw over the Iris boy."

Margritte sat back and looked at the marble bust on the mantelpiece behind him. She thought of Bartholomew's kiss and the ache in her chest. Even if it didn't work out the way Rupert said it would, it was better to play the long game and have a Sorcerer on her side. She nodded. "We have a deal, Rupert."

Will fiddled with his new mobile phone as he waited at the café. The sun had almost set and the mundanes were hurrying past in the rush hour. The cappuccino was nothing like the one he'd had in Rome on his Grand Tour but it was warming at least.

He was hungry, but too tense to eat. He stirred the coffee, looked out of the window and tried not to think about what the corruption of the Arbiters could mean. He would get information first, then draw his conclusions. It was the first rule of managing anxiety: don't speculate.

At least he'd come to a decision about Cathy and her secret life: to leave it well alone. He'd considered challenging her about it but she would only dig her heels in and be stubborn. She'd close herself off from him again and the little progress he'd made before the attack would be lost. The mundane had been warned off her, Carter was going to keep her out of Mundanus anyway and, besides, if he told her he knew, she'd replace the flat and the rest of the arrangements with new ones he knew nothing about. This way, if she did run off, he'd know where to look. If things deteriorated between them he would send one of his people to watch the property, and the Agency were already monitoring the phone line and bank account for any activity. He didn't like having to rely on them but he didn't have anyone in Mundanus with whom he could share such sensitive information.

He just hoped he could win her over and render all the precautions unnecessary. He needed an ally and he needed her to be his wife. And he wanted her to be someone he could trust, no matter how unlikely that seemed.

A couple walked in holding hands and Will felt a pang of jealousy until he spotted a familiar man behind them. Will raised a hand to catch his attention.

The Arbiter approached slowly, scanning the other people in the café. "Let's sit over there," he said, pointing to a corner table at the back.

Will picked up his coffee and followed.

"I was the one who came to the hospital," the Arbiter said.

"Yes, I remember you." When a man had a face like a frog it was hard to forget.

"My name is Faulkner."

Will remembered Cornelius saying his name. Why hadn't he noticed at the time? "Thank you for coming so promptly. Would you like something to drink?"

The Arbiter shook his head and sat down with his back to the wall. His wide-set eyes scanned the other customers again, the door, the barista and then Will. He studied Will's mundane garb, what he was drinking and the wedding ring on his finger. "What did you want to see me about?"

Will suppressed the urge to approach the conversation gently. There was no need to win this man over, nor to take any interest in his feelings. He'd been told the Arbiters had none, though he didn't know why. It was unnerving sitting in a coffee shop with one. It was like looking at a copy of a man, rather than a real person.

"I understand you effectively work for me now."

"That's one way to put it."

"Is there another?"

"I work for you *too*. You're not the only person I'll take orders from."

Will nodded. He suspected that if he asked Faulkner to do something that a Sorcerer disapproved of, the order would be ignored. He wondered what the Arbiter made of it. Wasn't he effectively doing the exact opposite to what he should? Perhaps he was nothing more than a soldier, happy to follow orders without questioning why. "This is a new situation for me," he continued. "I wanted to know if this is new for you."

"I've never helped the Irises before, if that's what you mean."

"Any other families?"

"Yes. If you want to know if I've lied to you, just ask me. This arrangement will be much more efficient if you just state plainly what you want to know and what you want me to do."

Will appreciated his candour. "Did you lie to me at the hospital?"

"Yes," Faulkner said. "That was before my new orders arrived. It won't happen again. Unless something else changes."

Will's heartbeat felt like a drum roll in his ears. "I want to know the truth about what happened to my wife. I want to know everything you do about what happened, who told you to lie to me and why."

"Cornelius White gave me the order to come to the hospital and tell you that Tulipa magic was detected at the scene."

Will gripped the sides of his chair below the table. Cornelius was involved? After all he'd done for him?

"My Chapter was already aware of a serious attack. I went to the scene before coming to the hospital because it happened in my ward. No Tulipa magic there; it was all Rose. I didn't expect that, considering what happened to that family, but that's what I detected. Large amounts; it was either Lady Rose or one of the Thorns. Most probably one of the brothers; she doesn't get involved with anything bloody. Enough for a powerful Glamour, and there was a strong residue in the bushes, which makes sense. There was a child injured with puncture wounds consistent with thorns."

"Then you came and told me it was Tulip magic?" Will struggled to keep his anger in check.

"That was my order. Cornelius was very clear."

"But he told me it was his cousin. He killed him."

Faulkner nodded. "Standard Rosa technique, I've seen it before. Glamour an assassin to look like a fall guy. Commit the crime and, if there are no witnesses, it's done. But if someone sees, or someone survives, they give a description and the fall guy is blamed. The cousin either pissed Cornelius off or was just unimportant enough to kill without repercussions from others in the family. What interests me is why the attack failed. From the police report it sounds like there was someone from the Elemental Court there, someone allied to Iron or Iron himself. Your wife has interesting friends, Mr Iris."

But Will was still struggling to understand Cornelius' betrayal. Were old family loyalties playing out? Was it because of the affair with Amelia? His stomach twisted. "Was his sister, Amelia, involved?"

"I can find that out easily enough," Faulkner replied. "I can bring the brother in and question him. I'm assuming you want that?"

Will nodded. "I want to know why. And what else he's done." Bastard, he thought. You bastard. And then he knew he was going to kill him, once he had all he needed from him, and he felt better. The rage had somewhere to go.

"Are you aware you're under the influence of a potent Charm?" Faulkner asked.

"What?"

"Your pupils dilated, your cheeks flushed and your lips went red again when you thought and spoke about Amelia White. Tell-tale signs of a love or lust Charm, probably a mixture of the two."

"I..." Will stammered, struggling to manage nausea as well as his anger.

"Did she engineer repeated exposure over a short period of time shortly after you first met?"

Will pushed his mind back to the beginning of the season in Aquae Sulis. The first moment he saw her on the balcony he'd been attracted to her. "She's very beautiful, it makes sense–"

"Did she make sure she had frequent access to you after you first met?" Faulkner repeated.

The memory of the crush in the hallway at the Peonias' party flooded back. She'd smelt of rose water and had made his chest almost burst with lust. They'd had tea and he couldn't stop watching her. Then the meetings to help them integrate into Aquae Sulis, the dinner parties, the way she smiled at him and made it so easy to help her. She was beautiful, but he'd met dozens of beautiful women all over the world and none of them had had the same effect on him.

"Damn it!" Will yelled and smashed his fist against the table. The Whites had played him and he'd lapped it all up. He slept with her on his wedding night! That night of all nights – why didn't he question his own decision? And the day Cathy was attacked, Amelia lured him up to her room when he'd been set on leaving. If he had left then...

"If you let me take a sample of your hair I can confirm it," Faulkner said. "From the way you're acting I assume I don't need to."

Will looked up from his fist to see the rest of the people in the café staring at him. "You don't need to," he said, twisting away from them and blocking his peripheral vision by resting his head in his hands. There was no one he could trust. Not even Amelia, who he thought loved him. He'd saved her and her brother, given her everything she needed... but even though she'd stolen his senses, it didn't mean she'd been complicit in the attack. He had to be certain.

"I need to know whether she knew Cathy was in danger," he said, rummaging in his pocket for his wallet. "I'll send a message to Cornelius to meet me at Black's in one hour. You'll take him into custody there and do whatever it takes to get everything out of him. Free rein."

"And when I'm finished with him?"

"Report back to me and don't let him go." He pulled a fiver out of his wallet and tossed it next to the coffee cup.

"There's something else," Faulkner said. "A message for your wife. We'd appreciate it if she were more subtle in her use of Charms in such public places."

"I beg your pardon?"

"She cast a Charm on the statue of Nelson in Trafalgar Square earlier. It seems she went straight out to test your new authority."

But he hadn't even told her yet. Will stood up, masking his ignorance with the movement. "I'll be sure to tell her." Why hadn't Carter stopped her? He'd given explicit instructions. How was he supposed to run Londinium when no one did as they should?

"Anyone else and we would have personally escorted them to the Patroon and pushed for their expulsion from Society."

"I understand," Will said. "You can go now."

He waited until Faulkner had left then went to the nearest underground station, one with multiple entrances and exits. If Faulkner knew where he was it meant the other Arbiters of his Chapter did too, and they might be following him. Whilst he wasn't afraid of them now, he didn't want them to know his business.

After a swift detour through the station and out by one of the more crowded exits, Will walked to the Bathurst stables and opened the Way to the Nether reflection. He penned a message and sent the head of the stables to take it to Cornelius. After a brief stop at the Emporium of Things in Between and Besides he instructed the driver to take him to Cornelius and Amelia's house. The journey gave him time to think it all through and calm down. He'd deal with the Whites first. He needed to root out the lies and make sure that his family was safe. Then he would work out what to do next. He only had the throne because of betrayal and manipulation, the former by Cornelius, the latter by his own patron. His wife was lying to him and was, it seemed, determined to have herself thrown out of the Nether. He'd been ordered to appoint the wrong man as Marquis and the Court would be against his reign from the start. His temples throbbed. If only he could be back in Sicily again. If only he could be that man running on the shore line, the beautiful girl dancing in and out of the surf ahead of him, with nothing to worry him in the Worlds. Will felt heavy with the knowledge that he could never be that young man again.

When the carriage drew up he slid the feather from its envelope and brushed it across his eyelids, under his nose, across his lips and his earlobes as the Shopkeeper had instructed. He felt no different but had been told it would be so. The protection would last a day and a night. He checked his pocket watch as the footman lowered the step. Cornelius would be in Faulkner's custody by now.

When the door was opened he climbed out. "You're to come inside and wait in the hall," he said to his footmen. They were the same men he'd brought to the house before and, just as they had been then, they were armed.

The front door was opened by the butler who bowed low. Will entered, his men behind him, and asked for Amelia. She was already at the top of the stairs.

"Will!" she called and hurried down. She was dressed in a peach-coloured damask silk and looked bright and healthy. Will appreciated her beauty as one would that of a painting, not as a man in love. As she took each step he became more and more aware of how deeply he'd been in her thrall. There was no need to harden his heart against her because there was nothing real there at all. Memories of being in love with her felt just like that: memories, something faded and already tarnished. The briefest urge to embrace her felt more of a habit than anything genuine.

"Amelia," he said and forced himself to smile.

"I'm so delighted to see you. It's been so long since you last visited!"

He hadn't been there since the day of the attack. He'd been in Exilium for two weeks then had been at Cathy's side every spare moment.

She stopped halfway down the staircase, studying his face. Then she curtsied deeply. "Your Grace," she said and then winked. "Would you be so kind as to wait for me in the drawing room? I'll be with you in a moment. I'll have tea sent and..." She fluttered her eyelashes in such an obvious way. "There's something we need to discuss."

He was tempted to just have it out with her, then and there, but he wanted to see if she was doing what he suspected.

Tea was brought but he didn't touch it. Amelia arrived a minute later in a cloud of rosewater scent that sparkled about her, confirming his suspicion. The protective Charm was doing its job well; not only was it preventing its effects, it was showing him when the love Charm was at its strongest. It was likely infused in her scent and when she saw he was different, she'd dashed back to her room and doused herself in it, desperate to have him malleable once more.

"Darling, how naughty of you to send for Cornelius so we could be alone."

"I wanted to see you by yourself," he said, standing out of habitual politeness. "There's something we need to talk about."

"I beg you to let me speak first. Please."

So she was going to confess. It would make it easier. She was shrewd and could sense the game was up. "You first then."

"I'm pregnant."

It felt as if the floor was falling away in front of him. Could the day get any worse?

Her face fell. "You're not pleased. Oh... oh, dear."

"Are you telling the truth, Amelia?"

Her shock appeared genuine. "I would never lie about such a thing! I'm going to give you a son. He'll be born in July next year. A summer baby."

A son. From the wrong woman. His guts twisted. "How could this have happened?" he whispered.

"What did you expect?" Amelia said sharply, then drew in a long breath. "Love has its consequences, darling."

She was looking different. There was a fullness in her cheeks and a pink glow that hadn't been there before. Her hair was shining. His son was growing inside her. Will looked away.

"Have I lost my appeal?"

He said nothing.

"I thought you'd be pleased. I'm going to give you a handsome and strong son, darling."

"I know what Cornelius did." There was a long pause. "And I know what you've been doing to me since Aquae Sulis. I'm going to give you one chance to tell me the truth, Amelia. One." He looked at her. She was sitting rigidly upright, hands clasped in her lap, still enveloped in a sparkling cloud. "Did you know Cornelius was planning to kill my wife?"

She held his gaze, as still as death. "Yes," she said. "He forced me not to tell you, even though I wanted to, Will. I wanted to warn you."

Will's breath felt like it had turned to ice in his throat. He'd expected her to deny it, but she was no fool. She'd realised why Cornelius wasn't there and why he hadn't touched her since he arrived. "Why didn't you?"

"He's my brother! And I wanted to take her place. I don't want to be locked away like a private whore. I want to be the wife at your side! She doesn't deserve you."

"Catherine has never manipulated me and never conspired to kill another. Don't you dare imply you are better than her!"

Will's voice rose to a shout. "She's my wife! You used me, you twisted me up and made me think I loved you when I should have been devoting myself to her!"

"Oh, don't be so melodramatic." She smoothed a wrinkle in her silk dress. "You men are all the same. I didn't need to use a Charm to get your attention. I didn't force you to come here on your wedding night. You did that all by yourself. You wanted it all; me in the background to satisfy your needs whilst you kept your family happy. Catherine's so ugly you would have taken a mistress without my involvement."

He was on his feet. "You will not say another word about my wife. You're not fit to speak her name. This is how it's going to be: you won't see Cornelius again. He will be kept a long way from where the two of you can cook up any more conspiracies and you'll be sent into Mundanus for the pregnancy. You will be watched twenty-four hours a day and if you do anything that could jeopardise my son's health, I will have Cornelius killed. If you try to escape or do anything to hurt me or my family, I will have Cornelius killed. He will understand that, if he does anything other than regret his actions, you will be killed. Your mutual good behaviour will ensure each other's survival. Do you understand?"

She was shaking and her hands twisted the pearls at her throat. "And when your son is born?"

"He'll be taken from you and will never know your name. You won't be able to poison him with your ill spirit. You'll live out the rest of your days in Mundanus."

"No!" She threw herself forwards and clutched his jacket hem. "Don't make me old, Will, don't–"

"Don't be so melodramatic," he said as she sobbed. "I could have you sent to the Agency, sold off to a foreign brothel or simply killed. Be grateful that I'm merciful." He freed himself from her. "I wouldn't bother," he said, going to the door. "It doesn't matter how much you cry, I won't be moved."

The tears stopped and she twisted to look at him. "You're making a mistake, William. She isn't capable of being a decent Duchess and you know it. Forgive me, forget her and make *me* your wife. I'll give you everything you could ever need or want from a woman."

Will smiled sadly and shook his head. "No, you can't, Amelia. There wouldn't be any trust."

He left the room and closed the door behind him. The matter was almost finished. Once he had a full report from Faulkner there would be only one decision left with regard to the former Alba-Rosas: the manner of Cornelius' death.

8

Sam sat in the doorway of the forge, cradling the cup of tea in his hands. The birds were singing and the breeze was fresh and cool. He wiped his forehead and looked at the grimy sweat on the back of his hand. The only time he'd ever got this dirty through hard work had been the day he'd helped his grandmother clear out an old shed when he was a boy. She was long dead and he hadn't thought about her for years. She was just a collection of fragmented impressions now: blue-rinsed hair, the smell of lavender soap and camphor mothballs, and a jar of pear drops that never seemed to run out. She died when he was seven, the same summer he'd cleared out the shed. He could still remember seeing all the things that he'd pulled out for her on the grass in the back garden when they went back to her house after the funeral. He had no idea what had happened to it all. The house was probably sold and other people lived there now, people who had no idea who she had been.

That was the thing about death, he thought as he sipped the tea. It made everything seem so poignant. He couldn't remember anything now without some reference to it. Leanne was still on his mind for what felt like every minute of the day he wasn't hammering the iron. He knew, intellectually, that his life had once been normal but it was so hard to recall. The bereavement was like the camphor in his grandmother's clothes; it perfused everything and the smell just lingered on and on long after the mothballs were gone.

The heat from the forge felt good on his back. It was like sitting between two worlds, one cold, one hot, and on the threshold between the two was his aching body. He'd become aware of muscles in his arms and back and shoulders that he never knew existed. Iron had hired a masseuse to stay as long as Sam needed her and three times a day she worked the knots out and made him groan in the place between pain and relief. Every day he got up, he walked to the forge and he hit metal all day long.

What surprised him was how much he'd taken to it. He'd never been particularly practical and always avoided the DIY jobs around the house until Leanne got impatient enough to hire a bloke to come and do it for them. He wrote code in front of a screen all day and then most evenings she was out and he played games on another screen. He hadn't looked at a computer since the funeral. Nothing seemed as real now as standing over the anvil, beating the shit out of lumps of iron.

He finished the tea and set the mug down. He stood and stretched, worked a crick out of his right shoulder and decided that once the piece he was working on was finished, he'd open the letter Leanne had left him.

Cathy took her seat in the carriage as Will spoke to the footmen. It reminded her of when they'd been newly married; she was dressed far more extravagantly than she'd ever choose for herself and feeling sick with nerves. Will didn't seem nervous on the outside, but he was more withdrawn than usual. She'd hardly seen him in the week since he gave her the library and it felt like the little moments of closeness they'd had were distant memories. But she was used to feeling awkward. In fact, it was comforting and the less at ease with each other they were, the less likely the chance of pregnancy.

"Would you like me to ride in the carriage with you, your Grace?" Carter asked him. Cathy sighed. Carter was a nice enough man, from what she could tell, but Will still hadn't dismissed him even though he knew Thorn couldn't attack her again.

"Take the place of the second footman," Will replied and Carter obeyed. The carriage rocked when he climbed onto the back.

Sophia came running out of the front door calling Will's name for a last-minute goodbye. As he embraced her, Cathy ran through her mental checklist: arrive, smile, say nothing stupid, swear oath to the city, survive the first Court, don't trip over anything and avoid the food. "I can do this," she whispered to herself. "I can do this." She groaned. Lucy's advice wasn't working. Perhaps positive self-affirmations were for Californians only. Perhaps the sarcasm and perpetual doubt wired into her British brain had made her immune to such tricks.

Will opened the door and climbed in, laying his top hat on the seat next to him. He was dressed in a rather austere Victorian-style morning suit with a deep blue cravat and waistcoat embroidered with subtle fleur-de-lys. It was the same colour as the trim on her dress, also in the late Victorian style and high-necked to cover the scar.

There was no more pain, thanks to some salve sent by Dame Iris. It was an expensive gift, the nurse had told her, and, whilst Cathy didn't want to accept it, she knew the Dame would be informed of her recovery. The note sent with it had said Dame Iris was delighted to receive the invitation to the first Court of William's Dukedom and hoped the salve would make the evening easier for her. It hadn't fooled Cathy; no doubt there was another agenda at play, as there always was with Dame Iris.

Will knocked on the roof of the carriage and they pulled off. Cathy waved to Sophia, who was sitting on her uncle's shoulders and waving a lace handkerchief. Cathy hadn't told anyone that every time she looked at Sophia she saw the thorns about her neck and felt the pain in her hands again. It wouldn't make the memories fade any faster.

"We're not going directly to the Tower," Will said. "Don't worry, we're just taking a more circuitous route."

"Are you worried about another attack?"

"I discussed it with Carter. It's best to be unpredictable." He looked at her properly for the first time. "I like your gown. How are you feeling?"

"Fine," she replied, resisting the temptation to make a comment about what he'd said to her before: "If you're well enough to gallivant around London causing chaos, you're well enough to be Duchess."

For a few minutes they sat in silence. She wanted to tell him about Bennet, but merely taking a breath to start made her cough. The curse was too strong. After a brief concerned look, Will stared out of the window into the mists, his mind evidently far away from the carriage. "Are you still angry?" she asked. "About the Animation Charm?"

It took him a moment to look at her with any focus. "What?"

"Because, like I said, I'm sorry. I should have done something more subtle."

"It's behind us now."

He'd been furious but it wasn't anything like her father's rage. Where her father rattled like a pot filled with boiling water before blowing up and beating her, Will just got colder and asked piercing rhetorical questions to make her feel like a total idiot. He accepted that both she and Carter had had to do as the Arbiter had asked but he still made the point that she could have chosen something that wouldn't have caused a viral YouTube hit. And he was right, she hadn't been thinking like an Iris. She hadn't considered the family and the impact it could have on their reputation. She'd had the feeling there was a lot more on his mind than he'd said but she hadn't wanted to draw it out any longer. She'd learned from her father that it was best to admit fault and apologise to make the storm pass as quickly as possible.

She didn't actually regret any of it, but she had to get him on side if she was going to achieve any real change in her new role. Will was looking out of the window again. He was so quiet. "Are you nervous?" she asked and he shook his head.

"I don't get nervous about things like this," he replied. "Everyone knows what they're supposed to do and when."

"But what about after the ceremony?"

"What about it?"

"Well... that's not scripted."

It was one of the many, many things that terrified her about the evening ahead. Small talk was bad enough but small talk with absolutely everyone watching and paying attention? She couldn't imagine a social situation harder than that. She started to shake and clasped her gloved hands tight on her lap. It all seemed too soon. Once Will had decided she was ready to be sworn in, the huge social machine had gone into motion. Poor Tom had only just moved to the city and had had less than a week to come to terms with the new position. He'd still looked pale when she saw him that morning to go over the last details of the ceremony.

"You're more capable than you think," Will said. "Remember, you're the Duchess. You don't have to seek their approval. They should be seeking yours."

"I'm only Duchess because I'm married to you, not because I'm better than them."

"Irrelevant," Will replied.

She wanted to bite her nails but they were trapped under silk fingertips. "What if someone says something about the new venue?"

"What are you worried they'll say?"

She shrugged. "I don't know. I think Tom had a point."

"Your brother's an academic, he sees things differently."

"No, I think he was talking sense. The Tower was built to crush the rowdy Londoners and lots of people know that."

"Somerset House was built to run an Empire that only exists in the Nether now," Will replied. "It reminds everyone of what we've lost in Mundanus. Everywhere has a history. And the White Tower is perfect for us. Lord Iris himself made its reflection in the Nether and it was the first property in Londinium. The Rosas never used it because of its Iris roots but we can feel safer there than in any building they commissioned."

"Oh, come on." Cathy wasn't willing to be fobbed off. "I'm not stupid, Will. Your ancestor – your namesake – had that Tower built for a specific reason. It's a statement."

"Is that a problem?"

"Is it really the kind of statement you want to make? 'The Iris family will crush any resistance just like the good old Normans did' is a bit… I don't know… brutal, isn't it?"

"A strong statement is the best way to begin a new reign."

"You don't have to distance yourself from Bartholomew this much, though." The brief creasing between his eyebrows showed her she'd struck a nerve. "It wasn't your fault. If you'd known what that bastard Cornelius did, you never would have duelled Bartholomew. You only acted on the information you had at the time. You thought you were doing the right thing."

"Did I?"

She found it hard to remember the warmth she'd seen in him. When he told her what the Whites had done, he'd shaken with rage, and he hadn't been anything but tense since then.

"Will," she said softly, leaning across the gap to take his hands, "why don't we tell Margritte what happened? She has a right to know and you need to be free of this guilt. His name should be cleared."

"We've been through this," he said but he didn't push her away. "If anyone else finds out what happened they could argue I have no right to the throne."

"But it doesn't change the fact you won the duel and that's why you have the throne, not because of what you thought he did."

"It changes the reason why I challenged him and then I'd be known as the fool who's easy to trick. And not only me; Lord Iris would be seen as fallible too and that is simply unacceptable. He wants me to rule here and that's what I must do. He didn't want me to just take the throne, Cathy, he wants me to keep it." He squeezed her hands. "Don't tell anyone. Swear it to me."

"I just don't think that–"

"Swear it!"

She saw the fear in his eyes and felt the desperation in his touch. The guilt was chewing him up inside. It wasn't the time to talk about Bartholomew's honour. "I won't tell anyone," she said, but there was no relief in his eyes. "You can trust me, Will."

"Can I?"

She knew that feeling. She'd tasted that fear, that need to have someone on her side and how bitter it was to be alone. A thousand times in her childhood she'd looked for someone who'd stop her father's violence but there was no one willing to help her. Tom was just as frightened of him, and her mother and sister didn't care. She knew the loneliness of struggling to find a way out, not being able to tell a soul of her plans and the sheer terror of seeing them through. He didn't want to be Duke, she could see that, no matter how hard he tried to look like he was born into the role. He was only avoiding Lord Iris' wrath, as they all were. The system held him as tightly as it held her and she didn't want him to feel that he was just as alone as she had felt.

"Will, I want to tell you something but I don't want you to freak out or anything until I've finished, all right?"

He gave a single nod, still holding her hands as tightly as she held his.

"I was planning to leave you. I was trying to find a way back to Mundanus with enough protections so that Iris couldn't find me. I managed to hide from Poppy before, for a couple of years before the engagement was announced. That's why everything was so tense at the first ball in Aquae Sulis; my family only just managed to get me back before you came home. I wanted to do it again. That's why I was so angry with you for wanting to marry sooner. But I'm not going to try to run away again."

He felt like he was really there with her for the first time since they left the house, staring deep into her eyes as if searching for something. "Why not?"

"Because I want to change Society rather than run away from it. And I've been thinking about being Duchess and it scares the living shit out of me and I'd rather go and live with my parents again than have to be on show in the Court but I've started to think this might be a chance to change things."

"What things?"

"How women are treated, for a start. Look, in Mundanus everything changed in the last hundred years or so because of external factors like the world wars and the industrial revolution and all kinds of other stuff. But in the Nether there aren't the same pressures. It's a closed system that endlessly propagates itself, do you see? People aren't supposed to live for hundreds of years and the way they think isn't supposed to dominate for as long as it does here. It's a stagnant pond, so we have to change it from within. We could do that. Together."

She held her breath as she waited for his response. She hadn't planned to raise it then even though she'd tried to think of a way to bring up the topic so many times and in so many different ways.

He kissed her gloves, closing his eyes as he did so. "I don't want you to leave me. I can't do this by myself and I can't keep worrying that you're not on my side."

"But I am, Will. I can see you're not like the others. You've respected my wishes and not forced yourself on me and I really do appreciate that, I do. I've met Iris, I know how scary he is and I know he's putting you under pressure too."

He pulled a hand away to curl it behind her neck, pulling her in to kiss her. "I haven't been a perfect husband. I'll try harder. And thank you for being honest with me."

"If we can't trust each other this is all going to fall apart," she said. "I'm not sure I even know how to really be with you, but I want to try now. I want to make things different and I need you to be on my side too. Are you?"

This time she was searching his face for something to cling to. He broke eye contact, bringing her hands together in her lap and closing his own over them to hold them tight. "We can't do anything radical. Not yet, Cathy. We have to establish ourselves, we have to have a child and we have to survive. We can't do anything outside of what's expected of us or we'll draw even more attention and we don't need that now."

"But we'll be the most powerful couple in Londinium – who better to lead by example? Who better to start a dialogue and bring these issues into the public consciousness than us?"

He shook his head. "No. The Patroon wouldn't support this and neither would the Dame."

"Fuck them!" Cathy balled her fists beneath his hands as he winced. "They're part of the system – of course they won't like it. That's the point!"

"Cathy, listen to me. We need to secure our position here. We need to make alliances and deal with the mess I made – that Cornelius made. We can't think about anything else and we can't make it harder by bringing in another agenda that will alienate the very people we need to bring on side. There's too much to lose."

"But that's exactly why nothing ever changes here – because people are scared. Don't you see what we could gain by having a Society with women contributing as much as men? We're wasted on bloody embroidery and taught to worry about what we look like all the sodding time. And it sucks for the men too! You don't have any real freedom either. It could be so much better."

"I agree, but we have to protect our own interests. If we try to change things like this without being in a strong position then we'll destroy ourselves without achieving anything."

She took a breath to argue back but reconsidered. They were on their way to the first test of his Dukedom, it wasn't the right time. She'd find a way to bring him round and in the meantime she had the other names in Miss Rainer's file to track down. There were allies out there, she was certain.

Will was still holding her hands, their foreheads were almost touching. He smelt of vanilla and musk and she wanted to kiss him but she didn't dare. "I admire your ambition and your passion but you need to redirect it, my love," he said. "We mustn't forget that Iris expects a son in the first year of our marriage."

"Haven't you wondered why?"

"He always wants sons in every generation. Everyone does."

"But why the rush? We're going to be together for hundreds of years. It's not like we're racing the menopause."

"I… I don't know."

"And why were we paired off in the first place? I mean, it's madness. If this was just about sealing an alliance between the Papavers and Irises, they'd have married Nathaniel to my sister. They're perfect for each other. You're leagues above me. When you were eligible they could have married any daughter they wanted into your line. Someone beautiful, someone hugely wealthy or strategically important but no, they marry you to me. The misfit. The ugliest girl in Aquae Sulis."

"Cathy–"

"No, it's true. There has to be a reason and it's something to do with the child we'd have together, I'd bet money on it. Why else do it?"

He frowned to himself and then shook his head. "I don't know. But it doesn't change anything. And surely it wasn't so bad before?"

She leaned back. "It isn't that I don't want you, Will, really." She tried not to laugh. "That's not the problem. I just can't allow myself to get pregnant."

"Why? Every woman–"

"No," she cut in. "Don't you dare say that's what every woman wants. My father said that on the morning of our wedding and I could've punched him. I just don't see myself as a mother and besides, there's no way in hell I'd want to bring a child into our Society."

"Why ever not? Our child would want for nothing."

"Except the freedom to do whatever they want. Come on, Will, think about it. I'm not going to bring a girl into this world to be sold off as property and I'm not going to raise a son to think that's all women are good for. It just isn't right."

"It doesn't matter how we might feel about it. Consider the consequences of disobeying Lord Iris."

"But what are the real consequences of giving him what he wants? For all we know, he may have plans for any son we might have."

"But he'll get what he wants, one way or another. There are a hundred different ways he could force this to happen. Let's not open ourselves to that kind of misery." He released her hands and cupped her face in his. His kiss was tender and deep. "Let's make a child the right way, without anything else interfering."

Cathy cursed the way her body betrayed her, and the fact that he wasn't listening to her. He didn't really understand why she didn't want it to happen. He was just frightened of Iris and, whilst she was too, she was determined to keep her body her own for as long as she could.

The carriage was slowing down. "Oh, shit," she whispered. "We're there."

9

As soon as they entered the room, Will knew he'd made the right decision in moving the Court's location. The ducal thrones had been reupholstered to the Iris blue and a golden fleur-de-lys was set into the top of the chair backs. The room was smaller than the one at Somerset House but it was still large enough for the assembled and there were many other rooms in the White Tower more suited to dances and dinners. He was even considering moving the family there. The thick stone walls were reassuring and it felt right to be in a place created by the man he'd been named after. It had a different sense of grandeur, one older and with more gravitas than the stuccoed reminders of Empire. These walls had seen over a thousand years of power and it felt right to weave his reign into that ongoing history.

He cast his eye over the room as people relaxed and conversed after the tight formality of the ceremony. All had gone to plan. Tom had hidden his nerves well and actually looked the part. He had the same military posture as his father, even though Tom had never served. As far as Will knew he hadn't even been on his Grand Tour.

Lucy, his wife, seemed happy and supportive and in fact the only one of their family who seemed utterly delighted with Tom's change in status. He watched her accompany Tom around the room, moving from introduction to introduction with ease and warmth.

Sir Iris had said his goodbyes after the ceremony was over, leaving Dame Iris to stay for the rest of the evening. Whilst Cathy had barely been able to hide her dismay at the news the Dame would be staying, Will was glad. The Dame would no doubt dissect the evening with Cathy at one of their meetings and help her to read the politics of the room. He was glad his Patroon had elected to make his excuses. It was an awkward situation; Will was the most powerful man in the city and now one of the highest-status Irises in Albion – above even his father – but the Patroon was still the head of the family. It was hard to be deferential to his authority whilst trying to stamp his own on the room and he appreciated the tact demonstrated by leaving him as the only high-ranking male Iris there. The Dame, whilst still someone he would obey without question, didn't cause the same problems with visible pecking order.

Dame Iris was talking to Georgiana, Freddy Viola's wife, who was doing her best to extricate herself from the inevitable social disaster he would cause when drunk. Will recalled his appalling behaviour at the dinner party the Tulipas hosted when they first moved to Londinium, and Cathy's fork-based solution.

He glanced at Cathy and checked that she was managing her nerves. She was gripping the arms of her throne rather tightly but no one else would be able to see that and thankfully her presumably white knuckles were hidden by her gloves. They only had to sit there for a few minutes longer before they could leave the dais and mingle. Not that it would be a consolation to her, but being stuck there with everyone watching was rather odd.

He'd offered the room the opportunity to come and speak to them with any pressing matters that were of importance to the city as a whole before the proceedings became less formal. No one had approached them yet and he hoped no one would. He just wanted this evening to be simple so that Cathy could see that nothing terrifying would happen. Over time she'd get used to it, he was certain. At least she was trying her best; if she hadn't had the change of heart she'd confessed in the carriage it could be so much worse. He brushed the baby finger of her right hand and she looked at him, alert and ready to be tested. He just smiled and with palpable relief she returned it. If you meant what you said in the carriage, he thought, we could not only survive this, we could thrive.

Then Freddy's voice cut through the moment. "That's terrible!" he boomed. He'd been relatively quiet up until that point and in all the places Will expected him to cause trouble he'd been mercifully silent. But now there was a glass of wine in his hand and a familiar red flush across his nose and cheeks.

He was talking to Mr Lutea-Digitalis, the former Marquis. He'd seemed relieved to be released from the post, knowing it would be a difficult position to hold in a hostile Court. Had he planned to cause trouble with Freddy?

Freddy's younger brother crossed the room swiftly and spoke to his elder. Will noted how different they were and how hard the younger was working to try and contain Freddy's outburst. He watched the room divide between those who thought it best to ignore Viola's latest bout of hot air and those who enjoyed good social sport. Georgiana excused herself from Dame Iris and went over as Freddy said, "But this is something you should take to the Duke. This is something that affects all of us!"

When Georgiana tried to speak to him he brushed her off and then told his younger brother to leave it all to him. Freddy planted a hand between Digitalis' shoulders and propelled him through the parting crowd to the foot of the dais.

"Something you need to hear. Your Grace," he added a beat later.

Will looked expectantly at Digitalis. "Is there something wrong?"

"My wife and I were robbed yesterday whilst travelling on the Nether road between Somerset House and our residence."

Now everyone was paying attention. "Were you hurt?" Cathy asked.

"No, your Grace, thankfully," he replied as his wife joined his side, as crimson as her dress. "When I saw their weapons I decided it was best to hand over what they demanded so we would be left with our lives."

"Our driver was struck," his wife said. She looked quite distressed at the memory of it. "He has a black eye, poor chap."

"I'm very sorry to hear of this," Will said.

"Being sorry doesn't do any bloody good," Freddy said.

"It isn't the Duke's fault, Freddy," Digitalis hissed. "Thank you, your Grace."

"He might not have been the robber but he's responsible for our safety, isn't he?" Freddy turned to address the room. "That includes the roads, surely?"

Tom stepped forwards. "Actually, it does not. There are no edicts, documents or records of any previous Dukes adopting responsibility for the roads between Nether properties and the location of the Court."

"Oh, read them all, have you?" Freddy scoffed.

"Actually I have," Tom replied, impressively calm. "As Marquis, it's my role to know such things, as I'm sure Mr Digitalis is aware."

"Yes, I am very aware of it," Digitalis spoke with obvious irritation towards Freddy. "Do stop making such a fuss. There have been highwaymen preying upon Londinium for hundreds of years and the Duke has only just taken office. It seems rather unreasonable to expect him to remove a problem the Rosas couldn't solve in all that time."

The old faultlines in the Court were being laid bare; the Violas were rich but they weren't socially successful, thanks to Freddy's lack of self-control. Will noted the younger brother's baleful stare at the back of Freddy's head.

It seemed Freddy hadn't anticipated the lack of support either. "Well, seeing as everything's changing, why not make another?" He turned back to look at Will. "Of course the Rosas didn't solve the problem, they were lazy, corrupt and didn't give a toss about anyone except themselves. I was pleased to see a new Duke on the throne. Someone I knew could make the kind of changes Londinium has needed for hundreds of years."

He meant Bartholomew. Freddy was no fool, as much as he liked to make people think he was. Will knew he was trying to back him into a corner and make him promise to do something, fearful of being seen as less capable of change than Bartholomew. For anyone else it would be madness, but Freddy didn't know about the power he had over the Arbiters. It would be a risk but, if he could pull it off, it would silence any doubters.

"Change is a powerful thing and I agree that the problem has existed far too long," he said. "I take my responsibilities as Duke very seriously and believe it's an omission to declare the Nether roads outside of my protection. Without them there is no city to speak of. Let it be entered into the record that my first promise to you as Duke of Londinium is to make the roads between your homes and the White Tower safe to

travel in the Nether. I will not have any person within my
domain be afraid to travel. I can't say how long it will take,
nor can I say it will be without its setbacks and difficulties.
But I will deal with the highwaymen and give the residents
of this domain the security they deserve."

There was a spontaneous burst of applause and he couldn't
resist a quick glance at Dame Iris to gauge her reaction. She
too was clapping politely but her expression was inscrutable.

Freddy was easy to read. He made a couple of gruff
comments which were inaudible above the applause and then
downed the contents of his glass. His younger brother, standing
behind him, moved aside with obvious contempt when Freddy
launched himself back into the crowd to find more wine. He
made eye contact with Will and bowed deeply. Interesting, Will
thought. The younger Viola is someone to watch.

Max got off the train at Bath Spa, having delivered the
package to Catherine. It contained several files on people
she'd requested after their abortive attempt to get a London
Arbiter to come and talk to her. He'd pulled them from the
Agency without mentioning it to Ekstrand, something the
gargoyle had talked him into.

He couldn't request a messaging tube from Ekstrand
without having to explain and he couldn't use the Letterboxer
Charm she'd suggested. He proposed a dead drop location
that she could send a servant to, but she didn't trust any of
them enough. She even seemed nervous of them.

Max spent a couple of hours patrolling the city centre but
saw nothing suspicious. There could be people disappearing
into Exilium all over the kingdom of Wessex for all he knew.
They were blind without the information network the Bath
Chapter used to manage and there was no one on the street
day in, day out like they needed. They were failing in their duty

of care and it had to be the same all over Albion, apart from Mercia. It was only a matter of time before the Fae noticed.

He'd been trying to speak to Ekstrand for almost a week, sending messages via Petra and Axon but receiving nothing in reply. The gargoyle was constantly on edge and had begun to wear a groove in the floorboards of Max's bedroom from the endless pacing. No progress was being made and Ekstrand was the problem.

Satisfied that nothing untoward was happening in the centre, Max headed back to Ekstrand's house. The gargoyle was waiting for him in the lobby and ran up to him like a dog who'd been shut up in a house alone all day. "Ekstrand's come out of his room!" it said. "He's in the ballroom with the apprentices!"

The gargoyle bounded down the hallway ahead of him before running back and then on again as if it had too much energy. As he approached the ballroom Max could hear Ekstrand's voice clearly through the door.

He knocked once and then entered, the gargoyle at his heels. The apprentices were gathered and looking down at something covered by a dark cloth in the middle of the room. Ekstrand was standing next to it dressed in a tweed suit with leather patches on the elbows.

"What sort of things could the Sorcerer of Mercia have neglected to ward his property against? Be creative now."

Gordon, the most enthusiastic apprentice, bobbed up and down with his hand in the air. Ekstrand pointed at him.

"Small mammals, sir."

"I beg your pardon?"

"Guinea pigs… hamsters, that sort of thing."

"No." Ekstrand cut him off. "Bombarding the Sorcerer's house with… otters is not creative, it's absurd. He will have warded against projectiles, even living ones. Next!"

"Acid," another suggested.

"Rubbish," Ekstrand said. "Is that the best you can all come up with? Acid is first on my list of things to ward my property against, not just because my list is alphabetical. The first things that spring to any Sorcerer's mind are destructive substances, so of course he'll have protected against all of them, including fire, ice – and jellied eels, before anyone suggests that foul substance."

"Sir," Max called from the back. "I must speak with you."

"Not now, Maximillian, I'm in the middle of an important lesson."

"But sir, it's about the Sorcerer of Mercia."

All of the apprentices turned to look at him.

Ekstrand held up a hand. "You're far behind me. I've been going through some old notes and I've already found out something desperately important about him. Well, two things actually. No, three. Three, yes. The first is his name: Rupert! I knew it was something that sounded like a currency, and I was right."

"Will that be useful for fighting him, sir?" Gordon asked.

"That his name sounds like Rupee? No, of course not."

"No, sir, knowing his name."

"Oh. No, not at all, but it was bothering me. Now the second thing I found in my clearing out was a notebook in which I wrote two very important lists. One is a list of places I would like to visit one day. The other – more important for the war – is a list of places I never, ever want to visit. And do you know what's at the top of the list?" When Max, the gargoyle and the apprentices shook their heads in unison he said, "Oxford."

He beamed at them all. No one had anything to say for a moment until Gordon said, "Oh! Oxford is in the kingdom of Mercia!"

Ekstrand nodded. "I started that list a long time ago, I remember writing that city down after I had a rather difficult Moot at which we were all discussing the civil war. Rupert was defending his decision to let the royal Court convene in Convocation House and the Sorcerer of Northumbria was furious about it. They shouted for hours until Rupert said something along the lines of it being his property, in his domain, so he could do what he wanted there. I had completely forgotten until I saw that list. Convocation House is one of the rooms in the Bodleian Library quadrangle. I'd wager the library is his anchor property too. It's certainly one of the largest in central Oxford, the only one that could contain his monstrous ego."

"But surely he wouldn't give away the location of his home, sir," Max said. All Sorcerers were fiercely protective of their privacy, especially with each other.

"Ah, but he wasn't thinking about such things at the time. He wasn't being careful at all. Of course, there's every possibility that he lives somewhere else now, given it was several hundred years ago, but it's the best place to start."

"What was the third thing?" the gargoyle asked. "You said you found three."

"Did I? Oh. I can't remember. It'll come back to me. So you see, Maximillian, I know everything I need to know about that ne'er-do-well."

"But sir, I don't think he's behind the attack on the Moot."

Ekstrand blinked rapidly. "Preposterous. Rupert of Mercia is a villain from an order of pond scum so low it hasn't even made it into any phyllotactic classification of plant life. He killed the others to take over Albion, as he's always wanted."

"But everything points to the Sorcerer of Essex."

"Dante's dead!"

"Exactly!" the gargoyle said. "He was already dead when the others were murdered. Petra told us that."

"Thereby making it impossible for it to have been him," Ekstrand replied. "So it must be Rupert. I didn't kill them and they wouldn't want to kill themselves – at least not in such a sociable manner – so it has to be Rupert."

"Fae magic can animate inanimate objects and make them behave in a way the caster of the Charm expects," Max said. "Someone must have animated Dante's dead body so the other Sorcerers would be tricked long enough to be killed, a way that the wards couldn't protect against. The only people who could have access to his dead body are one of his apprentices or someone from the Essex Chapter – which we already know is corrupt."

"But that doesn't change the fact that Rupert didn't go to the Moot!" Ekstrand said, his right index finger pointing up at the ceiling. "Why? Because he had to stay outside to cast the foul magic on the building."

Max could hear the gargoyle's stone teeth grinding with frustration. Ekstrand simply wasn't applying logic to the evidence. "No, sir, I believe he may have stayed away for the exact same reason as you; he suspected foul play. His absence from that meeting isn't enough to place him under suspicion."

"Yes, it is." Ekstrand folded his arms. "He's been planning this for years, I know he has. It all started with killing my Chapter. Not anyone else's – mine. Why? Because he's always coveted Wessex and wanted to weaken me!"

"No, sir." Max shook his head. "I think the Chapter was destroyed by someone from London – it only happened after I discovered the corruption there. That's where our efforts should be focused. Not Mercia."

"There's only a tiny amount of effort left to spend on dealing with Rupert," Ekstrand said. "Then once he's gone I can turn my mind to other matters without fearing for my life."

"But sir–"

"Enough." Ekstrand held a hand up at him. "You're defending him too much. Should I be concerned about corruption in the remnants of my own Chapter?"

The gargoyle gasped. "You crazy son of a bitch!" it yelled. "You're supposed to be calm and clever and look at facts without emotional crap and look at you! You're obsessed with this Rupert bloke when the rest of the country is going to shit because of something going down in London! London, not the sodding Midlands!"

For a few moments Ekstrand didn't say anything, he just stood with wide eyes and lips pressed so tight together it looked like his mouth had disappeared. "You," he said, so quietly the apprentices leaned forwards en masse to listen, "will not speak another word in my presence or I will destroy you and the shell left behind. Get out."

The gargoyle looked at Max who pointed at the door. Ekstrand wasn't going to listen and there was nothing he could do about it. He had the briefest flash of seeing the gargoyle leaping at him and some nebulous idea of a coup but it unravelled in the cold light of good sense. The gargoyle slinked out silently, its tail between its legs, chin so low it was almost scraping the floor.

"Now, let's move on," Ekstrand said as Max backed away until he was pressed against the wall by the door, watching silently. "We've wasted enough time so I'll give you the answer. The one thing Rupert will not have protected himself against is protection itself and that is how I am going to kill him. I will protect him from the very things he needs to survive."

10

"Maggie!" Rupert waved to her from the door at the far end of the Divinity Schools, one of the many parts of the Bodleian Library she'd never visited before. As she walked towards him she glanced up at the beautiful medieval ceiling, covered with carved stone bosses reflected from the anchor property.

He beckoned to her and then went ahead into Convocation House, a place she'd heard was much plainer in design but with just as much historical significance, especially for the mundanes. Whilst she knew there would be less grandeur, Margritte didn't expect a mezzanine floor constructed out of glass and steel cable. It was one of the greatest crimes to interior design she'd ever witnessed. The new floor severed the remarkable interior of Convocation House in two, breaking all of the lines that the medieval architecture naturally drew to the eye. The bright electric – electric! – lighting was harsh to her eyes and made her squint. It was like stumbling into a sliver of Mundanus in the centre of Oxenford and she didn't like it one bit. The main floor space below was divided into different areas, one containing large sofas and a fireplace that seemed to hang from the ceiling in a most unnerving manner. There was an area filled with strange machines, only one of which resembled anything she could understand: a bicycle without proper wheels. She wondered if all Sorcerers had such appalling taste.

"What do you think?" He threw his arms out open and wide.

"It's certainly not what I expected."

"I've got a generator out the back. I don't know what you people have against electricity, it's fantastic stuff. Come up and I'll show you my den."

Den? He made it sound like an animal's nest. She stopped at the bottom of the stairs, also made of glass, that seemed to float at the side of the room. She couldn't see how they were attached to the wall and had no idea how they could be strong enough to take her weight. He laughed at the way she tested the bottom step.

"They're safe – they're cantilevered through the wall. I went to a gallery in Mundanus that had them and just had to have the same here. No sorcery, I promise. Not for the steps anyway."

Margritte lifted the front of her black skirts and climbed the steps with care. Most of the wall facing her as she arrived on the upper floor was covered by three massive screens. The two on the outer edges were displaying pieces of art, some of which she recognised, fading from one to the next every few seconds. The screen in the centre was black. A huge desk filled one corner, covered with paper, and with something she thought might be a computer sitting on top of it. She remembered seeing one in a mundane catalogue a friend's son had brought back from his Grand Tour. She and Bartholomew had looked through it late into the night, marvelling at how grotesque things had become in Mundanus. The computer on the desk bore only a slight resemblance; it was smaller and white and almost elegant in design.

Two reclining chairs made of black leather faced the screens and there were shelves of books filling the rest of the wall space. He watched her take it all in, a big grin plastered across his face. "You should see yourself." He laughed. "Maggie in Wonderland."

"Is this why you invited me over? To marvel at your mundane toys?"

He was wearing baggy jeans and a hooded top. Margritte was certain it was the same one he'd been wearing the first time they met. He gestured at one of the chairs. "So you wrote to your friends in Londinium then."

"Yes." She sat down and, before she could stop herself, slid down until the seat back moulded itself to her. Rupert pressed something at the side of the chair and she squeaked as it tipped back a few degrees and the lower front part rose into the air until she was almost lying down. It felt most improper. He jumped into the chair next to her.

"These are the best chairs you can get in Mundanus," he said and opened a compartment in the arm of his chair that she hadn't even noticed. He pulled out a can. "Beer?"

"I think not."

"Oh. Don't drink?"

"I drink wine, Rupert. Not ale."

He laughed. "Sorry. I'll remember that for next time." He angled his chair back as far as hers. "One of your friends visited today. I had one of my favourite students from the university give him a tour of the town."

The plan was working. "That's excellent news. Who was it?"

"Freddy Persificola-Viola. There is no fucking way that twat is going anywhere near any of my colleges."

Margritte sighed. "Did he offend you?"

"Not in person, I didn't meet the guy. No one knows about me until they become part of the university, otherwise it's a hard secret to keep. I made an exception for you."

"Because I was causing you such a headache?"

"Because you're exceptional."

Was he trying to win her favour? Surely not whilst she was still in mourning. But then he had the manners of a savage; he probably didn't even know that it was unacceptable. She shouldn't really have come to his residence alone. But she was a widow, not a debutante. "Did Freddy offend someone else?"

"Worse," he replied. "I'll show you."

Ekstrand pulled away the cloth with a flourish, revealing a small cannon. "And this is how it will be done."

Max was still pressed against the back wall, doing his best to not draw attention to himself. If he still had a Chapter Master he'd be seeking him out. He had no idea if there had ever been a situation in which a Sorcerer was deemed unfit to hold his post but it was irrelevant now. There was no superior to take his concerns to and no one to enforce an intervention even if it were possible.

"But sir," Gordon was saying. "Whilst I have every confidence in your ability to make a cannon powerful enough to send a shot all the way to Oxford, how would it be possible to calculate the trajectory? Only some of the variables would be known and the risk to mundane lives would be high, too."

Max considered going to warn Rupert but there were several problems, aside from the fact that he would have to truly betray the man he was sworn to serve. The first was that it would be very difficult to even reach the Bodleian. He'd heard from colleagues at the Chapter that the city of Oxford was one of the most tightly controlled in Albion. Nothing happened without the Arbiters there finding out and responding in minutes – they were rumoured to be the most successful Chapter in the Heptarchy. Secondly, even if it were possible to get to Rupert, how could he convince him of the threat? And there was always the possibility – even though it seemed incredibly remote – that Ekstrand was right.

Rupert's best chance was that Ekstrand's unravelling sanity would make him incapable of striking an effective blow against him. There had been many sorcerous wars in the past but all were before his lifetime and he had no idea if Ekstrand had ever formally battled with any of the other Sorcerers when they were alive.

"Firing from outside my house in Bath would be a truly idiotic thing to do," Ekstrand said. "Really, Gordon, I do wonder why you're here sometimes. No. I've used mundane maps to calculate the exact distance between my garden and the Bodleian Library quadrangle. I'm going to open a Way and fire it through."

Max stopped doubting whether Ekstrand was capable enough. It might only be on a couple of days of the week at most, but on those days he was still brilliant.

"This cannonball–" Ekstrand hefted one up from beside the cannon "–is inscribed with warding formulae." He held it out to Gordon. "If you can't interpret any of the variables your apprenticeship is over."

The young man pored over it for a few seconds. "This is true genius, Mr Ekstrand."

"Are you stalling?"

"No, sir. There are several strings of formulae. I can see one that would change the composition of the cannonball when it hits stone, changing it to something like… clay – to stick! And here, that's to make it blend into its surroundings so it's hard to find. When embedded into a building it would activate wards for the entire Nether structure against nitrogen, oxygen and several trace elements. In other words, air. This one…" He bit his lip. "I think it would force carbon dioxide into the structure – something he can't have warded against because it's a natural by-product of breathing. And this here... a ward against silver for the entire structure. Now that's devilish. And this clause renders the external and internal doors incapable of being opened and the windows from being opened or broken, so it would seal the building completely. The Sorcerer of Mercia would suffocate to death."

"*Will* suffocate to death," Ekstrand said. "Grammar should never be overlooked."

11

Rupert pointed a slender black chunk of something like Bakelite at the central screen and an image of the Oxford High Street appeared with the back of Freddy's head at the centre of the shot.

"You have to understand I can't let one of the Fae-touched just wander around the city without being watched."

She nodded. "I do. Especially when it's Freddy. The person who followed him took pictures without him noticing?"

"More than that." He pressed something on the Bakelite and the image started to move. The sound of cars and sirens blared out of nowhere, making her jump. "Surround sound," he said. "The bass makes the chairs shake. Listen to this."

"So," Freddy was saying to a girl walking beside him with a backpack on. "Are you one of the maids at the university?"

"I'm reading English Literature at Trinity College," she replied and gave him a sideways glance. "I came top of the year in my prelims."

"Really? What does your pater think about that?"

"My father? He's very proud of me."

Freddy grunted. "Bloody waste if you ask me. You're pretty enough to marry off easily. Why fill your head with books when all you need to do is have babies?"

The image paused and Rupert looked at Margritte. "He's just warming up."

Margritte didn't know what to say. Freddy had the same opinions as most of the men in Society; it seemed a little unfair to single him out.

Another button was pressed and the images sped up without sound. "Kay was a bloody angel – I would have punched him," Rupert said. "Look at this."

The image froze on a shot of Freddy's hand on the girl's derriere. The images moved in slow motion and Margritte watched the girl step away swiftly. Freddy seemed to laugh and said something to her – addressing her bosom rather than her face.

"Kay was pretty damn eloquent when she came and reported on him," Rupert said. "Did you know he was like this?"

"He's never been so brazen at any of my dinner parties or soirées," Margritte said. "I suppose he felt free of the strict social rules of the Nether." As Rupert's frown deepened she added, "That's no excuse, of course. He can be rather… trying."

"Then why the buggeration did you invite him to check out Oxford?"

"Because he's rich," she replied, spreading her hands. "One of the wealthiest in Londinium, now the Rosas are gone. I thought a college would be expensive to run and his deep pockets would be an asset."

"Maggie." Rupert shook his head. "I'm a Sorcerer. Money really isn't a problem. I wonder if you were thinking about how much of a dent in the Londinium tithe his defection would make."

Margritte put on her most charming smile. "I would be lying to you if I said it hadn't crossed my mind."

"Well, the others who come had better be more civilised than him or else this isn't going to work at all. I don't want any of your kind treating the women here like that. Mundanus has moved on and if they can't handle that, they don't have a place here."

She noted the flush in his cheeks, the way he waved the Bakelite stick around. He really meant it. "You aren't what I expected at all," she said.

He frowned at her. "I don't know how women like you survive there."

"What do you mean by 'women like me'?"

"With a brain. With some fire in your belly."

"Not all men are like Freddy." The ache returned to her breast.

"I met Bartholomew," Rupert said, putting the Bakelite into a pocket at the side of his chair. "He seemed like a decent guy."

"When did you meet him?"

"Oh… years ago. Before you were married. He grew up here. You knew that though. I knew his father better, of course. He was a brilliant man. Shame about Queen Anne… that really fucked him up."

"That was the Irises," Margritte said. "They cursed her. Bartholomew's father couldn't cope with the fact that he couldn't do anything to break it." She shifted onto her side, ignoring the tiny voice at the back of her mind complaining about the indecency of it all. "Tell me what Bartholomew was like when he was young."

Rupert tucked his hands behind his head. "He was quiet but not shy. Earnest. Bloody clever." He sighed. "Shame the Fae had their hooks in him, otherwise he would have made a brilliant apprentice."

"He didn't want to leave Oxenford," she said. "But the Patroon insisted he establish himself in Londinium."

"I'm sorry you lost him."

"Thank you. And I'm sorry about Freddy. He would have heard about the letters I sent to my other friends and I couldn't let him feel left out. He drove us mad but he was a loyal friend. Still is."

"Like those dogs, you know, the really big ones that slobber everywhere and stink the house out. You want to get rid of them but it's hard when they're so fucking happy to see you when you come home."

As she watched him speak, Margritte tried to unpick the knot of the man sitting next to her. He was hundreds of years old and yet acted like a mundane with the most appalling manners. Why do that? Did he want to shock her? Did he want her to form a bad opinion of him? Men rarely did, they were all so needy, so vulnerable in their own way.

"Did you have a dog?"

"Me?" He laughed. "I hate dogs. And the people who love them."

She planned to leave but somehow the conversation held her. He told her about the city, about the research being done at the university, about the students. She wanted to ask him about sorcery but held back. They hardly knew each other and it was something he'd never tell anyone, let alone someone from Society. He remembered a bottle of wine he'd put away and it was a fine vintage. They shared memories of what they'd been doing the year it was bottled and for a few hours she forgot the Irises and the plan to destroy William. Rupert told her about quantum physics and she told him about the art he was displaying and yet knew little about.

When the headache started she assumed it was the wine. The conversation had lulled and they were both flopped back in the chairs, staring at the ceiling. She felt warm and sleepy and tried to find the energy to announce she should leave.

Rupert was rubbing his eyes. "It's getting stuffy in here, I'm going to open a window."

"Alex will be wondering where I am," she said, drowsy and heavy-headed. "I won't tell him I've been with you."

"Why not? There are people in this city who'd cut off their baby finger to have an evening with me."

"Who?"

He shrugged as he went down the floating stairs. "People."

She listened to him swear as he fumbled with one of the latches. When the expletives increased in frequency she pulled herself out of the chair with effort and looked down on the floor below. "Something wrong?"

He abandoned the window and went to the next one along. "I don't open them very often."

"Would you be very offended if I told you this mezzanine doesn't work?"

"What do you mean? It works perfectly."

"I mean aesthetically. It cuts the space in two."

"But I like that. Oh, for fuck's sake, what is going on with these bloody things?"

"But it breaks the flow of the–" She stopped when she saw the irritation on his face shift to worry. "What's wrong?"

He went to the next window and then crossed the room and tried three on the other side. "They're jammed." He glanced up at her. "Come down."

She took the stairs slowly, feeling sluggish and uncertain of her footing. The wine had been stronger than she thought; she'd only allowed herself one glass. Rupert went to the door and tried the handle. His concern lit a flicker of worry in her chest. "Are we locked in?"

"Seems that way."

"But it's your house. Can't you unlock the door?"

"Nope. Something is very fucking wrong here. The air isn't

right…" He turned in a circle a couple of times, hands on top of his head. "Fuck this for a game of soldiers."

Margritte wrapped her arms about herself, regretting having stayed so long. Rupert patted the pockets in his trousers and she noticed the sheen on his forehead and upper lip. He pulled something round and silver out of one of the pockets and after a moment of fiddling, flicked a yo-yo out from his hand.

"Fuck."

"What are you doing?" She went to him, her legs leaden. "This isn't the time to play with toys! Open the door, I want to leave!"

"So do I," he yelled. "And this isn't a toy." He flicked it out again and then wiped the sweat from his face. "Shit. I can't open a Way. Something's locked this place down, I don't think anything's getting in or out."

"Including the air?"

He nodded and then his eyes shifted to the right. "Are your earrings silver?"

"Yes, but what does–"

"Give one of them to me."

"This is most–"

"Just do it!"

His shout echoed around the room. She struggled to unhook the earring with shaking fingers but finally dropped it into his outstretched hand. He gave it a brief inspection then threw it on the stone tiles.

"Rupert! That's–"

"Oh, holy fucksticks," he said and knelt on the floor. He picked up the earring and threw it again, cheek pressed to the tiles as he did so. "It's not even touching the tiles. Someone's warded the building against silver. Only a Sorcerer would know to do that. I'm being attacked."

"By another Sorcerer?" Margritte struggled not to shriek. "Are you sure?"

He pulled her down next to him. "Watch," he ordered and she stared at the earring as it was thrown again. There was no tinkle of metal against stone and when she moved to only inches away she could see it hovering half an inch above the stone.

"It's floating," she whispered.

"It's a fucking disaster," he said and then hurried to the door leading to one of the partitioned-off areas. "Locked too," he muttered. "Makes sense." He came back to her and dropped onto his backside. "I never should've locked Benson away. I tidied up because you were coming and I didn't want you to see him."

"Who's Benson?" she asked as she retrieved her earring and put it back where it should be.

He didn't answer. He was staring at the floor, head in his hands, elbows on his knees. She sat next to him, waiting for him to come up with a suggestion, but he said nothing for what felt like hours.

"I don't feel right. We shouldn't be feeling anything like this so soon, there's enough air in here to keep us alive for at least twenty-four hours, if not longer. The place is warded against all the–" He hit his forehead with the heel of his hand. "Fuckshitbollocksandwank. It's carbon dioxide. The place isn't warded against a natural by-product of breathing and whoever did this knows that. It must be being pumped in somewhere." He stood and looked at the ceiling. "All right," he finally said. "I don't have anything here that can help. It's all locked away because I'm a twat and I didn't want you to see any of my sorcerous stuff."

"Can't you just do some sorcery to make some fresh air?"

He snorted. "It's not like that."

"Oh!" She searched for her reticule in the folds of black satin. "I have a key that–"

"Fae charms won't work in here. It's warded to fuck against all their shit."

"Oh, Rupert, must you swear so much in an emergency?"

He half-smiled. "There's no better time. I've been royally shafted here, but there's a chance we can get out. I have some emergency mechanisms in place, but we'll have to wait."

"What's the use of emergency mechanisms if they don't work in an emergency? What in the Worlds are you waiting for?"

"To die."

He appeared to be serious. "I beg your pardon?"

"It'll only kick in if I get into real difficulties. If I lose consciousness and my breathing is too shallow it'll start then."

"What if it doesn't?"

"Then this is the last time we'll be drinking wine of an evening."

"What kind of Sorcerer suffocates in his own house?" Her voice was getting higher but she didn't care. "I thought you were supposed to be all-powerful."

"I am, in the right circumstances. I don't know how much longer we've got before the air quality gets too bad so we need to do a couple of things now, and then wait, all right?"

He shuffled back until he reached the wall. "Come over here," he said as he undid his belt.

She stayed still. "Chancellor, I have no idea what you have in mind but there is nothing I want to participate in whilst you are not wearing your trousers."

"Come over here, Maggie, for fuck's sake. I'm just taking my belt off."

Her ears were buzzing and she just wanted to lie down and go to sleep but he kept calling her and there seemed very little else to do. "If I die in here I'll never forgive you."

"You're not going to die like this," he said as he straightened his legs out. "But I want to make sure that you're saved too, not just me." He patted his lap. "Come and sit here."

"Right, that's it." She started to get up but he caught hold of her arm.

"Maggie, I'm not making a totally shit pass at you. We're probably going to die. I'm feeling about as randy as a mathematics professor. Now do as I ask, please."

She wondered what Bartholomew would make of it all. How in the Worlds had she got herself into such an absurd situation? "If I think for a moment you're planning to take advantage of me I'll go and die in one of the more comfortable chairs upstairs. Alone."

He held his hands up as she sat on his lap. She didn't know where to look and shook with embarrassment. She remembered a parlour game they'd played the season before in which they had to sit in laps and imitate animals but they were all tipsy and besides, it was only a game. This, however… what was this?

"I'll be taken out of here if the mechanism works," Rupert said. His breath smelt of Cabernet Sauvignon. "I don't want you to be left behind. That's all." He gathered up the front of his top as if about to take it off. Margritte considered slapping him but then he stretched the opening and brought it down over her head so they were both effectively wearing it.

"What do you think you're doing?" It was definitely a shriek.

"Move your arms up a bit," he said, pulling the belt around his back. "I'm going to see if this'll fit round both of us."

He manoeuvred her waist until she was pressed right against him and managed to pull it in enough to reach the first hole. He wrapped his arms around her and let out a long sigh. "I'm really sorry about this. For what it's worth, I just want to promise I didn't plan this in any way. I didn't even think you'd stay for a drink."

"If this thing does work, I want you to promise me you'll never tell a soul about this."

"I promise. And you can relax. Lean your head back if you need to."

"I do not."

She sat with her back as straight as a poker, trying to keep as much of her body away from his even though it was proving impossible. His breath tickled the back of her neck and she felt hot and sleepy and slightly sick. It was like her corset had been laced too tightly and, no matter how deeply she tried to breathe in, it never felt enough.

"If I'm going to die, though," he said after a while, "having a beautiful woman sitting on my lap whilst I suffocate is a great way to go."

"I think you're insane," she mumbled back. She felt his chest rising up and down, up and down and then she realised she was leaning against him, her head on his shoulder. "Rupert," she whispered after a while. "Are you frightened?"

He didn't reply and she tried to twist around to look at him properly but didn't have the room. Her chest was hurting and her lips were tingling and she had the sudden thought that if their bodies were found like this it would be the scandal of the decade.

A loud bang against the partition wall made her yelp. There was another and cracks appeared in the plaster. The third made glasses smash on the floor above and the cracks widen. She watched paint flakes fall as her vision was peppered with blue lights. Something broke through as her sight tunnelled, something made of metal as tall as a man moving towards them at great speed before she slipped away with Bartholomew's name on her lips.

12

Carter filled most of the seat opposite her in the carriage and Cathy had taken to staring out at the mists to feel less crammed in. He rode in silence and seemed quite content once he'd checked the carriage over before they'd left the house.

The kiss Will had left on her cheek was still on her mind. He'd come out to the lobby when he saw the carriage pull up and saw her dressed for visiting. "Where are you going?"

"To see Charlotte Persificola-Viola," she said, noting the way Carter stood to attention whenever Will was there. "Freddy's sister-in-law."

"Oh. Did she invite you?"

"...No. I just wanted to meet her. It's part of what I should be doing, isn't it? Getting to know the women of the Court."

He smiled and embraced her. Carter looked away. "That's exactly right. Why are you starting with her?"

Her heart had smacked the inside of her ribs as she wondered what to tell him. She couldn't risk telling him about the files Max had delivered to her, but staying as close to the truth as possible was the best policy when dealing with the Fae and probably husbands too. "She employed the woman who was my Governess to teach her children. I thought it would be a good thing to talk about... you know... something in common."

He kissed her forehead. "I knew you'd be a fine Duchess. You're too clever not to be. Just make sure you don't overdo it, and rest if you need to."

She'd wanted to comment that finding something in common with Charlotte hardly required a university-level education but kept it behind her teeth. He was just trying to encourage her and bolster her fragile confidence. She smiled back at him. "I'm trying. In every sense of the word."

He'd asked her to tell him all about it at dinner and she fiddled with the buttons at the wrist of her gloves as she wondered what would come after they'd eaten. The previous evening he'd elected to stay at the Tower for private audiences after the Court was done and she was asleep by the time he'd got home. If he was home for dinner, there was no chance of such an easy way to avoid him.

Then she remembered Lucy's excitement, her exuberant speculation about which one of them would fall pregnant first and how wonderful it would be to have children close in age living in the same city. She and Tom had been married for months and trying for a child just as long. She was horribly open about it with her. The only good thing about enduring the conversation was hearing that it took some couples a while to conceive. She still didn't want to take the risk though.

Cathy sighed at the mists. Committing to staying with Will made it almost impossible to avoid having children, especially with the additional pressure they were both under. She'd considered trying to find a way to get contraceptives from Mundanus. Even though she'd been cursed she'd still read all the literature provided by the universities she'd attended, so she knew exactly what she needed and how to get it. But there were two major obstacles. The first was getting to a family planning clinic without any of the staff seeing it and reporting to Bennet. Another visit from Max was risky enough. The second was the fear that if Lord Iris summoned her back into Exilium he would be able to detect what she was doing and she couldn't bear to think about the consequences.

"Is something wrong, your Grace?" Carter asked. "Is the carriage making you feel unwell?"

"I'm fine." She smiled. "Carter, did you ever know anyone who changed their job?"

"Well... house servants progress through the ranks, if that's what you mean, your Grace?"

"No, I meant someone who changed specialism."

He shook his head. "I've never heard of anything like that, your Grace."

Charlotte's was the first name that had leaped out from Miss Rainer's Agency file. She had employed Rainer as a lady's maid, then four years later Miss Rainer became her governess. The two roles were completely different in terms of status and had different implications for the member of staff. As a lady's maid, Rainer would have lived her whole life in the Nether, never being expected to fetch and carry in and out of Mundanus. But as a governess she would only sleep in the Nether while her working hours would be spent in the nursery wing in Mundanus. If Carter was anything to go by, Miss Rainer wouldn't have initiated the change and for her mistress to insist the Agency allow her to change positions – and thereby shorten her life significantly – seemed rather odd.

"Are all Agency staff given a specialism when young?" she asked Carter.

"Yes, your Grace, apart from those brought in later of course."

She nodded. "Like the Rosas." She wondered where they'd ended up.

"And the people who grew up in Mundanus."

Cathy sat forwards, all attention on him now. "What do you mean?"

"There are some staff who join the Agency after being born as mundanes. There's one in your household, your Grace. Coll Jones was a mundane and entered the Agency just under two years ago. I hope you don't mind me knowing, it's just that I reviewed all of the staff when I took on my position."

Had he chosen to live as a servant? Why in the Worlds would he want to do that? "But how do they end up at the Agency? Surely that's a breach of the Treaty?"

"I'm certain the Agency wouldn't do such a thing." Carter seemed genuinely appalled at the implication.

"Of course not," she said lightly. He wasn't the person to speculate with.

The carriage was slowing down and Cathy looked out of the window to see a large Georgian house, one built of Portland Stone rather than the Bath stone she was used to. It had neat ornamental hedges at the edge of the drive, a subtle way to demonstrate wealth, and a stylised violet set into a stained-glass panel above the front door.

As the step was lowered she reviewed what she knew of Charlotte and her husband Bertrand. He was the younger brother of Freddy Viola and, from what she saw of him at the Court, seemed to be the exact opposite. She couldn't remember seeing him with his wife, probably because he'd been managing Freddy's attempts to sour the room against Will the whole evening.

Dame Iris had told her that Charlotte was one of the most beautiful in the Court but when beauty was the standard Cathy didn't really think it was anything of note. She wanted to know if she held the same ideals as Miss Rainer and, if she did, whether she would be a good ally. All she'd learned from the Agency file was that she married Bertrand almost one hundred years ago and aside from a problem with her first lady's maid – one that Miss Rainer had been brought in to replace – there was a standard turnover of staff. There was nothing mentioned about her maiden name or family, which surprised Cathy, but other than that everything seemed normal. They were sidelined politically, thanks to Freddy's constant bad behaviour, and lived quietly enough not to merit more than a passing mention in the Dame's Londinium Who's Who. The only reason Dame Iris had mentioned them at all was because of their wealth, something Cathy had already learned from Margritte. Cathy wondered where she was and how she was coping with the grief. The guilt she carried with Will sat like stones in her stomach.

Carter helped her down the steps and she smoothed out the creases from her skirts. The dark blue gown was wider in the skirt than most of her clothes and had a large collar with wide lapels. Her maid had chosen it to cover the fact that her corset wasn't as tightly laced as normal, on the insistence of the nurse. It was the only time the nurse had said something she'd been glad to hear.

The footman pulled the chain for the doorbell and Cathy took her time to go to the door. She'd sent a message ahead that she intended to visit. It was strange to think that Charlotte might be worrying in the same way she dreaded every time Dame Iris came to the house. Cathy didn't like the thought of people being similarly terrified of her. She wasn't going to be like that.

A butler answered the door and she was invited in. Carter went first, eliciting a sniff from the butler. She followed, amused by Carter's diligence. No family would be stupid enough to attack the Duchess of Londinium at their own house when both households were aware of her visit. It would no doubt get back to Bennet, but it was one of her duties as Duchess to visit other wives. She just had to make sure that none of the servants overheard their conversation.

The house interior was pleasant enough with black and white chequered tiles on the floor and portraits hung on the walls. She noticed one of a man who looked just like Freddy, so much so that she wondered if it was him, but the woman standing next to him in the painting didn't look anything like Georgiana. There were, unsurprisingly, vases of violets on pedestals and little tables that smelt of summer and made her long for blue sky again.

Charlotte Viola came to the main doors leading off the lobby. She was indeed beautiful, strikingly so, with high cheekbones and flawless skin. She appeared to be in her late twenties but Cathy had no idea what her real age was. Her brown hair was arranged in the classical Greek style and her dress was Empire line, making her look like she'd stepped out of the Regency. It bothered Cathy that she was noticing these things. Dame Iris had clearly infected her thinking.

"Your Grace," Charlotte said and gave a deep, elegant curtsy. "It's a pleasure and an honour to welcome you to our home."

Cathy's hand twitched as she almost gave an uncertain wave. Instead she inclined her head and smiled, just as she'd been taught the day before the Court. She felt like a fraud. "Thank you. And please call me Cath... erine."

"And, of course, please call me Charlotte. Would you like to come through to my drawing room?"

"I'm sorry about the short notice," Cathy said.

"Oh, it's no bother at all," Charlotte replied. "Quite the contrary. I'm afraid my husband had a prior engagement and wasn't here when your message arrived."

That suited her just fine. Cathy glanced behind her, suspecting that Carter was about to follow her in. "You can wait outside, Carter."

"But–"

She glared at him and he backed down. She couldn't remember that ever working on anyone before. She followed Charlotte into a richly furnished drawing room with a cheerful fire and a table already laid out for tea. The butler closed the door behind them. There was an embroidery frame in the corner with a partially completed country garden design. It seemed that women kept in the Nether developed a passion for embroidering and sewing the things they could no longer enjoy in Mundanus.

"Do you like to embroider?" Charlotte asked, having noticed Cathy's attention.

"No," Cathy said as she sat. "I'm not nearly as gifted as you."

"I find it passes the time so pleasantly," Charlotte said. "Would you care for a cup of tea?"

Cathy nodded. Charlotte wasn't what she'd expected, but she wasn't even sure what that had been. Someone more like Miss Rainer? She reminded herself to be patient. Charlotte was hardly to going to open the conversational dance with an observation about the subjugation of women in society.

"May I compliment you on your dress," Charlotte said as she handed over the tea. The cup and saucer were the typical dainty porcelain favoured in Society, with tiny violets incorporated into the design. "It's such a beautiful colour."

Cathy sipped the tea after an embarrassed smile. Small talk was still agonising, even when she was trying instead of daydreaming herself away from it. Charlotte served sandwiches and cake as Cathy struggled to think of a way to talk about something worthwhile.

"How are you finding Londinium?" Charlotte asked. "I understand it's quite different to Aquae Sulis."

"It is," Cathy said after hurriedly swallowing a mouthful. She felt the lump moving towards her stomach and fought the desire to belch. "Have you been to Aquae Sulis?"

"Sadly not."

The crackling of the fire filled the room as they both sipped and took dainty bites. Cathy put her teacup down, determined to end the agony. "I wanted to speak to you about Miss Rainer."

"Oh!" Charlotte's face became radiant with happiness. "Miss Rainer is an excellent governess. She taught my daughter and son."

"Yes, she taught me too," Cathy shifted to the edge of her seat now she was on topic.

"How splendid," Charlotte said.

"She taught me very well. I understand you were the one who… made her into a governess?"

Charlotte's smile lingered and she seemed to be searching for words. "Miss Rainer is a very intelligent woman."

"Is that why you suggested she change career?"

"She was a superlative lady's maid too," Charlotte said. "However, she excelled in her later role. She was so passionate about things that matter."

Cathy paused. She had the impression she was having a conversation slightly out of sync. Was Charlotte trying to tell her she knew about what Miss Rainer used to teach but didn't feel safe enough to say it to her directly? "Have you been in touch with her lately?"

"I understand she's been very successful and taught in many households since she was here, thanks to my recommendation."

Why hadn't she answered the question? "I saw her, only a few weeks ago, and something terrible has happened to her."

Charlotte's smile was rapidly replaced by concern. Cathy could see there was something else... fear?

"She's a scullery maid now," she continued. "And she isn't herself at all, it's like someone sucked out her personality and replaced it with a job description."

Charlotte's eyes became round and she looked away, her cup rattling in the saucer, but she still didn't say anything.

Cathy was losing her patience. Just because she was the Duchess it didn't mean they couldn't talk properly. "I think the Agency did something to her because my parents reported her unorthodox lessons."

"Miss Rainer was a superlative teacher who gave only the best lessons," Charlotte said with a voice suddenly bright and cheerful.

Cathy frowned. "Please, can't we speak candidly? I know I'm the Duchess but you don't have to be afraid of talking to me about this." Charlotte remained silent but was still unable to meet Cathy's eyes. Cathy lowered her voice, in case the servants were listening in, ready to report back to Bennet. "Don't you understand? I think the Agency did something terrible to Miss Rainer because she was teaching me about equal rights for women, the Suffragettes and Peterloo and all the other things we're not supposed to be taught. The people who run the Agency are... are..."

She couldn't find the right words. What were they doing? Removing a problem reported by important clients or participating in a wider conspiracy against women? Was she mad to even consider the latter? Bennet had blackmailed her because she'd caused problems, not because of her sex.

"The Agency are always so helpful and are marvellous at providing just the right staff." Charlotte's cheerful voice made Cathy feel nervous.

"Are you afraid that something you say to me will get back to your husband?"

Charlotte took a deep breath and seemed to force herself to look Cathy in the eye. "My husband is a very powerful man. He always gets what he wants because he's so clever and resourceful."

Cathy shivered. "Did he do something to you?"

Charlotte looked away. "My husband is absolutely devoted to me."

"Oh, bollocks," Cathy muttered beneath her breath. "He's put a curse on you, hasn't he?"

Charlotte giggled and covered her mouth with a shaking hand as if Cathy had told a silly joke.

"Is there anything at all you can tell me about Miss Rainer? Did you realise she was special and help her get out of the Nether as much as possible by being a governess? Is that why you did it?"

Charlotte stared down into her teacup. "It's so lovely that we have someone so special in common," she said, the cheerfulness switched back on like a sprite's glow after a hammer had struck the globe. "Would you like to see where she used to teach my children? It was such a happy time."

Cathy hoped this was a ploy to get them somewhere more private, or perhaps into Mundanus. Maybe the curse she'd been put under only worked in certain circumstances. "I'd like that very much."

Charlotte put her teacup back very delicately and as they both stood she reached across and caught hold of Cathy's hands. "I'm so delighted you came to see me. And I would be so very happy if we could be friends."

There was an intensity in her eyes as she spoke and it moved Cathy to squeeze her hands back. "So am I. And I would like that too. I have a feeling that I could be friends with anyone who knew Miss Rainer well."

"She is very talented," Charlotte said. "She always had a knack for working out who could be a good friend."

Charlotte led her out. Before Carter moved, Cathy ordered him to stay put and followed Charlotte up a wide staircase, both of them looked down on by dozens of portraits as they climbed. They passed a maid who bobbed a curtsy and hurried away. Clearly they hadn't expected the mistress of the house to take the Duchess on an impromptu tour.

"Miss Rainer was such a valued member of the household," Charlotte said when they reached the top floor. "Come and see how neatly she kept her old room. It hasn't changed since she left."

She opened the door of a room next to the green baize door that would lead out to the nursery wing. It seemed Charlotte didn't want to take her out into Mundanus.

The room was quite large and had several empty bookshelves. There was a single bed stripped of its linens and the personal effects were gone from the dressing table. Charlotte closed the door behind them as Cathy scanned the room, looking for anything unusual.

"Miss Rainer was such a neat person – we could always rely on her," Charlotte said, crouching down by the rug at the centre of the room. She flipped the corner over and revealed the joint between two floorboards. Cathy knelt down next to her. "She was always so particular about everything having its place, even this rug."

Charlotte was looking at what Cathy had thought was a knot in the wood but on closer inspection its edges were too uniform. It was a diamond-shaped hole between the two floorboards, large enough to put a finger into. She reached towards it, glancing at Charlotte for any protest and finding she was smiling at her, then tucked her finger into the hole.

The section of board closest to her was easy to pull up, revealing a cavity underneath. There was nothing there.

"She packed everything so neatly too," Charlotte said. "I'm sure all of her other rooms were kept just as beautifully."

Cathy had a sudden memory of Rainer outside the house the last time she saw her and the diamond-shaped scar on her thigh. She'd spoken about something important in the floor. She snapped her fingers. "The floor in her old room! At my parents' house! That's what she was trying to tell me! They had her taken away so quickly she didn't even have a chance to pack. I bet whatever it is she used to hide is still there!"

Charlotte beamed and put the wood and rug back into place. "It's so amazing, the effect a good teacher can have."

"It really is," Cathy said. She frowned at Charlotte, trying to work out the nature of the curse. If she knew exactly what it did, she could see if the Shopkeeper had something to break it. "I don't suppose you can tell me anything about the curse you've been placed under."

Charlotte giggled and covered her mouth in the same way as before. The curse was so powerful she looked genuinely amused, even though she must be raging inside.

"I'll work it out and I'll find a way to have it broken, I promise," Cathy said. "I'd like to have a real conversation with you."

"It's a deep pleasure to be able to talk with you," Charlotte replied. "I do hope we can do so again."

They said their goodbyes once they were downstairs and Cathy got back into the carriage with Carter. "Change of plan," she said as she waved goodbye. "We're going to Aquae Sulis. To my parents' house."

"As you wish, your Grace."

She settled back in the seat and thought about how much Charlotte had been able to convey despite the odd conversation. She hoped Miss Rainer's room was still relatively untouched and tried to imagine stepping foot in that house again. She'd hoped she'd never have to go back there; it held too many awful memories. Even though there had been the beginning of an understanding between her and her father on her wedding day it wasn't enough to quell the dread of seeing him again on home territory. She looked at Carter, who smiled back at her. At least this time there would be no fear of being beaten.

13

Sam had opened the envelope in the entrance to the forge. After building himself up to it for days it had been an anticlimax. He'd expected a more personal letter from Leanne but there was just a small key and an address for a bank with a contact person. On the back of the piece of paper was something more cryptic, in her handwriting, saying "The lady will want to know where you proposed to me and the gift I gave you on our wedding day before she gives you access to the box."

He assumed it was a safety deposit box key. The security questions were surprisingly sentimental for Leanne but at least he knew the answers to them. Mr Ferran was away again and it was simply a matter of asking the butler to arrange a car so he could go back to Bath. He'd had a hire car in mind but wasn't surprised when the chauffeur-driven limousine arrived.

He found the right person at the bank and when he showed her the key she seemed to know that Leanne had died. Condolences were offered, he answered her questions and then was taken to a room away from the public areas, full of deposit boxes. He wondered what was kept in the others as his was unlocked. Stolen diamonds? Wills written by paranoid millionaires? He didn't want to think about what would be in Leanne's.

The banker put the box on a small table and left him to remove the contents alone. He took a deep breath and lifted the top, finding another envelope inside with his name on it.

It contained a short note, a plastic keycard and an address for a storage company, the kind of place that had different-sized lockers for hire.

Dear Sam,

Sorry to make you run around like this, but it's necessary. Only you would know the answers to the security questions so I know it's you reading this and I know I must be dead. I hope you're all right. Everything you need to know about is at the storage place. When you go make sure you're alone and that no one else knows where you're going and why. That's really important, darling.

Leanne xx

He thought of the limousine parked on double yellow lines outside. The storage building was a taxi ride away; he'd get rid of the limo, walk home and then order one. He tucked the keycard and letter back in the envelope and slipped it into his inside jacket pocket.

Walking through Bath felt like being in a film set. He felt utterly detached from it. Sam rubbed the callouses on his hands with his thumbs as he walked, trying to work out what Leanne had been thinking when she'd set up the deposit box. What could possibly merit something so silly as all the cloak and dagger stuff? She hated Hollywood thrillers.

He was tempted to not go to the storage locker. He didn't want to find something that would shake him up again after he'd only just found something to drown out all the thinking.

The "For Sale" sign outside his house made him stop. It felt like coming home and yet, at the same time, it felt like it wasn't his any more. Holding both states made him feel exhausted. He needed a beer.

Sam unlocked the door, trying to ignore the machine-gun fire of memories. The air in the house was stale and it already smelt unlived in. The removals company that Iron's people had sorted for him had cleared everything out – including the hallway mirror, much to his relief – and cleaned it. He'd had messages that the estate agents had reported interest and were certain it would sell soon but he felt nothing. He was as empty as the house.

He walked from room to room, listening to the echo of his footsteps. Then he called for a taxi. There was no point wallowing and putting off going to see what Leanne had hidden away. He needed it all to be over.

Cathy looked out onto the streets of Aquae Sulis and reddened when she saw some Peonias stop and stare at her carriage. The ducal coat of arms was emblazoned on the door and she hadn't appreciated how much attention it would attract. She'd assumed that they would just go through a Way to the stables outside Aquae Sulis and hire a carriage there, like anyone else would. But her footmen insisted on the Glamour to make the carriage exactly the same as her Londinium one, to ensure they were treated with the proper respect in the city. So much for a quiet flying visit.

She saw Elizabeth's face pressed against the window as the carriage stopped outside the house in Great Pulteney Street. Cathy couldn't help but glance up at the top-floor room she'd been locked in before the wedding and the sight of it made her feel nauseous. One footman rang the bell whilst the other lowered the step and opened the door. Carter got out first – she was used to the drill now – and by the time she'd got out and straightened her clothes again the butler was at the door and Elizabeth was pushing past him.

"Catherine!" she squeaked.

Cathy endured the embrace Elizabeth forced upon her. "Hello." Her sister had never pretended to be excited to see her, even after the years she'd spent in Mundanus.

"What are you doing here? You didn't say you were coming to visit. What's it like being a Duchess? Can I come to the Londinium Court for the Season? Is there anyone eligible you want to introduce me to? How's Thomas?"

"Tom and Lucy are fine. Can I go inside?"

Elizabeth tittered. "Sorry." She noticed Carter, her large eyes going up and up until she reached his face. He made her look even more childlike.

"That's Carter, my bodyguard," Cathy said. "Are Mother and Father at home?"

"No, they're with Uncle Lavandula."

Cathy brightened. "Ah, well, never mind. I just wanted to get a few things from my old room. I don't have long anyway."

Elizabeth buzzed around her like an ambitious mosquito searching for the perfect spot to suck out what she wanted. Cathy felt exhausted by the time she got into the house. The scent and sight of the poppies in their vases made her stomach turn over. She had to get this done as quickly as she could.

"I should offer you tea," Elizabeth gasped.

"I just had some," Cathy replied. "Could you… go and send a brief message over to Uncle's house to say I can't stay and I do apologise? No doubt someone has told him about the carriage."

"I'll get the butler–"

"No, I want you to do it," Cathy said. "It's a family thing, after all. And you do have such beautiful handwriting."

Cathy watched her hurry off and thought back to the night Elizabeth told their father what Miss Rainer had been teaching them. She'd never hated someone so much and that old resentment was still there, buried under years of distance and the sure knowledge that Elizabeth would never appreciate – or even care about – the damage she'd done. Miss Rainer's lessons had never managed to penetrate the thick fuzz of being constantly approved of for the most vacuous things. Elizabeth was perfect in the eyes of Society and Cathy had accepted a long time ago that there would never be any real relationship between them.

She left Carter posted at the bottom of the stairs and headed for the nursery wing, checked no one was in sight and went into Miss Rainer's old room. She knew her personal effects had been stripped out by the Agency staff so she was expecting it to be bare, but she still felt a tug of grief at seeing the empty bookshelves.

Knowing there wasn't much time, Cathy lifted the rug and searched for any diamond-shaped knots but the floorboards were pristine. She moved to the edges of the room, crawled under the dressing table and felt under the wardrobe, but all was smooth. As she ran her fingers under the bed she could hear Elizabeth calling her name downstairs. Her finger caught on the edge of something and a section of board lifted up. With a kettledrum heart she felt a sheaf of papers, pulled them out, stuffed them down her bodice, replaced the board and dashed out of the room on tiptoes as Carter was telling Elizabeth she was upstairs. She darted left and through the green baize door as Elizabeth started up the stairs. The tingle across her face made a grenade of childhood moments explode back into her memory.

She was in her room with a doll in each hand by the time Elizabeth made it to the doorway. Whatever had been stashed beneath the bed was now prickling her skin with its creased edges but Cathy did her best to ignore it.

"Why do you want those?" Elizabeth asked. "You never played with them."

"I thought they'd be a nice gift," Cathy replied. "If Tom has a girl."

Elizabeth's hands flapped. "Is Lucy pregnant?"

"Not yet," Cathy said. "I like to plan ahead."

"You might have a girl first," Elizabeth said, coming to her side.

"I doubt that," Cathy said. "I'll take these two. Mother won't mind, they're only gathering dust."

"Catherine…" Elizabeth began with a low voice. "What's it like?"

"What?"

"When… a man… does…"

"You mean sex?"

Cathy got the scarlet blush she'd aimed for. "Why do you have to be so crass?"

"I haven't got all day, I told you that. Besides, you'll find out for yourself soon enough."

"Does it hurt?"

"I'm going now." Cathy plucked a third doll from the shelf and marched out of the room.

"But none of my friends know anything and I can't ask Mother."

Cathy stopped and faced her. "It all depends on who you're with and whether they care about you. If you're lucky it will be wonderful."

"And if I'm not?"

Cathy shrugged. "Lie back and think of Albion. That's what they tell you to do, isn't it?" Elizabeth looked small and nervous. Cathy couldn't remember ever seeing her this way. "You'll be fine," she said, feeling bad for brushing her off, but unable to bring herself to have such a conversation with her sister.

"Will you come and visit properly soon?"

"Probably." Cathy hurried back into the Nether and down the stairs. "But I'm so busy, you know, doing... Duchess stuff." She handed the dolls to Carter, who tucked them under one arm as if he'd been asked to carry dolls every day of his working life. "Take care. And give my regards to the parentals."

Elizabeth gave her a swift peck on the cheek. "It may cheer you to know that I'm horribly jealous of you. It's a rather strange feeling."

Cathy didn't know how to respond to that, so she kissed her back and left. Moments after she got back into the carriage she took the dolls from Carter and put them on the seat next to her. "Oh! I think I left my reticule in my old room. Could you ask Elizabeth?"

Once he was out again she turned her back to the house and pulled out the pieces of paper. They were all the same: vouchers for something called a "book spa" at Mr B's Emporium of Reading Delights. There was an address in the centre of Bath. She checked the back for any secret messages but there was nothing except a tiny star and the name "Jane" written in the top left corner of each one.

She just had time to stuff all but one of the papers back into her bodice and tuck the single voucher into her reticule before Carter returned.

"It isn't in the house, your Grace."

"I found it." She waved it at him. "Sorry, it was in the carriage the whole time, silly me." She couldn't go to a mundane bookshop dressed as she was and Carter would never let her go there anyway. "Let's go home," she said. It was time to take another risk.

Sam looked for the right door inside the soulless warehouse. Everything was brightly lit and numbered but still felt abandoned. The keycard gave him twenty-four-hour access and there wasn't even a person to check who he was. By the time he'd got to the right floor and found Leanne's storage space he felt like the last man left alive.

The keycard opened the door and he put it back in his pocket, then switched on the light. It was a five-metre-square cube containing about fifty cardboard boxes. They all had lids and handle holes, like the ones used by offices to store files. There was still space to go in and close the door. A couple of boxes sat in one corner with a large envelope resting on top addressed to him.

His mouth was dry as he opened it. There were several sheets of A4 paper inside, the top one a letter in Leanne's handwriting. He sat on the floor and leaned against the boxes to read it.

Dear Sam,

I've been writing these letters every three months for the last five years and I still find it hard. All of the others are in the envelope, the most recent on top, the first at the bottom. I couldn't bring myself to throw them away.

So you'll be wondering why I've made you come here in secret when I hate those kinds of films and it's because I've been doing something dangerous. Now I'm dead (that's still so weird to write) I have to tell you and that could make things dangerous for you too, for a short while. Just follow the instructions below and you'll be all right.

We've had a tough few weeks lately and it's so hard not to tell you what's been going on. I hope that when you know what I've been doing you'll forgive me for not being there. I think the Brussels trip was the final straw for you and I've been finding it tough too. All the stuff in these boxes has driven us apart but it's much bigger than the two of us. That's a horrible thing to say but if you decide to read it I hope you'll agree.

I've been gathering evidence for a friend in an environmental group. He's someone you met when we were at uni: Martin Barclay. I think you bought some gear off him once. Anyway, he and I cooked up a plan which came to fruition shortly after you and I got married: I got a job at Pin PR. His dad knew they were covering up stuff but all of his friends and family were known by CoFerrum Inc so they couldn't infiltrate. They didn't know me, so I went in with the plan to uncover some data, get it to Martin and his dad and blow the lid on it all.

The more I found out the deeper I realised the cover-up went. Pin does the PR for CoFerrum and several other major international companies involved in the minerals and metals trade and they've been fucking up the planet and the people who work for them for many, many years. In these boxes is enough evidence to cause a scandal and embarrass them into stopping some of it. I just want to carry on a bit longer to see if I can get close to the famous Mr Ferran. He's the kingpin and he's bloody hard to get close to, but I think Neugent is one of his lieutenants so I'm hanging on and going as high as I can to nail him. Martin knows I want to play the long game and he's persuaded his dad to let me do it my way, but when they find out I've died they'll need to know what happened. His contact details are with the instructions. Please follow them so you're not dragged into this any more than you have to be. CoFerrum is massively powerful and they've killed people to keep things quiet in the past. They may have done that to me – I might have just had an accident – obviously I don't know at the time of writing this.

Sam, I want you to know I love you and I'm sorry I put this before our marriage. I wanted to tell you, so many times, I really did, but I couldn't. I wouldn't let myself because I had to believe my own lie day in day out. Does that make sense? I couldn't open up to you and then pack it all away every morning to go and pretend to be who I needed to be to get this evidence.

You're probably angry with me and I understand that. You have every right to be. I hoped that once I got everything I needed to nail Ferran I could just come clean with you and we'd work it all out. I guess we don't have that chance now. Please don't be angry with Martin, this was all my choice and every time I spoke to him he told me to stop. The only thing I ask is that you make sure this information gets to Martin and his dad so something can be done. I may not have got Ferran, but we could still do them a lot of damage with what I've collected here.

I love you. And I know people say this and don't really mean it but when you're all right again, go and find someone to love who'll treat you better than I did. I just want you to be happy, Sam. God knows you deserve it. And I'm sorry.

Leanne xxx

P.S. There was never anything between Neugent and me, in case you were ever worried. He's an odious little shit and I can't stand the man.

At the bottom were Martin's contact details and the whereabouts of an inventory and report on the data in the boxes to pass on to him. Sam went back to the beginning and read it again, then flipped through the pages, seeing letter after letter, filled with the same apologies, the same instructions but a different note about what had been happening in the weeks before the respective letter. There were mentions of birthdays and arguments, reconciliations and the knowledge they were drifting apart. Their marriage's decline was there on several pieces of paper in front of him and the whole time he'd had no idea why she'd stopped loving him nor why she'd turned into a different woman. She hadn't, in fact, done either. He had no idea how to feel or how to handle it. So he sat there, staring at the letters and surrounded by boxes, as his mind churned and a headache grew.

Dressed in the mundane clothes provided for her honeymoon, Cathy dashed from the Victoria Art Gallery in central Bath to John Street. She didn't have much time; Will was at the Tower and she had two hours until dinner. Carter was posted outside her bedroom thinking she'd gone to lie down and there was a risk that someone could check on her at any time. But she couldn't get so close to finding what Miss Rainer had been up to and not act immediately.

She'd entered the mundane anchor property via the nursery wing and used a Charm of Openings keyed to Bath. She'd ordered it from the Emporium as part of the household order, knowing it wouldn't draw any attention as she used to live in Aquae Sulis. Many people sent their staff to shop in Bath after they moved away. If questioned she could say it was for sending the footman to buy soap from a particular shop and no one would give it a second thought. She wished she'd thought of it before.

The voucher for the book spa was clutched tight in her hand. The bookshop was tucked in one of the Georgian back streets, not far from the Assembly Rooms, and after a brief stop-off to buy a new mobile phone with cash taken from the household budget, it didn't take too long to find. She liked it as soon as she walked in. The smell of books made her feel excited and at home all at once. There was a man with blonde hair and blue eyes behind the counter and another man, tall and balding, talking with a woman with long red hair wearing an eclectic mix of mundane and period clothing. For a moment Cathy couldn't help but stare at her, wondering if she was from one of the Great Families on a day out, but then she realised that one of them would never wear a corset on the *outside* of her blouse.

"Can I help you?" A woman approached with a friendly smile. Her greying hair framed her face with a tumble of gentle curls.

Cathy held out the voucher. "I have this voucher for a book spa. I don't really know what it is though."

"Present, was it?"

"...yes."

The assistant flipped the voucher over and looked in the top left corner. "Well, you're talking to the right person. I'm Jane. This way, please."

She led Cathy through the shop and they passed an old roll-top bath which had been filled and converted into a bookshelf. Cathy decided that it was probably the best bookshop she'd ever been to.

They went up a staircase at the far end of the shop and Cathy was led through the first floor, which was filled with wooden bookshelves and books. The floorboards were uneven with age. They went through one room then through an alcove to a second with a fireplace and two comfy chairs. A door with a stained-glass panel was set in the corner and Jane was heading straight for it.

"We usually do the mundane book spas here," she said, glancing at the chairs as she pulled a key out of her pocket. "You should try one. I'll give you a leaflet all about it when you leave, if you like."

"So I won't be having the same thing?"

Jane smiled but said nothing. She picked up a glass lantern with a small candle inside and lit it. Cathy watched her turn the key once, unlocking the door, and then she whispered a Charm as she turned the key a second time, opening a Way into the Nether. It was a similar Charm to the one the Shopkeeper had taught her for getting to the Emporium from Mundanus.

"Do you have anything to do with the Emporium of Things in Between and Besides?"

"No, we're totally independent."

After checking there were no customers in the room, Jane opened the door and stepped through the familiar haze marking the threshold between Mundanus and the Nether. Cathy followed and found herself in another room that could easily have been part of the mundane bookshop, with walls covered by book-laden shelves. There was a fireplace but the grate was empty and two armchairs. Jane lit two more lanterns and handed the first to Cathy.

"I'll leave you to browse. Are there any topics in particular you'd like to read about?"

Cathy looked at the books on the nearest shelf and many were familiar – several had been at her flat in Manchester. They were the books Miss Rainer had taught her from: essays on feminism, social-political history and the works of several remarkable men and women. "I don't suppose you have the collected works of Aphra Behn?" she asked in a moment of nostalgia.

Jane crossed the room and pulled a weighty tome from a shelf. Cathy recognised the edition instantly. "Will you be coming on Thursday?"

"What for?"

"Miss Rainer didn't tell you? We haven't seen her for such a long time. There's a group of like-minded people who meet on the third Thursday of every month. Just come to the shop at 7 o'clock and ask for me."

Cathy felt tears spring in her eyes. Miss Rainer had already done the hard work for her; there were people like her in the Nether and they were already meeting and they would have a plan she could get behind.

"I'll be here." She took the collected plays from Jane. "I can't stay for long. I'll only need five minutes."

"Just go through the door when you're ready."

Cathy sat down after Jane left and flicked to Miss Rainer's favourite play, *The Forced Marriage*. It was easy to find the right place; the spine naturally fell open at the page. She remembered the day Miss Rainer had climbed onto the table and said the words out loud, declaring that they were written to be spoken on a stage, not read silently in a classroom. Cathy kicked off her shoes and stood on the nearest chair. "This is for you, Miss Rainer," she whispered and then read, "'Love furnish me with powerful arguments: Direct my tongue that my disorder'd sence, May speak my passion more then Eloquence.'"

Her hands tingled as a pulse of magic rippled through the book and the pages flipped over rapidly until they fell open at the end of the play. As she stared at it, a piece of paper slotted between the pages came into view and on it a list of names in Miss Rainer's handwriting. Cathy would bet her own library that they were people sympathetic to the feminist cause.

Cathy dropped into the chair and pulled the paper out. Scanning the list she saw several were crossed out, names she'd requested files on after seeing them in Miss Rainer's. They had all had a form inserted at the top of the file filled with obscure abbreviations she'd planned to ask Max to decode at the Agency. Now she was even more determined to find out what they meant.

Charlotte's name was there but hers was crossed out with a wavy line – perhaps to indicate she was still around but unable to speak her mind. Cathy flipped the page over to find more and the first to leap out at her were Margritte and Bartholomew Tulipa.

"Oh, God," she whispered. "Fucking Roses." If it hadn't been for them and the way they'd manipulated Will, the ideal Duke and Duchess would have the throne and would already be working to change Society. Then she remembered the day, once she'd escaped life in the Nether, she went to Aphra Behn's grave and laid flowers there. There was a bunch of tulips already there; she could still see the ribbon tied around them, blue against the grey stone. Cathy slapped her forehead with her hand. Why hadn't she asked Margritte if she'd left them?

She had to go and talk to her. She was the first person she'd met in Londinium – in Society – that she'd genuinely wanted to befriend. There had to be a way to make things right without destroying Will, and the only way to find it was to find Margritte and talk to her. Just the two of them, away from Society, as equals.

14

Margritte woke with an excruciating headache and a sense of total disorientation. She opened her eyes and looked straight into two black discs in a silver oval. It took a moment to realise it was an approximation of a face, only inches away from her own. She cried out and the oval withdrew.

"The patient is awake. Shall I dispose of her?" The voice was male but it didn't sound like a real person, more like a recording of one heard through an exceptionally high-quality gramophone.

"Benson, for fuck's sake, Maggie's my guest, not a kebab wrapper."

She became aware of something over her face and in a panic pulled off a clear mask that was cupped over her nose and mouth. After a few blinks Margritte could see that the strange pseudo-face was fixed on the metal shape she'd seen before she'd blacked out. It was standing next to Rupert. He came over as she realised she wasn't in Convocation House but instead on a makeshift bed in the corner of a very plain room. There were no windows, only a large open doorway leading off into a wide corridor lit by electric lamps.

"That's oxygen," Rupert said, picking the mask up from where she'd dropped it. It was connected to a large metal cylinder. "You might want to keep it on a bit longer." She shook her head. "How are you feeling?" He offered her a hand.

She accepted the help in sitting up. The bed felt springy and wobbled as she moved. "Awful. Where are we?"

"In the Stacks."

"That means nothing to me."

"Under the University. We're in the Nether, we'll be safe here. Take these." He handed her two round white pills and then fetched her a glass of water from a nearby table.

She frowned at the tablets. "No, thank you."

"It's just ibuprofen for your headache."

She shook her head again. "I just want to go home, thank you."

He dropped them into a pocket with a shrug. "Soon. I'm just waiting for the Proctors to get something to me."

The Proctors were the university police. Unlike the mundanes, Margritte knew they were also Arbiters. "Do they have any idea what happened?"

"They've found something important but I haven't seen it yet. Oh, Maggie, meet Benson."

She stared past him at the metal man. Aside from the two black discs suggesting eyes there was only a rectangular grill where the mouth would be on a man's face. Its head was shaped like a soup tureen with a large black bowler hat on top. Its body was a large cylinder, the arms and legs thick metal tubes. The legs ended in wheels, the arms in a collection of tools, from a corkscrew and bottle opener to a small saw. There were different tools at the end of each arm but she could only see small parts of them when tucked away out of use.

"Isn't he great?" Rupert said. "I wanted him to look kind of retro, you know, a homage to those Fifties sci-fi B-movie robots, but also a bit like a Proctor."

"But… what is he?"

"A robot." When he saw she didn't understand the word he added: "An artificial man."

Margritte was horrified. "But he spoke! Does he have a soul?"

"Christ! No! That would be bloody awful, being trapped inside…" He shuddered and then unclipped something at the back of its arm. Margritte realised the metal was just a cover, like armour. Beneath she could see its arm was made of something clay-like, every inch of it covered with symbols she didn't recognise. "It's not really a robot, I'm just yanking your chain. It's a golem, with bells and whistles. It might sound like they know what they're saying, but they don't, it's all just programmed responses, like a computer. No… that won't help you understand." He jerked a thumb at one of the doorways. "Hedges is over there. Say hi, Hedges."

"Hi." The voice sounded identical to that which had come from Benson.

Margritte felt nauseous. She was trapped underground with a Sorcerer and armoured golems and, if she wasn't careful, she could panic. She checked her posture was correct. Going to pieces wasn't going to achieve anything. "Could I trouble you for a cup of tea?"

"Benson, get us some tea, will you?" The golem rolled out of the room.

"How long was I asleep?"

Rupert sat on the bed next to her, making it creak. "A few hours. Benson picked both of us up and opened a Way to Hedges. You're officially the first Fae-touched to have been rescued by any of my staff. Congratulations."

"But how did he open a Way when you couldn't?"

"It's all to do with anchors. I was blocked from making contact with anchors in the building but it doesn't matter for those two; they're each other's anchors, so Benson can always find Hedges and vice versa. Even if one of them was drifting in the Nether, nowhere near any reflected buildings, they'd still be able to find the other."

"What if they were both drifting in the Nether?"

He grinned. "Then I would have majorly fucked up. One of them is always here. Can you walk?"

She stood up and, whilst her head was pounding, she was otherwise all right. "Yes. Are we leaving?"

"Let's go to my office, it's more comfortable there. I just kip here if I can't be arsed to go home." He offered his arm and she slipped her hand into the crook of his elbow, more out of politeness than anything else.

They walked out of the room and into a corridor lined with books from floor to ceiling as far as she could see, lit at regular intervals by bright lights hanging from the ceiling. "My goodness," she said. "You meant the Bodleian's underground book stacks, didn't you? I thought that was just a myth."

"That's what I want everyone to think. There are miles of them under the city, all reflected into the Nether."

"The books too?"

"Only the good ones."

Hedges followed them as they walked and there was no sound save the golem's wheels and the clip of her heels. The books they passed were uniformly bound in leather with dates embossed on the spines. She wondered why he was telling her so much and letting her see the place he slept in. The Sorcerers were famously reclusive – she didn't even know the name of the Sorcerer of Essex though she'd lived in his domain for over two hundred years – but Rupert seemed more approachable than the majority of people in Society.

"I hope you don't mind my enquiring, but why did you make Benson and Hedges? Don't you trust real people?"

"The trouble with human beings is human error," he replied. "Don't get me wrong, I think people are great – the clever ones, that is – but that doesn't mean I'd want to rely on them. Here we are."

Tucked between two bookcases was a door that he unlocked with a key fished out of his pocket. He flipped a light switch and revealed a room with a huge desk, a few filing cabinets and a sofa. The walls were covered with photographs and paintings of Oxford, and there was a framed Dali.

"The Metamorphosis of Narcissus," she said. "One of my favourites."

"I like most of the stuff he did before his religious phase," Rupert said, sweeping food wrappers off the sofa and onto the floor. "Shame that got to him too. Got a bit out of control, all that God stuff. Never mind. Sit down, make yourself at home."

"A package has been deposited, sir," Hedges said. "Would you like me to collect it?"

"Yeah, do that." He looked at Margritte. "You warm enough?"

She nodded.

"That's all, then," he said to the golem and it rolled off.

Just as the lull in conversation was getting uncomfortable, Benson arrived with the tea. It was in a large earthenware mug, rather garishly painted, and stronger and with more sugar than she liked, but it still made her feel better. Rupert slurped his tea and gave a loud sigh of pleasure, which Margritte did her best to ignore.

Hedges returned soon after with a small box. Rupert abandoned his mug and opened the box on the desk. He pulled out a letter, read it quickly, then rummaged around in the top drawer of his desk until he found a pair of thick leather gloves covered in strange marks.

Margritte cupped her hands around the mug and watched Rupert lift a lump of clay out of the box. It had unfamiliar symbols carved into it and she realised it was something sorcerous. She looked away, choosing to stare at the Dali painting rather than something she probably shouldn't see.

"Well, fuck me sideways with a toothbrush," Rupert murmured. "If this hadn't been designed to kill me I'd think it was a thing of beauty."

"Do you know who made it?"

"Not yet. Wessex or Northumbria, I reckon, they're both pricks. Hedges – magnifier."

The golem rolled over to him and the tools attached to its left arm rotated until a magnifying glass clicked into place and was extended into a position between the clay and Rupert's eyes.

"Ekstrand, you sonofabitch!" He dropped the clay back in the box and swatted the magnifying glass away. Hedges rolled backwards into a corner as Benson left the room at speed, as if it had been frightened away by Rupert's outburst. "The Sorcerer of Wessex tried to kill me! Us! What a bastard!"

"Is that a… usual problem?"

"Not without a declaration of war – in triplicate. It was totally out of the blue! He's a weird bugger but even so, trying to murder someone because they're better at solving riddles than you is a bit fucking extreme, don't you think?"

Margritte just nodded. She wanted to go home.

"He's always had it in for me." Rupert's rant was building up steam. "He got it into his head I wanted Bath. Why would

I want that place? Boring shitty little city at the bottom of a valley with a few natural springs. Whoopdy-fucking-do! Nothing—"

"Wait!" Margritte held up a hand. "He's the Sorcerer of Aquae Sulis?"

"It's in his domain, yeah."

"Oh, my." She put the mug on the floor, having lost her appetite for tea. "William Iris helped him to rescue the Master of Ceremonies, just before he moved to Londinium. That was the night the Rosas fell. Ekstrand turned up in the middle of a party because of William."

"Ekstrand working with an Iris?" Rupert shook his head. "Nah, he hates the puppets, always has."

"It's true. William found out what the Rosas were doing and got Ekstrand to rescue Lavandula. Or so they wanted everyone to believe."

"What are you getting at?"

"What if it was all a ruse to remove the Rosas so William could take Londinium?"

"Nah," Rupert shook his head. "Ekstrand playing politics with the Fae-touched? Not his style."

"But let's look at what's happened so far. The Rosa Duke of Londinium falls because William pins Lavandula's disappearance on them and convinces Ekstrand to report it to the King and Queen. Then William turns up in Londinium, makes a half-hearted attempt at running for the Dukedom, realises he can't get the support and so frames Bartholomew and legitimises his murder. Now Ekstrand attacks you, out of the blue. If you were killed, Oxenford would be thrown into chaos, making it ripe for the plucking. Ekstrand and the Irises move in and take it."

"Why haven't the Irises taken over Aquae Sulis?"

"Because they don't need to. They have the city sewn up with the Papavers. Oxenford is next on their list, I'm certain of it."

"I don't like the way you're making sense." Rupert looked back into the box. "I want to think you're just obsessed, you know, grief-stricken and seeing Iris plots everywhere but... fuck. It sounds plausible. I heard a rumour the Prince was pissed off with Iris – maybe it's because of this." He shook his head. "I'm sure there was something important I had to remember about Ekstrand..."

"Sir," Benson was back at the doorway, holding several volumes of the leather-bound books with a sheet of paper on top. "Recent incidences of Northumbria, Wessex and Ekstrand. The most recent entry indexed under 'Ekstrand' is marked 'critical' – would you like me to read it to you?"

"Yeah, go on."

"Ekstrand has called a Moot. No fucking way I'm going to that when everything has gone tits up here. I'd rather f–"

Rupert snapped his fingers. "The Moot! Pull the footage the drones took and bring it to me on my laptop."

"Moot?" Margritte asked.

"It's when all the Sorcerers get together on neutral ground and have arguments about pissy little things when they're not allowed to kill each other. Ekstrand called one a few weeks ago but I had my hands full here with all the Rosa fallout. I thought it would be a waste of time – he never brings anything interesting to the table. So I sent some of my drones to film it."

"This seems like Sorcerer business," Margritte said, getting up. The talk of drones and "filming" things made such little sense it was making her headache worse. "Perhaps it would be best if I went home now."

"Soon, soon. I just want to see if anything – ah, put it here, Benson."

The "laptop" appeared to be a smaller version of the computer she'd seen in Convocation House. She sat back down, regretting staying for that drink. She didn't feel like she was being held prisoner, but he was hardly respecting her wish to leave. Did he need an audience? Perhaps he'd forgotten what it was like to have a human being around and couldn't bear to have it end yet.

She'd learned more about the Sorcerers in the last ten minutes than in the last two hundred years. Was it simply that the Sorcerer of Essex was a recluse and the others weren't, thereby giving her a skewed impression? It was a taboo subject in Society, the Sorcerers effectively being the jailers of their patrons. She wondered what Lord Tulip would make of it all. Was there any way she could turn it to her advantage?

Rupert was hunched over the screen and after a few minutes said, "But Ekstrand didn't even turn up. What kind of arsehole calls a Moot and then doesn't even show up for it?"

Margritte peered around his side and saw grainy pictures of the entrance to a castle's inner keep. "Perhaps he was just late," she suggested.

"I'll fast forward." He pressed a button and shoved his hands in his pockets. The picture didn't change but numbers in the bottom right corner sped through minutes then hours. "Looks like they went ahead without him; none of them have come out again. Hang on…" He tapped a button and the numbers froze. "What the fuck is that?"

Bizarre markings were appearing on the wall. Rupert moved his finger about on a square below the keys and the area being written on filled the screen. The symbols glowed briefly then disappeared.

"I don't know what the fuck is writing that," Rupert said. "Doesn't look like a ward kicking off. Not one I know anyway."

"Are they sorcerous symbols?"

He scratched his chin. "Kinda. Some of them." They watched the writing appear briefly all along the wall until it went out of sight down the side of the keep. Rupert sped the pictures up again. The symbols made a brief reappearance after presumably being written around the whole building, then went out of sight.

Rupert cracked his knuckles as he watched and it made Margritte shudder. "This is a bloody long Moot."

"Could that strange writing have trapped them inside?"

"Maybe. Oh, hang on, someone else has arrived."

Margritte sat down, not wanting to watch. He could realise how much she'd seen already and she didn't want to give him any more incentive to keep her there indefinitely.

"That's Ekstrand and one of his Arbiters. The Arbiter's checking the symbols disappeared – Ekstrand must have cast them out of shot. What the... is that a walking gargoyle?"

Margritte twitched, then resisted the urge to look, no matter how bizarre it sounded. She closed her eyes and let her head fall back onto the sofa cushion.

"Oh, Jesus. Oh, shit, no."

She opened them to see Rupert twist to face her, as white as bone china.

"What's wrong?"

"Ekstrand killed them."

"Who?"

"The Sorcerers. He's checking they're all dead. Ekstrand and I are the only ones left." He paused the footage and dropped onto the sofa next to her. She carefully laid a hand on his shoulder, wanting to console him, having been ripped apart by her bereavement so recently. She couldn't help but feel sorry for him. He didn't notice and she discreetly withdrew, thinking it better to keep her distance. "I can't believe this. That's why Ekstrand missed the Moot: he killed them all – except me. Look how pissed off he is – it's because my body isn't there."

She glanced at the screen, saw the bodies laid out, then looked away again. "So Londinium is without a Sorcerer? North or South?"

"Yup."

"And William Iris, friend of Ekstrand, is rather conveniently the Duke. How interesting."

"That's why Ekstrand tried to kill me," Rupert said. "He wants to take the whole Heptarchy – make it one domain under him. And the Irises have two major cities in the Nether now. If they're working together they'll take Oxenford and then Jorvic. This is fucking huge."

Margritte took a deep breath. "We need to work together. We have to protect Oxenford from the Irises and from Ekstrand."

He nodded. "Hell, yeah. All right, let me get the Bod' sorted and better protected. Then I'll kill Ekstrand and help you take Londinium back, all right?"

"How will you do that?"

"Cut off the head of course," he said. "We'll get William Iris." He stared at the screen. "After I've twatted Ekstrand." He frowned. "I shouldn't have let you see all this. But I wanted you to. That's not good."

Margritte's mouth went dry. "You have my word that not a single detail of my time here, or what has happened to the Sorcerers, will leave my lips once you let me go home."

He stared at her. "I shouldn't have wanted you to stay. Maybe I should kill you, just to be sure."

She leaned back. "Is that really necessary?"

He jumped up, making her heart fly into her throat. "Nah. That would suck. I like you, Maggie. Seems there's enough death at the moment without me adding to it. Right?"

She steadied her breathing and nodded. "Yes, Rupert. You're absolutely right."

15

Sam rubbed his eyes and checked his watch. He'd been reading the files for almost six hours and it was the first time he'd paused. His stomach growled like a wild bear and now he was tuning back into his body he realised how thirsty he was. He slid the file into one of the boxes, replaced the lid and put it back in its place.

It felt like someone had gouged out his chest with a spoon. The things he'd read about would never go away, he would never be able to live his life in ignorance any more. There were people dying, suffering and struggling – that moment – all at the hands of Lord Iron and the other companies he worked with. If the devil was going to own a company, he'd be happy with CoFerrum Inc.

He went out and closed the door, leaving all of Leanne's letters there and taking only the keycard with him. As he walked through the warehouse, past other lock-ups containing other people's secrets, he decided not to call that Martin bloke yet. He didn't want to hand all that stuff over to a stranger and lose control of the real legacy Leanne had left him. No wonder she'd set up such a generous life-insurance package; she was always expecting to be found out and removed. Everything in that room had destroyed their marriage and he wasn't going to just pass it on and get on with his life like it had never happened. She could have set things up to give Martin the location of the stash, but she didn't, she trusted *him* with it. She wanted to explain what she'd done in such a way as to give him the chance to see what she had discovered. There was no way Leanne would ask him to help directly, no way she'd want to put him at the same kind of risk she'd lived with, but some part of her wanted to hand it over to him. She wanted him to act, he was sure of it.

She didn't know that the head of the very corporation she was investigating had taken him under his wing. He had an advantage over the environmentalists, who would need the media and politicians to act, and Sam knew all too well they wouldn't do a thing. Iron's wealth probably had them all sewn up and Sam had no faith in them. Besides, the atrocities spanned continents and the international entanglements would need multiple governments and agencies to cooperate for anything to change. It would take months, if not years – even if they were able to do anything about it. He could go straight to the top and see if Iron was even aware of what his company was doing, and then threaten him with exposure if he refused to do anything.

He was just starting to formulate a plan when his mobile rang. It was his voicemail service so he listened to the message, relieved he wouldn't have to speak to anyone.

"Hi Sam, it's Cathy. New number again, I've texted you so you've got it. I lost my old one when we were attacked. I was just calling to make sure you're all right. Max came to see me and said you saved me from Lord Thorn and that your wife died and I wanted to say… I don't know, that I was thinking of you and hoping you're coping and stuff. Can you call and leave a message to let me know you're all right? I don't know when I'll next get a chance to–"

The message cut off – she'd run out of time – but there was a second one.

"Sorry, I was talking too much. I'm staying in the Nether, Sam, I'm not going to find a way out. The system is fucked here and the more I learn about what's going on, the more I know I need to change it, but I can only do that from the inside. I'll pick up any messages you leave. If there's an emergency, or if you really need somewhere to be away from family or stuff like that, come to Spencer House near Green Park in London and ask for Morgan. He'll let you in and get me, but only do that if you really need to, all right? Take care, Sam. And thanks for helping me and Sophia."

He ended the call, and the text message with her number arrived. He called it straight away.

"Cathy, it's Sam. Don't stay there, you have to get out. I know you're scared of the Fae, I am too, but there has to be a way to be free of them. I have some stuff to take care of, then I'll be in touch."

When he pressed the key to end the call he realised he was shaking. Leanne had spent all those years thinking she could just get that little bit closer to the top and change the world; now Cathy was falling into the same trap. He almost called her back to tell her that her husband had threatened him, but decided against it. If she lost her temper at her husband he'd know they'd been in touch and she'd only get into trouble.

"It's all a fucking mess," he muttered. He had to go back to Lord Iron and sort him out. Then he had to go and find Cathy and make her realise she needed to get out before she ended up losing her life to a struggle she couldn't win.

••••

The first thing Max saw when he woke was the gargoyle. It had been sitting in the same place all night, having gone there after Ekstrand's threat.

"We're going to do something, aren't we?" Its question sounded more like a statement.

Max nodded, dressed and went down to breakfast. There was no sign of Ekstrand. "He's in his study," Petra said when he checked the living room. "We're not to disturb him."

"There are Chapters all over the Heptarchy without a Sorcerer," Max said. "He needs to take charge."

Petra put down her book and looked at him properly. "I'm sure Mr Ekstrand has a plan."

"Are you?"

"Are you going to patrol again today?"

"I want to see if Mr Ekstrand is going to give me any new instructions."

"I told you, we're not allowed to disturb him."

Max was about to reply when Axon came to the doorway. "I think we need to." He was holding a newspaper. "Look at this."

He went to the coffee table and laid it before Petra, pointing to an article.

"Oxford scientist discovers Ekstrand syndrome." Petra read the headline and looked up at Axon with surprise.

"Go on," he said and she looked back at the newspaper.

"An Oxford psychologist, Dr Rupert Superior, has announced the discovery of a new psychological disorder, one he claims could put the entire country at risk, if not the world, were it to go untreated. Coined 'The Ekstrand Syndrome' and identifiable by a simple set of psychological tests, this discovery, Dr Superior asserts, is the most significant since the work of Sigmund Freud. 'The Ekstrand Syndrome consists of certain personality traits which can appear relatively harmless in isolation,' Dr Superior said, 'but when presenting as a cluster in one individual can pose a significant threat to society. I discovered it in a patient with long-term trust issues and an inferiority complex. He began to commit violent acts in order to further his own egotistical fantasies and delusions about taking over the country. Unfortunately this patient is so dangerous that rather extreme measures needed to be taken to ensure the safety of others, but I believe that now the full extent of his problem – and the threat of the syndrome itself – have been identified, the individual will pose no further danger to innocent members of the public.' When asked how sufferers of Ekstrand Syndrome can be identified, Dr Superior replied, 'They are always men who believe themselves to be more intelligent than their peers despite repeated evidence to the contrary. They dedicate significant time and effort to trying to remove those considered a threat to their schemes and refuse to accept they might be wrong. Aside from the patient in question it's my belief a not insubstantial number of Conservative Party members also suffer from Ekstrand Syndrome.' Dr Superior has yet to publish a paper on the disorder."

The gargoyle was wheezing with suppressed laughter but Petra was ashen. She looked at the date at the top of the page. "He's still alive then. How did he get this into today's newspaper?"

"Maybe he put it in before the attack," Max suggested.

"I thought the same thing," Axon said. "Then I noticed this." He flipped forwards a few pages. "There's a piece here on a student prank involving a clay ball thrown at the Bodleian Library. It says, 'No damage was caused and the students in question will be severely reprimanded.' And in the puzzles page... here, there's a wordsearch that's clearly been tampered with."

Max moved to read the list. "Idiotic. Sorcerer. Failed. Murderer. Attempted. Inferior. Revenge. Retribution. Pride. Justice."

The gargoyle sniggered.

"This isn't funny!" Petra said. "When Mr Ekstrand knows it didn't work he's going to be distraught."

"He's going to keep being obsessed," the gargoyle said, not laughing any more.

Max didn't want Axon and Petra to hear anything else the gargoyle might say. He had to find the person behind the murders before the last two Sorcerers in Albion killed each other. "I'll leave you to tell Mr Ekstrand," he said to Axon. "I have things I need to do."

Will covered the letter he was writing when there was a knock on the door to his study.

"Mr Bertrand Persificola-Viola," Morgan announced.

The younger Viola walked in, dressed in a Regency-style outfit with a superbly cut single-breasted tailcoat and high cravat. He was so much smarter than his brother Freddy, in more ways than one, Will suspected. Bertrand gave a formal bow and entered, heading for the chair on the other side of the desk that Will gestured to.

They shook hands before he sat down. "Thank you for accepting my request to speak with you, your Grace."

"I assume it's something important or you'd have said something at Black's, earlier." Will sat down. He also expected something was about to be raised off the record, or Bertrand would have visited him at the Tower.

"I wanted to be discreet, and to ensure a private conversation didn't become the subject of gossip."

"Would you like some brandy?"

"Thank you, your Grace, but no. I don't drink alcohol."

Will inclined his head in acknowledgement. The younger wanted to distance himself from Freddy in every way, it seemed.

"May I say, before we go on," Bertrand said, "I understand the Duchess was kind enough to pay a social call to my wife earlier today. Charlotte was deeply touched and quite thrilled that Her Grace singled her out for the honour."

Will smiled. Cathy's gesture was perfectly timed. "My wife said she enjoyed the visit immensely." He had no idea if that were so, but was planning to quiz her on the subject later.

"Your Grace, something has come to my attention that I believe you should be made aware of, if you haven't been informed already. Several people are considering leaving Londinium to go and live in Oxenford."

Will pressed his fingertips together, keeping his expression neutral. "People are free to live wherever they wish, if the ruler of the city permits it."

"They've been personally invited to consider moving by Margritte Tulipa."

He hadn't expected that. "How many?"

"I know of ten but there may be more. All influential families, including my brother."

"I know Freddy took Bartholomew's death badly."

Will watched a muscle work in Bertrand's jaw. "My brother speaks first, thinks last. I apologise for his appalling behaviour at the first Court."

"There's no need for you to apologise for him. His actions aren't your fault."

Bertrand looked down. "He's been to Oxenford and is waiting on the Hebdomadal Council for a formal invitation to move there. He's trying to persuade others to come with him and take their tithe from Londinium's coffers. I felt you should know."

Will almost thanked him, but stopped himself. He didn't want Bertrand to know it was the first he'd heard of it, or to appear beholden to him. "Have you received a letter from Margritte?"

"No, your Grace. It seems I've been overlooked."

Will didn't miss the bitterness in his voice and felt Margritte's omission had little to do with it. No doubt he'd been overlooked many times. "Older brothers can be difficult," Will said, adopting a more relaxed position. "Mine is said to be the most able swordsman in Albion. Every time I picked up a sword I was compared to him. I always fell short, but I didn't mind."

"Why? If I may be so bold."

"Because he deserves the acclaim. He *is* the best swordsman. If I was to be judged poorly thanks to his *inability* to wield a weapon it would be a different matter altogether. I wouldn't just be overlooked, or compared unfavourably, I'd be suffering an injustice."

Bertrand's eyes flicked over his face, as if he were searching Will's expression for any sign of something other than solidarity. "I had the impression that you're going to be a Duke with a strong sense of justice."

"Indeed." Will nodded. "A Duke must do all he can to ensure the people under his care are able to be all they can be. Whether that's ensuring they can travel safely or simply helping them to solve their personal problems, it's all equally important." Bertrand was nodding slowly, listening with total attention. "Wherever I perceive an injustice it's my duty to ensure something is done."

"You've already demonstrated that, your Grace. So many in Londinium are nothing but words, but you act decisively to protect those under your care."

Will smiled to mask the uncomfortable flash of memory. He had acted decisively but he'd killed the wrong man. "I do all I can to make sure those I love – and those who are loyal to me – have the very best of my protection and care. I hope, when people realise this, they can feel confident and secure enough to act decisively themselves, to make their lives all they can be."

"Even if they had to do something... radical?"

"If I believed it was for the good of Londinium, yes. Sometimes a forest has to have a great tree felled to give enough light for others to grow. It's a radical act, but for the good of the whole."

Bertrand's chest swelled and his eyes glistened with the implicit permission he'd just been granted. "I won't take a moment more of your time, your Grace, I'm sure you are very busy."

Will stood and extended his hand which Bertrand shook enthusiastically. "My door is always open to you, Bertrand. I'm better able to help if kept well informed."

"I'll bear that in mind, your Grace." Bertrand bowed and left.

Will sat back down and took up his pen. There was another knock on the door. "The Marquis of Westminster is here, your Grace."

"That time already?" He covered the letter again. "Show him in, Morgan, and bring us a bite to eat."

"Very good, sir."

Tom soon entered and they shook hands. Whilst he wasn't as uptight as Bertrand had been, Tom was far from relaxed. "I trust you're well, your Grace?"

"Tom, please. We're in my house. Call me William."

He went to the tantalus on the sideboard behind him. "Brandy?"

"No, thank you. I have the report. Would you like me to leave it with you?"

"How about giving me a summary now? Do you have time?"

"Of course."

Will waved a hand at one of the twin sofas in front of the fire and sat opposite Tom. Whilst he settled into the corner with an arm on the rest and his legs crossed, Tom remained bolt upright as he looked through the sheaf of paper in his hands. That he and Cathy had been brought up in the same household still amazed Will.

"I've interviewed all the victims who came forward and some interesting findings have emerged. One of the most important is that there's more than one team of robbers."

"That's interesting," Will said. "How–"

There was one knock on the door and it opened. Cathy marched in. "What's going on?"

"Catherine!" Tom stood. "The Duke and I are having a private meeting."

Cathy's hands were on her hips. "So this is how it is, then? The ladies sit and embroider while the men talk about all the important things?"

"Catherine," Tom's voice was stern. "Don't be so rude."

Will watched with interest as the old family pattern emerged. Cathy continued to ignore her brother, her eyes fixed on Will.

"I can contribute," she said. "If I'm clever enough to be a good Duchess, let me be more than someone who sits next to you in the Court and has tea with wives."

Tom turned to Will. "I'm so sorry, she's always been difficult."

"Tom!"

Will held up a hand. "You're right," he said to Cathy. Tom would be on his side no matter what, but he had to win Cathy over completely. He couldn't bring himself to use anything that overpowered her emotions again, especially not after having been a victim of it himself, so he needed to do all he could to bring them closer together. And she was right, she wasn't stupid.

Her smile made her features softer and he found himself smiling back. "Thank you," she said.

"Come and sit next to me, my love. Tom was telling me what he's found out about these highwaymen."

Tom sat down, took a deep breath and focused on the pages again. "As I was saying… there are several groups of robbers – the attacks on multiple carriages are simultaneous and in different parts of Londinium. Jewels and money are stolen, as would be expected. The carriages are never attacked on the way to or from the Court. Only large banquets, balls and soirées."

"I wonder why that is…" Will said.

"There must be something that people don't take to Court," Cathy said.

"There's a tradition in Londinium," Will said with a snap of his fingers. "No Charms in the Court that can influence the way one looks or how persuasive one might be to others. That's why the old room at Somerset House was lined with mirrors, so people could always check a person's reflection if they were in doubt."

"So they want jewellery that's Charmed," Cathy said. "That's interesting. Did you get descriptions of the things stolen?" she asked Tom, who nodded.

"Yes, a mixture of Charmed and plain jewellery. All sorts of things, from tiaras to cufflinks."

"Will," Cathy said, "you should get someone to look at the mundane auction houses."

"What for?"

"I doubt the highwaymen are stealing jewels to wear themselves. I bet they're selling on the pieces that aren't Charmed, and they'll be going through a fence to do that."

Will and Tom frowned at her. "A what?" Tom asked.

"A fence is someone who takes stolen goods and sells them for a profit, taking a cut for themselves. The good ones can get fake proof of ownership for the really expensive pieces and they have loads of contacts willing to take stuff off their hands in return for a lower price."

"How the devil do you know that?" Will asked and Tom fidgeted.

"I saw it in a TV show in Mundanus," Cathy replied. She noticed Tom's discomfort. "Don't worry, Will knows all about that."

Tom's surprise was evident. "Oh. I see."

"Auction houses are the best place to sell good pieces," Cathy continued. "They're more likely to have specialist buyers and collectors who'll pay more for rare jewels. Necklaces and so on that we wear in the Nether are usually the highest quality, so they get better prices, too."

Will was glad he'd let her stay. "All this from a TV show?"

"Oh… well, the fence stuff, yes. I used an auction house…" She glanced at Tom. "I sold my coming-of-age jewels to fund my time there."

"Catherine Rho–" Tom cut himself off. "That's a terrible, terrible thing to do. Those were a gift, not to mention a family heirloom you should pass to your daughter."

"I felt that freedom was a more valuable gift," she replied. "But of course, you never did understand that."

The tension between them was something Will had only glimpsed in the past. He recalled the time Tom had dropped her off at the restaurant in Aquae Sulis after the first ball of the season. No wonder their relationship had been so strained, and still was – Tom was ashamed of her behaviour. The amount of stress that must have been endured in the household before that first ball must have been intense. He wondered if that was why he'd never heard anything of Tom's Grand Tour. Had it been sacrificed in the search for his runaway sister? No wonder there was animosity between them.

"I think that's very useful information, Cathy, thank you," he said and squeezed her hand. "Tom, do you have anything else?"

"Only a theory," he replied, all business again. "I've been considering how multiple groups of highwaymen could possibly know when and where to target carriages on miles of roads in the Nether. I thought about various military campaigns and how even the seemingly insignificant parts of a system can actually provide critical intelligence. I think they must have contacts at the stables. There are seven reflected into the Nether in London, and all the people robbed used one of them on the night they were attacked. It would be a simple matter for a spy to see people set off in their finery and send a message detailing who was inside and where they were going."

Will nodded. "Yes, it makes perfect sense. No one would ever think of the staff either – they're always overlooked. This is excellent work, Tom, thank you." He smiled at Cathy. "And thank you, my love. It seems we can make a good team."

She gave Tom a nervous glance. "I'm sorry about the jewels."

Tom gathered his notes, not looking at her. "Don't tell Mother what you did, for goodness' sake."

"Of course not. I'm not an idiot."

"I think I can handle it from here," Will said. He stood, shook hands with Tom and they watched him leave. Will caught hold of Cathy's hand, pulling her up into an embrace. "Your poor brother," he said. "You traumatised him with your wilful behaviour. He didn't know how to handle you coming in like that."

A moment of sadness crossed Cathy's face. "We used to be close. Not any more. I don't think he'll ever forgive me. You didn't seem to mind though, and you're the Duke."

"And your husband," Will said and kissed her, weaving his fingers into her hair and holding her waist tight against him. He felt her tense up at the initial contact and then soften into the kiss. He closed his eyes and tried not to think about Amelia.

16

Max pulled the ivy around the gargoyle's neck, adjusting it until the soul chain was hidden. "If you don't move too much and keep most of your body behind the guttering it should be out of sight."

"This is going to be brilliant," it replied.

"Don't get carried away. As soon as we spot one of them you need to tone it down, and when they get close you need to keep still so they use the Sniffer. When he tries to climb up then you need to use the–"

"I know, I know," it replied. "Don't worry, it's going to work." It took the Opener from Max and put it between its teeth.

"I'm not worried," Max said but the gargoyle was already climbing up the wall. When it reached the top it leaped across to the top of the portico and up to the guttering at the corner of the church. Once he was satisfied the gargoyle was in position, the Opener tucked away and the soul chain still hidden, Max hid in the doorway across the narrow London street. It had taken hours to find the right place but once he had it had been no trouble to bring the gargoyle through from Aquae Sulis and formulate the plan. Now it was just a matter of waiting for an Arbiter to turn up so he could be tracked back to the corrupted Chapter's cloister.

"Hey!" the gargoyle shouted at a young man walking by. "Hey you, short-arse! Hey, look at me when I'm trying to insult you!"

The man stopped and looked at the church. The gargoyle waved and the man jolted.

"Yes, it's me," the gargoyle yelled. "What are you wearing? Is that supposed to be a hat? You put your Mum's tea cosy on instead."

As expected, the young man pulled his mobile phone out of his pocket and began filming as the gargoyle blew raspberries at him. "Are you another actor?" he asked. "Are you from the same people who did the Nelson stunt?"

"Nelson?" The gargoyle pulled a face as if he'd just smelt a rotten egg. "Nelson was an amateur. No charisma. I'm so much more interesting than him."

"Don't take it too far," Max whispered under his breath.

"That's so cool," the man said. "I'm posting this right now."

"Yeah, you do that," the gargoyle said. "Make me famous."

Max hoped the ivy was doing a good enough job. Whilst it wasn't ideal having the gargoyle made famous on the mundane virtual library network, it wasn't as if anyone in the Nether used it and besides, he could hardly take the gargoyle out and about in Mundanus anyway. There was no other way to find one of the London Arbiters so efficiently.

Then he saw Faulkner at the end of the street. He remembered him from the cafe on Judd Street. Max got the bug ready, activating it so the claws sprang open, ready to catch onto the fabric of the Arbiter's coat. He had a spare in case he missed, but he still needed Faulkner to get closer.

"Have you seen this?" the first man asked and then looked back at the gargoyle, disturbed by Faulkner's manner. "He was saying a lot more a few minutes ago."

Faulkner got out a mobile phone and made a call as he walked down the street to stand next to the other spectator. The gargoyle pulled faces for a minute or so, then stopped when Faulkner ended his call.

"Aw, show's over," the young man said. "I'm going to see if I can find the wires or the battery. No one knows how they did Nelson, maybe–"

Faulkner shook his head. "I wouldn't if I were you." He flashed an ID at the young man. "Move along."

"Bloody hell, it's just a bit of fun," the man said. "The filth are all fascists these days!" He ran off.

As predicted, Faulkner got out a Sniffer and began winding it. He was less than ten feet away. Max placed the bug on the palm of his hand, lined it up as best he could and then flicked it with his forefinger. It landed just above the belt of his coat and crawled away beneath the waistband, geared as it was to seek out a dark crease upon landing. Satisfied, Max gave the gargoyle a curt nod and slipped away, limping without using his stick so the sound wouldn't alert the Arbiter. By the time he was in the next street he knew the gargoyle had opened a Way in the church roof and escaped into the Nether driveway of Mr Ekstrand's house whilst Faulkner had been trying to find a gate into the churchyard. Mission accomplished.

Sam pulled the iron out of the coals and laid it on the anvil, then, pausing only to wipe the sweat from his forehead, he struck it with the hammer. He'd barely slept, he'd hardly eaten but when he worked the iron he didn't feel it. It was the only thing he could bear to do as he waited for Lord Iron to come back from his latest trip.

The strikes upon the red metal rang through the forge and he felt each one through the gloves, up his arm and into his chest. His blows were hammering the blunt stump into a flatter point, "drawing down" as the blacksmith had taught him. He didn't have a particular piece in mind; he just wanted to practise the basics. He'd made a few curls, slit a few pieces and made some holes, each time the technique felt easier. At school he'd barely been able to wield a coping saw in woodworking class yet here he was, doing something totally practical with relative ease. His teacher wouldn't recognise him.

"I hardly recognised you," said a voice at the door. "I thought you were Bob."

Sam left the hammer where it had last struck and looked at Lord Iron. "I've been waiting for you."

Iron was dressed in his usual Savile Row suit, looking effortlessly immaculate as he always did. His shoes shone against the muddy stones at the threshold. "Looks like you're well on the way to becoming a blacksmith. Bob said you'd taken to it well."

"Seems I'm good at something after all," Sam replied, thrusting the metal's tip back into the coals. "Shame it's not two hundred years ago. How was the trip?"

"Very good. Made some progress with a European partner and scoped out some–" He smiled. "You're not interested in all of that."

Sam just worked the bellows and watched the fire, not knowing how to start to say what he needed to.

"I understand you went back to Bath. Are you satisfied with the way everything's been handled?"

He nodded.

"If the house doesn't sell in the next week I'll get a team of stagers in. They dress the house neutrally, apparently it makes it easier for people to imagine living there themselves."

Sam pulled out the metal and laid it on the anvil. He beat it again and tried to ignore the fact he was being watched.

"Drawing down," Iron said. "It looks like you've been doing it for weeks rather than days. You really do have a gift. What about the other six?"

"Six what?"

"Bob must have taught you the seven core skills; splitting, curls–"

"Yeah, all those."

When he paused to see his progress, Iron came closer to inspect the work. "This is the only craft that every other craft depends upon, and the only one where functionality and art are truly fused." When Sam didn't say anything, Iron carried on. "People used to fear blacksmiths, you know, as much as they needed them."

"Bob told me about that."

"Good. It's important to know these things."

The metal had cooled too much to be worked any more. Sam picked it up to put back into the fire, but changed his mind and lay it back down on the anvil. "I know more about you, too. I know what your business does, all over the world."

"I've never hidden that from you. I gave you that tour–"

"You gave me a tour of the clean bits, the offices and the paper work and the fucking PowerPoint presentations. You didn't tell me about the stuff you're doing in the Congo and the things you've been covering up in South Africa and Chile. The acid rain and thousands of hectares of land you're just fucking up forever to make a quick buck. You make out that you're refined and the whole time you're living off the blood and deaths of people and nature, and helping your mates to cover up their shit too. I know all of it."

Iron appeared to be unmoved. "They say childhood ends when you understand the ugliness of the world."

"Don't fucking patronise me! Your company has committed atrocities that make BP and Shell look like humanitarian organisations! And don't tell me your company is so huge that you don't know everything that happens at the lower levels because I won't believe it."

"I do know. I know everything that happens, in ways you can't possibly appreciate. Yet."

"So you just don't give a shit as long as the wheels keep turning, is that it? Profit is more important than people, right?"

"It's not the profit."

"Oh, so you get a sense of personal satisfaction from being the most evil man in the world? The obscene wealth is just a bonus."

Iron looked down at the foot of the anvil. There was no defensiveness, no anger, just... Sam couldn't work it out. Resignation? Was he so at ease with himself and the awful things he did that he felt nothing?

"There's a lake in Chile that's so acidic everything in it has died and the land for miles around it can't support any life. There are conditions in a mine in South Africa that are so bad the average life expectancy of the men who work there – work for you! – is less than forty. Doesn't any of that make you feel anything?"

"It makes me feel incredibly sad."

Sam chucked the hammer to one side and jabbed him in the chest with his gloved finger, leaving a black smudge on his tie. "Then why don't you do something about it?"

"I can't."

"You won't, more like."

"No, Sam, I'm literally incapable of stopping all of this. I've wanted to, for a long time, but it's... just what I am."

Sam gripped the metal he'd been working tight. "That's such bullshit. You're incapable of picking up the phone and saying, 'Let's pay those people proper wages and, while we're at it, let's spend some of these profits on cleaning up the mess we've made.'"

Iron shook his head. "Have you ever known anyone with an addiction? You can find them over a toilet, throwing up their guts, losing everything in their life and say to them, 'Just stop drinking' and it's simply impossible for them. Even when it's obvious it's killing them."

"Alcoholics can recover," Sam said, the metal rattling against the anvil as he struggled to rein in his anger.

"Neugent killed Leanne, but I was the one who made him into the thing he is now." Iron stared at the anvil. "I do that. I'm poisonous without even trying to be. Everything I've ever done in my life has been part of this... this natural talent. When I became Lord Iron it was amplified – the company machine grew and took over until it propagated itself endlessly. It isn't just me, it's the people I've hired, the ethos of the companies I own. I'm the root of all of it and it won't change just because I have a moment of clarity."

Sam didn't know what to make of what he was saying. Was it depression? Self-pity? Or was there something else involved, something unbelievable like the Fae and that world they lived in? Questions and worries surfaced again about the wedding rings and the railing at the park and the plugs that formed in his wounds, but he didn't want to lose focus. "Of course you can change it. We could go to the house, right now, and you could close the business down."

"It doesn't work like that."

"Oh, for fuck's sake!" Sam lifted the metal and struck the anvil with it, the dull clang filling the forge. "People are dying, people are being murdered and poisoned by the only air they have to breathe and you have to take some responsibility for it!"

"I am," Iron said, looking at him in the eye again. "That's why you're here."

"Eh?"

Iron lifted the tip of the metal, ending its vibrating song, and inspected its tip as Sam wondered whether to pull it away from him and whack him over the head with it. "I've tried so many times to find the right one and they end up killing the best people around them. Neugent was the last. I realised it was all my fault – when I got too involved the poison in me would leech into them. Just like CoFerrum, just like everything else in my life. But I have the solution now, and that's why I've brought you here and tested you and had you taught. Because you can take on the mantle and do something better with it." He smiled. "Everything's going to be all right, Sam."

And then he threw himself forwards, still holding the tip of the metal and directing it to his chest. It pierced him before Sam even fully registered what he was doing and he tried to let go of the other end of it with a horrified cry. His hand didn't co-operate, as if his fingers and palm were magnetised to it. Sam staggered backwards as Iron pushed himself forwards, further onto the spike of metal, an awful wet gurgling erupting from his throat as bubbles of blood emerged from his mouth and died on his lips.

Sam hit the wall of the forge, the blunt end of the metal now against his own chest, Iron's eyes still fixed on him and now only inches away from his own. He could smell the blood and felt it spray onto his face as Iron coughed. The metal felt hot again, even through his glove, and he feared his own heart was going to be pierced as the pressure built.

Iron's smile was fading and his skin looked like it was made of wax. Sam struggled to breathe as the heat from the metal penetrated the thick leather apron, then his shirt, and flooded into his chest. He shook violently and felt a warm liquid running down his leg as the last rattling sigh escaped from Iron's lips and he became a dead weight at the other end of the shaft. As he collapsed Sam was pulled down with him, still unable to release the metal. Iron's blood ran down the shaft and over the gloves, dripping off the cuffs and onto his wrists as Sam heaved his chest up and down, feeling like the air was drowning him.

17

Cathy waited for Carter on the lower floor of the bookshop, conveying her apologies and embarrassment with one glance at Jane. His footsteps clumped across the floor above them, did a circuit of the room with the fireplace and then made their way back. When he came down the stairs, Cathy hoped he didn't have something on him that would detect the Charm to open the Way to the Nether reading room.

"Everything seems in order," he said. "I'll sit here whilst you browse, if that doesn't get in your way?"

"That's fine," Cathy said. "We'll be upstairs, that's where… the best books are."

"And the comfy chairs," Jane added. "Shall we go up?"

"It's so kind of you to open after hours for me," Cathy said to her as they went upstairs, purely for Carter's benefit. As long as he didn't come up too – which she doubted – everything would be fine.

They went to the stained-glass door at the far end of the shop and Jane got the key ready. "If he starts coming up the stairs I'll tell him you're in the reading booth." She opened the door to reveal a little cubby with another comfy chair in it. "Then I'll come through and warn you, all right?"

"Thanks," Cathy said as the door was closed and the key inserted. "I'm sorry to be a bother. It's such a pain in the arse, all of this bodyguard bobbins, but it's the only solution I could think of."

"It's no trouble," Jane said and then unlocked the door. "Everyone else is already here. Enjoy!"

Cathy stepped across the shimmering threshold and into the secret reading room. This time it was full of people; she counted ten men and women, all evidently from the Great Families. A young woman who looked very much like Charlotte stood up.

"Your Grace!" she said and the conversation died, along with Cathy's confidence.

Cathy reminded herself this wasn't like a normal salon. "I'm Cathy," she said. "Miss Rainer was my Governess and... and I think she used to organise this, am I right?"

Everyone nodded but they were still staring at her. She could feel the skin on her neck burning, and in moments the sensation reached her cheeks. "Um... I don't want to screw this up, just because I'm the Duchess. I knew Miss Rainer before I became Duchess, it shouldn't get in the way."

"Of course not!" the woman said. "We're so sorry, we knew a new person was coming but we had no idea it was you! I understand you've met my mother, Charlotte? I'm Emmeline and this is my brother, Benedict."

Emmeline made the introductions and Cathy rapidly forgot all the names. Only two others were Londinium residents; the others came from all over Albion. A woman said she was from Aquae Sulis but Cathy didn't recognise her.

"This is so exciting!" Emmeline said, leading her to one of the chairs. "We haven't had a new member in four years! How is Miss Rainer? Where is she teaching now? Why hasn't she been in touch with us?"

"We feared something had happened to her," Benedict said. He was handsome but still boyish. Cathy suspected he hadn't yet been packed off on his Grand Tour.

Everyone was looking at her. "She's not... herself any more," Cathy replied. "My parents discovered she was teaching me something worthwhile and complained to the Agency. I managed to track her down and... well, it's not good." There was a collective sense of grief. All of their lives had been touched by Miss Rainer. "But I promise I'm going to find a way to restore her."

"She's not the first," Emmeline said, glancing at her brother.

"We need to stay positive though," Benedict said and others agreed. "It's what she would want."

"I couldn't agree more," Cathy said as she sat down. "So. What have I missed?"

"Emmeline recited a very moving poem," said the woman from Aquae Sulis. "And Benedict has brought something to share, haven't you?"

"I've written an essay," he said, patting a leather wallet resting on his lap. "And Alicia, didn't you say you had some thoughts about the Suffragettes you wanted to discuss?"

Alicia, a lady from Jorvic, nodded. Cathy looked at the others but they just seemed to be waiting for something. "And then what happens?"

Emmeline frowned. "And then we have tea and decide what next month's theme should be."

"Hang on... is this just a discussion group?"

"Yes," Benedict replied. "Were you expecting something else?"

"I didn't know what to expect, I just found an old invite. I thought there would be planning, you know, working out what to do about Society. Taking action!"

Emmeline sank in her seat and Benedict took a sudden interest in his shoes.

"I mean, why else are you meeting?" Cathy pressed. "Surely you're trying to work out how to change things for the better?"

"There used to be more of us," Benedict said. "Men and women who were like you. Who wanted to be more… active and vocal about our cause in Society."

Cathy wondered if they'd split and she'd found her way to the cowardly half of the group. "Where do they meet?"

"No, you don't understand," Emmeline said. "They were removed from Society and replaced by less troublesome spouses, or cursed in such a way as to make it impossible for them to cause any scandal. Like our mother."

"Charlotte was such a pioneer," Alicia said. "When she spoke, we felt like we could do anything!"

"But she took it too far," Benedict said. "She was too passionate and she humiliated Father. If she wasn't Lady Violet's favourite she would have been replaced like all the others."

Cathy thought back to her visit, how lovely Charlotte was. She could imagine the Fae adoring her beauty and the trouble that would bring. "Which family was she born into?"

"She was from Mundanus," Emmeline said. "She was spotted by our father on the way home from a Suffragette rally. He had no idea what she'd been doing."

"He stole her," Benedict said, the anger straining his voice.

"But that's a breach of the Treaty," Cathy said.

"It happens all the time," Alicia said. "Didn't you know?"

She didn't. Cathy sat back, appalled at how naive she was. From ignoring where the servants came from and how they could be treated, to discovering that mundane women could be kidnapped from Mundanus without anyone caring or doing anything about it, made her feel sick. What else was she ignorant of?

She considered telling Max about what had happened to Charlotte, but if she'd been taken in the early nineteenth century her family would be dead. Would she want a life in which she had the freedom she'd been fighting for without knowing a soul? And modern life was so different, it could be too much of a shock. It explained why she'd changed Miss Rainer's fortunes; Charlotte had brought radical ideas into Nether Society with her and Rainer had been spreading them ever since.

"What happened to the others? You said they were replaced." She'd heard of that at least, but she wasn't exactly sure what it meant.

"They're sent away and never come back," Emmeline whispered. "No one knows where they're taken nor what happens to them."

"We don't even know if they're still alive," Benedict added.

Cathy worried a button on her glove, the sombre mood of the room being the last thing she'd expected. "I don't suppose one of them was Clarissa Arvensis-Ranunculus?" She was one of Miss Rainer's students, one whose file ended abruptly with the cryptic code she'd asked Max to decipher in her last letter to him.

"Yes!" Emmeline said. "Do you know what happened to her?"

"No, she was just someone I hoped to meet." She ran through the other names she could remember and the assembled confirmed that all had been replaced. None of them had been Londinium families, at least none of any note, so Max was the best bet in tracking them down. "I'll look into it," she said.

"Shall I read my essay now?" Benedict asked.

"No, wait," Cathy held up a hand. "I know I've just got here but I'm sorry, I'm not taking the risk to sneak out just to listen to an essay." When Benedict's young face displayed his sadness she said, "I'm sure it's really interesting, but I can read essays at home."

"We can't," Emmeline said pointedly.

"But what I mean is that if we're all taking the risk being here, let's put it to better use. Let's work out what we can do to find others like us. And we need a way to communicate securely with each other. We need to plan who we need to talk to and get on side, what we can say to them and who we think might be sympathetic."

The group wouldn't meet her eyes. No one said anything. Alicia took a breath but only to cough delicately into a handkerchief.

"I'm sorry, your Grace," Emmeline finally said. "It's too dangerous. We take comfort in each other and this keeps us from madness, but we aren't the kind of people you're looking for. They stood up for our rights and look what happened."

"What do you think the Suffragettes endured?" Cathy stood up, unable to keep calm in the face of such cowardice.

"The Suffragettes didn't have to contend with Charms and the Fae," Benedict said.

"No, they had to contend with the police and prison officers who force-fed them and people jeering at them on the street and their own families turning against them. What kind of feminists do you think you are if all you're prepared to do is just hide away in a bloody bookshop and talk?"

"Living ones," Emmeline said, now standing too. "I'm sorry we haven't met your expectations, and I'm sorry we're not as brave – and reckless – as my mother, but we've lost people and seen with our own eyes what horrors can be committed."

"So have I!" she shouted and immediately regretted it. Cathy held up her hands, ashamed of herself. "I'm sorry. I thought that if there were other people who had the same values we could actually achieve something."

"Having the same values does not mean we believe the same action should be taken," Benedict said. "If this group isn't what you want then, respectfully, your Grace, perhaps you need to look elsewhere."

She scanned the faces. All were nervous and tense. They were probably afraid she was going to force them into doing something by virtue of her status or that she'd do something that would lead others to them who would cart them off too. They were frightened and she didn't have the right to tell them how to protest, any more than she had the right to be angry with them for not being what she'd hoped.

"I think I do," she said. "I'm sorry I... sorry to disrupt your evening. I won't bother you again."

"Oh, your Grace, you'd be most welcome to discuss and debate with us," Alicia said nervously. "Just... nothing more."

Cathy managed a sad smile. "It's not enough for me," she said and left them to it.

Jane was waiting on the other side of the Way. "That was quick."

"It wasn't what I was hoping for," Cathy said. "Thank you for being so accommodating though."

She went down the stairs slowly, heavy with disappointment. Carter stood as she approached the door. "Did they not have any books to your taste, your Grace?"

"No," she said. "I need to find what I'm looking for elsewhere."

Will looked at the house through the raindrops rolling down the taxi's window. Why did it always rain when he had business in Mundanus? It looked unassuming enough, a terraced townhouse in Pimlico with iron railings outside and a neat row of clipped hedges in a window box. There were steps down to the basement level and steps up to the black front door.

He couldn't have found it without Tom, who may not have had the political connections but did have a talent for investigation. Tom's instincts about the stables had been correct and he'd followed each of the leads diligently, writing it all up and delivering the evidence to him in a dossier that read more like an academic paper. The house he looked at now was at the root of the criminal network.

"This the one then?" the driver asked.

"Yes." Will paid him and got out, opened the umbrella and directed it against the wind.

There was a light on in the living-room window and he could see an alcove full of books and a potted plant. The walls were white with a bold piece of modern art dominating the space above the fireplace. He couldn't see much more but it was already evident that the woman living there was wealthy.

He had several Charms ready to use, should the woman elect to fight him instead of accepting her fate. He wondered whether to use the Clear Sight Charm he'd purchased only an hour before, but didn't want to suffer the ill effects afterwards. He took a deep breath, adjusted the way the Glamoured sword rested against his thigh, and crossed the road.

The door knocker was a traditional lion's head holding a thick circle in its jaws. It made a satisfying clunk against the door. He heard footsteps in the hall and the door was opened by a woman in her thirties. She was slender with long black hair and wore a suit. There was a smile on her face which faded when she saw him.

"Not who you were expecting," he said.

"No. And you are?"

"The Duke of Londinium."

She paled as she looked him up and down. "Come in."

He looked at the threshold carefully before stepping through. It appeared to be clean and very mundane. The hallway had a polished oak floor and a cat sat on a console table, watching him with large amber eyes. Its fur was the same colour as the Nether's mists. The sight of it reassured him he would just be walking into the house as opposed to an unknown location in the Nether, so he went in. She closed the door behind him after a quick glance out onto the street.

"What do you want?"

"You haven't even shown me into your living room yet, Dr Tate. We may be in Mundanus but surely we don't need to behave like savages. I know you were brought up well at least."

He could see she was terrified. It made him more certain the conversation would go his way but didn't make him feel good. He'd had his fill of destroying lives. No, he corrected himself, it may not come to that.

"I would offer you a drink but I doubt you'd accept it," she said as he followed her into the living room.

"That's right. And I'd rather you didn't either. I'm sure you understand why."

"So you know all about me." She sat in a leather chair near the window. "Or so you want me to believe."

He sat on the sofa. It was a nice room, tastefully decorated. "I know you have a lucrative business underpinned by crime. I know you used to live in the Nether until your father decided it was more important to bed the wife of a friend than protect his family. I know you somehow managed to escape the Collectors and have been missing for over ten years, presumed dead."

He watched her throat move as she swallowed. "I can only assume, seeing as you're paying a personal visit, that you don't plan to turn me over to the Agency."

Will nodded. "The ones you paid to rob the people of Londinium are in their custody now."

"All four teams?" she asked.

"All five," he replied. "Nice try."

She licked her lips. "Sure you don't want a drink?"

"They stole jewellery for you. You sold on the plain pieces and kept the Charmed ones to extract the magic trapped inside them whilst you obtained the other ingredients needed to make new products. These ingredients include a vast range of human emotions, from despair to love. I understand you take your time and cultivate your... patients until they're ready to be emotionally harvested."

"So you do know everything," she sighed. "But you don't want to turn me in. Which means you either want to kill me or use me. Which is it going to be?"

The door creaked as the cat pushed it open further and rubbed against her legs. She picked it up and put it on her lap. "What's she called?"

"*He* is called Henry. And I'd rather you just get on with it."

"I'm not going to kill you," Will said. "What do you think I am, some sort of gangster?"

"You're an Iris, right?" At his nod she smiled. "You're a gangster. Perhaps Daddy hasn't told you yet."

He stiffened, then laughed. "It takes more than that to upset me. I'm not going to kill you because I admire your work. The operation is really quite remarkable. It's also mine, now."

She tickled the cat behind his ears and purring soon filled the room. "But you've destroyed one of the most critical parts of my supply chain."

"I'm merely replacing it with my own. I will supply all the Charmed artefacts you require. And I know exactly what you've stolen and when, so I know what kind of demand there will be. I won't have to rob innocent people to satisfy your quota."

"Innocent?" After a moment's thought she added, "The pieces need to be first generation – Charmed by the Fae themselves – can you handle that?"

"Yes. That won't be a problem." He was planning to request pieces as part of his tithe and any shortfall could be made up by Lord Iris, he was certain of it.

"And your cut will be...?"

"Modest. You can continue to live your illegal life in the manner to which you have become accustomed."

Tate looked at the cat and smiled as it looked back up at her. "And what about our two customers? I'm not sure they'll be very happy about this. It does muddy things somewhat."

He'd been fascinated to discover the criminal operation supplied the Agency and the Emporium of Things in Between and Besides directly. "Oh, there's no need for you to worry about them." Will smiled. "It's not as if there are alternative suppliers for them to go to. And the Shopkeeper's no fool. He'll understand that to accept this new arrangement is to survive."

"Hmm." Tate looked unconvinced. "The Shopkeeper. Not the man best known for liking change."

18

Sam couldn't stop shaking. Even though he'd managed to stagger back to the house and had had a bath and been given hot sweet tea, he trembled at his very core. Iron's lawyer sat on the other side of the table, watching him and waiting patiently.

"I didn't kill him."

"I know, sir," he said slowly. "You've seen the video and you've seen the instructions he left me. No one is going to accuse you of anything."

Iron had planned it. There'd been a concealed camera in the forge from the first day he went there and the entirety of Iron's bizarre suicide had been recorded. But none of it made sense and Sam was terrified the police would walk in any moment. It was just so unlikely, so silly, that he simply couldn't believe anyone would accept that the owner of a global corporation and one of the richest men in the world would choose to walk onto a metal stake. Once it was obvious what Iron was doing, they'd certainly want to know why he hadn't been able to let go of it. Sam wanted to know that himself.

"I mean... what the fuck?" he asked out loud.

"Mr Ferran, I can see you're still in shock–"

"What did you just call me?"

"Mr Ferran. I went through this with you, sir. You've been designated the official heir of the previous Mr Ferran and exist legally as Mr Samuel Ferran, his sole benefactor." When Sam continued to fail to reply, he added. "As his son would be."

"He wasn't my father." Sam gripped the edge of the table, wondering when he was going to wake up. "My father lives in Australia and collects stamps. He's living off a shitty pension."

The lawyer sighed. "I think it's best we resume this tomorrow, after you've had time to rest. It seems the previous Mr Ferran didn't appreciate how traumatic his actions would be."

The noise of a helicopter landing on the grass outside made Sam look out of the window, his chest tight at the thought of the police flying in to arrest him.

"Ah, she's here, good." The lawyer stood up. "I'm sure Lady Nickel will want to speak to you in private. I'll tell her where you are."

"Next you'll be telling me Lord Copper will be turning up and we'll have a big old party." A pathetic half-laugh slipped from his lips. "Maybe Lady Gold will be there."

"I understand that Lord Copper hasn't yet been informed of your new status," the lawyer replied. "And the current incumbent is *Lord* Gold. You'll be meeting them all soon. And please, don't worry about Lady Nickel's arrival. It was all part of the instructions left behind."

"Oh, good," Sam said flatly. "That makes me feel so much better."

The lawyer smiled as if he'd never heard a man be sarcastic and left the room. Moments later Sam watched him leave the house and walk to the edge of the lawn as the helicopter's door opened.

The woman who climbed out exuded power and confidence. She was wearing a trouser suit in a style more casual than Lord Iron's used to be, but it looked just as crisp and just as expensive. Her hair was black with some grey at the temples and cut in a short afro, her brown eyes made striking by her bold make-up. She pulled out a briefcase, spoke to someone still inside the helicopter and then strode over to the lawyer. They shook hands and when he spoke she looked at Sam through the window. They talked for less than a minute and then she was escorted in as two small suitcases were unloaded from the helicopter. It was taking off by the time she entered the room.

Sam stopped shaking. She walked in, set her briefcase down and looked at him. "So you're the one," she said, looking him up and down. "You're not what I expected, but I suppose that's the point."

He stood up, wondering if he'd met her before, seen her on television perhaps, or in a newspaper. "I'm Sam," he said.

She came over and they shook hands. Sam felt reassured she'd know what was going on and that, if things weren't OK, she would fix them. There was such self-confidence, such an aura of authority that he felt safe for the first time since Iron's death. Perhaps since Leanne's too.

"My name is Mazzi, but your predecessor used to call me Nicky."

"So you've got lots of names too?"

She nodded. "All of us do," she said, pulling out the chair next to his and sitting down.

"Which one would you prefer me to call you?"

"I think Mazzi for now. Let's keep it away from the Court for as long as we can. That's best, I think, by the look of you." She reached across and patted his hand. Her nails were painted a dark red. "It's all going to be fine."

"That's such a lie," Sam said, but he still felt better.

"So, what did he tell you?"

"Nothing."

"Not even about the Elemental Court?"

Sam shook his head. "No, but I've heard other people mention it. What is it anyway?"

Mazzi pursed her lips and looked out of the window. "He asked me to help, but I didn't realise I'd be babysitting. No offence."

"Look, I'll be OK. I'll just... go back to Bath and try and get a job. Stuff will work out. He was obviously mental. No need for him to screw up my life any more."

Mazzi stared at him as if he'd said something utterly ridiculous. "Oh, God. He really didn't tell you anything. There's no easy way to tell you this... you're Lord Iron now."

"That lawyer was saying some bollocks about me being the heir but I thought he was..." Sam stopped. "Oh fuck. This isn't... I mean... this is something more than just some loony leaving me money, isn't it?"

"You don't seem like you have a head for business," she said, stroking her chin with one of the shiny red nails. "Are you an artist? An engineer?"

"I'm a computer programmer. What's that got to do with anything?"

"No natural affinity for iron in any way?"

"Oh. Seems I'm a good blacksmith. And there was this weird thing that happened in a park when my friend was attacked and oh, shit – you're not like the Fae, are you?"

"Absolutely not." Mazzi grinned. "You could say we're the opposite. Especially you."

"Me?"

"Yes, because you're Lord Iron now. Come on, Sam, keep up. What was the weird thing that happened in the park?"

He told her about when Thorn attacked Cathy and the child in the park, how the railings had broken beneath him, how he'd been able to throw one like a spear so accurately. He shook as he described the iron plugs that had formed in his wounds and how he'd never found the right moment to confront Lord Iron about it before he died.

Mazzi was nodding, looking like she'd heard it all before. "You're definitely attuned. That probably caught his attention. You're a complete unknown to any of us – that's unusual but it makes more sense now."

"Are you saying I did that? I made the railings change?"

She shrugged. "We all have different ideas about how it works in the Court. Honestly, you have to make your own mind up about how you want to explain it, but it sounds like you manipulated the metal. I know blood is important for iron."

Sam thought of Leanne and Neugent and the apartment they'd given her to live in. He remembered that night in Bath, held stretched between the Brothers Thorn, and how his wedding ring had burned Thorn's skin. They would have killed him, and Cathy would have been killed if he hadn't intervened.

"Iron hurts the Fae," he whispered, looking at his wedding ring. He could feel its iron core in a way he couldn't before. It wasn't the ring Leanne had made for him; it was too perfect. The ring she'd died wearing wasn't made by him either. Neugent must have had them swapped.

"Yes, and when it's pure, it breaks their magic."

Sam realised the ring's core alone wasn't pure enough to protect him from the Charm Thorn's faerie placed on him, nor to stop Lord Poppy's interference.

"Copper makes them inert," Mazzi added.

Sam remembered the gloves Max put on, the night of the party in Aquae Sulis, before going through to take Lady

Rose into custody. "I've seen an Arbiter wear gloves covered in copper."

Mazzi nodded. "It's been used by Arbiters for over a thousand years to imprison the Fae. The very anchors that hold the Worlds apart are made by iron and copper. You'll never be at risk from them – they'll be terrified of you."

"Even if I'm not wearing pure iron?"

Mazzi smiled. "Sam, you *are* pure iron now, in the way that matters to their magic."

Sam was relieved he hadn't turned into metal. He didn't fully understand what she was saying, but it felt right. Did that mean Poppy would have to destroy the contract between them? He liked the thought of that.

"And I'll be able to protect other people from the Fae?"

"Yes."

He stared at the wedding band. "But it didn't protect my wife."

"Amir told me about her. He was trying to find a successor for decades but he corrupted all of them. Neugent was the last. That's why he did this, Sam. I know it's a shock but he did the best he could. The best for everyone."

"Was Amir his real name?"

She nodded. "We have the name we were born with, the name passed to us by our predecessor – but only the most powerful of us have that – and the name of our position in the Elemental Court."

"And what exactly are the people in the Court?"

She leaned back and looked out the window again. "We are the ones who have the closest affinity with one of the elements. It usually manifests in three different ways, and this is how we find potential successors: an aptitude for getting the most of that element out of the ground and in use, an aptitude for engineering or science that increases its use, or artistic ability. You'll become more attuned as you settle into it. You develop instincts… desires… ambitions. It's different for each of us."

"What about the Sorcerers? It sounds like the kind of thing that would freak them out."

"They're so out of touch they have no idea what we really get up to. They know there's something deeper to it, but they seem to think of us like a guild of master craftsmen. They'll make requests for pieces from you, by the way. They know it's the purest iron they can get, and that's used in their artefacts. They don't ask very often. They know very little about what it's really like to be in the Court, to be one of us, and that suits us just fine. We've never caused them any trouble, we help them keep the Fae in check and we're polite. They're the only people who could interfere, so the less they know, the better." She frowned at him. "How come you know about the Fae and the Sorcerers and not us?"

Sam sighed. "I took a piss in the wrong place at the wrong time and got sucked into all their crap." He didn't want to raise the Poppy stuff. He didn't want her to know how badly he'd screwed up.

"If you have any relationships with Sorcerers or Arbiters, keep it purely professional now."

Sam nodded. "No worries there. So if it's not what the Sorcerers think it is, what does the Elemental Court actually do?"

"Business. We make deals, we talk about what we're up to and how we can help each other. It's in a different place every year. Last year we met in Rio, the year before was Toronto. We're due to meet in Manchester in six months' time, but that'll be brought forward when you're announced. There's a week's grace, to give you a chance to get your head around it."

"What if I don't want to go?"

"Not an option. You're one of the most powerful people in the world now. All of Amir's estate, all of his companies, all of his power and influence is yours."

"But that's mental," Sam whispered. "He was mental. He must have been."

Mazzi held up a hand. "I won't have you say that about him. He was a brilliant man. Just because this is all new to you doesn't mean it wasn't planned carefully. You need to decide what you're going to do with what you've been given, and you need to decide fast. When the rest of the Court find out he's passed on the mantle, they'll want to meet you and they'll want to know how things are going to change. They always do when there's a new member."

Sam rubbed his wrist, remembering the feel of Iron's blood dripping from the gloves. He'd wanted to persuade him to change and it had seemed so hopeless. Now he was being told he was in charge of the very companies Leanne had sought to expose. A pulse of elation rippled through him. He could actually do something about it.

"I know exactly what I'm going to do with his business," he said. "I'm going to shut it all down."

Mazzi shook her head. "You can't do that, not for at least ten years – it's built into the rule of succession. If we let every new member make changes as drastic as that, the world would be in chaos."

"But I own it all now, that's what you said."

"There's a small army of people waiting to speak to you. They'll explain it all," Mazzi said. "Don't worry. It will get easier."

Sam nodded, not really listening to her properly. If he couldn't close the corporation down he could still change it. And he could protect people from the Fae too. There was one right at the top of the list, the one they'd treated as badly as him. He would give Cathy the freedom she'd always wanted.

Margritte tossed the letter onto her desk and walked away from it, cursing the Peonias. She went to the window and looked down on Turl Street, wondering how busy its anchor was in Mundanus. She wanted distraction, she wanted people to watch to rid her of her tense loneliness, not the silent streets of Oxenford. Only twice had she seen anyone walk past; there were few parties in these troubled times.

She went back to the letter and scanned it for any hidden messages or even a subtext from which she could squeeze some hope, but there seemed to be nothing.

William Iris may be young and may have achieved the throne in unfortunate circumstances but he's already proving himself to be an admirable Duke.

She read the line twice. Was it supposed to be an insult? Was she supposed to infer that opposing his reign was the wrong thing to do?

… and that is why we've decided to remain in Londinium rather than suffer the upheaval of moving to a new city.

It was the fifth letter that week and it was clear no one was going to make the move to Oxenford. Georgiana was the only one who seemed genuinely upset at the prospect of staying in Londinium, though that was probably because Freddy had yet again ruined her chances to do anything exciting. Her letter had explained what William Iris had been doing to win the fickle Court over and Margitte was sickened by tales of his success. It seemed friendships spanning hundreds of years meant nothing; all forgotten when a handsome boy tackled a few robbers. How in the Worlds could he have managed to track down their stolen jewellery and return it? He was getting help from someone other than his patron to achieve that; Lord Tulip had secured a promise from the Prince that Iris would be prevented from helping him directly again.

Margritte scrunched up the letter and threw it into the fire. As she watched the edges char and then catch alight she wondered if she was wrong to want to pursue her revenge. Her son didn't want to be Duke, her friends – or at least those she thought were friends – seemed all too happy to be charmed by the boy, and Rupert was so busy planning his own revenge she hadn't heard from him in over a week. Not that she wanted to see him.

She wanted to see Bartholomew. She wanted to hear his voice and smell his skin and feel his hand cup her cheek. She looked up at the painting over the fire, hidden beneath a veil of black silk so only his painted shoes could be seen. She sobbed every time she saw his face and so she'd covered it up and tried to get on with things. She'd been working hard trying to rejuvenate old alliances in Oxenford to gain support but her relationship with the people there needed to evolve. They had to think of her in some way other than as the grieving widow or she would be marginalised and–

She sagged. What did it matter? What was the point of keeping herself in social circles when she had no desire to socialise? She could go to her sister in Jutland and disappear from Albion's memory. She could appeal to her parents and ask them to give her something to do for the family, something that wasn't riddled with anger and hatred. She could do many things, but none of them appealed. A new life in Jutland would be *without* him, a new task for the family would be done *without* him. Everything was defined by his absence. Even herself.

Margritte shook her head. She couldn't just run away or ask someone else to keep her busy – she already had a clear idea of what she ultimately wanted to achieve and losing Bartholomew didn't mean that she should let go of everything in her grief. There was the monthly group at Mr B's to consider and she still hadn't been able to track Miss Rainer down. She'd hoped that once she was Duchess she'd have new resources with which to search for her, another thing William Iris had denied her.

But the thought of fighting for women's rights alone was something she'd never had to face. Once she'd realised Bartholomew felt the same way they'd planned everything together, discussed it and steadily increased their influence in the hope that one day they'd have the opportunity to really make a difference. When the chance of the Dukedom presented itself they'd spent hours talking excitedly about what they could do. Now she was alone and without any power of her own. What could she achieve now? She'd already lost Charlotte and Rainer, now Bartholomew and so many others. She missed them all so much she could feel it in her chest like a heavy block of granite where her heart used to be.

A loud knock startled her and she realised how maudlin she'd become. She took a deep breath and called, "Come in" as cheerfully as she could.

Rupert walked in, dressed just as untidily as usual, this time with stubble. He looked like he hadn't groomed himself since the last time she saw him.

"Maggie!" he cheered. "You're not doing anything, are you?"

"Well, I–"

"Good." He held out a hand. She didn't want to take it, not being certain it had been washed recently, but it was too rude to ignore. "Come with me."

"Where are we going?"

"My place. Don't worry, it's safe. I want you to see something." She placed her hand in his and he clasped it tight. "You look like you need some fun. There's nothing more fun than killing a traitorous fuckpig Sorcerer, I reckon."

"You really want me to come and witness you killing another Sorcerer?"

"It'll be brilliant. Really. I've got popcorn. And afterwards we can get ice cream from G&D's, you know, that place opposite Somerville, and then destroy William Iris. Sound like a plan?"

Margritte nodded, chilled by how casually he spoke his intentions but not wanting to alienate the only person she knew who could get past Lord Iris' protection Charms. But then she could hardly judge, considering what she wanted to do. "It's certainly more appealing than what I had in mind."

He pulled the silver yo-yo from his pocket and winked at her before aiming it at the wall. It felt strange to hold a man's hand again and she wished it wasn't his. A Way opened and he pulled her through as if he were a child running towards a table laden with cakes. She'd hoped the recent silence had been an indication that he'd lost interest in having her as an audience but nothing seemed to have changed in that regard.

The Way led straight into his office in the Stacks and she was relieved it wasn't Convocation House. Some of the equipment from the den had been moved there including the computer and a projector screen. He finally let go of her hand as the Way closed behind them. One of the metal men was in the corner but she didn't know if it was Benson or Hedges.

"Before you start, Rupert, may I ask you a question?"

"Yup." He grabbed a large glass bowl filled with popped corn, something she remembered tasting on a trip to the Colonies across the Atlantic. He stuffed a handful in his mouth before holding the bowl towards her. She declined.

"Whilst I'm flattered to be asked, I must confess I'm not sure why you wish me to see any more of your sorcerous... business. When I came here before, it was in the most extraordinary circumstances, however this time you elected to bring me here. Is there something you need me to do?"

"Well," he began, speaking around a mouthful of popcorn, "I was talking to one of the people in the psychology department a couple of days ago about grief and trauma and that kind of stuff. From what she was saying, I started to worry that you might not be sleeping, or that you had what they call flashbacks – intense memories that can be triggered after a traumatic event. We did nearly die, after all."

She shook her head. "I haven't had any." At least, she hadn't had any about the events in Convocation House. She'd seen Bartholomew run through a thousand times since that awful day. "It was distressing but we recovered."

"Oh. Right. Cos I thought if you saw me hand Ekstrand his arse, it might be a good kind of closure for you."

"I see. I don't feel I have any need of it." His hand, full of another load of popcorn, stopped halfway to his mouth. "But if you feel I should be here..."

"I want you to be here," he said, more calmly than usual. "I like you. I shouldn't, but I do."

Margritte tensed and silently berated herself for accepting his invitation so readily. "But I'm in mourning."

"That doesn't stop me liking you. It stops you liking me back, I know that – I'm not a complete twat. I'm just... trying to be more honest and open. Like the Yanks."

"The who?"

"The... colonials, I think your lot calls them. The Americans. You ever met one? They're so fucking open. Probably because they didn't live through Victoria's reign. I don't know what their Fae-touched are like, but the mundanes are fantastic. There are loads at the university." He shrugged, her silence wearing his words down. "We hang out. Sometimes."

Margritte had no idea why he'd taken such a liking to her but it made everything far more complicated than it needed to be. She didn't want to manipulate him like one of the Rosas would without a thought, but she didn't want to lose him as an ally. Could he detach his strange affection from the way they could work together to achieve their own goals? Either way, she had to be truthful and she had to try and keep him focused on what was important.

"I'm sorry, Rupert, I just can't think about anything like that at the moment."

"Shit, yes! I know, it's cool, I... Let's just kill Ekstrand, shall we?"

To her immense relief he set down the popcorn bowl and activated the screen. After a moment the white screen changed and displayed a map of a city. Once she saw a couple of the street names she realised it was Bath.

"The thing about Sorcerers is that they're bloody hard to find, especially when you want to kill one." Rupert pressed another button and the map was overlaid with dozens of red dots. "I've always known he was somewhere in Bath, just from the way he talked about the place, but I had no idea where. I sent some of the Proctors to release some of my gadgets down there to see if they could find anything that might be an anchor. I found something much better instead."

"What are the dots?"

"Sensors, ones that Ekstrand has placed all over the city to monitor the Fae-touched there. See, this is what happens when you have a Sorcerer who doesn't have a fucking clue what's going on because he doesn't work *with* you people. I realised – hundreds of years ago – that you weren't the enemy. The Fae are the ones who cause all the problems, you guys just get roped into doing stuff for them. You can't turn around and say bugger off to the Fae so you're just as much victims as the mundanes are."

Margritte just nodded, keeping quiet. She'd wondered why Oxenford was run so cooperatively.

"I figured that if we worked together the innocents would be more likely to stay that way. But Ekstrand is a paranoid little shit and has set up this network all over Bath so he can track the residents of Aquae Sulis going in and out of the Nether."

Margritte didn't have to fake her surprise. "And they have no idea?"

"Nope. It's probably why his Arbiters are so low profile," Rupert said. "Now, my boys did a bit of work on these things and they're all wired – he's so nineteenth-century! – to send the data back to this location." He tapped another key and all the dots disappeared, leaving one large house highlighted on the outskirts of the city.

"Is that where he lives?" she asked and he nodded, his eyes bright with excitement. "What are you going to do?"

"Watch and see."

The image changed from a map to that of a house in Mundanus. It was a beautiful property with a fountain in the centre of the drive and stone pillars either side of the door. A bird flew out of a tree and she realised they were somehow watching what was probably the anchor property of the Sorcerer's home. Margritte clasped her hands together in an effort to keep her nerves under control. She didn't want to watch a man being murdered, even if he had tried to kill

Rupert – and her, albeit inadvertently. Rupert was acting as if he was about to show her a music-hall performance he'd enjoyed, rather than an act of violence, and it made her feel unsafe. If he succeeded, he would be the only Sorcerer in Albion. What would that mean for the other Nether cities?

"Fly, my pretties," Rupert whispered, and Margritte saw a dark cloud appear in the top left corner of the image, which headed straight for the house.

"Are those insects?"

"Really fucking amazing nanotech insects made of a completely new material he can't have possibly warded against."

"Are they going to sting him to death?"

Rupert laughed. "No, they're going to give me control of the anchors in his property. Once I have that…" He focused on the screen, forgetting to finish the sentence.

The swarm landed on the house, giving it the appearance of being smudged with charcoal, then coalesced in certain places until it looked like the house had been splattered with huge ink blots.

"Go on, go on!" Rupert sounded like a man watching a cricket match.

A couple of minutes crept by and Margritte wanted to go home. She wasn't interested in facilitating his fantasies; she didn't want to be there just to smile at him when it was over and congratulate him on winning this lethal game. That's all it was; even though he was a Sorcerer, he was still a typical man wanting the approval and adoration of someone he liked but considered beneath him. He didn't realise she was only there because she hoped he'd help her deal with William Iris. But now, watching his attempt to kill another man, she was losing the desire to make the boy suffer. She just wanted him to clear Bartholomew's name. She didn't want to get sucked any further into this downward spiral of hatred and bitterness. She didn't want to be like Rupert.

"What the fuck... come on!" Rupert glanced at a wristwatch and then back at the screen. "Why's it taking so fucking long?" He jabbed at the computer keyboard and the image switched to the back of the property with a different distribution of ink blots.

The back door opened and a man dressed as a butler stepped out, holding out a hand to test the weather. Margritte sucked in a breath, fearful that the poor man – only a servant – was about to be bitten to death. But he simply went back into the house and emerged moments later wearing an overcoat.

"Rupert..." she whispered. "Don't hurt that man."

He didn't reply. They both watched the butler walk a few steps and glance back at the house as he probably did every time he left it. He stopped and wheeled around, his back to them as he scanned the house and its infestation. Calmly, but with more speed than when he'd left, the man went back inside the house.

"Shit," Rupert said, scratching the stubble on his neck. "They'd better break through soon or–"

"You have to call them off," Margritte said. "That man's in there now. If you do whatever it is you plan to, he'll be killed as well."

"All staff know the risks," Rupert said, keeping his eyes on the screen. "I could have had staff in my place when he attacked – I had a guest! He almost killed you."

"That doesn't give you the right to murder a man who happens to work there."

"A man who knows what Ekstrand is like and helps him to murder–"

"Don't be so ridiculous." Margritte went to him and touched his arm. "This is wrong, Rupert, you must see that."

He looked down at her hand and stared at it until she started to pull it away. He pressed his own hand over it and held her there, now staring into her eyes. She saw that his were hazel, with flecks of brown around the iris, and her instinct was to get away before he tried to kiss her. As his eyes started to close and his head leaned forwards she looked at the screen, desperate to see something that would distract him.

The door opened and the butler emerged, this time wearing an apron and long rubber gloves, holding something made of brass that looked like a cross between a plant sprayer and a rifle.

"Look!" she said, as grateful for the distraction as she was concerned for the butler.

Rupert let her go and clasped the sides of his head with his hands. "That can't be–"

Margritte backed away, as slowly as she could, so as not to draw his attention. When she was out of his reach she watched the butler spraying at the clusters of insects. Whatever was in the device was cleaning the insects from the stone walls as easily as water washing chalk off a blackboard. Rupert made a series of agonised groans, transfixed by the sight of his failure. He hung his head when the last of the swarm was removed and didn't look up again until the butler came back out of the house with a dustpan and brush and proceeded to sweep up the detritus left by Rupert's failed assassination attempt.

"Fuck!" He yelled and slammed his fist onto the keyboard, making the image of the butler play backwards, before he threw an empty tea mug at the button at the corner of the screen and made it black again. He leaned against his desk, hunched over the computer, shaking his head and muttering to himself.

Margritte stayed still and silent, as did the golem.

Eventually Rupert straightened up and turned to her. "Well. That was fucking embarrassing." He shoved his hands in his pockets. "That cock always was good at warding. Seems he actually deserves that reputation. I brought you here for nothing."

She didn't agree but she didn't say so. "Perhaps you should open a Way for me. I think you need to be alone."

He sighed. "I said I'd sort out William Iris after this. Ekstrand's going to be a hard nut to smash into fucking smithereens but I don't see why you should have to wait any longer."

"I don't want to kill William," she said hurriedly.

"Not right away, I understand that," Rupert said, nodding. "You need him to clear Bartholomew's name first. I just figure that if he's tied to a chair, horribly sleep-deprived and scared out of his tiny mind, he'll be more willing to do that for you."

Margritte nodded. She didn't want the boy to just carry on with his life with no punishment for his crime but after seeing Rupert's behaviour she was feeling less certain of how to go about it. Asking nicely wouldn't get what she needed, though. "He'll be protected by his patron, I don't see how I could get him to–"

Rupert held up a hand. "Don't worry about that. All you need to do is get yourself alone in a room with him. Let me know the time and place and I'll do the rest."

"And what about the Irises that live here?"

"When we move against William we'll take them into custody too, otherwise Iris will use them against us. I won't hurt them – they've been good to the university for a long time. But you said it yourself – William Iris is working with Ekstrand to take over Albion. We can't be too careful about the other Irises already here."

"Are you sure you want to do this, Rupert? The university has already lost the Rosas."

He shrugged. "Shit happens. I was thinking about giving you Magdalen when the Irises go down. If you want it."

She would be the first woman to have a position of power in Oxenford. "Not Lincoln?"

"I want Alex to stay as Vice-Chancellor and you to have your own college."

So that was it; he wanted her to give up on taking the throne back. "I'll think about it."

He opened a Way for her and she stepped through, greatly relieved to see him remain on the other side. "See you soon," he said and gave a sad smile before it closed.

She let out a long breath and rang for tea. Getting William Iris to meet her seemed impossible; he would expect revenge or foul play. The rattle of a Letterboxer made her jump and she realised how tense the time with Rupert had made her. He was offering her the chance to show everyone that a woman could have responsibility outside the household. If she made a success of it, the cause could be reignited. But could she accept in the knowledge that Bartholomew's dream would never be realised and there would never be a Tulipa on the Londinium throne?

Once the letterbox disappeared she picked up the letter and was surprised to see a fleur-de-lys on the wax seal. She opened it and looked at the end of the letter first: "Catherine Reticulata-Iris", with no mention of her new title.

She wanted to meet. Margritte knew it was the opportunity she needed to get to Will. Just as she was about to pen a reply there was a knock at the door.

"Please don't be Rupert," she whispered and then invited the caller in after tucking Catherine's letter into the top drawer of her bureau.

Georgiana Persificola-Viola swept into the room wearing an austere black dress and the first genuinely joyful smile Margritte had seen on her face for many years.

"Georgiana?"

"Oh, Margritte," she said, rushing to clasp her tight. "The most wonderful thing has happened. Freddy is dead!"

19

Max decided to put his efforts into learning more about the Agency whilst waiting for Ekstrand to have a good enough day to tell him where the tracker was located and thereby the location of Faulkner's Chapter. The gargoyle had managed to wait two days before convincing Petra to go into Ekstrand's study and take the reading herself. Max had been in the middle of the tour of the upper floors of the Agency Headquarters at the time, aware of what the gargoyle was doing but unable to stop it. By the time he'd got back the gargoyle had the location and Petra hadn't seemed concerned about their activities.

As Max followed Derne into another room lined with more filing cabinets, the gargoyle was posted in the Nether, watching the Chapter Master's movements. It was the third day of the gargoyle's surveillance and a pattern had already emerged. Max planned to make his move the next day.

Max located the right drawer and pulled the file from the cabinet as Derne watched in silence. Cathy had led him on an interesting paper trail and between them they were uncovering more dirty nooks in Fae-touched society than in an abandoned house. The latest was a secret asylum in Mundanus.

"This isn't a breach of the Treaty," Derne said as Max scanned the top page. "There's nothing to state that those who are no longer innocent cannot be returned to live out the rest of their days in Mundanus."

"Are you concerned about something, Mr Derne?" Max looked up from the page at him. "I never said anything about the Treaty, or any breaches."

Derne cleared his throat. "I find this rather difficult."

"Yes, I suppose you would," Max replied. "This asylum is staffed by your people?"

"Of course. No innocents are involved at all."

"There's no information about visiting hours."

"Of course not. Nobody visits these people."

"What if someone wanted to."

"I find that highly unlikely."

"I find it hard to believe that these people have no loved ones who worry about how they are." Max flipped a page and saw the latest name Catherine was looking for in the list of patients. "Or do the loved ones have no idea where this place is either?"

Derne's frown deepened. "The Patroons know where it is and whether they choose to share that information with the relevant parties is up to them. We merely provide a safe environment. Being alive for hundreds of years can take its toll. Some people simply cannot maintain the clarity of thought required to survive in Society and so it's kinder to them to let them rest in a quiet, peaceful location."

"Far away from the rest of Society," Max said. "To die."

"To age naturally," Derne said.

Natural aging terrified the puppets and Max wasn't under the impression they would voluntarily choose it over life in the Nether. The Chapter had speculated about the fate of various individuals who'd been picked up in Mundanus confused and terrified by how it had changed. Now he knew where they'd gone, but had no Chapter to report back to. "So you put them in Green Dale Asylum when you know they can't be put to better use here?"

Derne merely smiled.

"The techniques you use on the ones in the basement don't work on them, I assume, otherwise this asylum wouldn't exist. And you don't have any ethical concerns about the way you brainwash the people taken by the Collectors?"

"Should I?" Derne asked without any hint of remorse. "No one else has complained. We take great care and give a great deal of thought to where people are placed once they've come to terms with their change in status. Society requires a steady turnover of staff, Mr Arbiter. Better that we take them from within the Nether than from the streets of Mundanus. Surely you would agree with that?"

"But there are staff from Mundanus."

"Only a handful and only taken in when a breach made it imperative. Never against their will, I can assure you."

Max closed the file. "I'm taking this with me."

Derne sighed. "Can I at least take a facsimile so that our records aren't damaged any further?"

"I'll return it soon," Max said, not wanting to give them a chance to cut or change any of the information within. "I want to see your files on the children born into the Agency."

Catherine had told him what her bodyguard had said and asked that it be looked into as well. The gargoyle had been dying to go and see her in person, no doubt to tell her how the Agency ran their premises, but Max had been deliberately keeping them apart. Max hadn't anticipated children being involved with the Agency other than the ones who had the misfortune of being young when their family was cast out of Society, but that happened very rarely. No doubt there was a current glut of minors, since the Rosas had fallen from grace en masse, but Catherine had made it sound like they were born and raised there.

Derne hadn't moved. "Could that be another time? I have a meeting."

"Then get someone else to show me."

With a grim expression Derne mumbled, "Follow me."

The main reason Max hadn't anticipated children was because of the strict segregation he'd observed in the upper floors of the building. The male and female staff-in-training slept in separate dormitories divided by a corridor policed by a guard. Considering that some of those people must have known each other in their previous lives Max could understand the caution.

Another room, again full of files. Max scanned the drawer labels, which contained date ranges instead of alphabetical ordering. "Where do you get the babies from, Mr Derne?"

"Hasn't anyone explained to you how children are made?"

"I'm immune to sarcasm as well as Fae Charms," he replied. "Let's get to the point. You keep your employees separated. Everything is so tightly controlled here I can only assume these babies are planned."

"They are."

"So people in marriages before their change in status are llowed to continue to sire children?"

Derne looked away, scratching the bridge of his nose.

"You'll get to your meeting much faster if you just lay it all on the table, Mr Derne. Surely you've realised by now that we're going to learn everything about what you do here, whether it's with your cooperation or not."

Derne's nostrils flared. "We match the parents to obtain the children most likely to have the qualities we require." When Max remained silent he added, "Every new arrival is evaluated and allocated to the positions they would suit the most. You've seen the notes made using our annotations at the front of each file. Those with a very specific cluster of skills and natural abilities are filtered into the programme you saw in the basement to maintain the building."

"You breed the kind of people you need and raise them to be servants," Max said.

"Yes," Derne replied, relaxing when he realised there was going to be no need to justify himself to an emotionless man. "It's most efficient."

"And the parents? Do they have any say?"

"No. And they're not involved in the lives of their children. It's less complicated that way." Derne sniffed and rolled onto his heels and then onto his toes. "Charms are used so it isn't traumatic for those involved. We're not barbarians."

Max wondered how Catherine would react when she heard about this. He knew the gargoyle would have a lot to say. It always did.

"How long have you been doing this?"

"Hundreds of years. The only people who've done it longer than us are the Fae themselves. But you must know all about that."

Max didn't say anything. He knew the puppets arranged their marriages but had always assumed it was just as it was for the innocents: for the mutual benefit of the families to increase their wealth and influence. That the Fae might be involved in pairing people off to have children suggested they planned ahead and that was not something that sat well with his idea of them. They were flighty and mercurial, obsessed with a person one minute only to abandon them in disgust the next. If they were selectively breeding it meant they were looking for a particular combination of features, like the Agency. Like dog and horse breeders. But what for?

"Thank you for your cooperation," Max said. It was time to go and meet Cathy.

Will read the letter a second time and leaned back in his chair. Amelia had been telling the truth. Even though he'd believed her at the time, there was still a doubt, still a fear she was saying whatever she needed to at the time to stay his hand. He would have a son within the year, just not the one Iris wanted. For the briefest moment he considered a ruse to pass off the child as Cathy's but immediately dismissed it. Lord Iris would be able to tell, surely? It was too much of a risk.

Amelia was tucked away in a mundane country house, under guard and stripped of all Charms and artefacts. His man's report said she was eating and sleeping well and wrote to Cornelius every day, handing the letters to the butler in the hope that she would gain permission to send them at some point soon. They were burned straightaway, in accordance with his instructions. She didn't know her brother was already dead.

"It's a merciful death," he'd said to Cornelius as he poured the hemlock into the glass. "The way Socrates died."

"It's *bloodless*, not merciful," Cornelius said. "You prefer to kill me like a woman would. It seems you've lost your taste for swords."

"No," Will said. "I just want you to die slowly."

Cornelius didn't beg for his life but just picked up the cup and drank it swiftly. "You can go now," he said with stained lips but Will shook his head.

It was a long time to sit in a room with a dying man but Will had to see it done, had to be certain he really was dead. Near the end Cornelius said Amelia would never forgive him for killing her brother and Will had simply smiled. "I will never forgive her either."

He took the report on Amelia to the fire and threw it into the flames. He wanted the child to be brought to him immediately but what would he tell Cathy? There had been illegitimate children in both Mundanus and the Nether for as long as there had been marriage. Other families took the children in, even though they could never reach the higher echelons of Society, but he knew that was an impossibility in his own. His patron would not approve and his firstborn son would have the dubious status Sophia endured: an open secret within the household, yet hidden from the Patroon and without recognition in Society. No doubt Cathy suspected Amelia was his mistress before the revelations about their treachery, but bringing physical proof of it into her home would be so hurtful. He only wanted her to be happy.

A footman brought him a note on a silver tray. It had been delivered by a messenger who was waiting for a reply. Will recognised Faulkner's handwriting and opened it.

Frederick Persificola-Viola was found dead in a mundane massage parlour in Soho in the small hours of this morning. He appears to have suffered a heart attack and the mundane emergency services were unable to resuscitate him. I found traces of Charms suggesting foul play. In light of our previous conversation regarding this individual, would you like me to pursue?

"Tell the messenger the answer is no. No further attention required."

"Yes, your Grace," the young man replied and left after a swift bow.

Will threw that note on the fire too. Bertrand had picked an excellent location; the family would be keen to keep the circumstances of the death as quiet as possible and it was in keeping with Freddy's unsavoury habits. It was the third death he felt responsible for, even though he hadn't committed the murder itself. Would there be more? The first was the only one he truly regretted, the second was unpleasant but justified and the third was... business. Was that reason enough?

He closed his eyes and rested his arm on the mantelpiece, thinking about what Tate said about his family. He wondered whether his father had done anything like he had to protect their influence in Aquae Sulis. He would never know; it was hardly the sort of thing his father would elect to tell him and he could never ask. But even though Will felt heavy and sickened by his own behaviour, he couldn't deny it was achieving the results he wanted. Londinium was falling into line after his success with the highwaymen problem, Bertrand would be a powerful ally and the Shopkeeper had barely reacted to his announcement that he would be supplying his products now – he hadn't given him any reason to worry. Once he and Derne were happy that Will's taking over wasn't going to affect the quality of the products he would start to turn the arrangement to his advantage.

Tired of politics and plans, Will felt no desire to go to Black's and be roped into a conversation about the city. Cathy was meeting Margritte, something he'd only agreed to in an effort to demonstrate he trusted her. Margritte was of no concern now that her efforts to disrupt his Court had failed but Cathy seemed to think it was important to at least try to open a dialogue.

He went to the nursery wing and knew it was the right thing to do as soon as he stepped through the door to Mundanus. Sophia's laughter was echoing down the corridor and sped his steps. She was in the schoolroom with Uncle Vincent, trying to catch bubbles he was blowing from a loop of plastic.

"Will-yum!" she cheered and raced to him with open arms. He did his best to ignore the scars that covered her throat.

He scooped her up and soon his face was covered in tiny kisses. His uncle smiled and set the bottle of bubble mixture down. "Hello, Sophia," said Will.

"Cathy brought me some dollies, do you want to see them?"

"I would love to," Will lied, and she ran from the room.

"She's healed well," Uncle Vincent said. "And she's sleeping better too."

"Good," Will said. "Is she bothered by the scarring? I've got some plans for removing them." He'd put in an order with Tate at the end of their meeting. She said it would take between three to six months to gather the ingredients but it was worth the wait.

"No, she doesn't mention it." Vincent pointed at the small bottle. "Catherine gave that to her. You should have seen her face when I blew the first bubble. She thought it was magic."

Will smiled. "And Cathy bought her dolls too?"

"Mmm." Vincent sat on the windowsill. "Catherine means well, I'm sure."

"Look!" Sophia was back and thrust a doll towards Will. "This is Josephine. She has the same hair as me!" Will took it from her, surprised to see it dressed in safari gear with its own little pith helmet. "She's an explorer. That's why she's wearing trousers, like a boy, so the creepy-crawlies don't bite her legs and so she can climb trees to take pictures of elephants and dinosaurs."

"Climb trees?" Will looked at Vincent who shrugged.

"Yes. Girls are allowed to climb trees, Cathy told me, but Uncle Vincent won't let me." She pouted in his direction.

"And what about the other dolls?"

He put the explorer down and Sophia pulled out the other two from under her arm. "This one is called Jessamine and she's an ark... leegist. She finds old things and puts them in museums. That's why she has a brush and book. The brush is for the dust on the treasure and the book is to write it all down. That's very important."

"Archaeologist," Will said and Sophia nodded.

"That's what I said. And this is Jemima."

It was the only doll that looked like any his sister had owned. She was wearing a silk ballgown and tiny jewels. "Ah. Is she a princess?"

"Yes! She's a princess who can fire laser beams from her eyes and fly and she can lift whole houses! She finds bad people and locks them in prison and everyone loves her because she's good and strong."

"I see…" Will didn't know what to say. "And you thought this up all by yourself?"

"No, Cathy told me all about them. She said I could be anything I want to be, not just a princess. I said I want to be one and be pretty and she said it was better to be a princess who can fire laser beams! Anyone can wear a dress and look pretty but only super-duper girls like me can explore Africa and find treasure because I'm clever."

"Has Auntie Cathy been playing with you then?"

"Yes and I love her and I don't want to go home, Will-yum. It's boring there and no one plays with me. I can write my name and read books too, shall I show you?"

"Yes, but put the dolls away first, darling."

When she ran out he looked at Vincent. "Cathy's been busy."

"So it seems. I talked to her about those dolls and she said Sophia needs to aspire to more than getting married."

Will folded his arms, irritated that Cathy was imposing her own views on Sophia.

"I think she's right, Will. We both know that Sophia can't be married off like Imogen will be. I'm not even sure she can have a life in the Nether."

"What have Mother and Father said?"

"Nothing. I don't think they want to deal with the problem. She can't be hidden away forever."

"They haven't even visited her." Will hadn't bothered them for fear a reminder would prompt them to take her back. Now he wondered if they wanted her back at all. He'd expected them to insist on taking her home after the attack and he'd dreaded the accusation that he was incapable of providing a safe environment for her, but there had been nothing of the sort.

"Well… they know I'm here and I keep your mother informed." Vincent looked out of the window at the rain. "But I think they don't know what to do either. The family is more high-profile than most. I have the feeling they'll ship her off somewhere eventually."

"They will not," Will said. "She has a home here and I'll inform Mother she can stay indefinitely."

"You're even more in the public eye, Will. It's a risk."

"Hang the risk. Besides, I think it does Cathy good to have her here." He looked at the bottle of bubble mixture. Whilst he wasn't sure about the strange dolls, he was touched by how she'd clearly been spending time with Sophia when he hadn't had a chance to do so. She was thoughtful, in her own way. "I just want her to feel safe and be happy," he added.

"Sophia or Catherine?"

Will smiled. "Both."

20

Margritte didn't want to go back to Hampton Court ever again but there seemed to be no other locations suitable for meeting Catherine. As Duchess it was unreasonable for her to be expected to leave Londinium and they needed a private place to keep the gossips at bay. She didn't expect any threat to her personal safety but she still wanted to feel secure.

She picked a room they seldom used when Bartholomew was alive and went in through the servants' entrance for fear of triggering memories that would leave her incapable of keeping a clear head. There was only a skeletal staff in residence and the palace felt horribly empty but she managed to keep her composure whilst waiting for Catherine to arrive. She had to keep her mind focused on what she wanted: a meeting with William in person, away from the Court.

The sound of a carriage on the driveway brought back memories of waiting for dinner-party guests to arrive. She looked down at her black dress, trying to remind herself that it was different now and there was no need to keep thinking of the past. Instead she tried to work out why Catherine had requested a meeting. Was it a strange sense of guilt for being the cause of William's actions without being responsible for them? Was it simple concern for someone who was becoming a friend before everything went so horribly wrong? There was the possibility that William had sent her to determine whether she intended to cause any more trouble. No doubt he knew of her attempt to lure residents away by now; Georgiana had told her that those she'd written to were the first to receive their stolen goods back.

"Her Grace, the Duchess of Londinium, Catherine Reticulata-Iris," announced the footman and Margritte readied herself, still uncertain how to play it when Catherine entered.

She looked well and was dressed in a deep burgundy dress with a high collar and the narrow line of the late Victorian period. She also looked as nervous as a debutante at her first ball.

"Your Grace," Margritte said and curtsied deeply, as Georgiana had to her that night she'd briefly been Duchess.

"Margritte, thank you so much for agreeing to see me."

"Would you care to sit down?"

Catherine did so and Margritte gave the nod for tea to be brought. She hadn't entertained formally since the bereavement and she was a little uncomfortable. It felt too soon, and therefore disrespectful.

"How are you finding your new role?" she asked and Catherine squirmed.

"Umm... oh, God, this is awkward."

Margritte almost smiled. She'd forgotten how open the girl was.

"I asked to see you because we need to talk," Catherine said, her words slow and carefully chosen. "But before I get to that, I wanted to say how sorry I am about... what happened. It was such a shock." She grimaced. "It must have been so much worse for you, I don't want to sound like... oh, for the love of..."

"I understand, and thank you." Margritte wanted to make her feel more comfortable. She wanted her to let down the flimsy guard.

"Are you… coping? That didn't come out right. I mean, are you all right? No, of course you're not all right, I mean…" She released a long breath. "I'm so sorry, I'm making a complete mess of this."

"Bereavement is difficult for everyone," Margritte said. "One never knows what to say."

"Exactly!" Catherine smiled. "It's just that Bartholomew was such a wonderful man and you were both so very kind to me and I…"

Margritte clenched her teeth at the sound of his name. And she was right; they had been so kind to her – and William – yet it had meant nothing. She used the arrival of the tea to mask her anger.

Catherine fell silent as she watched it being poured. "Have you been here the whole time?"

"No, I've been spending some time with my eldest son in Oxenford."

Cathy knew of the reflected city but had never been there. She said as much, adding, "Is it nice?"

"It's a beautiful city." She handed over the cup of tea. "Now, you said there was something you wanted to tell me. Is it about who attacked you?"

Catherine's cup rattled in the saucer and she set it on her lap so quickly that some of the tea slopped over. "No."

"Have you fully recovered?"

"Almost."

"I understand you were very badly hurt. Did your husband catch the perpetrator?"

Catherine just stared at her, a terrible flush rising up her face from her throat. How, Margritte wondered, could this girl be a Duchess?

"It's all… in the past now. All of it."

"But it's left scars. On both of us."

"Will didn't–" She looked down at the spilt tea. "Please, I don't want to talk about it."

Margritte watched Catherine attempt to compose herself. It was clear she was hiding something, but what? Did she know who had really sent an assassin? Or perhaps she'd discovered the man behind the attempt was her husband, or even the Sorcerer of Wessex, creating the perfect excuse to attack Bartholomew. She decided to let it go until the girl had settled down.

"I… wanted to see you to talk about the group that meets at Mr B's."

It was the last thing Margritte expected her to say. "I beg your pardon?"

"The one started by Miss Rainer. She was my governess and I found her again and she managed to tell me about the group. And I know you and Bartholomew were members."

Margritte set her cup down with a loud chink. "Where is she? We looked everywhere!"

"She's in a household near Kew Gardens. She's a scullery maid. The Agency did something terrible to her. And Charlotte too – I think that was her husband. I'm tracking down where they took the others, the ones who dared to speak out."

"You're… you're one of us?"

Catherine's face transformed with the most beautiful smile. "Yes! And it's just eating me up that you and Bartholomew would have been perfect to change everything – that's what you were going to do, wasn't it?"

Margritte nodded, struggling to adapt to the new course the conversation was taking. "Is William a progressive?"

"Not yet. But I think he will be. He's gentle and thoughtful and–" She stopped and the usual awkwardness resurfaced.

"You must think he's a monster but he really isn't. He wouldn't have done that if... he wouldn't have normally..."

Catherine's eyes were filled with the need to tell the truth. "Your Grace, everyone believes that my husband sent another to kill you. They think he's a base creature who obtained the throne by attacking his competitor's wife. Do you realise how hard that is to live with?" Catherine nodded silently. "You know it couldn't possibly have been Bartholomew. You spent hours talking to him, you know he was a good man, now you know just how remarkable he was. Surely William must be told to look elsewhere for the villain behind this terrible affair?"

"It's... complicated."

"Is it? It seems very simple to me. Bartholomew's name must be cleared. We've lost everything, and the least William can do is restore his honour."

Catherine was blinking rapidly, unable to look her in the eye. "I don't think I can speak for Will. I wanted to ask you if you'd help me with the cause. If we worked together..."

Margritte stiffened. "You want me to be your adviser in Londinium when I cannot even show my face in the Court?"

"What I'm trying to say is that we need to try and salvage what we can."

"I'm trying to salvage my entire life! You come here, wife of the man who murdered my husband, to talk about changing Society for the good of women and you can't even offer me the most basic reassurance that my family's name will be cleared?"

Catherine was shaking. "I can understand how angry you are. I shouldn't have... I should have given you more time. It was selfish of me to think you'd be able to help, I'm sorry."

Margritte forced herself to calm down. She'd pushed Catherine too far. "I'm sorry too. It wasn't your fault. And

I'm truly... heartened that you see the need for change in Society. But it will come to nothing unless William can be brought onside. The Patroons will dismiss anything we do, but they won't be able to ignore the Duke of Londinium."

Catherine nodded, crushed. "You're right. But it's not going to stop me trying. The men and women who've been silenced need my help and it will carry on happening if we don't actively strive for change. I'm not asking you to forget your husband – nor what Will did – and I'm not asking you to come back to the Court and act as if nothing happened. But is there nothing I can do to convince you to help our cause? This is a difficult time for Will but I'm certain he'll come round. The more I can achieve before then, the better, and you're the perfect person to help."

Margritte felt the briefest sadness at Catherine's earnest plea. If she abandoned her need for justice and took up the position in Oxenford she would be free to help her and the others in the secret group. She knew it was the noble thing to do. But, as she took a breath to agree, the thought of William Iris keeping the throne made it catch in her throat. Of course he would never clear Bartholomew's name; he didn't want to risk his own reputation. He would live a long, long life and because of his barbarity she was forced to live without the man she loved. She had to at least try to restore her husband's honour, otherwise she would never forgive herself. "How can I help when all I can think about is the injustice committed against my husband?"

"But... surely you see how hard it would be for Will to say anything about what happened?"

Margritte nodded, seeing the way to get what she wanted opening up before her. "I do. He needs to preserve his own reputation, I understand that. But if he truly is the gentle man you believe him to be, surely he feels some remorse?"

"Oh, he does!" Catherine seemed convinced at least.

"Then would it be possible to ask him to express that remorse to me – in private – and offer his personal regret? If he could do that, my heart would be eased and the Duke of Londinium would no longer be monstrous to me."

"I…"

"It would also offer proof that he could indeed be persuaded to support our struggle. I would have hope for the future once more."

Catherine stood. "I'll ask him. I'll do all I can to try and change things for the better, for you and for all of us."

Margritte kissed her on both cheeks, stifling the guilt rising in her chest. "Thank you, your Grace. We must all do what we feel is right."

Ten minutes into the meeting and Sam was still there at the head of the table. No one had told him it was all an elaborate hoax. He'd been waiting for someone to tell him that for the last twenty-four hours, but it seemed he really was Lord Iron.

The problem lay in the fact that even though the suited lawyers, accountants and directors seated at the table treated him like their new billionaire boss, he still felt like an unemployed computer programmer from Bath. Now he truly understood those people who looked shell-shocked after a massive lottery win and why they said their lives wouldn't be changed. It was simply impossible to grasp how different everything could be, so they clung to their old life out of terror, like it had been taken out of a bathtub and chucked into an ocean.

All of the things he used to worry about, from paying the bills to whether he could really justify getting a new games console, had been replaced by a whole set of new worries that he simply didn't understand yet. The men and women seated around the table were showing him spreadsheets and pie charts and projections and statements as if they could mean something to him.

"... and if you continue with this program of expansion in this–"

Sam held up a hand and Susan, the woman giving the presentation, stopped speaking. "I'm sorry, I'd prefer it if you just left the materials with me to look at in my own time."

"Of course, Mr Ferran."

"And I want to use this time to ask a few questions."

Pens were picked up, some activated tablets and laptops, all poised to take notes.

"All right... governments and international agencies have different laws about preventing environmental pollution. Some have laws that need clean-air tech installed as standard, for example. Am I right?"

Susan nodded. She had brown hair and hazel eyes and looked like an English teacher he'd had at secondary school, but dressed in a much more expensive suit. "That's right, Mr Ferran. There are also differences in the amount of monitoring and the pressure to prove compliance."

"Good." Sam smiled at her, glad to have someone to focus on instead of the whole group. "So would it be possible for someone to write me a report..." He faltered. Did he really just ask that? "...on what the most stringent requirements are and how many of the mines and factories and things in the corporation adhere to them?"

Susan frowned. "Do you mean a report on which operations meet local compliance? If that's the case there's no need – all of our operations comply with local environmental code."

"No, I mean, which ones comply with the strictest codes in the world. Not local ones. I want to know exactly what the most strict environmental protection measures are and I want all of the global operations to be measured against that standard. Does that make sense?"

The scrawling and touch-typing stopped before his last sentence did.

"It shouldn't be too hard, should it?" Sam asked.

"It will take some time to compile," she said. "CoFerrum Inc owns hundreds of operations around the world."

"But there must be a central database containing information about them. If there isn't, I'll build one."

They all laughed, then realised he wasn't joking. "There is," she replied as people fiddled with their pens and gadgets, "but I don't think it necessarily contains detailed information on that sort of thing."

"Why not?"

"It's never been a priority."

"Why not?"

A man with a large nose who looked a little bit like an American bald eagle raised a finger to get his attention. "Mr Ferran, you've made an interesting request and I'm sure it isn't just a matter of curiosity. What do you plan to do with the report once it's completed?"

Sam smiled, imagining Leanne seeing him now, able to actually do something about the things she'd been unearthing over all those years. "I want all of the places that aren't using the very best anti-pollution technology to have it fitted as soon as possible."

Looks were exchanged around the table. Susan was frowning at the tablet computer beneath her fingers as the Eagle stared at Sam.

"That would cost a huge amount of money," he said. "And it's not even necessary – we already comply with local code."

"You're telling me that clean-air technology isn't necessary in the places where there's the most pollution? Really? That doesn't make any sense. And anyway, you told me right at the start of this meeting that this corporation makes billions in profit every year. Are you seriously telling me CoFerrum can't afford to do this?"

"I have no idea how much it would cost," the Eagle replied, "but CoFerrum's continued success depends upon minimising costs to maintain those profits."

"What for? So you all get massive bonuses? So I get to live like Amir did?"

He'd hit a nerve and every person around the table – with the exception of a jowly ginger-haired man at the far end – looked distinctly uncomfortable. Sam tried to remember what job that man did, but failed.

"It's all a question of return on investment," the Eagle said.

"Correction." Sam was getting into it now. "It used to be all about return on investment. That's going to change now."

The Eagle looked at Susan and so did several others. When she noticed she set the tablet down on the table and smiled at Sam. "Mr Ferran, CoFerrum is a huge global corporation composed of multiple subsidiary companies and interests. It's like a fleet of aircraft carriers. You can't just change course and take off in another direction as fast as you could if you were in a private yacht. Like that fleet, CoFerrum needs to be carefully coordinated in terms of its mid- to long-term direction and each part – each ship, if you will – needs to be given enough notice in order to be able to change direction without crashing into each other. It takes time to implement a radical change in priorities."

"That's just what corporates say to keep things the way they like them."

She smiled, but it wasn't to reassure him. "Mr Ferran, it really isn't like that. There are multiple factors that need to be considered, not the least of which is the fact we're halfway through the financial year and budgets for this one and the next have already been allocated."

"Oh, come on, surely we can just change that!"

"No, we can't. You have to understand that once budgets are set it enables multiple levels of management to allocate spending in accordance with their division's needs. That involves procurement of services and products from hundreds of suppliers not owned by CoFerrum. If we suddenly withdrew millions of pounds and told the directors to spend them on different things it would create all sorts of contractual problems and destroy a lot of excellent working relationships."

"But–"

"Not to mention a ripple effect that could cause the collapse of many SMEs who depend on the work we give them. Mr Ferran, please appreciate that the decisions you're talking about have many, many ramifications that may not be immediately apparent. In effect, we're not only responsible for the continued employment of the thousands of CoFerrum employees, but also for the companies we pay for goods and services."

Sam tried to work out whether she was telling the truth or just being obstructive. He realised that it was probably both. The image of Leanne watching him with a proud smile on his face evaporated. "It doesn't change the fact that I want things to be different."

"Of course not," Susan said smoothly. "It's natural for you to want to put your own mark on the company. You may have to accept that it will take longer than you thought."

"And you might have to accept that these environmental considerations aren't in keeping with CoFerrum," the Eagle said.

Sam wondered if he could sack him, then and there.

"I don't know," the ginger-haired man said. "I think Mr Ferran's vision could prove immensely beneficial to the public image of the corporation."

"Oh, for Christ's sake, Duncan," the Eagle said, evidently reaching the end of his patience. "This isn't PR fluff! A change in environmental compliance policy could cost the corporation millions and millions of pounds."

Sam remembered Duncan was the head of PR, several levels above Neugent. "You're right," Duncan said to the Eagle. "It's not fluff. It's bold, it's radical and it's in tune with the public, who are more aware of these issues than ever before. I've had to lock down some serious incidents which could have cost the corporation millions of pounds, and that expenditure would have just been to get our arses out of the bear-trap with no other benefits whatsoever. If we repositioned CoFerrum as the world's most socially and environmentally responsible corporation, it wouldn't just be a PR exercise, it would make it easier to–"

"Why don't we take this one step at a time," Susan said. "Let's get the report compiled for Mr Ferran and look at the costs involved. It may be that we could prioritise certain operations that would have the greatest PR impact whilst we look at the plausibility of a global change in policy."

The Eagle and Duncan nodded and Susan looked back at Sam. "Is there anything else, Mr Ferran?"

"No," he said, wanting to go to his local in Bath and have a beer or six with Dave. "That's it for now."

He slumped in the chair as they all packed up and left, the Eagle the first to leave. Duncan looked like he was heading towards Sam but Susan diverted his attention and they left together in close conference. Sam was left at the table with abandoned crystal glasses, a couple of jugs of water and the beginning of a headache.

"How did it go?"

He swivelled in the chair to see Mazzi in the doorway. "I have no idea. I thought it was going well at one point. I think I freaked them out."

She smiled. "Probably not a bad thing to shake them up a bit. Drink?"

He stood and stretched. "God, yes."

"Find one you want to sack?"

"Yeah," he went over to her.

"That's normal," she said and rested a hand on his shoulder. "It will get easier. I promise."

He didn't believe her.

21

Cathy adjusted the seat in the car Max had hired and checked the positioning of the rear-view mirror as he went round to the passenger side and got in. The last time she drove it had been to London to rescue Josh, and Tom had been the passenger. So much had changed since then, including, she realised with a tension in her chest, herself. She'd been so determined to find a way out of Society and now she was Duchess, a bigger cog in the machine she'd stopped trying to run away from. Was she doing the right thing in trying to stay and change things for the better? Or had she lost her way and forgotten what it was like to be alone and truly think for herself?

"We need to get onto the M4," Max said, looking at a map.

"We'll head west then," she replied and started the engine.

It felt good to be back in a car and mundane clothes again. "Thanks for letting me drive," she said but Max didn't reply. Now she was getting used to being around him she enjoyed the lack of pressure to make small talk. She suspected the gargoyle was hidden in the boot.

She was grateful for a trip out of Londinium too. The meeting with Margritte had made her feel guilty and inept and she couldn't stop berating herself for bothering her at such a time. Of course Margritte would be angry and grieving; it was stupid to have even thought of contacting her for anything to do with the secret group. It only served to remind her that she was no good at the people thing. It had taken Lucy to point out there were other women who felt the same about Society. Her inability to think about anything other than her own frustrations had been revealed again.

"Take the left lane," Max said, and she indicated after checking the mirrors.

The roads were busy. Negotiating the traffic and following Max's navigation was a welcome distraction from worrying about Margritte and what would be reported back to Bennet. At least Will had left before Max arrived. He'd be on his way to meet Margritte now, unaware of this secret excursion until Carter reported it all to him.

"Poor Carter," she said aloud. "He'll be worrying."

"I told him I would take full responsibility."

"Those magic words," she said with a sigh.

Cathy had no idea what arrangements Will had made to meet Margritte; once she'd talked it through with him he'd agreed to meet her as soon as possible and handle the rest himself. She took that as a good sign. He seemed relieved she'd made contact with her, thinking it was in the hope of reducing the animosity between their families to avert any further disruption. Cathy hadn't been able to bring herself to tell him she'd had her own agenda, even though she'd wanted to share it with him. Worrying about what to tell and what to keep to herself was exhausting. She'd rather share it all with him, but that was unwise until she'd convinced him of the need to change the status quo.

Will was kinder than most but he was still one of them, a product of their patriarchal society and so concerned with keeping Lord Iris happy that he couldn't contemplate anything remotely controversial. She could sympathise, but she couldn't wait for him to feel secure enough in his position before she did something herself.

Max was a good navigator and they made it to the slip road onto the M4 without any wrong turns. "So," she said, once she was at the right speed and feeling more confident in the faster traffic. "Can you tell me where we're going now?"

"You asked me to look into a code you found in several files. The code 'GDA' refers to 'Green Dale Asylum' and several of the people you've requested files on are there."

"An asylum in Mundanus?"

"Yes, run by the Agency. Only they and the Patroons know about it. I suspect the mundane authorities are oblivious of its existence too. It's in the Cotswolds. I have the address and I thought it best to go there via mundane means."

"I bet they're not put in there because they're mad," Cathy said, gripping the steering wheel tighter and pressing down on the accelerator.

"Some of the people there may have lost their faculties," Max said. "But I suspect the ones you're looking for haven't."

"No, they wanted to hide them away so they would stop saying things the Patroons didn't like. Are they just left in Mundanus to get old and die?"

"It seems so," Max replied.

"So you're coming along because you're curious?"

"I doubt they would let you in without me. And I want to understand everything the Agency does."

"Are they breaching the Treaty?"

"That's one of the questions I want to answer."

She almost asked him what the other questions were but decided against it; he wouldn't tell her anyway.

So the men and women who'd disappeared from the secret group had been sent to a mundane asylum to die quietly, just because they'd spoken out. Perhaps the remaining members were right to be so cautious. Margritte had spoken of needing Will on her side and Cathy resented the fact it was true. But would Lord Iris sanction having her packed off when he was so keen for her to breed?

"I wonder if the Fae know."

"They must. They would notice their puppets were missing." Max said.

"I don't know how much attention they pay. Lord Poppy probably didn't even know I existed until he heard about me going to university."

"Was he involved in securing your marriage to William Iris?"

"I know Lord Iris was. Will told me the Patroon said he wanted us to marry."

"Do you know why?"

"To breed is my theory." Out of the corner of her eye she could see Max nodding. "But I have no idea why it has to be Will and I."

"You must both have qualities Lord Iris wants to see in one child. Or several," Max said. "The Agency do the same – they breed with certain pairings to make it more likely that certain qualities will be seen in the – keep your eye on the road, Catherine."

She yanked the wheel back, realising she'd started to drift across a lane. "The Agency have a breeding program? What the fuck?"

"The head of the Agency told me the Fae have been doing the same for generations. Were your parents matched by the Fae?"

"I don't know. God, this is awful. Will doesn't think it's the norm for his patron to be so involved. I've heard marriages are arranged by the head of the families and it's all to do with money or politics. I'm certain they married Tom to Lucy for the money – the Californicas are loaded."

"They probably needed it for your dowry," Max said and Cathy felt nauseous.

"Shit. You're right. That's the only way the Irises would have been happy to have their golden boy married to a dud like me: a tonne of money. Bastards, the lot of them." The clouds and greenery of Mundanus seemed to have reawakened the joy of swearing too.

"Which qualities do you both have that would make Lord Iris interested in your children?"

"I don't have a clue. I don't have any qualities. None that Society wants anyway."

"The Fae are not the same as those in your Society though. He may want something different."

Cathy breathed deep, hoping her breakfast would settle in her stomach again. Even though she'd already suspected it, it terrified her to hear an Arbiter talking about the possibility she and Will had been matched for that reason. "But what would Lord Iris want the child for? Assuming he got the combination of qualities he wanted."

"I don't know. We only monitor theft of children from Mundanus, not the Nether. Have you heard of children from the families being taken by the Fae?"

"I've heard all kinds of stories, but I always assumed they were to frighten us into being good. Are you convinced that people in Society need protection yet?"

"No," Max replied. "You people are still not protected by the Treaty."

"But why? We're just as human as the people in Mundanus."

"But not innocent."

"You make it sound like we're guilty of something. I didn't choose to be born into that Society. And I tried to get away from it. If you'd helped me that first time I met you, I wouldn't be in the mess I'm in now."

The conversation died and she focused on the road. She would have to tell Will what Max had said. Please don't be pregnant, she thought, trying to detect any change in the way her body felt. Between the nerves and the anger, it was hard to tell whether there was anything else going on.

They drove for over an hour without saying anything. It was almost like driving alone; there was no sense of there being someone with her unless she actually looked at him.

"Do you want to listen to some music?"

"No."

"Do you mind if I do?"

"No."

She flipped between radio stations but was unable to find anything she liked so she switched it off again. "So... what's it like being an Arbiter?"

"We need to take the next exit," he said, looking down at the map again.

"Did you always want to be one?"

"Take the third exit off the roundabout."

She changed lanes and followed a bright yellow car for a while. "How do you even become an Arbiter anyway?"

"There's a crossroads coming up," he said. "Turn right and then take the second left."

She stayed silent for the rest of the trip. They ended up driving down a bumpy single-lane road that turned into a glorified track through fields populated with cows. Just as she was about to tell him he must have got it wrong they saw a set of wooden gates with a letterbox in one of the supporting posts. "Green Dale" was carved into the stone above it.

Cathy stopped the car in front of them and Max got out. The gates were unlocked, which surprised her. He got back in and she drove forwards slowly, avoiding potholes in the gravel-covered road.

"I have nothing to say about what it's like to be an Arbiter," he said out of the blue. "I was selected from a large group of potentials. I passed the tests."

"Were they hard?"

"...Yes," he finally replied.

She drove slowly, wanting to ask more but knowing it would have to wait for another time. There were landscaped gardens on either side of them with large, mature trees at the boundary. As they rounded the corner a huge house came into view, obscured from the road by the trees at the edge of the estate. It had an extensive terrace and Cathy could see people sitting on chairs with blankets over their laps.

"Park over there," Max said, pointing to an empty parking area on the left. "I'll go first and make sure there isn't going to be a problem."

"Can I look for the people I wanted to find?"

He nodded. "Keep me in sight if you can. I doubt they'll do anything to the Duchess of Londinium, but it pays to be careful."

"Don't tell them who I am," she said and they got out of the car.

He went ahead as she locked it. A nurse was already hurrying into the house from the terrace, probably to raise the alarm. As she got closer she could see several elderly men and women watching the new arrival with interest.

They were dressed like they were still in Society and it looked so odd to see the period clothing in Mundanus. A woman came out of the house to intercept Max on the steps up onto the terrace and a short exchange resulted in Max being shown in. He turned and gave her a curt nod and Cathy took that as a confirmation that she could go ahead. She only hoped she would find answers instead of more questions.

••••

By the time Will had finished casting each Charm he felt invulnerable. No blade could cut him, if anything containing poison came near him the pendant resting on the skin over his heart would grow hot, and no Persuasion, Lust, Love or Hate Charms would have any effect on him, nor would any others created to alter his opinion. Tate had prepared the assortment for him and given a lengthy description of each one's benefits, and instructions for either casting them or placing artefacts in different places on his body. He'd used several before and heard of all the rest but had never used them in concert. He'd sent a bottle of the finest champagne and an obscenely expensive box of chocolates in return.

He was dressed in a modern suit and wearing a long coat to protect him against the mundane wind and rain as he stood in a doorway across the street. He'd opted to arrive early and keep a low profile, blending in with the mundanes as much as possible. He was waiting for one of his footmen to return and assure him that all was well at the hotel he'd chosen for his meeting with Margritte. It was easy to hire a private room with no Nether reflection halfway between London and Oxford, something he hoped would show his willingness to accommodate her needs. He wasn't going to tell her what really happened but he was happy to give her condolences if the conversation went well. Cathy was convinced it would be best for everyone and the decent thing to do. He hadn't argued with her on that point.

Nevertheless, he wasn't going to be complacent. He'd taken every precaution, preparing for the meeting as if it were with the head of a rival family rather than simply a grieving widow. Margritte was no fool and there was always the possibility she'd convinced the Tulipa Patroon to support her should she wish to humiliate him in some way. He'd denied their family true political power and that wouldn't be forgotten for a very long time.

"It's clear, your Grace," the footman said. "No trace of any Charms and nobody has been in the room since it was cleaned early this morning. None of the guests in the lobby nor any of the staff on duty have been Charmed and all staff identities have been confirmed."

"Excellent," Will replied. "How are you bearing up?" He'd cast a Clear Sight Charm on the man that morning, giving him the ability to see anyone or anything that had been Charmed or Glamoured. Tate had sent it for him to use but Will didn't want to suffer the side effect: severe depression for a few days once it had worn off.

"It's… interesting, your Grace. I'm glad to be of service."

"You'll be on reduced duties for the next week, should no emergencies arise," Will assured him. "I'll wait in the meeting room. When Mrs Tulipa arrives check her whilst she's being escorted and report to me should there be anything I need to know. You know what to look out for."

"Yes, your Grace. I'll escort you there now."

Will knew he was skating the fine line between caution and paranoia; even if she was wearing an artefact it was highly unlikely it would be able to affect him whilst so well protected. Better to be safe and home in time for dinner. He'd just finished reading *The Time Machine* and planned to discuss it with Cathy over a special meal he'd planned with the cook. She'd been working so hard to be everything he needed her to be; it was time to show her how much he appreciated it. And he wanted to see the smile the gift of the library had brought out again.

They crossed the street and the footman took him through to the meeting room after a brief exchange with the receptionist. Being back in a hotel made him yearn for the Grand Tour again, for that feeling of arriving somewhere new and knowing that fresh delights were soon to be discovered.

"This is the room, your Grace."

There was only a small table and two comfortable chairs near the window. They'd followed his instructions precisely: no mirrors, only one door in and out and secure windows. The first was to reduce the opportunity to open a Way into Exilium, the latter two to provide better mundane security.

"Good. Tell the others to take their positions."

Margritte arrived on time and Will was given a chance to compose himself as she was escorted to the room. His footman informed him she was wearing a simple Charm to keep her clothes clean and dry, one commonly used by those visiting Mundanus, but nothing else.

When she entered in her widow's garb Will found it more unsettling than he'd anticipated. As they went through the motions of polite greetings he was forced to see the impact of his actions. She was evidently still in deep mourning; not only was she wearing black, she was pale and had lost weight. More than that; she'd lost the joy he hadn't realised – until now – she'd radiated before.

His footmen followed her in and stood just inside the door. He felt safe.

"Thank you for agreeing to meet me," she said. She was tense. So was he.

"Catherine told me you were keen to speak. It may be meaningless, given the circumstances, but I am very sad about what happened between our families."

She stared at him, as if weighing the worth of his words. He hoped she would see his sincerity through grief's veil. "Have you found the person who really tried to kill Catherine?"

Will breathed out and in again, wondering what he could say to ease her pain without condemning himself in the process. "I consider the matter behind us."

"You have that luxury," she said. "I, however, do not. William, I believed you to be a decent man, as did Bartholomew. Surely you cannot think it right to leave things as they are. We both know Bartholomew was innocent. Tell me you know that to be so. Explain to me how you were led to believe otherwise, so I can find some peace again."

"There's nothing I can say that will bring him back."

"You can restore my family's honour."

"I'm sorry. I can't. I feel wretched about what happened but there is nothing I can do to change the situation we find ourselves in."

"I'll ask you one last time." She took a step towards him but most of the room was still between them. "Please tell the truth in the Court and clear his name. Let him be remembered as the man he was and let me mourn him in peace. He was not a murderer."

Will kept his lips pressed together and shook his head.

"So be it," she whispered and took a step back again.

There was a tremor in the air and his men had hands on their pistols in moments. Will reached for his sword, drawing it enough to break its Glamour, and felt a dampness on his chest. Thinking it was blood, he looked down to see a blue stain penetrating the cotton of his shirt in the place where the artefact had rested against his heart, as if the glass it was made of had turned to water.

The feeling of speed and sharp reflexes left him and he realised the Charms he'd so carefully prepared were failing. As Margritte watched he felt a sudden pressure on his ring finger. The wedding band – looking like oak once more – burst as if filled with too much air and his hand and fingers were filled with the sharp stab of hundreds of tiny splinters. The blade of his sword crumbled, one forged hundreds of years before, given to him when he came of age.

"Your Grace!" one of the men had time to shout before a tear in the air revealed another room, windowless and unfamiliar, through which stepped several suited men wearing bowler hats. They were followed by a scruffy mundane man who was grinning.

Before Will's footmen could reach him they were cut off by the hatted men, all of whom had modern pistols trained on their faces.

"Who–"

"You are in the Kingdom of Mercia, under jurisdiction of the Oxford Chapter and in the domain of Rupert, Sorcerer Guardian of Mercia," one of the hatted men announced.

"That's me," the scruffy man said.

"Any further action will be considered a breach of the Split Worlds treaty and you'll be prosecuted accordingly."

The unlikely Sorcerer looked at Margritte. "You OK, Maggie?"

She gave the slightest nod. "He won't clear his name."

"Well, we knew that would be the case, didn't we?"

"This is none of your concern, Sorcerer," Will said. "I am the Duke of Londinium and this is a private meeting with no risk to any innocents."

"This is my domain," Rupert said. "Everything that happens in Mercia is my concern. I don't give a flying fuck that you're the Duke of Londinium – that's thirty miles away and you're here, right now, not doing the decent thing."

Will looked at Margritte, still reeling from the fact that a Sorcerer seemed to be involved in her private affairs. Cathy had mentioned she lived in Oxenford now, but nothing about a Sorcerer. "How is this to play out, Margritte? If you act against me, the entirety of the Iris family – including Lord Iris himself – will seek–"

Rupert blew a loud raspberry. "Oh, blah, blah, blah. Yes, you're not happy and it's all most irregular and all of that arse." He flicked the fingers of his right hand and a silver yo-

yo dropped from it to bounce straight back up again. "Do you have a yo-yo?" he asked when he saw Will watching it.

"I did when I was a child."

"Could you do tricks?" Rupert caught the string on the forefinger of his left hand. "This one is called 'Round the World'." The yo-yo did a circle around his head and segued perfectly into the next bounce. "This one's called 'Walking the Dog'," he said before Will could get a word in. He crouched and the yo-yo rolled along the rug before being jerked back up the string. "But this one is my favourite. It's called 'You're fucked'."

Faster than his eye could track it, Rupert jerked the yo-yo towards the floor in front of Will's feet. Then he was falling through a hole that had opened in the floor, and landing with a loud thud in an empty room. He toppled, a terrible bright pain shooting through his right ankle. There was no door, no window, just a box-like space dimly lit by the light coming through the hole above him.

"You've no right to do this!" he shouted up at the opening.

Rupert was peering down at him, the hateful grin filling his face. "I absolutely do, Dukey boy. It's my domain. Ekstrand isn't going to help you now."

"But I haven't done anything!"

Margritte came to Rupert's side. "Neither did Bartholomew," she said and the hole closed, plunging Will into absolute darkness.

22

Max watched Catherine carefully as they walked out of the asylum. She paused when she was about to unlock the car, turning to look towards the trees edging the estate.

"Which way do we go?"

Max pointed to the drive, only metres away and in plain view. "The way we came in."

Catherine's eyes skimmed over it, like she hadn't even seen it. "Which way to get to the driveway?"

Max's suspicion was confirmed; none of the inmates tried to escape because there was a Charm to obfuscate the way out. "I'll drive," he said.

"There's the road!" she said once they were a mile or so away from the house. "Oh. That's why they don't escape, isn't it?"

Max nodded. The people at the asylum seemed to be treated well. At least they were clean, well dressed and well fed. Max hadn't built up any firm expectations but wouldn't have been surprised to find a Bedlam-like institution considering how out of pace with Mundanus the rest of Society was. The agency wasn't behind the times, even if their clients were.

When Max had said Derne knew he was there, he was introduced to the manager, a round-faced man who tried his best to understand why Max was there but was none the wiser by the time the tour was over.

The security was incredibly low-key, consisting of nothing more than a few burly orderlies who would be capable of throwing someone over their shoulder and carrying them back in the event of attempted escape. The manager said – several times – that no one had ever tried and that the residents were very happy.

As Max had suspected, some of the inmates had been placed there when life in the Nether had got too much for them. The latest arrival was a man called Archie, formerly of the Wisteria line, who'd been unable to control his cravings for fresh air and blue sky. He'd been found in a mundane hospital by his brother after suffering a nervous breakdown.

"He's very happy here," the manager had said cheerily. "It's everything he wanted and the family don't have anything to worry about. They couldn't afford the Charms to put him right, you see."

"What about the ones who haven't had a nervous breakdown?" Max asked.

"I'm sorry, I don't know who you mean."

"The ones put here because they have controversial opinions."

"They have just the same problems, Mr Arbiter. They're unable to cope with the demands of Nether Society and say the most outlandish things as part of their madness. Raging against accepted behaviour is simply a cry for help."

"A cry for help?" Catherine said when Max reported it to her. "Bollocks. I don't know what to do. It seems wrong to just go home and do nothing about it."

"The Patroons know, and some of the people there were placed by their families," Max said. "You would upset a lot of powerful people if you challenged it."

She nodded, chewing her thumbnail. She was silent for almost an hour, staring out of the window. "And all of that stuff you told me about the Agency breeding perfect staff and the way they treat them... like slaves. It isn't right. But it's all so big. I don't know what to do about it all. I just know it's wrong."

There was a thud in the boot and she twisted to look into the back of the car. "Did we just hit something?"

"No."

"I don't even know who's in charge of the Agency, or where they're based. Even if I did I wouldn't know what to do."

Another *thunk*, this time louder, as Max exited the motorway and headed into the outskirts of London.

"There's something wrong with the car," Catherine said and he shook his head.

"There isn't."

The back portion of the rear passenger seat was knocked into the foot-well and the gargoyle poked its head through the gap between car and boot.

"So you were in there." Catherine stretched back and clasped the gargoyle's paw.

"The whole bloody time." It clambered onto the back seat; at least it had the sense to stretch itself along the width of the car to keep out of sight of the other drivers. "We need to talk."

"We need to stay focused," Max said. "You know what we have to do after we've taken Catherine home."

"That's exactly the reason why," the gargoyle replied. "If we die without telling anyone about what the Agency is doing, nothing will put a stop to it." It shuffled about so its head was closer to Catherine. "I need to tell you so I know that something will be done. Ekstrand doesn't give a rat's arse and he's mental anyway."

Catherine repositioned herself so she was facing the gargoyle more comfortably. "All right. I'm listening." She looked at Max. "Are you OK?"

"He's fine," the gargoyle said. "Listen to me. The Agency headquarters is a place that only exists in the Nether without an anchor property and the only way it can make that is by keeping all these people in the basement like... like... machines." It described everything Max had seen, as if it had been in that room with him.

"My God, is there anything these people aren't doing?" Catherine said, and then asked questions about what they saw that day the Agency was taken over, which the gargoyle answered readily. Max focused on the road and the heavy traffic. The gargoyle was trusting her with sensitive information. Should he pull over and kick her out of the car? Why hadn't he done that already?

"It's because she needs to understand how bad this is," the gargoyle said to him. "It's because we know we need to do something."

"But they're not protected by the Treaty."

"Did I miss something?" Catherine asked but the gargoyle was focused on Max.

"But they're being screwed over like we were. Don't you get it? We're just the same as those poor bastards strapped in those chairs: we're nothing but a tool, made for a specific purpose. We didn't choose this, just like they didn't."

"What do you mean?" Catherine asked.

"This isn't the right time," Max replied.

"Why are you afraid of her knowing this?" the gargoyle asked. "You don't really think it's ever going to go back to the way it was, do you? Most of the Sorcerers are dead and the two that are left are trying to kill each other. Ekstrand is a fruitloop. We're on our own. We've come this far without his orders, why not do the right thing whilst we're being insubordinate?"

Max pulled over when he saw a parking space free at the rear of Catherine's anchor property. Catherine was staring at him.

"You can't show me the asylum and tell me all this stuff about the Agency and think I'll just forget about it."

"I don't."

"Then what are we going to do?"

"I have to speak to someone," Max said, thinking of Faulkner's Chapter Master. "I think he'll lead us to the root of these problems."

"And then will we do something?"

"I don't know. I need to think about it."

Catherine groaned. "I'm going." She glanced at the gargoyle. "I hope you come back. And I hope you can convince him to get off his arse and commit to taking action."

"I'll do my best." It grinned at her and she left.

They sat in silence for a few moments, then Max noticed the time on the dashboard clock. "We'd better get moving," he said. "The Chapter Master will be at the park soon. And we're already taking action," he added, prompted by the gargoyle's stare.

Sam pumped the bellows until the fire was hot enough and put in a length of iron. It was the first time he'd been in the forge since his predecessor's suicide. He'd been apprehensive about coming in, fearing it would trigger unpleasant memories. It made him think about what happened but he no longer felt unsettled. He just wanted to beat the iron until he was ready to go back to Exilium.

The meeting with the Directors wasn't a clear success or an obvious failure. He decided to feel good about starting the ball rolling at least and as time went on and he learned more about how it all worked he would make the changes he wanted. At least the PR guy was behind him. Instead, it was time to focus on the other benefits his new status accorded. Mazzi had said the Fae would fear him and he knew which one he wanted to terrify the most. But how to do it? How to get back to Exilium on his own terms, rather than at the summoning or permission of Lord Poppy? He wanted to take the Fae by surprise.

He looked down at the anvil, breathing in the sense of potential. What would he make as he considered his plan? A spear to run Poppy through? A sword to threaten him with, like Cathy's husband had wielded? He swore at the thought of her stuck with him, deluding herself into thinking she could do something about the way they lived. As soon as he was free of Poppy's interference, he'd go and free her too.

He went to pull out the iron but found himself drawn back to the anvil. The floor had been scrubbed and he noticed a feature for the first time: the anvil was resting on a solid circle of iron set into the floor. At its edges he could see slivers of what looked like copper, running at intervals around it. He pulled the length of iron from the fire and abandoned it in the plunge bucket, steam accompanying the loud hiss of hot metal meeting cold water.

Grunting with effort, Sam pulled the anvil off the circle, certain that, without the "affinity" Mazzi had spoken of, he'd never have been able to budge it an inch. He crouched down and scraped the black grime from the groove between the circle and the flagstones and had a sudden sense of its base being deep in the earth, so deep that the forge had been built around and on top of it, rather than being set into the floor as a feature.

He pulled the abandoned rod of iron from the bucket, tossed it aside and threw the water over the circle, washing away the outline of dirt left by the anvil base. It was solid iron and close to the diameter of a postbox. He thought of the pillar in Exilium, the one Poppy couldn't bear to be near. That had been a similar size and also had copper riveted to it. Then he noticed a haze in the air. He thought for a moment that it was steam from the cooling rod but that had already dissipated. He stared at the iron set into the floor and the haziness increased until it was as if a fog were forming in the air. He crouched down beside it as the tiny hairs on his arms and the back of his neck prickled, and reached towards the space above the circle. Where he thought his fingers would pass through the air, they instead brushed iron.

There was a terrific lurch in his stomach and he tipped forwards, his hands slapping against iron with copper bands riveted around it, familiar formulae etched into the metal. He was on his knees, palms still on the metal, and no longer saw the forge, only mists, as if the strange fog that had been rising now encompassed everything. Then he realised he wasn't in the squat little building in Mundanus any more. He was in the Nether and the iron was stretching ahead of him now, like a path through the void.

Cathy pulled off her gloves and dumped them on the chair, feeling exhausted and yet as tightly wound as a nervous man's watch. She felt as if she needed a release, like a long cry or the opportunity to scream at someone, but neither was forthcoming.

She was too full of terrible knowledge. How could she sit there in her library in front of the fire when so many people were being mistreated? Her efforts felt like they'd come to nothing; she'd found people who knew Rainer but they were either unwilling to help her or incapable of it. She knew about the atrocities committed by the Agency but felt powerless to act. Bennet had managed to curse her once already; if she moved against them she had no doubt he would see his threats through and she'd be hauled in front of Dame Iris and probably shipped off to the asylum herself. That Will knew her past would make no difference if the Irises were publicly humiliated.

Could she rely on Max to come back and form a plan with her? He was acting without the knowledge of the Sorcerer. Would he be able to take on the Agency without his Master's blessing?

There was a knock on the door and Morgan entered with a note on a small silver tray. Cathy recognised Bennet's handwriting before she touched it.

I am aware of the visits from a certain Arbiter and your recent contact with Charlotte Persificola-Viola. If you continue to pry into matters that are no concern of yours, I will contact Dame Iris and have a frank conversation with her about your previous interests.

"Morgan!" Cathy called him back from the doorway, planning to show him the evidence of blackmail, but by the time he'd crossed the room the ink was sliding from the page like mascara in the rain.

"Is there a reply, your Grace?"

"No," she said, crumpling the paper in her fist. "No reply."

Cathy went to the fire and threw the note onto it, then put both hands on the chimney breast, leaning over until she felt the warmth. She had decided to stay in the Nether with a head full of noble ideals but still felt powerless. Had she made the wrong choice? Was she deluding herself that anything could be done by one woman?

She shut her eyes, letting her head droop between her arms, thinking of the people she'd left at the asylum, the truths the gargoyle told and Max talking about the Fae and the Agency matching people for goodness knows what. She thought of Miss Rainer scrubbing pans, a shadow of herself, and Charlotte, trapped in her own body and living in a gilded prison. And what had she done since she'd made the decision to stay instead of run away? Looked for someone else to help her, looked for a group of people to get behind, looked to Will to stand up and fight the system so she could stand beside him.

"I'm still a coward," she whispered. She wasn't going to find someone to show her the way to change things because that person didn't exist. She had to do it herself. She would find a way to free all of the people held by the Agency, and she'd find a way to give women a voice and recognition and rights in Society even if it meant destroying her own life in the process.

A pulse of magic rippled out from her, making her fingertips tingle as it left her body. The third wish! She'd felt something similar for the first and second when they were cast, but when she told Lord Poppy her last wish she'd felt nothing. Until now. She knew what her true potential was: it was to change Society by becoming the force of change herself.

The place to start was the asylum and the main obstacle was Bennet. She needed to distract him long enough to go there herself and lead those people out. Out where? The flat in Manchester was too small and there would be no way to protect them there anyway. She thought of the empty rooms in the house and imagined them filled with illegal guests. The thought made her smile but the staff would report back to Bennet and she couldn't keep him distracted for that long. She needed to change the household into a safe haven by the time he realised what she'd done.

She straightened, took a deep breath and then called for Carter. He entered and stood to attention. "Yes, your Grace?"

"Carter… shut the door. The Arbiter wasn't here about the attack. He took me to a place in Mundanus where people are being kept prisoner even though they've done nothing wrong. People who used to live in Society. They're being left there to get old and die."

He looked appalled. "Why would the Arbiter do such a thing? And why did you go, your Grace? You could have been at risk."

She realised he was more upset about that than about the news of the place itself. "Because I asked him to find some people who disappeared. And we didn't tell you because I know that you report to Bennet." She paused, expecting the usual tightness in her chest that always came when she thought about Bennet and what he held over her. But there was no change. "He's been…" she took a breath, ready for the coughing fit to start any second. "Bennet has blackmailed and threatened me."

The curse had been broken! Of course, how could she reach her potential with that constraining her? Poppy's magic had actually done something useful!

Carter was gawping at her. "I had no idea, your Grace."

"He cursed me so I couldn't tell anyone."

"Mr Bennet said I had to report all your movements to him as well as the Duke to ensure your safety. He said all personal guards of people of your status have that duty." He looked down at the carpet. "I should tender my resignation. I failed in my–"

"Oh, don't be ridiculous," Cathy said. "You couldn't possibly have known."

"I can only offer you my word that I will not make any more reports on your actions to Mr Bennet. I trust you'll tell the Duke upon his return?"

"Yes, I will. But quite frankly there are much more important things to worry about now. I can't just carry on with my life knowing about that asylum. I have to do something and I want to free those people and bring them here, to stay, until they get back on their feet and work out what they want to do for themselves."

"I see, your Grace. This sounds like a noble thing to do."

"It's run by the Agency and Bennet is in charge of it."

His expression darkened. "But if the Agency are–"

"Listen, I need your help to get them out. The Agency don't have the right to keep them there, and it's only one of a long list of terrible things they're doing. They've been keeping all kinds of people silenced for the Patroons for far too long now and it has to stop. Now, I understand if you don't want any part of it, but I want to offer you a choice. If you want to help me do the right thing, I'll support your resignation from the Agency and I'll pay your wages myself. You'll have the same job security and–"

"I'm sorry, your Grace, I don't understand what you mean. I don't receive wages."

"But I've been paying the Agency thousands of pounds for everyone's…" Cathy shook her head. None of that money had been passed on to the staff and they had no idea the Agency were charging money supposedly for them. Of course not. Why in the Worlds would the Agency teach their indoctrinated slaves about the right to earn a living? "All right. You have the choice to come with me and free those people – if you do, I'll make sure the Agency don't take you away and you'll be my personal employee. That means I'll give you money for you to spend on whatever you like, and time off when you want it. Or you can let me go by myself."

"I should, in fact, stop you from going at all, with all respect, your Grace. The Duke gave me explicit orders."

She folded her arms. "That may be so, but unless you want to lock me in a box, that isn't going to happen. I know you're a good person, Carter, you just didn't know what the Agency is capable of. I need you. I need you to help me do the right thing."

She didn't take her eyes off him, hoping he would see her conviction. After what seemed like an age, he nodded. "I'll help you, your Grace. I trust you know what's best." She thought it would be harder to convince him. Was it the wish magic? "But if we're going to do something that might upset the Agency, we need to convince the rest of the staff it's the right thing to do too. I know enough about them to be able to advise you on the best way to approach it."

Cathy nodded. "You're right. I'll call a meeting. Everything's going to change now, Carter." When he frowned she smiled as confidently as she could. "But it's all going to be for the better. I'm sure of it."

It took only moments for Will to explore the boundaries of his prison, then he had no choice but to wait. He worried about the air running out, then decided Margritte wouldn't have gone to all the trouble to engineer his kidnapping only to leave him to suffocate in a large box. Besides, the Sorcerer or the Arbiters could have killed him just as easily as imprisoning him.

There was total silence, not even the slightest vibration in the floor. Will suspected the prison was a Sorcerous construct in the Nether and that rescue was therefore probably impossible. He sat in the corner and the fingers on his left hand started to sting. He tried to feel for any splinters but in the total darkness it was only possible to pull out the largest slivers of wood. It didn't feel like he was bleeding enough to be a concern. The fact that the Sorcerer wielded magic capable of shattering a ring made by the Fae King and Queen both impressed and frightened him.

Will stretched his legs out and felt his right ankle throb. It wasn't painful enough to be broken, but was still uncomfortable.

He rested his head against the corner where the two walls met and took a few moments to breathe deeply and steady himself. He'd had a shock and it was natural to feel frightened in the circumstances, so he permitted himself a few moments of unbridled fear. He blinked a few times, disturbed by how hard it was to know whether his eyes were open or closed, and wondered what they were going to do to him.

How had Margritte secured the support of a Sorcerer? And why had they mentioned Ekstrand? Will had only seen him for as long as the other people at the party; he hadn't even spoken to him. That night seemed like it was years ago but it was only a matter of months. He had the feeling there were other agendas playing out around him; the matter of the Londinium throne shouldn't be of any interest to the Sorcerer of Mercia, nor any of the others for that matter.

He heard the sound of a key in a lock and the adrenalin surged again. He managed to get to his feet before a crack of light revealed the opening of a door on the opposite side of the box. Whatever was about to happen, he was ready.

23

Cathy couldn't stop grinning as she penned the note to Bennet. She'd waited as long as she could bear for Will to return but was so afraid she'd lose her nerve she decided to press on with her plan regardless. What did she want from him anyway? Permission to save people? She knew she probably shouldn't have done anything without considering it all more carefully over a cup of tea, but since the magic had zipped through her she couldn't bear the thought of keeping still. There would never be a good time and the consequences of her actions would never be anything but frightening.

Mr Bennet,

It's imperative we meet urgently to discuss a matter regarding the Agency. My carriage will be waiting for you in the reflection of Bathurst Stables to convey you to Somerset House where we will be able to talk without my husband's knowledge. Please come as soon as you are able.

Catherine Reticulata-Iris

She folded the paper, sealed it with wax and pulled the bell cord beside the fire. When Morgan arrived she handed him the letter. "This needs to be sent by Letterboxer. Please inform the footman that Mr Bennet from the Agency will require transport in our carriage from the stables to Somerset House and that he should be conveyed via the longest route possible. I need to be told as soon as the carriage leaves the stables."

Morgan nodded and bowed. "At once, your Grace."

"Is everything in hand?"

"Yes, the bedrooms are being prepared for guests, and extra food and fuel is being fetched from Mundanus."

"Any word from Will?"

"No, your Grace. I'll inform you as soon as he arrives."

"Thank you, Morgan."

She paced as she tried to think of ways to tell Will what she'd done. "Darling," she said as if he was there. "While you were visiting Margritte, I secretly convinced the staff to break away from the Agency and form an independent household. The Agency doesn't know yet."

Cathy shook her head. "Darling," she started again, imagining Will standing in front of her, frowning like he had when he asked her why she'd animated Nelson's statue. "The Agency – no – Mr Bennet, from the Agency, has been blackmailing me and I thought it best to take away his control over our household by employing the staff myself, including the bodyguard you've been using to spy on me." No! Too confrontational.

She tried a few more permutations but none of them sounded any good. She just wanted to get moving. The waiting was the worst thing about it all.

A knock on the door made her jump and Morgan entered. "Mr Bennet has arrived at the stables."

"God, that was quick." She took a deep breath and smiled at him. "This is it then, Morgan. Are you sure you want to stay and be involved in all this?"

"I am, your Grace." He returned the smile. "In fact, may I say how pleased I am to have the opportunity to do so."

"You rock, Morgan. Could you bring my hat, gloves and cape? I'm going dressed as I am." She'd changed back into an outfit appropriate for the Nether, knowing that the people at the asylum wouldn't believe she was the Duchess if she was wearing mundane clothing like she had been before.

Whilst she waited for him to return she realised how nervous she was. She'd set things in motion and there was no turning back; the staff were depending on her now in a way they didn't need to before. She had to see it through, no matter what Bennet did. She had no doubt he was going to reveal her secrets to Dame Iris, but the consequences of that seemed less important now than doing her best to free those people. She wondered how far Poppy's magic would protect her.

The slam of the front door made her heart race for a different reason; Will would have to be told and she didn't have time to explain it all to him.

"Get out of my way, fool!" The voice that penetrated the wood was not her husband's – thankfully not Bennet's either. She heard Carter's low rumble and then "I'm the Duke's brother, idiot, stand aside!"

The door banged open and Nathaniel barged in like a man about to leap into a brawl rather than enter his sister-in-law's company.

"Would you like me to remain in the room with you, your Grace?" Carter asked at the door, his cheeks a deep red.

"This is private!" Nathaniel slammed the door in Carter's face.

Cathy backed away from him until her skirts brushed one of the armchairs by the fire. She sat in it and tried to look as composed as possible. "Would you like to sit down and tell me what has upset you so?"

Nathaniel looked horrified. "Don't pretend you're ignorant of this!"

She sat. "Of what? Please, sit down and–"

He crossed the room and leaned over her chair, planting his hands on the arms and effectively caging her in. "Where is he?"

"Who?"

"William!" He glanced at her left hand and frowned at the wedding ring. "You really don't know?"

"He went to meet Margritte." Nathaniel didn't move. "Margritte Semper-Augustus Tulipa. I don't know where."

"Why?"

"Because she wanted to speak to him. Will you please sit down?"

"William has disappeared and we think he's been kidnapped."

"What?"

"The Patroon has tasked me with finding him and bringing the kidnappers to justice."

"Margritte wouldn't do anything like that."

"How can you be so sure?"

"Because I spoke to her and–"

Nathaniel moved so swiftly she didn't realise he had until his hand was gripping her jaw. The last of the bruising from the attack twinged as he made her look up at him. "Did you lead him into a trap?"

"Of course I didn't, you prat, let go of me!"

He squeezed tighter, until tears pricked at the corners of her eyes. "I know you didn't want to marry him. Did you and your friend come up with a plan to–"

"Let me go!"

The door opened and Carter's hand was on his shoulder in seconds. Nathaniel released her so he could bat the huge man away. Carter put himself between her chair and Nathaniel as she composed herself, rubbing her face. With a horrified jolt she realised it was the first time another man had touched her since the wedding day, but Nathaniel didn't seem to be burned.

She stood up and Carter looked down at her, frowning at her face. There were probably marks. "Thank you," she said to him and then stepped to one side to look past his bulk at Nathaniel. "I know Margritte has a son in Oxenford. She said she was staying with him. But I really can't imagine she would do anything like this and I'm deeply insulted by your suspicion. I've been away for the day and had no idea anything has happened to Will."

She expected an apology but there was nothing of the sort on Nathaniel's face. "I'll go and look for him there then."

"How can I help? Perhaps I could write to her and see if–"

"I think you've done enough, useless woman." He gave her a look of absolute contempt. "If I find that you're responsible for his being harmed I'll personally–"

"May I suggest you leave, sir?" Carter shifted until he blocked the way between them again and Cathy heard Nathaniel leave the room, slamming the door behind him. Carter turned to face her again. "I'm so sorry, your Grace. Mr Reticulata-Iris is one of the individuals permitted to see you. Had I any idea he would be so... despicable I never would have let him enter."

"It's all right, you weren't to know. Would you be so kind as to find out if Will came home after he met Margritte?"

"I'll come straight back, your Grace."

Trembling, Cathy opened and closed her mouth carefully, feeling the bruising again. She fumbled with the opening of her reticule and pulled out the small mirror compact inside and looked at her face, expecting to see marks, but there was only the usual red. Had they lied to her about the curse or had the third wish broken that one too? The ring still looked the same though, and the curse was bound into it.

Only an Iris man may touch you now…

The memory of Will's mother breaking the news to her returned with a sharp clarity. An Iris man – she had made out that it meant only Will, but what if it didn't? Her hand flew to her mouth as she realised why Vincent had been so keen to stay and take care of Sophia. He was her father. Will's mother had had an affair with her brother-in-law.

After a single knock the door opened and Carter returned. "Your Grace, the Duke hasn't yet returned and neither have his footmen. The Steward is going to the meeting place as I speak, a mundane hotel halfway between here and Oxford, to see if there is any evidence of foul play."

"Perhaps they just got talking and lost track of the time." She didn't believe it even as she said it. Something had happened to him; Nathaniel wouldn't have been sent by the Patroon unless they were sure. She could write to Margritte but what would it achieve? If she had done something terrible she was hardly likely to confess it to her victim's wife.

"I'm sure everything will be fine, your Grace."

It felt wrong to do anything but wait for word of Will's safety but Bennet wouldn't be distracted for much longer. Morgan arrived with her hat and gloves. "We have to go to the asylum," she said to Carter. "We've only got an hour or two at the most. We'll go through to the edge of Aquae Sulis, then you'll pick up a hire car for us in Bath, it's much closer to the asylum than London. You can drive, can't you Carter?"

"Yes, your Grace."

"What will happen afterwards?" Morgan asked as she put on her hat.

"Hopefully, I'll turn up with a bunch of people who'll need lots of tea," she replied.

"And what about Mr Bennet?" Carter asked.

She sighed. "I'll face that problem when I come to it."

Max waited at the edge of the park, watching the gates as the gargoyle hunkered down in the bushes. The Master of the London Camden Ward Chapter had a habit of taking a stroll and eating a chocolate bar there every day at 3 o'clock in the afternoon. It was overcast but not raining and the man's favourite bench was free.

Not wanting to look like an Arbiter waiting for someone to arrive, Max sat down on another bench with his back to the gates. The gargoyle had a clear view of them so it would know when the Chapter Master arrived, and meanwhile Max's face would be hidden. He checked his watch. Three o'clock.

He had a brief vision of the Chapter Master walking into the park behind him from the perspective of the bushes. He was a tall and rather gaunt man who didn't look in the best of health. There was a newspaper tucked under one arm, a take-away coffee cup in his left hand. He was dressed in a suit and wearing a heavy woollen coat with a thick woolly hat that had a large red bobble on the top. Max had a sense of the gargoyle finding it funny, but had no idea why.

Free of the pressure of fieldwork, Chapter Masters were able to live a relatively normal life, their souls intact and lifespan extended by living in the Nether. Many avoided entering Mundanus unless absolutely necessary, hoping to prolong their lives as much as possible, just like the puppets. Unlike them, Chapter Masters wanted longevity to protect the innocents. It seemed this one wasn't so keen on staying alive as long as possible.

The Chapter Master sat on his usual bench, rested the coffee on the wooden slat next to him and opened the newspaper. Max got up and approached slowly, expecting the man to look up, alert and ready to flee as soon as he detected him. But when the man's brown eyes peeped over the top of the paper he simply lowered it and smiled.

"You must be Max," he said. "I've been waiting for you."

"You're the Chapter Master of the Camden Ward?" Max wanted to be certain before they spoke about anything sensitive.

"I am. My name is John. Come and sit down. And I feel I should say now, in case you had any concern, you're not in any danger."

Max sat next to him. "So you've decided I'm not a threat any more?"

"You misunderstand me. We haven't tried to kill you. Whoever put you in hospital wasn't one of mine."

"Let's go back to the beginning," Max said. "Montgomery contacted me because he suspected your Chapter was corrupt. He was right."

"Going right back to the beginning," John echoed, "I instructed Monty to contact you."

"You wanted me to find out." Max nodded. "Yes, that makes sense. I wondered what could have motivated him to reveal it, when he didn't feel any guilt. But if you sent Montgomery, why did Faulkner give me the brush-off?"

"Faulkner didn't know what I'd done. I couldn't risk anyone finding out, and that's why I'm still alive today. Monty is dead."

"Who killed him?"

"The same people who tried to kill you, I imagine. You'd left the hospital before my people had a chance to reach you, and then you were back in Wessex. There was nothing I could do without seriously rocking the boat."

"Someone followed me and tried to finish the job."

"Again, not one of mine."

"But it was an Arbiter. Both times. And my Chapter was destroyed."

John fiddled with the edge of the newspaper. "This is troubling news. I was depending on you to inform your Chapter Master, in the hope the Sorcerer of Wessex would intervene. My orders to turn a blind eye to the activities of various families became unbearable when it was the turn of the Rosas. They took it too far."

"Is it the Irises now?" When John nodded, Max asked, "And there have been other families?"

"In the past I've been instructed to ignore the Wisterias, Peonias, Ranuculi, Digitalis and a few other very minor families. The Irises are the last ones – all of the puppets have had their turn over the years."

"But how could you sanction that?"

John was staring at one of the trees. "I haven't been happy about it. But I couldn't disobey a direct order from the Sorcerer. Surely you understand that?"

Max nodded. "Did you question it?"

"The first time, yes, I did. He told me there was a bigger picture and that whilst it seemed contrary to my remit, it was for the greater good. You said your Chapter was destroyed… is that why the Sorcerer of Wessex hasn't intervened? Because you haven't been able to get a message to him?"

"Mr Ekstrand knows," Max said. "But he's been distracted by the war with Mercia."

"War?" John appeared to know nothing about it.

"Ekstrand believes Rupert of Mercia killed all of the other Sorcerers. Have you been in contact with the Chapters in Sussex or East Anglia? How are you functioning without your Sorcerers?"

"I don't understand." John was even more pale now. "I received a message from Dante only this morning."

"But Dante died several weeks ago. I saw the body myself."

There was a long pause.

"Someone has been using a combination of Fae and sorcerous magic," Max said. "My theory is that an apprentice of Dante's is behind all of this. I don't know how and I don't know why. With your help I may be able to find some answers." John was still staring at the tree. "I need you to open a Way to the Sorcerer's house. I know you must have access for emergencies."

John stood up. "I can't help you."

"But you know something is wrong. Innocents are being taken, Arbiters and Chapter staff are being murdered – the Master of my Chapter was murdered along with everyone else. The last two Sorcerers in Albion are trying to kill each other whilst the true perpetrator goes free. If you don't help me, you're only going to put more people at risk."

John shook his head. "I'm sorry."

"You wanted this to be discovered. Now I'm here and willing to do something, are you really going to turn me away and let this continue?"

"Yes. I am."

Sam felt like he'd been walking for days. The mists of the Nether made it hard to mark his progress. There were no landmarks and no points of reference against which he could measure the distance travelled. He looked back at one point, seeing the iron path twisting in a huge corkscrew shape that made his heart flap like a dying fish. He only looked forwards from that point on.

He thought about the pillar he saw in Exilium on the day he tried to rescue the blondes. Poppy had been unable to look at it. Mazzi had told him that the anchors that hold the Worlds apart were made from iron and copper, as this path was. He was certain it had something to do with marking its edges – that's what he'd been looking for when he stumbled upon the pillar the first time. He was walking the chains between the Worlds. He smiled. That sounded pretty cool.

He wanted to understand more but Amir hadn't left anything for him to read about the esoteric aspects of his new position. It was all business. Mazzi said that each Lord and Lady of the Elemental Court was different, bringing something new to the role each time. He was probably the first one who'd had a previous run-in with one of the Fae Lords. Hopefully, he was about to become the first to bitch-slap one too.

Sam tried to focus on reaching the end of the path, just as he had focused on finding the edge of Exilium, but it seemed to have no effect. Then he realised the same rules wouldn't apply in the Nether. There was nothing to do but walk and not think about the fact that he was probably walking upside down at points on the corkscrew path without even realising it.

Just as he was wondering whether it actually led anywhere, Sam looked up from his feet to see that the path ran into a thick bank of fog. Hoping it was the boundary between the Nether and the edge of Exilium, Sam quickened his pace until he reached the point where the iron disappeared into the mists. He remembered the pillar stretching out of the ground in Exilium, so he got down on his hands and knees, expecting another stomach-churning sensation as he crossed the boundary.

His instinct was correct and, as he passed from the misty void into the Fae prison, his weight tipped back and he grasped the pillar, wrapping his legs around it like a child trying to shimmy up a tree trunk. He squeezed his eyes shut as he inched forwards until his body readjusted.

When he opened them again he wasn't in the Nether any more, but he wasn't convinced he was in Exilium yet either. There were trees and meadows, a blue sky and fluffy clouds but it could have been a spot in the English countryside. It wasn't as breathtaking; the colours were just normal – pleasant – but not supernaturally beautiful.

He was about a metre off the ground and beginning to slide towards it, so he let go of the pillar and stood on the grass. It looked like it was the same pillar he'd seen before and was incredibly cold to the touch. Scanning the horizon, Sam couldn't see any clusters of trees to suggest Lord Poppy's or anyone else's domain, nor any of the tell-tale flowers. He did see lots of tiny things in the air, seeming to be fleeing from where he was. Or were they fleeing from *him*?

Sam started to walk, holding at the centre of his thoughts the desire to see the enslaved blondes he couldn't save before. He would find them, he would free them, that was all he wanted to do. After a while he wondered why the ground was still flat. All the other times he'd looked for people the meadow would rise into a gentle hill, then the person he was hoping to find would be on the other side. Nothing like that seemed to be happening. Maybe he was just in the middle of the Sussex Downs and not in Exilium at all.

Then he saw someone walking towards him, someone tall enough to be Fae, wearing a long cloak. Sam stopped and waited until he got closer. He looked behind him to make sure no one was creeping up on him whilst he was distracted and saw a couple of tiny flowers he'd brushed as he went past, now brown and shrivelled. He faced front again. He was in Exilium, he was certain now, but he wasn't the same man he was before.

The Fae had green eyes in contrast to the solid black Sam was used to in Poppy. He was covered in thousands of oak leaves, woven into a cloak and wrapped around him from neck to floor, trailing after him and spilling around his feet as he walked. There was a circlet of oak leaves too and Sam wondered if he was some sort of royalty.

The Fae stopped a few metres away, further than one would normally when speaking to another person. He bowed, very deeply. "Lord Iron, Master of the blood and star metal, protector of the innocent, brother to the binding metal and friend to the Sorcerers, as Prince of the realm it is my honour to welcome you to Exilium."

Sam rubbed the back of his neck, feeling like an impostor. "Right. Thanks." After a beat he returned the bow, as embarrassed and hesitant as the Prince's was elegant.

"May I ask why you have chosen to grace us with your visit?"

"I want to speak to Poppy."

"I will see that he is brought to you immediately." The Prince pulled one of the leaves from his cloak and blew it off the palm of his hand. It fluttered away and was swiftly out of sight. "Has he caused offence?"

"Oh, yes," said Sam, nodding. "I'm going to give him the chance to put it right."

"That is most generous of you. I'm sorry we have to wait. I'm sure you understand it isn't possible to bring him so close to your presence in the usual way."

Sam nodded, even though he didn't understand, being ignorant of how the usual way worked.

The Prince stared at him but remained silent. Sam was about to ask how long it would take when he saw Poppy hurrying towards them.

"Your Royal Highness," he said when he reached them, bowing so low his black hair brushed the blades of grass. He looked at Sam, his expression mutating into one of absolute horror. "...Lord... Iron?"

"Lord Iron wishes to speak with you," the Prince said and then turned to Sam. "I will be close by, should you need anything else."

Sam thanked him and then looked at Poppy. The Fae was leaning back, as if trying to stay as far away from him as possible without looking like he was trying to do so. "I've come to put things right."

"Oh, of course." Poppy smiled and clicked his fingers. The faerie appeared behind him, peeping from behind his shoulder. It managed one look in Sam's direction before squealing and diving out of sight. "The hourglass!" Poppy hissed at it as the Prince backed off, still watching.

The faerie fluttered to a spot on the grass further behind Poppy and gave Sam another nervous look before waving its tiny hands to make the dreaded hourglass appear. The pile of sand in the bottom half of the glass was so small it was noticeable by its sparkling rather than its size.

Poppy hurried over and tapped the top three times. The sand poured into the bottom half so fast it had all run through by the time Poppy straightened up again. He grinned and held it out towards Sam. "Ah, it seems there was a little blockage at the neck. Oh, look! Now I've cleared it, it seems the debt has been paid already. How quickly those minutes seemed to pass!"

"That's a start. Where are they?"

"Who?"

"The slaves, the ones I tried to save. I want you to bring them here."

"Oh, *those* slaves!" He tittered. "I've grown so tired of them. I don't suppose you'd like to take them off my hands? I'd be so delighted if you could."

"Stop stalling."

Poppy twisted to look for the faerie. It had gathered a clump of grass together to hide behind. "See to it!" He smiled at Sam again. "It seems you've... risen in the Worlds. Of course, I always suspected there was something special about you. My favourite wouldn't care about just any mundane."

"Bullshit," Sam said. "You had no idea and don't try to say otherwise."

Poppy's laugh was weak and unconvincing. He flung the hourglass up into the air and it turned into a cluster of poppy petals that settled at his feet. He twisted his cane and attempted another smile. "Not long now."

The slaves soon came into sight and Sam went towards them, closing the distance as fast as he could. They were dressed in poppy petals clinging to their bodies, leaving no curve undescribed. They looked healthier than the last time he saw them, but far from happy.

"I really am going to rescue you this time," he said to them, but none of them looked convinced.

He knelt in front of Clare and pulled at a poppy petal clinging to her ankle, covering the sparkling band he knew was there. As soon as his fingers touched the petal's softness all of the others fell. It revealed the band marking her slavery, but also every other inch of her body. Sam kept his eyes fixed on her ankle, muttering an apology, but she seemed unconcerned. None of the others seemed to react either. Perhaps they were too beautiful to be bashful.

He worked the fingers of both hands under the band and it lost its diamond sheen. When he pulled outwards it snapped like it was made of baked clay. Clare shuddered, took a deep breath and looked around her as if she'd just woken up. Then she blushed and accepted the blacksmith's apron Sam offered, giving him a grateful smile. Sam didn't have enough items of clothing for all of them, so he called to the Prince and asked for something to protect their modesty before he broke the spell on them too. He didn't want anything belonging to Poppy to touch them again.

Soon they were all free and wrapped in green blankets made of the softest moss imaginable. Sam faced Poppy again. "Why couldn't they eat or drink in Mundanus before?"

Poppy twisted the cane as if he were trying to screw it into wood. "Well... I suppose there could have been a teeny tiny curse put on them – I hear it happens to mortals when they visit here. But now you've touched them they'll be free to eat and drink whatever horrors are in Mundanus."

Sam grinned at Clare as they all thanked him. She went to embrace him but he stepped back. "Let's wait until you're not wearing a magic blanket, eh?" He called the Prince over again. "Could you get them all back home in Mundanus and guarantee that no one does anything to them on the way?"

"It would be my pleasure," the Prince said. "They will be given into the care of one of the most trustworthy mortals I know, and conveyed to wherever they wish in Mundanus without any Charms cast upon them."

"Because I'll hear of it, if anything does happen to them."

"You have my word that it will be done as you wish."

Poppy was watching the Prince's deference with great interest, but said nothing. Sam told the group to make sure they had each other's contact details before they parted ways and that he'd be in touch as soon as he was home. No doubt his army of staff would be able to track Clare down and from her he could find the others. "Don't mention me to anyone," he added.

The Prince led them away and Sam breathed in deeply, newly aware – by virtue of its absence – of the weight he'd been carrying since he'd failed to rescue them the first time.

Not only were they going to be reunited with their families, he was never going to be summoned and messed about by Poppy again. He was no longer afraid.

"Well, if that's everything…" Poppy took a step away.

"There's just one more thing, Poppy," Sam said, enjoying the fear that crossed the Fae's face in response.

Poppy clasped his hands together, dropping the cane as his face twisted with anguish. "I had no idea what she would wish for, truly – how could I? And I did all I could to divert her energies. I told her to paint! It isn't my fault the wish will come true now!"

Sam frowned. "You're talking about Cathy?"

"Yes, my favourite! I had no idea what potential lay beneath the damage and layers of insecurities and self-doubt and misery caused by her–" he stopped. "That is what you meant by 'one more thing', isn't it?"

"What will happen now the wish is going to come true?" When Poppy hesitated Sam took a step towards him.

Poppy shrank back. "She'll destroy everything!"

"She made a wish to do that?"

"She wished to reach her true potential and that's what it is! But don't tell anyone, especially her husband! He'll only tell–" he lowered his voice to a whisper "–her new patron, and he wouldn't have to wait for their child, he'd be able to take what he needs from *her*. He knows what potential she has, but he doesn't think her capable of bringing it to fruition. But I've made that possible." He covered his mouth with his hands and spoke through his fingers. "It's exquisitely terrifying. I haven't been so excited in such a long time."

"Is she in any danger?"

"No, she made a very clever wish. It really wasn't my fault."

Sam decided he would ask Cathy; he was planning to see

her anyway. "The last thing I want from you is the memory you took from me the first time I came here."

"That little thing?" Poppy pulled his cane from the ground and took another step back. The faerie, which had been hidden behind him, zinged off into the distance. "It's not worth your trouble to–"

"Poppy, give it back to me, or I'll take it from you."

"I have no idea how to give it back to you, now that you break–"

Sam launched himself at Poppy's throat, unable to stomach being messed about a moment longer. They both crashed to the ground, Poppy screeching for help and flailing ineffectually as the urge to push Sam away warred with the one to avoid any contact.

Sam could feel the skin of Poppy's neck beneath his hands. It was cold and didn't feel like the throat of a man, being disturbingly free of the feel of an Adam's apple and muscles beneath the skin. Instead, it felt more like holding a pillow stuffed full of down; too soft and with too much give. He could crush it, he realised, but wasn't convinced it would choke the Fae like it would choke a man.

"Give it back to me, or I'll drag you to the Prince and tell him you've been uncooperative."

"You're burning me!" Poppy wailed and then coughed so hard his entire body shook.

A wisp of smoke with hints of gold and green in its tendrils escaped with the next cough and before he could move away, Sam breathed it in. Appalled by the thought of it, he released Poppy's neck and clambered off him, leaving the Fae to moan quietly.

Then he was with Leanne, laughing so hard they were holding each other up as Pete kept asking what a douchebag was, over and over again. They were drunk but not too much, and Leanne's hair was flowing back in the breeze.

Then Sam was on his knees in Exilium, and he drew in a harsh breath to stop the grief from flooding out of him. Poppy hadn't just taken a memory of a perfect afternoon, he'd stolen the meaning of the photo in the hall of their house, the reminder to fight for the marriage even when Leanne was moving on.

But he couldn't let it overwhelm him then and there. Sam forced himself onto his feet and went back to where Poppy lay with his fingers gingerly exploring the skin on his neck. "If you ever come near me again, or try to fuck up my life ever again, I'll make a cage of the purest iron and lock you in it and then… I'll eat the key. The same goes for Cathy. Don't you ever do anything to her again. Understand?"

"She isn't mine any more," Poppy whispered. "You're threatening the wrong Lord." When Sam leaned towards him, he whimpered. "But I do understand your desire."

Sam walked away, free of the Fae yet burdened by grief. He had to see Cathy safe before he could rest. He couldn't save his wife but he could save his friend and that would have to be enough.

24

Max and the gargoyle looked down at the Chapter Master's body, watching the thin trickle of blood run from the wound on the back of his head. They were in his office, having followed him back into the Nether from the mundane park. Max didn't realise the gargoyle would hit him that hard.

"Is he dead?" the gargoyle asked.

Max felt for a pulse, found it. "No."

The gargoyle's shoulders dropped a couple of inches. "We've crossed a line, haven't we?"

Max nodded. "Now we're here, we need to make it count for something. Every Master has a means to get to their Sorcerer's house in the case of an emergency. We need to find it."

"Will it be an Opener?"

"Probably," Max replied. He wasn't sure how else a Way could be opened by anyone other than a Sorcerer, using legal magic at least.

They both began to rifle through drawers in the desk and then in the cabinets behind them. It was a modest office, decorated with a few paintings of seascapes. The desk was free of personal effects. A tidy man.

"Nothing." The gargoyle abandoned searching the drawers and instead began to sniff about the room. It lifted the corner of the rug with a claw, then pulled the whole thing aside with an excited flourish, revealing nothing but floorboards. With a disappointed snort it moved back towards the desk as Max completed his search of the last filing cabinet.

"It might be something hidden in one of the walls, or even the door." Max checked the doorknob but it was only what it appeared to be. There was nothing but wall behind the paintings and thick curtains.

"Hang on," the gargoyle said. It was sniffing the desk.

"I checked the drawers," Max said.

"Did you check the hidden one?"

The gargoyle reached underneath and there was a quiet click. The top centre panel of the desk slid back, explaining why the desk was so free of the usual objects people filled them with.

"Rookie error." The gargoyle grinned at him. "Fancy missing the old hidden-desk-compartment trick."

Max ignored the teasing and reached inside, closing his fingers around a standard doorknob-shaped Opener. It had the usual pin that would be easy to stick into any surface and enough formulae to convince him it was the one they were looking for.

He went to the wall next to the window and lined the pin up ready to push in. "Ready?"

The gargoyle came to his side. "Wait a sec. What if we go through and the evil apprentice is there, ready to kill us?"

"If it is one of Dante's apprentices, he'll think only the Chapter Master can come through this way, and he wouldn't without sending word ahead. He'll be caught off guard."

"So I just go for him, knock him out and we drag him to Ekstrand? No, hang on, that won't work, will it?"

Max shook his head. "No. If he's involved in something as dodgy as all this, he'll be protected. Most Sorcerers are anyway. The best scenario is that we get into his house and find some evidence to prove to Ekstrand that the Sorcerer of Mercia is innocent. If the apprentice is there, we should leave straightaway and get Ekstrand." He paused. "Maybe we should just do that anyway."

"No way!" the gargoyle said. "First, we'd have to explain how we got this Opener and second, there's no guarantee he'd do anything. I mean, he doubted us before, what's to say he wouldn't do it again? And anyway, it's Sunday, and he's batshit on Sundays. Well, more batshit than usual. We've got to do this now."

"Will a few days make a difference?"

"They could to the Sorcerer of Mercia! Hell, if we wait, Mercia might kill Ekstrand before he's useful again."

Max nodded and pushed the pin into the wall. He twisted the doorknob and the burning outline appeared of a Way being created.

"I'm scared," the gargoyle whispered as the door appeared.

"It won't serve us now," Max replied. "Focus on the goal."

He opened the door and a large hallway stretched ahead of them, containing an impressive staircase that split into two smaller ones halfway up to reach the upper floors. It looked like a wing of the house stretched to either side. It was a substantial property and far more extravagant than Ekstrand's Georgian mansion.

Max pulled out the Opener, let the gargoyle go through and then went through himself, keeping the Opener in his hand in case they needed to leave in a hurry. He waited a moment, expecting an assistant or butler to challenge them, but no one came. He turned to see a normal front door now the Way had gone.

The gargoyle was sniffing again. "No one's been here for a long time," it said. "The air is too stale."

"I doubt there have been any visitors since whatever happened to Dante happened," Max said. "Let's see if we can find a part of the house that's still in use."

"Maybe the dodgy apprentice doesn't live here any more." The gargoyle sounded hopeful.

They took a wing each, only Max's shoes making a gentle clicking sound. The house was silent enough to suggest it was empty and they tried each door on the ground floor of both wings in turn. All were locked. The marble tiles were dulled by dust and, the further they went from the large windows in the central hallway, the darker it got. There were candles in the chandeliers, but they too were dusty.

Max went back to the staircase and the gargoyle reported the same as he had seen. They climbed the stairs together, the gargoyle's ears twitching.

They split up again to search the upper floor of the two wings. Again, locked doors and dust. They regrouped and went back downstairs, Max keen to find the kitchen and see if there was any sign of servants. There was none.

"Bugger," the gargoyle said as they went back to the entrance hall. "Of course this dodgy apprentice wouldn't stay here, not when he could be found by the Chapter Master. This is all a bloody waste of time. I gave that bloke a concussion for nothing."

They stood at the bottom of the staircase. Max wondered if it was safe to use his own Opener to go straight from the house to Aquae Sulis. If the culprit returned, would he be able to trace their destination? He wasn't sure if it left a residue. He looked up the staircase and saw a large window they'd passed without even looking outside. It was a habit of living in the Nether; one got used to there being nothing to look out at. "There may be outbuildings," he said. "I'll go and–"

The gargoyle was already bounding up the stairs. "There's a great big bloody tower!" It pointed out of the window with a claw. "And there's a light on at the top!"

Max didn't need to look out of the window to see the tower, seeing it through the gargoyle's gaze. It looked like a turret of a castle but was unattached to any other building or curtain wall. It was close enough to walk to without risking getting lost in the mists.

"This house must have been where the apprentices lived and had their lessons, and where Dante met with the Chapter Master," he theorised. "That tower might be his private residence."

"Do you think the other apprentices are dead?" The gargoyle was peeping over the sill more cautiously.

"Probably."

"Are we going to risk going to the tower?"

"Yes," Max replied. There was a direction they could approach from without being overlooked from one of the tower windows.

"But won't it be warded to hell and locked and really dangerous?"

"Probably."

The gargoyle padded down the stairs. "If I could, I'd be shitting pebbles."

"Let's go now, it won't get any less risky."

They broke out of the locked house and made their way to the tower, taking care to keep out of the line of sight of any of the arrow-slit windows on the top floor. It was four storeys high and the top floor's narrow windows glowed with a pale light. It had a larger diameter than the average castle tower and Max wondered where its anchor was.

"I'll try the door," the gargoyle volunteered as they reached it. "You know, in case it's designed to burn people who aren't evil."

"I'm not certain that would be one of the criteria written into the formulae," Max said but let the gargoyle do as it had offered.

The door opened inwards. "Well, blow me down," the gargoyle said. "It's not even locked."

"All the people who knew it's here are probably dead," Max said. "After you."

The gargoyle went inside, paused to see if it collapsed into dust or spontaneously combusted, and, when neither happened, beckoned Max onwards. Max pulled out his penlight torch and switched it on. There was a staircase curving upwards and one that went down.

"Wait here," the gargoyle whispered. It took the torch and went downstairs.

Max saw an image of a small kitchen, untidy and recently used. The gargoyle sniffed at a small puddle of milk on the table. It was fresh. No one else was there. Dante's murderer was satisfied with fending for himself, it seemed.

Once the gargoyle was back with him, Max hooked his walking stick over his arm and climbed the stone steps until he reached a wooden door into the room on the next floor. It too was unlocked and there was a lantern hanging from a hook just inside the door. After a brief sweep over the room with the torch to check it really was empty, Max took a moment to light the candle inside.

The room contained a couple of armchairs, a single bookcase crafted to fit the curve of the wall, and a fireplace. There was a table, again curved, upon which were piled all manner of artefacts. Max recognised Peepers and Sniffers from his own Chapter, presumably looted from the cloister. They looked the same as the ones in his pockets and – something he hadn't appreciated before – distinct in design from others on the table. They had the same function, but side by side it was clear that each Sorcerer had his own design.

There were several items the likes of which he'd never seen before, things he assumed weren't tools used by Arbiters but personal artefacts made by and for the Sorcerers themselves. Max took care not to touch them; that lesson had been burned in deep by his training. One Opener had several interlocking circles embedded in the doorknob and upon inspection Max found they could be moved to spell out the principle cities of the Heptarchy: Bath, London, Oxford, York, Norwich, Colchester, Winchester and Canterbury. He'd only ever used an Opener that was keyed for a specific location, or could open a Way into the Nether version of the anchor property he was already at; not one that could open Ways to multiple locations. Useful. He wondered which Sorcerer it had belonged to.

"We shouldn't get distracted," the gargoyle said.

It climbed the next section of the stone staircase a few steps ahead of him, paused to listen at the next door and then looked through a keyhole. The room beyond was empty, so it opened the door and they crept inside.

The first thing Max noticed was the lack of any more steps. He looked at the ceiling, searching for a trapdoor and signs of a ladder, but there were neither, only thick wooden boards. Even though the floor above appeared to be lit and presumably occupied, there were no sounds of anyone's footsteps, not even a creak. There was a lantern but he didn't want to light it when they were so close to the room above.

"Shine the torch down again," the gargoyle whispered and Max did so.

The circle of light picked out a wardrobe, a washstand, a mirror and a bed. On top of the bed's rumpled sheets were several items of clothing.

Women's clothing.

Max saw a bra, petticoat, skirt and blouse. He swept the room for any sign of male clothing but there was none. The gargoyle went silently to the wardrobe and opened it slowly, lest its door creak. Only women's clothing hung inside.

"I don't understand," he said as the gargoyle closed the wardrobe again. "How could a woman be behind this?"

It was one of the fundamental rules of the sorcerous arts: never teach a woman the secrets of sorcery. He recalled people at the Cloister speculating about the reasons why, and the confusion caused by the fact Ekstrand had a female librarian. The distrust, the refusal to contemplate a woman being a Sorcerer – or an Arbiter for that matter – was universally accepted in his world and yet they were some of the best researchers he'd worked with.

"Perhaps Dante fell in love," the gargoyle suggested. "With the wrong kind of woman."

Max tried to reconcile what he knew. The perpetrator was a master of sorcery and Fae magic and female. Was she Fae-touched? It would explain how she knew of Lady Rose and how she would have the means to contact her and make the deal Thorn had told him about. Had one of them managed to infiltrate Dante's household? It would explain the corruption – but then surely they would have engineered the protection of only their own family from the Arbiters in London, not many families over the years. Why favour the Irises now?

"There's something over here." The gargoyle was on the far side of the room and Max sought it out with the torchlight. It was standing beside a painting, one of a man and a woman sitting close together, looking at each other lovingly. Max recognised the man from the body he saw after the Moot: Dante. The woman had the same colour hair and too similar a mouth for her to be anything but his sister. They appeared to be very close in age.

The frame had something embedded in the centre below the painting and Max went closer to inspect it. A small dome of glass enclosed two locks of hair twisted around each other. He went to the bed and scoured the pillows until he found a long strand the same dark blond as the subjects of the painting. He didn't need to hold the strand next to the locks to see they were the same.

"Dante's sister," he said, and then gave the torch to the gargoyle to hold whilst he put the strand in an evidence bag pulled from his pocket and then tucked both away.

"She murdered her own brother?"

"Perhaps. Or perhaps he died of natural causes."

"And she preserved his body for later use?" The gargoyle shook its head. "No way."

Max gave the room another sweep with the torchlight but still couldn't find any way out other than the staircase they'd climbed up.

"So…" The gargoyle came to his side. "Now we know who's been causing all the trouble, we can report back to Ekstrand, right?"

"Wrong," Max replied, examining the ceiling again. "We know who but we don't know why."

"That's obvious: to be the last Sorcerer."

"But why?"

"To be the most powerful."

"But what for?"

"Umm… isn't that enough?"

Max looked at the gargoyle, giving up on finding a secret ceiling hatch. "People want power for a reason. What does she want to do with it? What's the point of being the only Sorcerer unless you want to do something that the other Sorcerers would prevent?"

"Isn't being a female Sorcerer exactly that? If they found out about her, they'd kill her. There you go: perfect motive. Now let's get out of here."

"Not until I know what's going on up there."

The gargoyle's eyes followed Max's finger upwards. "Bollocks."

"There has to be a way to get to that floor. Have a look around."

As the gargoyle sniffed, Max looked at the painting again, examining the details of their clothing and the room in the background. It looked like it had been painted a long time ago, but he couldn't put a date to it, not being an expert on such things.

"Look, even if we do find a way up there," the gargoyle whispered in his ear, "look at the size of this place. No way we can walk in without being seen or heard."

"I'd rather peep than walk in," Max said. "I just need something to use the Peeper on."

"I reckon it's that." The gargoyle jabbed a claw at the painting and Max nodded.

Carefully he swung the frame to one side and then the other. The wall was intact behind it. He ran his fingers around its edge, feeling for a button or depression of some kind that could trigger something. He found nothing and took a step back, shaking his head.

The gargoyle went close up to it, sniffing it like a dog would a table of food, and then pressed the dome containing the locks of hair.

The painting, and the entire section of wall it hung upon, shimmered and, before Max realised what was happening, he and the gargoyle were looking through a Way into another circular room. Dante's sister was standing in front of a huge pane of glass, thankfully with her back to them.

She didn't react, absorbed in painting something onto the glass which seemed to be scrolling sideways by arcane means. She didn't have to move as she painted on symbols and strings of formulae; they just appeared to float away to her left, as if the glass itself was a moving portal onto another surface. She was wearing a loose white dress and was barefoot, her dark blond hair so long it reached the floor.

The scent of flowers tickled Max's nose. It was such an intense mixture he couldn't single out one in particular.

Either side of her, two large lenses were held in ornate brass stands and seemed to be focusing light reflecting from the pane of glass to such an intensity that Max could see the light passing through them, creating the pale glow they'd seen from outside the tower. Each of the focused beams was striking the back of what looked like some sort of scrying glass, also held in their own frames a few feet above the ground. Each scrying glass then had a modern digital camera on a tripod pointed at it, and, judging from the small viewscreen on each one, they were filming what was being displayed on the scrying glasses.

At first Max thought the scrying glasses were simply displaying a copy of what she was painting onto the glass, but then he realised the background was different in each one.

The mirror on the left showed the outside of Ekstrand's anchor property in Bath, while the one on the right showed the exterior of the Bodleian Library in Oxford, the Sorcerer of Mercia's anchor property. In both images, the formulae were appearing on the walls of the buildings, a couple of feet above the ground, just for a second or so before fading from sight.

Another movement in the one displaying the Bodleian quadrangle made him focus on it. A man in a black coat and black bowler hat had noticed something happening to the wall. An Arbiter. He pulled out a mobile phone, pressed a button and then dropped dead, in the way Max imagined his colleagues had when the Chapter was attacked and the soul jars destroyed.

It was all Max had a chance to take in before the gargoyle yanked him away. The Way closed again but the gargoyle didn't let go of Max's arm, pulling him to the steps and not letting go until they were in the room below.

Max leaned against the wall, waiting for the residual panic to pass that had leached through from the contact with the gargoyle. The gargoyle was still caught up in it, grasping the sides of its head and pacing up and down silently, thanks to the formulae in its bracers.

"She's going to kill them!"

"I know." Max got his Opener out of his pocket and then went to the table to find the other one he'd spotted before.

"Oh, shit, this is terrible! She killed that Arbiter – the whole Chapter's probably gone down! She's turning their hearts into stone, isn't she?"

"The spell was moving where she painted from left to right, which suggests it's either a very long thing to write or it needs to surround the entire building," Max said, his fingers hovering for a second above the strange Opener as he battled with his training to overcome the urge to leave it where it lay. "Ekstrand and Mercia may still be alive if the spell requires completion of the formulae."

"So you want us to go back up there and... what? Rugby tackle her?"

"No, she'll be protected." Max knew they wouldn't have a hope; he could still remember his mentor's response when he'd asked what could be done if a Sorcerer needed to be stopped. "You find another Sorcerer and tell him the problem," he'd said. "You think Sorcerers would let us exist if we could be a threat?"

Dante's sister knew both Fae and sorcerous magic and she'd be able to destroy the soul chain with little effort if the gargoyle went for her, meaning the end for both of them. If he went in alone there were a hundred ways she could kill him if he managed to get close to her. Even if he managed to secure a gun in time, she'd no doubt be warded against projectiles and similar forms of attack.

"I'll use my Opener to get back to Mr Ekstrand's house and get everyone out before the formulae are completed. This Opener looks like it can get into Oxford." Max picked it up and showed it to the gargoyle. "The Bodleian Library quadrangle is in the centre of the city, it's likely to open a way near there. You go and find the Oxford Arbiter's body. He'll have a means to go back to his Cloister – use it to get to the Sorcerer of Mercia–"

"No." The gargoyle snatched Max's Opener from his hand. "No way you're going to Ekstrand, flesh-boy, your heart will be turned to stone. Only I can go through."

"But there's only one of you. There's not enough time. One of them will die."

The gargoyle nodded. "I know. So which one are we going to save?"

25

Margritte stood outside the large black box, twisting the key Rupert had given her. It looked bizarre beneath the beautiful vaulted ceiling of the Divinity Schools. There was no door, neither were there windows. He'd said it wouldn't run out of air inside, that he'd thought of that. As long as they fed and watered him, he'd said, William Iris would last as long as they wanted.

As long as they wanted. She shivered, finding such power over a man's life unpalatable. Across the city three families had been taken from their homes and put into custody, just because they were Irises. They had children. They were probably terrified.

She'd made it all happen. At the beginning it had all made sense, but now it felt like some terrible accident unfolding around her.

"Do you want me to go in there with you, Maggie?" Rupert called from the doorway to Convocation House. "I already sent an Arbiter in there, he can't hurt you."

"No," she said. "I just need a minute."

He lingered, watching her hesitation, and it made her feel more flustered. It was too late now. She couldn't tell him to send William back home and carry on as if nothing had happened. She pressed the key against the black glass and it sank in, a keyhole forming around it. She opened the door that appeared moments later, keeping the key in the palm of her hand in case she needed to get out again quickly. If she turned it to the right once she was inside it would let her back into the larger room she was in now. If she turned it to the left, it would open a Way to her room at Lincoln. She had the feeling he was trying to be thoughtful, in his own strange way. She just hoped he hadn't made another to take him directly to her room whenever he wanted.

The light that spilled in from the new doorway was the only light in the box. It was the size of a very small room and the air smelt stale and laced with sweat.

William was sitting on a chair next to a small table. His lip and right eye were swollen and it looked like his hands were tied behind his back. There was an empty chair across from him.

"Light," she said and, as Rupert had promised, the ceiling shone, bathing the interior in a blue-white glow. She let the door close behind her and, as expected, its outline disappeared until there was a smooth surface once more.

William stared at her as she approached the empty chair. "You'll forgive me if I don't stand for you," he said. "I'm unable to."

She suppressed the urge to apologise or show any of her doubts. He would exploit any weakness. "It's within your power to improve your circumstances," she said as she sat opposite him.

"What have you done, Margritte? How did you persuade a Sorcerer to do this?"

"I simply told him the truth."

"Whose truth?"

"He knows you're in league with the Sorcerer of Wessex, he knows about Lord Iris' plan and your part in it. Of course he got involved."

"I have no idea what you're talking about but I do know what the ramifications of this will be, and none of them bodes well for you."

"You're the one in the worse position here, William. Your threats lose their power when you're just a boy in a box."

"My family will–"

"I don't want to talk about your family, I want to talk about what you need to do to get out. I'm sure you're keen for that to happen."

"I want to know one thing first. Did Cathy know what you planned to do?"

She considered lying to him, the angry, shadowy part of herself hoping it would fill him with despair to think he couldn't even trust his own wife. But she couldn't do that to Catherine, not now she knew how she felt about the cause. She couldn't destroy any more lives. "No," she said.

"So you exploited her better nature and betrayed her trust. I thought more of you."

Margritte curled her toes inside her shoes, focusing her anger into the movement to keep it from her face. It hurt because he was right. "You know my husband didn't try to kill her. All I want is for you to clear his name in front of the Court. It's not too much to ask. I shouldn't even have to, in fact. If you were as decent as Catherine seems to have deluded herself into believing, you would have done so already."

William's laugh was bitter. "You want me to clear your family's name when you've sunk to this? Kidnapping a Duke, destroying his possessions – including his wedding ring – locking him in a box with no food, no water for God knows how long, beating him, tying him to a chair? Do you even know where the moral high ground is any more?"

Margritte took a moment to breathe in as a burst of panic threatened to take her. "If you don't do this, I will invite the Patroons to Oxenford and cast a Truth Charm on you in their presence. You will be forced to confess–"

"They wouldn't come!" William laughed again. "You did all this to threaten me with that? What fantasy world do you live in? If they answered your demand they would be sanctioning this barbaric behaviour. The Patroons would close rank and force you to release me."

She stood, trying to think of something to say, something to frighten him, but she was too afraid herself. So she turned her back, thrust the key into the wall and went back out into the larger room, controlling herself until the door closed behind her.

Margritte went to one of the long wooden benches and sat, wondering if she was actually going to be sick. She slid the key up her sleeve, freeing her hands so she could weep into them. She should have gone abroad until the madness of her grief had passed. Instead she'd sucked Rupert into the maelstrom with her, and the entire city. All of her suspicions about Ekstrand and Iris were only that; there was no proof.

"Maggie?"

Her spirits sank further as she heard Rupert coming towards her. She hurriedly wiped away the tears.

"What did he say?" His hand was on her shoulder. Really, the man was insufferable!

"Nothing." She stood to break the contact but he was boxing her in against the bench. "I... it's harder than I thought it would be."

He nodded. "I thought so. You knew him before. That's bound to make it tough."

She had to find a way to untangle the mess she'd made without making Rupert angry. He could destroy them all, including her son. "Perhaps we need to take a different approach."

He nodded. "I couldn't agree more."

Rupert went towards the box, flicked his yo-yo at one of the sides and a door opened again. She hurried after him, fearful.

"Morning."

William watched him warily, the cockiness gone. Rupert was trying to make him feel disoriented; it was evening in Oxford.

"Good morning."

"So, I take it Margritte has explained what she wants from you?"

William nodded slowly. His lip had split and Margritte tried not to look at it. Rupert hadn't mentioned any violence. Had he provoked the Arbiter? Were they trying to frighten him?

"I refuse. This is no way to treat a Duke. I won't be coerced into anything."

"But that's what happens to you all the time, isn't it?" Rupert turned the chair around and straddled it, resting his arms on the back. "Your Patroons and patrons tell you what to do all the fucking time. Shit, I really hope you were coerced into killing Bartholomew, for your sake. Otherwise you wanted to kill him to take the throne. You don't want me to think that's true, do you?"

"I have no interest in what you think I may or may not have done. It's none of your business."

Rupert chuckled and fired a grin at Margritte who had retreated to a corner after the door closed behind her. "I like him. Cool under pressure, like all of the Irises. And–" he turned back to face William "–like all of the Irises in Oxenford, you're also in a box of my making. Now listen to me, Dukey-boy, there are two ways we can do this. One is like gentlemen, I'll even put on a posh voice so you feel at home. We can have tea and crumpets, laugh about who's just been rogered up the arse by who, and then you can sign a statement that clears Bartholomew's name and read it out in Convocation and in the Londinium Court. We could do that right now, and you'll be home in time for tea."

"No."

"All right, well, the second option is that I leave you in this box for a few days. I'll break up the sensory deprivation with periods of unpredictable loud noise that will only start when you fall asleep. After a week or so with no rest, no food, no fucking toilet, let's face it, you're going to be much more willing to meet Margritte's very reasonable request."

William looked at Margritte. "You want him to do this in your name?"

"I think I'm being one generous motherfucker." Rupert didn't let her reply. "I could torture you in ways your family haven't even discovered yet. And the longer you go on being an asshole about all this, the more likely that's going to happen."

"What have you offered him to make him do this?" William asked her and Rupert punched him so hard his chair fell back, taking William with it.

Rupert shoved the table to one side and grabbed William's lapels. "Listen to me, you misogynistic little shit. It may come as news to you but men can decide to help a woman because they think her argument is correct, not because she has different genitalia and has offered to do something with them. Don't insult my intelligence by making out that I'm incapable of making decisions without thinking about sex. That's fucking offensive, to me and to Margritte."

William coughed and blood splattered over Rupert's jumper. "There's more to this than Bartholomew."

"Yes, there is, but it isn't any promises of sex. Your patron is working with Ekstrand. I want you to tell me what he wants you to do and why."

There was a look of genuine confusion on William's face. "I have no idea why you think Ekstrand has anything to do with me."

"You helped him get the Master of Ceremonies back to Aquae Sulis."

"I helped an Arbiter get into a party, that's all. I made the people there think I did more to protect the identity of the person who really did help to rescue him. Now, will you please untie me or let me sit upright at least? I apologise for my remark, Margritte, but, for reasons I'm sure I don't have to explain, I'm feeling rather bad-tempered."

She waited for Rupert to meet with his request but he did nothing so she went behind William's back and untied his hands. Rupert frowned as she did so, but said nothing.

"This has gone far enough," she said, helping William to his feet. "Rupert, whilst I appreciate your sentiments, punching a man when you declare yourself to be above male stereotypes is hardly a way to prove the point." She righted William's chair and helped him to sit down. "I can't bear this to go on a moment longer. I was... and still am devastated by what you did, William, but all I wanted was to correct the injustice committed against my husband. I've gone about it the wrong way. How can I watch you be beaten and terrorised into doing what I want in Bartholomew's name? If he were to see me now and what damage I've wrought, he would be just as disgusted with me as I am of myself."

"Maggie, he–"

She held up a hand. "I'm sorry, Rupert, but this has to stop and I have to apologise to the Irises. I take full responsibility for my actions."

"So you're going to let him go back and sit on Bartholomew's throne and–"

"He sits on his own throne now. Nothing will bring Bartholomew back to me. I see no reason to carry on infecting everything and everyone around me with the madness of my grief."

William reached out and rested a hand on her arm. "I beg your forgiveness, Madam. I know your husband was a decent man. I was led to believe he wasn't and, like you, I acted swiftly in anger and filled with the desire to take revenge. I swear to you that I only discovered his innocence after the deed was done. It's something I'll regret for the rest of my life."

Margritte's legs wobbled beneath her, so she knelt on the floor in front of him, the black satin of her skirts disappearing against the black floor. "Who did it?"

"The Roses. When Thorn attacked Cathy he disguised himself to look like a minor Rosa, whom Cornelius White killed. He told me it was because he discovered he'd been hired by Bartholomew to kill Cathy. An Arbiter backed up the story and together I found their false evidence irrefutable. Lord Iris supported me but gave me no opportunity to calm down or uncover their lies. Once I learned of what they did, I killed Cornelius and banished Amelia to Mundanus. I'm so sorry."

The hard stone of rage-filled grief that had sat in Margritte's chest for so long burst and she couldn't help but sob. Bartholomew had been nothing more than a cog in a political machine, one that was pulled out to make something else break. No wonder William hadn't said anything; his own patron was part of the reason he'd rushed into challenging Bartholomew. Admitting he'd been tricked would reveal that Lord Iris had also been duped by the Roses – a family already broken – and William's life would be forfeit. They were all victims, in their own way, and the thought fuelled her grief. What else could William have done, believing Bartholomew had attempted to kill his wife? She'd done the same as him: acted without knowing all the facts, driven by passion and rage.

"I accept your apology," she said as the worst of the rush of emotion subsided. "And I offer you mine. I'll see that this is put right and I'll answer for my rash act."

"Now just wait a bloody minute," Rupert said. "The Irises won't just accept an apology, they'll want blood!"

"So be it," she said. She wasn't afraid to admit she'd made a mistake.

"Don't give me that noble bullshit! And anyway, he's my prisoner and I'm not letting him go until I'm certain he's not–"

A Way opened behind William, making her jump to her feet in surprise, William too. The gargoyle that she'd seen in the film of the Moot leaped through, looking left and right with urgency as it took the room in. "I'm here to get you out!" it yelled.

"I don't need to be rescued," William said. "It's all–"

"Not you! Him!" The gargoyle pointed at Rupert. "All of you, actually, if you don't want to die."

"I can't trust you, you're one of Ekstrand's–" Rupert began, readying his yo-yo.

"Dante's sister is about to kill everyone in this building," the gargoyle cut in. "Your Arbiters are dead. Now let's get out of here before you are too!" When Rupert hesitated, the gargoyle leaped onto the table. "Open a Way into Oxford, you idiot! We can't go the way I came, they're all dead in the Cloister already."

"I'm not going anywhere with you," Rupert said to it and then looked at Margritte, but she knew where she was going and it wasn't with either of them. She thrust the key into the nearest part of the wall and turned it to the left, opening a Way to her room. She reached for William's hand, he took it and she pulled him through, leaving Rupert to determine his own fate.

26

Cathy parked the car half a mile down the road from the gates to the asylum. She and Carter walked on to the entrance in the deepening twilight, silent for the first time in their journey. She'd talked so much on the drive from London that her throat felt sore. Excited by his change in status, Carter had bombarded her with questions and between them they'd drawn up a list of rights to announce to the staff once they got home.

She was grateful for something to keep her mind busy. Now she was just walking along a road her thoughts were tugged back to Will. The steward reported that he and his men had reached the hotel but never left and he'd ended up carrying out a rather hasty clean-up by Charming the staff on duty to believe that the group had paid and left to avoid any difficult enquiries.

There was nothing she could do to help, as Nathaniel had so forcefully said, so she had to keep her mind on the things she could change. She looked at Carter, who looked back and smiled. "Are you ready for this?"

"Yes, your Grace. Are you?"

She grinned. "Hell, yes."

They reached the gates and Carter had a quick look first. "We should walk along the boundary and approach across the grass over there, your Grace. It minimises the chance of us being seen before I cut the phone line."

She nodded and followed him in, noticing the orchids growing at the boundary between the trees and the lawn. She wondered if they had something to do with the disorientation she'd experienced on her earlier visit. Not that it mattered now; they weren't going to leave by the driveway.

Carter guided her along the best route, pointed out a place for her to hide whilst he cut the phone line, and then beckoned her over to the house. Lights were on inside, on both floors, and she saw the curtains being closed by the orderlies.

When they reached the front door and she held her finger above the bell, the doubts flooded in. Would the Patroons send people to stop what she was doing? Will would probably be furious when he got back... could she–

"Stop it," she whispered to herself, to the frightened child inside her still fearful of getting a beating for putting a foot wrong in a dance lesson. "This is the right thing to do."

She pressed the doorbell and listened to it clang inside. With one last glance at Carter, who seemed rather excited, she tried to prepare for what lay ahead.

Will let himself be pulled through into a room that smelt of freshly baked bread. As Margritte closed the Way behind them he noticed a painting over the fireplace with black silk draped over it, and the same drapes over the sprite lamps in the room, creating a dour atmosphere. There was fresh bread and butter, along with a glass of milk on a tray. His stomach rumbled.

"Please, sit," Margritte said and busied herself with buttering some bread after handing him the glass of milk.

He drank it all without pausing for breath, the cold glass soothing his throbbing lip. He took the plate she offered him, and the handkerchief. When he ran it around his mouth it came away red. He noticed the time on a grandfather clock in the corner. "Is it really morning?"

"No, he was just trying to disorient you. You were in there for about four hours. I'm sorry they hurt you." She went to the window, still sniffing. "Do you have any idea what that gargoyle was talking about?"

"No."

"I'll do everything I can to put this right, William. It got out of hand."

He nodded. "I know. We both will."

"We need to go to the Hebdomadal Council," she said after a few moments. "They'll be debating what to do next. We need to go there together and explain it's all... resolved between us." She turned to face him. "I am right in saying that, aren't I?"

"Yes." He stood, aching all over, his legs and arms trembling with fatigue and the residue of adrenalin that had rampaged through his body. "I forgive you, if you'll forgive me. I did far, far worse, of course, but they were both acts of passion, and both have far-reaching consequences. I'll make sure my family know my feelings on the matter."

She nodded. "And Bartholomew's reputation?"

"I will discuss the matter with my patron in person," he said. "If a way can be found to tell the truth without damaging Lord Iris' standing, then I'll do so. I hope, in the meantime, the knowledge that those behind this foul business have been punished will give you some peace."

Margritte's eyes were still reddened and shining with tears. "It will," she finally replied. "Are you able to walk? They'll be meeting at the Sheldonian. It's not far from here."

"I thought that was a theatre."

"It is, but it's also one of the main university meeting venues."

"And the city is run by a council?"

She pulled a shawl from a nearby chair and wrapped it around her shoulders. "Yes. It's very different to Londinium. When all of this is over, I would be delighted to explain it to you." She paused. "If I have the opportunity."

He went to her side and offered his arm. "I'll see to it that you do."

Cathy recognised the man who answered the door, but now she was dressed like a Duchess he didn't realise they'd already met. He was one of the orderlies and a big man, but not as huge as Carter – a fact he seemed to evaluate after they both stared at each other for a few moments. Cathy could almost smell the testosterone.

"My name is Catherine Reticulata-Iris and I'm the Duchess of Londinium," she said, channelling a memory of her mother at her most frightening. "I'm here to speak to the manager,"

It had the desired effect. "Come in," the man said and, as he went to a room down the hallway, Cathy exchanged a grin with Carter.

Soon after, the manager darted out, a short man with a paunch and receding hairline. A napkin was still tucked into his collar. "Your Grace?" He hurried over, tugging the napkin free and dabbing at his mouth as he walked.

"I'm here to speak to all the residents and all of the staff, yourself included. Is there a place I could address everyone?"

"This is… most irregular… We're serving dinner and–"

"Perfect. I assume everyone dines in the large hall at the end of the hallway?" He nodded, dumb with shock. "If you'd be so kind as to round everyone up? There's a good fellow."

Like her mother, like her father, like Dame bloody Iris, Cathy didn't ask for what she wanted. Instead she stated what he needed to do as if he'd already agreed. He could obey, as the social cues dictated, or he could refuse and risk embarrassment and confrontation. She held her breath, watching to see which way he would go.

"I... I need to speak to my superior."

"Is he here?"

"No, I need to make a phone call."

"That would take far too long and be most inconvenient. You don't need to phone someone to ask if one person can speak to the people here, surely? Certainly not the Duchess of Londinium."

A muscle beneath his right eye twitched. She felt sorry for him. "This way," he finally said after a glance at Carter's arms.

"Keep an eye on him," she whispered to Carter.

The manager had a brief hushed conversation with the orderly, who began to round up members of staff they came across on the way to the dining hall. Cathy's heartbeat became more frantic with every step. What if they didn't believe her? What if they laughed at her? What if her voice came out like air from a leaky balloon when she got up to speak?

But then she was in the dining hall, all of the residents assembled at long tables and the last members of staff being ushered in. She found a chair to stand on with a helping hand from Carter.

Cathy took a breath, trying to stop her knees from shaking as the assembled looked at her. There were about thirty staff and over a hundred residents and every single regarded her expectantly.

"Good evening," she began.

"Speak up!" someone called from the back.

"My name is Catherine and I'm the Duchess of Londinium. I feel you should know that, because it might make you believe that I can actually do what I'm about to." She glanced at Carter. He was busy watching the room, vigilant for foul play. "I know that many of you were put in this place against your will because you had an opinion that was dangerous to Society. I know that many of you have tried to leave and couldn't, because of a Charm placed on the boundary."

"I knew it!" a man cried out and was rapidly shushed by those around him.

"I also know that some of you are here because you need to live in Mundanus again. And I can understand that. But I don't think you should be confined to one part of it, and I don't think anyone has the right to keep anyone here who doesn't want to be, regardless of why you ended up here in the first place."

The room was silent, every face fixed intently upon her. The manager was drained of colour, nurses and orderlies gathered around him. Some looked terrified.

"And I say this to the staff too. There's more to life than doing what they've told you to do. You should have choices and you should have rights as employees. The right to earn wages, to resign and do something totally different with your life if that's what you want. I know how the Agency works now and it's wrong to just let them use you like slaves."

The staff looked at each other and then to the manager.

An elderly woman caught Cathy's eye, smiling away like she was watching a fabulous play. "Go on," the lady mouthed to her.

"I'm going to open a Way to my house in Londinium. Anyone who wishes to leave this place may come with me. I'll give you somewhere to stay that's safe from the Agency so you can decide what you want to do with your lives. If you don't want to leave Mundanus, that's fine – come with me and you can stay in the mundane wing of the house. I'll help each and every one of you to find a way to be independent if that's what you wish. No one has the right to keep you here. No one has the right to tell you how to live and no one has the right to control what you say or think. So I say... sod them! Let's find our own way. Who's coming with me?"

The streets of Oxenford were deserted, something Will found rather disconcerting. He was surrounded by the most beautiful architecture, reminding him of Aquae Sulis with its warm sand-coloured stone and neo-classical grandeur, but without people promenading and eager to be seen in their finery.

"Is it always this quiet here?"

The clip of Margritte's shoes echoed from the walls as they hurried down a narrow street, wide enough for only one carriage. "No."

"Who sits on this council? Anyone who'll be sympathetic?"

"To me or to you?"

"You," he replied. She was the one at risk; she'd convinced the Sorcerer to take not only him but several other members of the Iris family into custody. He had no idea what the Council was like, nor the kind of justice they dispensed, but suspected she'd be exiled from the city at the very least.

"My son is the Vice-Chancellor," she said.

"And the Chancellor, is he a reasonable man?"

She didn't reply. The narrow lane opened out onto a wider street and she guided him to the right. His ankle was throbbing but he could limp along well enough. He wanted to go home and have a brandy and a meal and put it all behind him.

In moments a curved building came into view on the right, surrounded by a set of high railings punctuated by stone pillars. On top of each one was a carved bust but Will didn't stop to examine them. He was too busy trying to think of a way to bring Margritte out of the situation unscathed. If they exiled her, he'd take her back to Londinium. He wondered whether anyone had noticed he and his men hadn't returned. Unlikely, if it was only the evening. He looked at his ring finger and the dried blood. There were still splinters to be pulled out. He thought back to when he felt it hurt when Cathy was attacked. Was she aware something had happened to him? Was Lord Iris aware?

As they reached the doors they both heard someone shouting within.

"I demand to see the Chancellor!"

"My brother," Will said. It was going to be more complicated than he hoped. Not only would they have to placate the ruling council of Oxenford, they'd have to talk Nathaniel down from a temper. "He sounds worse than he actually is," he said to Margritte when he noticed how nervous she looked. "Don't worry, I'll make sure he sees reason. There's no point making this into something worse than it needs to be. We can discuss compensation for the Irises who reside here. It can all be fixed."

Dreadfully pale, Margritte pushed the door open and they walked in, unchallenged by any guards, which surprised Will. To get into the Londinium Court one would have to pass through several guarded points. Here, it felt like anyone could walk in off the street and straight into the presence of those in power.

They walked through one antechamber to the sound of Nathaniel demanding to be treated with respect and then Margritte opened doors onto a large D-shaped interior with seating running in a horseshoe shape around the room. There were two levels of gallery seats, marble pillars and a fresco on the ceiling with dramatic orange clouds.

At the far end of the room, a young man – who looked so like Bartholomew that Will's breath caught in his throat – was sitting in a chair at the centre of a crescent of seated gentlemen nearing twenty in number. Nathaniel was shouting at him and he didn't seem to be taking the pressure well. It looked like he was trying not to be sick.

The other men, all presumably members of the Council, were either locked in hushed discussions with each other or studiously avoiding Nathaniel's glare. No one noticed they had entered.

"Oh, no." Margritte clutched his arm. "The torches are out."

He noticed two elaborate gilded stands, one on either side of her son's chair. It looked like small baskets at the top could hold flames when lit. "Why does that matter?"

"It means the Chancellor is dead."

But Will saw something that made him far more concerned: the sword hanging from Nathaniel's waist belonged to the Patroon. Sir Iris himself must have given it to him, meaning that Nathaniel was there with his authority, and an implicit blessing to use it where he deemed fit. That the Patroon had given it to the best swordsman in Albion was a powerful statement.

"Let's sort this mess out," Margritte said and strode down the aisle to reach the Council. She walked ahead bravely as he struggled to think of a way through that would see her safe and his brother satisfied.

"Mr Reticulata-Iris, I am Margritte Semper-Augustus Tulipa and I beg your forgiveness for interrupting you. As you can see, your brother is here with me, and we are both ready to explain what happened today. Please don't see it as a sign of disrespect that only the Vice-Chancellor is here. I assure you he is the highest ranking individual in Oxenford."

Nathaniel didn't turn straightaway, forcing her to address his back most rudely. He turned slowly as she spoke of the Vice-Chancellor, fixing her with such a hateful look that his face was monstrous.

"Perhaps William can–"

Nathaniel backhanded her with such force she was knocked onto the floor and for a few moments lay there without moving. Her son cried out but when Nathaniel turned and looked at him he sank back into his chair, cowed.

Horrified, Will started to walk towards Nathaniel, hoping Margritte would stay still and let him talk his brother down. "See, I am here, Nathaniel," he said as lightly as he could. "I know passions are high, but surely we do not need to strike a woman to express ourselves?"

Nathaniel's eyes widened at the sight of him and Will remembered the bruising on his face. "My brother," he said, stepping over Margritte. "I'm so glad to see you." In seconds he had strode over to Will and planted a hand on his chest. "Lord Iris intends that I take this city," he whispered. "Back me up." He turned around and went back to the Council as Margritte was struggling onto her hands and knees, clearly badly shaken. Nathaniel's signet ring that marked him as their father's heir had cut her cheek and Will felt himself spiralling into despairing panic. It was going to happen again; Iris was going to use them to take another city and destroy more lives.

Nathaniel put his hand between her shoulder blades and pushed her back to the floor. "Stay down, whore. You kidnap my brother, have him beaten and you expect me to listen to the lies that fall from your mouth? I know what you're capable of. Your husband tried to have my sister-in-law murdered. You haven't learned the lesson my brother taught your family, it seems."

"Your brother has been returned to you." Margritte's son finally found his voice. "I ask that you leave and we will deal with this matter ourselves."

"What's your name?"

"Alexander."

"I hardly think the son of the perpetrator will dispense any justice I find satisfactory, Alexander. Where is this Chancellor of yours?"

Alexander glanced at the others in the council and a few nodded to him. "My mother spoke the truth," he replied. "Oxenford is without a Chancellor. I–"

"Then whom do I duel to take the city?"

The men who'd remained silent burst into cries of indignation. "This is Oxenford, sir!" one of them shouted. "We are a civilised city – the paragon of enlightenment and learning. We do not duel for power like barbarians!"

Nathaniel stared at him. "Then how do you go about finding a new Chancellor? Don't tell me that lily over there will inherit the title?"

"The Chancellor is voted in by the Congregation of Oxenford. It will take several days to organise."

"*You* can't vote a new one in?"

"We are the Hebdomadal Council, sir," another man said in a tremulous voice. "It is not our place to do so."

"But…" one of them said, drawing Nathaniel's attention with the tone of his voice. "There is a statute dictating that, should an emergency arise, the Hebdomadal Council does have the right to elect a Chancellor." Ignoring the furious glares of his fellows, the man cleared his throat. "I do consider this an emergency."

Will was convinced the man was a Wisteria. There was something about his hairline that gave it away, and the way he was willing to ingratiate himself with whoever was on the rise. He could hardly feel superior to him though, standing there, doing nothing as Nathaniel loomed over Margritte and glared at her son. But to stand against him would be the highest treason; Nathaniel acted with the authority of his patron and Will had no power in the city to fall back on. He was stripped of Charms, had no sword and no desire to incur his patron's wrath. If he fell from grace, Cathy and Sophia would be put at risk and he had to protect them.

Nathaniel drew his sword and pointed it at Alexander. "Do I have your vote, sir?"

The poor man looked at his mother, who was curling into a ball, shaking as her world fell apart. The tip of the Patroon's sword pressed into his waistcoat and Will looked away, as disgusted with his brother as he was with himself. He listened to each member of the Council giving their vote under duress until Alexander said, "The Council recognises Nathaniel Reticulata-Iris as the Chancellor of Oxenford."

Will watched Nathaniel pull Alexander from the chair, shove him aside and sit in it himself. "You are no longer the Vice-Chancellor." He pointed his sword at the Wisteria. "You are." Looking back at Alexander, he said, "You'll go and free the Irises from wherever you've imprisoned them and you'll bring them here. If any of them have even a scratch upon them, I'll inflict twice the injury upon you."

Alexander took a step towards his mother, reaching down to help her up but Nathaniel batted him away with the flat of the blade. "She stays there until I have somewhere to put her. Go."

Will stepped aside to let Alexander pass. Nathaniel smiled at him. "Well, that's all been seen to. Let's get you home, shall we?"

"Margritte is a resident of Londinium," Will said. "I'll take her with me."

Nathaniel shook his head. "The crime was committed here, dear brother." His smile was cruel and it sickened Will. "I will dispense justice in the way *I* see fit."

27

Cathy felt sweat prickling beneath the high lace collar of her dress. The hushed tension in the room was becoming unbearable.

"But what about the Patroons?" a lady asked.

She'd worried about that herself but she tried her best not to show it. "I'll handle them. None of them will be able to come and take you away, I promise. You'll be safe."

"You can guarantee that?"

Could she? She was about to lie and say yes, she could keep them safe from anyone and anything, but of course she couldn't. "I can't," she said after a pause. "I can't predict everything they might do. All I can give you is the chance to stand up and say, 'No, you can't treat people like this'. I hope it will force them into realising the world has changed. As long as this place stays secret they hold the power. Do you really think that your friends and families will let anything happen to hurt you even more, once they discover what has been done? Do you think the Patroons could keep control if everyone knew you were no threat and yet were treated terribly again?"

People looked at each other, searching the faces of their friends for courage or fear.

"It's a risk," Cathy said. "But if we do nothing, more people will be silenced. You'll all die of old age. Nothing will ever change. Come with me. Make it happen!"

A woman stood up and tossed her napkin onto the table. Cathy had spoken to her earlier that day, when she was disguised. She was one of the women from the old group, one of those who disappeared from Society because she spoke her mind. Her name was Clarissa – one of the missing women she'd been looking for – and she looked like she was in her sixties. "I'm going with her," she announced to the room. "We have nothing to lose except a slow death. Let's do something with some meaning, for goodness' sake! If this girl is willing to put her neck on the line, then we should be willing to stand up for ourselves too."

Another woman stood up, then another who pulled a man onto his feet too and kissed him on the cheek. Several were looking towards the elderly woman who'd urged Cathy on, but she was still seated. When at least half of the room had stood up she did so too and then many more rose from their chairs. Cathy wished she'd met that lady earlier; she seemed influential. In moments, only one man remained seated.

When everyone else noticed, he shouted, "Why's everyone standing up?" The woman next to him explained in a loud voice and he beamed at Cathy. "Splendid. I want to give my son a piece of my mind and a good curse to boot."

Cathy looked at them all and took a moment to let what she'd done sink in. She soon realised that if she dwelt upon it she'd implode with anxiety and be unable to take another step forwards, so she considered the practicalities instead. "If you have any personal items you want to take with you, go and pack them now. We'll be leaving in ten minutes. If you need help to do that, let me know." Cathy stepped down from the chair. "Carter, go to the staff, answer any questions they have and let me know if any of them make calls on their mobiles. They may have them, seeing as they live in Mundanus all the time."

"Do you want me to stop the calls?"

"No, the Agency will find out very soon, one way or the other. If they want to turn up and curse me, you'll be able to stop them, right?"

"Yes, your Grace, I understand."

The elderly woman came to her side as he left. "You're one of Dame Iris' little poodles, aren't you?" The woman was peering at her through a lorgnette with a beautifully decorated handle.

Cathy wasn't sure how to react. "This hasn't got anything to do with Dame Iris."

"Oh, I know that dear." The lady continued to scrutinise her. "Duchess but recently wed, that's interesting, and someone the Dame really doesn't think very capable at all. You're not very graceful either. Oh, dear, I should imagine you're having a perfectly horrid time with her."

Cathy wondered why the lady was taking such an interest when there were more exciting things to attend to.

"Less than a year under her thumb, I see, that must be why you still have some spirit in you. Before you ask, I can tell by your dress. She had it made for you, didn't she?"

"How could you possibly know all this from a dress?"

"The trim is less than an inch wide and made from lace. She detests lace and only has it put on the dresses of those she likes the least. And your cuffs have three buttons at the wrist, indicating you need a great deal of attention. But don't be offended – take heart in the knowledge of her little system and the fact she needs to do these things. She has a terrible memory for new brides. You all blur into one for her, because she's so desperately bored of having to look after you all."

"It sounds like you know her well."

"All too well. Hateful woman, I hope she catches the pox and is scarred beyond recognition."

Cathy tried not to grin. "I'm sorry, but you are…?"

"Eleanor," she said with a smile. "Formerly Dame Iris herself, before that spiteful hag destroyed me. Do close your mouth, dear, I have no desire to see your tonsils. We have a great deal to talk about and I have nothing to pack, so I would like to speak to you as soon as we make our escape. I suspect you're just the person I've been hoping for."

So that was why so many people followed her lead. "I'm surprised you didn't stand up straightaway."

"I wanted to make sure people stood up because they wanted to leave, not because they thought I wanted them to." She took Cathy's hand and patted it. "That's the thing about authority, dear, it can get in the way when you want to be certain that people are doing what *they* want."

Ekstrand was lying at the bottom of the stairs when Max found him, his neck broken and his right leg bent at an unnatural angle. He hadn't been dead long enough to look wax-like. When Max closed his eyelids, it looked like he was asleep.

"He's here," Max called to the gargoyle and Rupert. "It must have killed him at the top of the stairs. It doesn't look like he tried to break his fall."

Rupert came and stared at Ekstrand as the gargoyle huddled in the corner of the entrance hall, its stone claws over its eyes but still seeing the body as he did now.

"I wonder if it really is him," Rupert said, crouching down to prod Ekstrand's cheek. "He could have done the same as me."

He was talking about the doppelgänger he'd had the gargoyle throw through a Way into his property. Max had seen that through the gargoyle's eyes as he waited in an Oxford street, wondering whether they'd chosen the right Sorcerer to save.

"But I doubt it," Rupert said.

Max agreed. "He's wearing his Sunday clothes. I can't see him having the time to pick the right outfit, nor would he have needed to in order to fool Dante's sister."

"Interesting that she just left the body." Rupert pulled at the smock and Max noticed a spot of blood on it. "Looks like she put a pin in him to test if his heart had turned to stone." He looked away for a moment. "I think the doppelgänger's heart would have done the same. Hard to tell, not knowing how she did it exactly. Of course, if she tried hard enough she'd be able to see it had never really been alive, but it looks like she isn't the autopsy type."

"Did you make it because you knew about what she did to the others?"

"I made it because he tried to kill me," Rupert replied. "I didn't know about this sister until today. What a fucking mess." He looked back down at Ekstrand. "Poor crazy bastard. Not even his famous wards were enough." He pointed at the gargoyle. "Is it broken or something?"

"We're upset," the gargoyle said.

"Don't feel guilty," Rupert said, straightening up.

"You would say that," the gargoyle replied.

"Look, if Ekstrand had listened to you both, he'd be alive now. Shit happens." He raised an eyebrow at the gargoyle's stare. "Wondering if you made the right choice?"

The gargoyle didn't answer, neither did Max. The Sorcerer of Mercia was so different from Ekstrand he wasn't sure what to say or do around him. His boss was dead. Arguably, Rupert had authority over him now, but he wasn't acting like he did. Once the gargoyle had persuaded him to leave the Bodleian he'd acted swiftly and clearly had an emergency plan ready to go at a moment's notice. Through the gargoyle's eyes he'd seen images of large artificial men carrying objects out of rooms. Then they'd rendezvoused with him and from an underground room the three of them watched Ekstrand's house through a scrying glass, debating what to do next. They said nothing as the Sorceress led a group of Arbiters into the house after breaking the formulae she'd painted on. It had taken her moments to break Ekstrand's wards and they were in the house for less than five minutes, leaving with surprisingly little. Perhaps Ekstrand's artefacts weren't anything special compared to the treasures she'd already accumulated.

After seeing her in action, Rupert announced he was going to fake his own death to everyone, not just her, and go underground. When the gargoyle asked if they could go to see if Ekstrand survived, there had been no argument.

"What do we do now?" Max asked.

"I've got a few things to take care of," Rupert replied. "Do you want me to open a Way for you back to Oxford? Somewhere else?"

"That depends on what you want me to do."

Rupert frowned at him. "Do what you want. I'm not your master."

"We'll stay here," Max said, wanting to look for Petra and Axon. "Someone has to bury him."

"You are going to do something about Dante's sister, aren't you?" the gargoyle asked.

"Yeah." Rupert put his hands in his pockets and rocked back and forth on his toes and heels. "Haven't got a Scooby what that'll be yet, but I'm not going hide for ever. It's gonna take a while to work it all out."

"Is there anything else you want to know from us?"

He shook his head. "The gargoyle told me where I can find her. Speaking of which, if you need any help, or if you find anything else out, call this number and leave a message with a way to get in touch." He pulled an old receipt from his pocket and grabbed a pen from the table on the other side of the hall to scribble a phone number on the back. "It's secure and checked three times a day. Give me yours."

"I don't have a phone," Max said.

"Get one. It's the twenty-first century, for fuck's sake. Then leave a message with the number. Just in case I need you."

Max nodded and put the piece of paper in his inside pocket.

"Thanks for getting me out," Rupert said. "For what it's worth, I think you made the right choice. Ekstrand was a relic, like all of the others."

"What about the Chapters and the rest of the Heptarchy?" Max asked. "No one is protecting the innocents."

"It sucks, but things change," Rupert said. "Long overdue, now I think about it. We had things nice and cushy for a thousand years, and that's probably too long. We got complacent but the fittest will survive. It's the law of evolution: adapt or die."

"Do you mean us or the innocents?" the gargoyle asked.

Rupert grinned. "Both. Take care, you two."

He opened a Way with a silver yo-yo and then they were alone in a silent house.

"The clocks have stopped," the gargoyle said, its stone ears swivelling like a nervous cat listening for trouble.

"Let's look for Axon and Petra and bury the bodies," Max suggested. It needed to be done and it was something they were capable of doing without having to make any far-reaching decisions.

Axon's body was at the top of the spiral staircase leading down to the library. A tray, smashed teapot and shattered cake plates lay beside him. A few slices of Battenberg had tumbled down the steps, leaving a trail of yellow and pink crumbs and fragmented ribbons of yellow marzipan. The gargoyle's dry weeping rasped through the room.

Max listened to the noise as he closed Axon's eyes. He felt nothing. The man at his feet had cared for him when he was a day out of hospital with a broken leg, he'd cooked for him, made sure he ate at least one hot meal a day and given the gargoyle privacy when it had hidden in the parlour or under the stairs, distressed on Max's behalf.

He'd died alone, doing his job, never a threat to anyone. Max had no idea who his family used to be, where he used to live before he became Ekstrand's butler or what his life was like. It had ceased to be relevant, like it had for Max. They did their work for the Sorcerer and nothing else mattered. There was no one to inform of his death and no one to mourn him.

Max sat on the top step and slowly reached towards the gargoyle's back. He lay his hand on the stone and let his own grief fill him. An ache bloomed in his chest, a physical pressure built, pushing up his throat as his skull felt like it was being gripped in a vice. He coughed once, twice, and then the third time there were tears with it. He thought of the house as it used to be, the quiet comfort that Axon provided, the sound of his gentle throat-clearing at the doorway and the eyebrow twitch when he disagreed but was too polite and well-trained to say anything.

Then he wasn't only crying for Axon, but also for his mentor, for the researchers and staff at the cloister. They were his friends before his soul was dislocated. They made him laugh, they cheered him on, they fought and argued with him and some competed against him for selection. All the people who knew him when he was a whole person were dead.

He was crying for himself, for the boy he used to be. He wept for everything he had lost, from the chance to have children to the moments of pleasure, relief, satisfaction and a dozen other emotions denied him every day. He was once an innocent. He was once a boy with everything ahead of him and nothing to fear but his mother's disappointment. She never knew what happened to him. She would have died wondering what happened to her little boy, perhaps even blaming herself for not watching him closely enough. He wept for her too.

For a time there were no thoughts. He was consumed by the physicality of his grief, unable to do anything but draw in the next breath to be released in violent sobs. When he finally came back to himself, he realised the gargoyle's arms were wrapped around him and his arms were clinging to its waist, his head on its stone shoulder.

"That's better," it said. "Are we all right?"

"Yes," Max said and thought about letting go but didn't. He was afraid, he realised. There was no one to tell him what to do and the case was solved, even if the perpetrator was still free. There were no more leads to pursue and nowhere safe to go. The Chapter was gone, it was likely the other Chapters would soon disintegrate or were already destroyed, and he had no means to find them anyway.

"It'll be all right," the gargoyle said, its arms still around him. "We'll work something out. We could… go fishing or something."

Max laughed at thought of the two of them in a rowing boat and the sound startled him. He let the hope that everything would work out fill him for a moment more and then pulled back. The gargoyle released him and Max settled back into the neutral state he was used to. His cheeks were still wet; he dried them with the sleeve of his coat and then stood.

"Let's find Petra."

They expected her to be in the library. Max sent the gargoyle down the steps, just in case any of Ekstrand's wards were still active on the doorway to the library. It was empty and there were gaps on the shelves. They searched the rest of the house, from the basement to the attic, even in the rooms that used to be out of bounds. None of the locks had been left unbroken by Ekstrand's murderer, but Petra was nowhere to be seen.

"Perhaps she was out when it happened," the gargoyle said. Max could hear the hope in its voice.

"Let's go and find the best place to bury Mr Ekstrand and Axon," Max said. "Maybe she'll come back."

They went out the back door, using the key Axon had used to get from the Nether house into Mundanus. It was becoming dark so Max headed for the bushy borders at the edge of the lawn to look for a place where they could dig without being noticed.

"Max!" Petra called from a far corner of the garden. By the time he had worked out the direction, she was running towards him. She threw her arms around him and sobbed until the gargoyle arrived.

"Were you in Mundanus when it happened?" Max asked.

"No," she said with a sniff. "I was in the library. I heard Axon drop the tray and…" She broke down.

After taking her into the anchor property, Max and the gargoyle managed to get enough out of her to piece together what had happened. She believed the library's wards – more extreme than any others in the house – managed to protect her from the initial attack. At first she hid, then when she ventured out she heard intruders in the house and barricaded herself in the library, carrying out Ekstrand's instructions to save the most precious books in the event of an emergency.

"And then I came into Mundanus and hid in the garden," she finished. "I couldn't go back in there, not by myself."

Max made tea in the Nether kitchen and brought it through, and they drank it on the back step of the house as the stars came out. Between them, Max and the gargoyle told Petra what they saw in the tower, and how they saved Rupert. Neither of them mentioned the fact they chose to save him instead of Ekstrand.

Unable to rest whilst the bodies were left in the Nether, the three of them dug two graves and buried Mr Ekstrand and Axon side by side beneath two giant conifer trees. Petra knelt at Ekstrand's graveside, weeping for hours, until Max and the gargoyle agreed to bring her inside and light a fire.

The gargoyle found food for them in the fridge and they ate in silence. More tea was drunk by the light of the fire in the mundane living room and the gargoyle lay at Max's feet, resting against the toes of his shoes like a faithful dog.

"I know what I want to do," Max finally said and Petra jumped. The gargoyle rested its head on Max's knee and he knew that he'd made the right decision.

"What is it?"

"I want to start my own Chapter. I want to protect the innocents. We might need to do it differently, but I want to find a way."

"I'll help you," Petra said. "Those books will be useful and I know how to read them safely. And I know where Mr Ekstrand hid some of his artefacts. They might still be there."

"We'll need a new cloister," the gargoyle said. "This place isn't safe enough. She knows where it is."

"Rupert can help us with that," Max replied. "We'll have to learn how to use the internet too. It might help us to find breaches whilst we recruit staff."

"It sounds like a plan," the gargoyle said and Petra agreed. "Can I just make one request?" it added. When Max nodded, it said, "Can we have just one day off first?"

"Yes," Max said. "We'll go fishing."

28

When the front door wasn't opened as he reached the top step, Will knew something was wrong. One of the footmen, returned with the released Irises in Oxenford, hurried to open it for him.

"Morgan?" Will called as he entered. He saw two maids rushing across the top of the stairs, bed linen piled high in their arms. There was the sound of people, lots of them, but scattered all over the house rather than the concentrated roar created by a party.

A grey-haired woman came out of a nearby room. "Who's Morgan?"

"Who are you?" He watched another elderly woman follow her out. "What in the Worlds is going on here? Where is my wife?"

The woman pointed down the hallway, towards Cathy's library.

"Find Morgan," Will told the nearest footman. "The rest of you stay nearby in case I need you."

He passed the two ladies, who were whispering to each other, and caught sight of more people in the drawing room with them. He quickened his pace as much as he could, feeling cheated of the warm and relieved welcome he'd anticipated, the pain in his ankle adding to his irritation.

He could hear Cathy as he approached the door of her library.

"Don't tell me what I have the right to do or not! You can't say I've stolen those people unless you claim to own them, and I'm certain you can't do that."

"They are the property of the Agency." The man's voice was familiar. Will stopped and waved a hand to his footmen to stay back. He would learn more if he stayed quiet and listened.

"Quite apart from the fact it's a foul claim to make, saying they are your property only proves that you've been conning us – and the entirety of Society – by charging for their wages. I know for a fact that since I established this household I've paid over twenty thousand pounds in wages and not a single penny of that has gone to my staff."

"You were paying for their time and our management of–"

"Don't try and wriggle out of this! And don't try and tell me that the people who have chosen to work for me don't have the right to do that, because I've given it to them. If you try to take them from this house, or threaten any of them, I'll tell every single wife that runs a household in Albion that they've been collectively paying the Agency millions of pounds for hundreds of years to do nothing but run a slave racket."

"You think they'll care?" the man laughed. "All they'll care about is whether the linen is clean and the chamber pots emptied."

Will didn't like the way he spoke to Cathy. There was no deference and no respect. It sounded like he was from the Agency. Was it someone he'd dealt with in the past?

"If you return the staff and patients to the asylum and accept that your staff will be replaced here, your reputation will remain intact," the man continued. "You know the consequences should you cause any further problems for us."

Blackmail! Will touched the door handle, about to open the door and slam the man against a wall when he heard Cathy speak.

"Your note stated, very clearly, that should I cause the slightest inconvenience or loss of income to your venerable establishment Dame Iris would be told about my past. I'm rather confused by this conversation. Why aren't you with her now, telling her all about my terrible secret?"

Her question made Will pause. He wanted to hear the answer. As the man hesitated, Will remembered where he'd heard that voice before: the hospital, the day she was stabbed. He was the Agency man he'd bribed to keep her mundane history secret. He'd done it to protect Cathy, and the vile dog had used the information to blackmail her. He gripped the handle tighter.

"I can tell you why." Cathy had got tired of waiting. "It's because as soon as it's no longer a secret, you don't have any power over me."

"Your–"

"In fact, keeping all of the terrible things the Agency does secret depends on my being afraid. Well, I've only got one thing I actually want to say to you about how you treat the staff, those prisoners you kept and the way you've been threatening me, something I learned in Mundanus: fuck off. Go, tell people whatever you want about me, I don't care. The only people whose opinions matter in all of this are my husband and myself. I'm glad I lived in Mundanus and Will didn't bat an eyelid when I told him, because he's better than all of the men in Society put together. So screw your blackmail. I'm not afraid of you any more."

"This isn't the last you'll hear from me."

"I should hope not," Cathy said as footsteps came closer to the door. "I expect a letter of apology. And a refund, you dishonest bastard."

The door handle turned but was released again. Bennet had changed his mind. His steps moved away from the door again and Will readied himself to burst in at the slightest hint that he was hurting her. "You may not care about your own reputation." Bennet sounded calm again. "It's clear you don't have the good sense to do so. But I imagine you care about the little girl you're hiding here. You may be able to convince your staff that she's your husband's distant cousin, but I know who his cousins are and she isn't one of them. In fact–"

Will opened the door. "Mr Bennet," he said. "I was struggling to recall your name. I won't forget it now."

"Your Grace, I'm so glad you're back, I'm afraid your wife–"

"I don't want to listen to anything you have to say," Will replied. He beckoned to the footmen. "This man has been threatening my wife. Remove any personal effects and take him into custody. Watch him and don't let him speak to anyone." As Bennet spluttered, Will suppressed the urge to punch him. He was tired and needed to recover before he could organise an appropriate punishment. Besides, he wanted the wretch to sweat a while.

"Will!" Cathy threw her arms around him once Bennet had been taken away. "What happened? You're hurt! Nathaniel said–"

He kissed the questions out of her, holding her close until he was sure he was really home. "Where's Carter? Why isn't he keeping the likes of Bennet away from you?"

"He's… running an errand for me. Where have you been?"

What to tell her? If he said anything about Margritte he'd have to admit he'd failed to protect her friend. "It's a long and unpleasant story, but I'm home now."

"Does Nathaniel know you're all right? He went a bit… mental."

"Yes, he does. Cathy, why are there strangers in the drawing room?"

"Oh… yeah, sorry about that. There's a very good explanation for that. I wanted to tell you before you came into the house, but I had to deal with that arsehole Bennet."

He watched her speak. There was something different about her. "I heard everything through the door. You were brilliant. Why didn't you tell me what he was doing?"

"He cursed me the day you gave me the library. He blackmailed me to the tune of a hundred thousand pounds and then, when I started to find out what he was really up to, he threatened to tell Dame Iris about my time in Mundanus. Bastard."

"You don't have to worry about that weasel any more. Cathy, what in the Worlds is going on here?"

"Your Grace," Morgan said from the doorway. "I'm dreadfully sorry to interrupt but a Mr Ferran is here to see you. He says it's urgent."

"Who?" Will asked, irritated by the way Morgan seemed to be looking to Cathy for a response.

"I'm very pleased to see you are home, your Grace," Morgan said to him. "I don't believe he's from the Agency," he said, focusing on Cathy again.

"All right, well…" she looked at Will. "Tell him I'm sorry but he'll have to wait."

Will frowned. "It feels like I'm not really home," he said, but, just as she was about to respond, Carter came in before Morgan closed the door.

"Did you find them?" Cathy asked.

"Yes, your Grace, and I followed the rest of your instructions. Both of them are comfortable." He smiled at

Will. "I'm glad to see you're back, your Grace. We were a little worried about you."

"I want to speak with you," he replied. "You have specific instructions regarding the protection of my wife."

Something about the way Carter looked at Cathy again made the anger spike.

Cathy put a hand on his arm. "We need to talk, Will. Come and sit down. We'll get some ice for your lip, you poor thing, it looks sore."

Carter took up his correct position, guarding the door, and that satisfied Will for now. He let himself be guided to a chair, soothed by her concern. He wanted to be cared for, he wanted to rest and have everything go back to normal, but underneath it all was the worry about what his brother would do to Margritte. Could he have done things differently and stood up to him better? Was it right of his Patroon and Iris to take the city? His head throbbed with doubts. He was so tired.

Cathy kissed his forehead once he was sitting down. The fatigue washed over him and he let himself rest whilst the ice arrived along with tea. He watched her wrap a few cubes in a linen napkin which she gathered up and then gave to him before sitting down. It made his lip sting but soon it was numbed enough to be an improvement.

"Bennet said something about an asylum," he said as she poured tea. "And those people in the house… what have you done?"

"I rescued people from the Agency."

He listened, aghast, as she told him what she'd discovered and what she'd done. By the end of it the fatigue had been superseded by a growing panic. Once the Agency broke the news to the Patroons, he'd be hauled in front of Sir Iris and made to explain his wife's actions. No doubt some of the people in the place had been put there to keep them out of Society and not just because they were feminists.

"You just went and did this, without mentioning any of it to me beforehand?"

"You weren't here."

"I was away for a day, Cathy! Those people have been there for decades, they couldn't wait just a few more hours?"

"No! Once I felt the curse break and the… wish kick off I knew what I had to do and I couldn't wait a moment longer."

Will's anger was diverted towards Poppy. "It was Poppy's magic influencing you to–"

"No!" She hit the arm of her chair with the flat of her hand. "This was me actually taking action and standing up to these bastards. Don't write it off as anything else but that."

"Cathy, you've set us against the entire Agency and by the sound of it, most – if not all – of the Patroons! With no forethought, no consideration of what it will mean for us and how this will affect anyone else. You want me to believe you're that naive?"

"I want you to see that as long as things like the asylum and this organised slavery run by the Agency stay hidden, the Patroons can carry on controlling us all. We need to stand up and tell everyone in the Court about this. And we need to show them there's another way to live – the best of both Worlds, so to speak. We need to prove that everything won't fall apart if they pay their staff wages and treat them properly. And we need to give women rights too."

"What about our patron? Damn it, what do you think Iris will say when he hears of this?"

She moved to the edge of her chair, hands balled into fists. "We have to stop being afraid. If enough people demand change, the Patroons and the Fae have to listen!"

"No, they don't. They'll Doll us or curse us or replace us altogether. How could you have been so thoughtless? I told you it was too dangerous to change anything so soon and you went ahead anyway."

"Will, I'm sorry I've sprung this all on you but I don't regret what I've done. This... this *feels* right. This is what I'm supposed to do with my life. If you want to replace me with some boring trophy wife then go ahead, I'll find another way to protect these people. But I'm not going to backpedal and I'm not going to keep quiet. You said you wanted a partnership. Well, it's not just you deciding what we can and can't do. It's got to be both of us sticking together and making a difference, or nothing at all. Sacrifice me to Iris and I'll face whatever that fucker has to throw at me, same for the Patroons. I refuse to live by their rules any more." She paused for breath, her face flushed with passion. "Or join me. It's going to be hard and they're going to try and stop us, but if we both commit to this, people will listen. If we can change this city then they have to pay attention."

Will closed his eyes, struggling to think clearly amidst the anger and worry. Bennet was a key player in it all and could be the perfect scapegoat. He could keep the Iris Patroon on side by giving him the news first and he probably had a little time to work out what to say; no one in the Agency would be rushing to tell their superiors what Cathy had done.

He hated being forced into it and he resented the way Cathy had stormed ahead without consulting him, but he was convinced the wish magic was influencing her, whether she liked the thought or not. To throw her to the wolves would make him no better than his brother. He thought about what Nathaniel did to Margritte, recalling the wretched feeling of powerlessness as his brother trampled a city into submission, and he knew he wanted things to change too. Cathy had forced his hand, but perhaps that was the best thing to do to drive away his guilt.

Cathy's eyes were brilliantly blue against the blush in her cheeks and there was power in the way she looked back at him, ready to face whatever was to come. He hadn't wanted to marry her, but now he was glad he did. She was alive in a way that so many of the women in Society were not. He'd always wanted someone to face the rest of the world with, rather than a decoration for his arm, to dance with at balls and give him children. The wish magic might have made her reckless, but she'd been brave enough to stand up to her Patroon at her Coming of Age ceremony and forge a life alone in Mundanus before that magic had been cast.

"What's it to be then?" she asked.

A knock on the door prevented his response. "My apologies, your Grace," Morgan said. "But Mr Ferran said it's urgent and that you may know him by his usual name – Sam."

"Oh! Show him in," Cathy said. "What's wrong, Will? There's no need to worry."

Will seethed. He'd be the judge of that.

"Mr Ferran, your Grace," Morgan announced.

"Carter!" Will called, spotting him next to the visitor, "escort this man from the house."

"Will!" Cathy gave him a horrified look. "He's nothing to do with the Agency, he's a friend."

"Oh, we've met," Sam said. He looked different too. He was dressed in a superbly tailored suit for one thing. He still looked tired, but he was clean-shaven and stood taller, nothing like the saggy-shouldered man he'd found in Mundanus. He doubted his earlier dismissal of him. Perhaps this was a man Cathy could have fallen in love with.

Carter hadn't obeyed his order, and was looking to Cathy for confirmation. Will felt like he'd come back to the same house but to a slightly different reality.

"You've met?" she asked.

"Yeah." Sam smirked. "He held a sword up to my neck and threatened to kill me if I ever saw you again."

"You did what?" Cathy turned to face Will.

"And yet here you are," Will said.

Sam looked him up and down. "You're looking a bit worse for wear. Did someone fight back?"

"I don't have to–"

"Stop it, both of you. Sam, are you all right? Has something happened?"

He grinned. "Yeah. I'm Lord Iron now."

"What does that mean?"

Will didn't like the way Sam looked at him. He was fearless, and ready to fight. He could see it in his stance, the way his fists were partially curled. He felt unprepared and uncertain of Carter's loyalty.

"It means you don't have to stay here any more." Sam smiled and held out his hand. "I break their magic now. I've just been to Exilium and freed those dancers we found – do you remember them? I got that memory back that Poppy took from me and that time debt he screwed out of me too. They're terrified of me there, Cathy. If you come with me now, there's nothing any of the sodding Fae can do about it, not any of their people." He looked at Will. "Not even him."

Will couldn't believe a man would dare come into his house and try to take his wife away right in front of him! Was he still in that awful black box, dreaming, having been driven mad by the Sorcerer?

It seemed Cathy didn't believe him either. At least she wasn't moving towards him. She was staring at Sam's hand, frowning.

"You don't believe me?" he asked. Before she answered, he went to one of the globes held in an ornate light fitting. He reached up towards it and the sprite inside dulled noticeably. When his finger touched the glass the tiny creature cowered away as far as the globe would allow, barely casting any light at all.

"I believe you," she said. "But I told you, Sam, I'm not going to run away."

"I know you said that." His hand dropped to his side. "But it must be because this twat put a spell on you."

"What did you call me?"

Sam ignored him. "I can break it. Just take my hand and all of their curses, all of the stuff they've done to you will be broken. And I'll keep you safe."

Cathy sniffed. "I've heard that before. How could you do that?"

"They can't come near me, nor anyone under my protection."

"So my safety would be dependent on you?" Cathy shook her head. "You want me to come and live in your cage instead?"

"No, it's not like that!"

Will stared at her. Was that all this life was to her? A cage?

She looked at him then, saw the hurt in his eyes and her face softened. "I'm not going anywhere," she said. "There's too much to do."

"Listen to me," Sam said. "My wife thought she could change things, and she put herself in danger every day and you know what happened to her."

"I'm not your wife," Cathy said gently.

"Don't you get it?" Sam's voice was louder. "We can stop all of this! We can get your friends, all of the wives treated like shit, like you are, and we can get them out of the Nether and the Fae won't be able to do a damn thing about it! You know what they do, how they steal people. If we worked together, we could stop it! The Sorcerers and the Arbiters don't give a fuck about people but we do!"

"We could stop the Agency," Cathy whispered.

Will brushed the back of her waist with his hand. "He wants to throw everything into chaos. If the Agency collapsed, hundreds of people would be left without any idea of how to care for themselves. Only a small fraction of their staff understand Mundanus. Destabilising Society would only encourage the Patroons to be more controlling. This 'Lord Iron' can't be everywhere at once. And what if someone falls out of his favour? Cathy, he's not offering freedom. He would be in control."

"I'm offering something better than being owned by some prick from the fucking dark ages who can't handle the fact his wife might have a male friend."

"Oh, for heaven's sake, shut up! Both of you!" Cathy held up her hands. "Sit down. Let's talk like adults. Will, I have no idea why you threatened Sam, but there's no reason for you to be so antagonistic."

"He wants you back!"

"Back?" Cathy looked at the ceiling and then groaned. "You thought we were lovers? We're just friends."

Sam came further into the room and sat on the other chair in front of the fire. Cathy moved away from him, taking care to make sure there was always something between them, as if she feared he would lunge for her. Will felt his fears ease. They weren't lovers and she was clearly trying to protect the magic bound in their wedding ring. He sat down too.

"Right, let's get this straight," she said to Sam. "I don't want you to break the magic on me, even though the Iris curse is offensive as hell, because there's other magic – wish magic – that I want to preserve."

"Poppy told me about that," Sam said. "He told me you were going to destroy everything because of the third wish you made."

"He did? But that's not what I wished for. My wish was to reach my full potential."

"Well, he thinks you're potentially destructive. Oh, fuck!" He slapped his hand over his mouth and looked at Will. "He also said you shouldn't know, because if you tell your patron, he'll be able to take what he wants from Cathy instead of your baby."

"I knew he wanted something from our child," Cathy said. "Well, that settles it. We are never having children, Will."

Will frowned at the declaration, disturbed by the thought of losing the chance to be a father. "Let's try not to worry about every single thing at once," he said, but he was quietly panicking. He couldn't let anything happen to any child of his, nor to Cathy. Perhaps he needed to accept the help Sam was offering, as galling as it would be. Perhaps fighting the system as Cathy wanted was the only way to keep his family safe. "Tell me more about this wish business," he said.

"There's no need to worry, you'll both be safe, whatever happens." Cathy grinned at Carter. "You too. The wish was to reach my full potential in such a way that wouldn't 'draw the attention of the Arbiters, nor endanger my life, nor that of the individuals I love and care for – be they Fae, a member of the great families or a mundane'. It's going to be tough, but we'll be all right."

Will knew there was a world of difference between endangering someone's life and simply making their existence miserable. She had a lot more faith in the strength of Poppy's magic – and its interpretation – than he did.

"But," Cathy added, "I would appreciate some help, Sam."

Sam nodded. "I can keep the Fae out for a start, and break any curses put on the staff, that sort of thing. But are you certain you want to stay?" His eyes flicked to Will. "Are you sure he won't stop you doing what you want to do once I've gone?"

Cathy looked at Will and he let her search his face.

"I'm certain," Cathy said. "Will, you'll be all right with Sam coming to visit in the future, won't you?"

Will nodded. It wasn't the time to complicate things with his doubts and he might need Sam himself. "I'm sorry we got off to a bad start," he said, mostly for her benefit. "Let's shake hands whilst I have nothing you can break upon me."

They stood, shook hands like gentlemen but looked at each other with the hard stare of men who knew nothing had changed at all. Cathy led Sam out, promising to be back soon. Carter followed her and Will was left alone.

Whilst he felt no warmth for the man, having Sam on side could be critical if he was indeed capable of what he claimed. And hearing of Iris planning to take what he wanted – whatever that might be – from his wife or his child made Will's teeth grind. Why fight to maintain a status quo in which it would be acceptable for either of them to be taken from him? It might not have been the schedule that he would have chosen, but it was clear to him now that there was no way – and now no desire – to find a way back to where they were before.

Morgan brought fresh tea and apologies for taking so long, explaining that he was trying to settle over a hundred people into the household, many of whom had extraordinary needs.

The tea made his lip sting but it was worth it. By the time he was on his second cup, Cathy returned. She looked radiantly happy and then seemed to remember what they were talking about before Sam interrupted.

"So then… what's it to be, Will? Are you with me?"

Will thought of the first ball of the season, how ungrateful she'd been and how the sight of the bruises on her arms at the Peonias' soirée had stirred something protective inside him. He recalled the gut-twisting guilt she'd made him feel after they'd married and the countless times she'd irritated him. He remembered the way she'd glowed in the Londinium salons when debating some point of philosophy and how she'd dealt with Freddy's attentions. He thought of the panic he'd felt when he learned of the attack, and the hours of watching her sleep as she healed, and the smile when he gave her the library. "There's a huge amount to talk about," he said, reaching for her hands. "But there's something I need to tell you first."

Her brow creased and she let him pull her down to sit on the arm of his chair.

"The next few weeks, no, the next few years are going to be hard, Cathy. I don't know if we'll come through this. Lord Iris isn't going to forget what he wants from us." She took a breath but he pressed a finger to her lips. "We'll sort something out, I'm sure. Having a friend like Lord Iron gives me some hope. But before we work out how we make the changes that need to be made, there's something I want you to know."

She looked frightened for the first time since he'd come back.

"I think you are the bravest, strangest, most infuriating, intelligent and fascinating woman I've ever had the privilege to know and…" he paused, uncertain whether to pin a single word to the mess of emotions she stirred in him. "And I love you, Cathy."

She laughed and a fat teardrop rolled down her cheek. "Oh. All right. That's better than I thought it would be." She looked up, nervous.

"What is it?"

"I was just waiting for a piano to fall on my head or something." There was a knock at the door and she jumped to her feet. "Come in."

A woman walked in, pale and red-eyed as if she'd been crying. She was dressed like a maid, her brown hair tied back in a bun, but she didn't curtsy and look away like a maid would.

"Will," said Cathy, "I want to introduce you to someone. This is Miss Rainer. She was my governess and she's the bravest person I know. Miss Rainer, this is Will, my husband."

Will kissed her hand, thinking it best to treat her as royalty, given the way Cathy clearly adored her.

Cathy gestured for Miss Rainer to sit. As she did so, Cathy leaned over and whispered, "I love you too" in his ear. Then, blushing, she tugged at her sleeves nervously and picked up the teapot. "Tea?"

29

Margritte listened to the scratching sound and tried to imagine it was something other than a rat. In the darkness, the sound could only come from claws against stone, and with thoughts of the claws came thoughts of the teeth and the whiskers and she drew her knees up under her chin. She must be imagining it. There weren't any animals in the Nether.

She couldn't stop shivering. The tower room was freezing cold, so much so that she wondered if it had been cursed, and the damp from the stones beneath her was leaching into her bones. It wasn't just the cold though. She was frightened, more so than she'd ever been in her life, even more than the time she and Rupert were nearly killed.

What could have happened to Rupert? He seemed invulnerable. Had Ekstrand finally managed to kill him? Was it yet another disastrous repercussion of her poor judgement? She thought of his awful manners and strange affection for her. She couldn't decide how she felt about his death. She was saddened, but not grief-stricken. She didn't really know him and they were at odds with each other when they parted. The interruption from the gargoyle was a relief at the time. Now Oxenford was in the hands of Nathaniel Iris, she wished Rupert was still alive.

Just the thought of Nathaniel made the shivering worse. After exiling her son – something for which she was grateful – he'd marched her out of the Sheldonian, his fist in her hair, making her stumble as she tried to walk without him ripping it from her scalp. He threw her in a carriage at the end of Broad Street and climbed in with her, forcing her onto her knees inside as they rode to the end of the city.

He made her watch as one of Lord Iris' faeries made a new road to Oxford Castle, a property outside the boundaries of Oxenford, and then made her walk along it as he held her hands behind her back.

"My ancestor built this," he said as they arrived at the newly reflected castle. "Lord Iris was very disappointed when he learned its anchors had been destroyed. He was delighted to restore them for me. A fitting place for my rule, I feel."

"I find it interesting that your brother was named after the conqueror, rather than you," she'd said. He'd pinned her wrists higher up her back the rest of the way. It had hurt so much but she didn't cry. Neither did she when they reached the castle and he showed her the tower. Even the mundanes had felt the evil of the place; she knew the anchor property had been a prison for hundreds of years.

"You'll rot in here," he said as he threw her in. "Unless," he said through the grill in the door after he'd locked it, "I can find another use for you." He'd looked at her breasts then, and below her waist, as if seeing through the black satin. For a moment, he looked as if he was going to unlock the door again, but someone called his name and he left, taking the only light with him.

The darkness was welcome then, but not any more. I deserve this, she thought. I should have let it go. She remembered Bartholomew teaching Alexander that it was better to rise above a feud than fuel it. Why hadn't she listened to that herself?

"Bartholomew," she whispered, needing to hear his name in the darkness. She tried to remember what her name sounded like when he spoke it but all she could hear was the awful scratching claws.

Then she imagined donning a silver cloak and escaping into the Nether, as Queen Matilda had donned a cloak the colour of snow and escaped across the frozen river almost a thousand years before. She held the image in her mind as she closed her eyes, arms tight around her legs and head on her knees, the silver cloak blurring into the white queen as she drifted towards sleep.

A noise made her stir. She thought the outline burning into the stone was a dream, so she closed her eyes again. When something touched her arm she jolted, banging her head against the stone as she saw a man's silhouette against a bright rectangle of light.

"Margritte, come with me."

"William?" She didn't trust herself. It couldn't be him.

"Yes," he replied, helping her to stand. "Come on."

She let herself be guided through the Way, out of the cell. She found herself in a large bedroom, with a metal bath full of steaming, sweet-smelling water, by a roaring fire. Fresh clothes were on the bed and tea was on a table alongside a box filled with bandages and dressings. She glanced back at the dank cell before the Way closed.

"Welcome to my home," William said, guiding her on unsteady legs to a chair beside a dressing table. "There's a maid ready to help you bathe, but let me see to that cut first."

"I... don't understand." She couldn't stop shaking.

"I told you that I'd do everything I could to put things right," he said, bringing a box over with a small bowl of water. "I wasn't prepared for what Nathaniel did and I couldn't say anything against him there. I didn't want him to take the city like that and do what he did to you, but to speak against him whilst he wore the Patroon's sword would have been treason."

"But isn't rescuing me just that?"

William smiled as he soaked a ball of cotton wool in the water. "Nathaniel would never guess his own brother did it. His arrogance makes him complacent. Besides, I couldn't trust him to treat you well. It seems I was right. He didn't... hurt you any more than this, did he?"

She shook her head and winced as he cleaned the wound.

"Your son is at Hampton Court and safe also. He doesn't know you're here. Of course, you'll have to hide until certain arrangements are in place." William dabbed at the cut with a piece of dry linen. "But you'll be safe here."

"Does anyone else know you've done this?"

"Cathy, of course. She's desperate to speak to you once you've refreshed yourself. And there are two others who know – they're waiting with her. But I'm under strict instructions to leave their identities as a surprise."

"Does she know what I did to you?"

"Yes. Especially the part where you untied me and got me away from the Sorcerer."

"She was right about you," Margritte whispered. "You are a good man."

Something flickered across his face, making him look away and rummage in the box. "Here we are. These aren't the prettiest accessories, but they'll keep the wound closed." He waved a strip of paper with what looked like tiny butterfly shapes glued to it. He peeled one off and placed it gently over the cut, then added a second. "There. You'll be good as new in a few days."

"Do you remember that first time we met? Cathy stuck a fork into Freddy and we had to send him home early."

William nodded. "Yes, I remember that."

"We sat up late into the night talking about you and Cathy. Bartholomew was so excited. We had plans, you see, and–"

"Please," his face crumpled. "I don't want to–"

"He knew the two of you could help us to change Londinium," Margritte pressed on. "I've come to realise, these last few days, that he was a very wise man. He saw the best in people. Had I held more of him closer to my heart in my grief, I wouldn't have destroyed everything my family had left. What I wanted to say, William, is that I don't blame you any more. You were used by your Patron and I want something good to come of all this."

William cleared his throat, looking up at the ceiling rose. "Cathy and I feel the same. We're making dangerous plans, Margritte. Cathy thinks that you'll be a great help to her, if you're willing."

She smiled. "I am."

"I'll fetch the maid," he said, closing the box and tucking it under his arm. "Once you're ready, she'll take you to Cathy. Then we can all rest."

"Thank you." She gave a gentle curtsy as he bowed, and watched him leave.

She bathed away the grime of the prison cell and ate for the first time that day. The tea eased a headache that had been steadily worsening. The dress she'd been given was a passable fit in a dark enough green to be acceptable for mourning in the unusual circumstances. A black shawl was given to her, for which she was grateful, and she followed the maid downstairs. The house was full of people; she could hear laughter and crying in rooms she passed and the staff were busy despite the late hour.

"Mrs Margritte Semper-Augustus Tulipa," the maid announced at the door and she was shown into a beautiful library.

"Margritte, I'm so glad you're here." Cathy came to her and gave her a swift, fierce embrace before she could see the other two people sitting by the fire. "I'm sure I don't need to introduce you…"

She stepped aside as the two women stood. On the left was Charlotte Persificola-Viola and on the right was the one she and Bartholomew had searched for and lost hope of finding.

"Natasha Rainer!" she cried and rushed forwards. "Charlotte!"

The three of them embraced and laughed and wept and then laughed again. Margritte pulled back and extended a hand to Cathy, drawing her into the circle. They stood, arms about each other's shoulders, taking in the sight of each other.

"In case you were wondering," Charlotte said. "My husband is still a troll of a man."

"The curse is gone!" Margritte cheered.

"I can say what I please again, thanks to a rather dashing friend of Cathy's. But I'll take more care than I did before."

"This is all desperately exciting and wonderful," Natasha said, "but we can't weep all night. It's already 3 o'clock in the morning and we don't have all of the proposed changes for the Court drafted yet."

"You haven't changed either," Margritte said, kissing her on the cheek.

"Before we get to work," Cathy said, going to the teapot, "a toast. Ladies, I will charge your cups." When they each had a cup of tea, Cathy held hers high and said "To…"

"Freedom of Speech," said Charlotte.

"The brave women – and men – who went before us," said Natasha.

"Absent friends and loved ones," said Margritte.

"The future," said Cathy, chinking cups. "And all who sail in her!"

●●●●

Sam pushed the keycard into the slot and adjusted the package under his arm as the door beeped and clicked open. He switched on the light, put the package to one side and took a brief look down the corridor before closing the door behind him.

The boxes were as he'd left them, along with her letters. He unwrapped the package and propped the photo of him and Leanne laughing in the field against a box, having reclaimed it earlier from the storage facility his house contents had been moved into.

He sat where he had before and read the last five letters Leanne had left him. He looked at the photo of her, letting the memory play out. He thought he would cry, having struggled to hold it in when he got it back in Exilium, but instead he felt calm.

He pulled out a notepad and pen from his rucksack and leaned back. He looked at Leanne's long hair, the way her head was tipped back and how the laughter had seized her totally.

Dear Leanne,

I suppose it's a bit weird, writing to you when you're dead, but seeing as you wrote letters to me that could only be read once you'd died it kind of fits.

I didn't speak very well at your funeral. I was all fucked up and angry and I think I was mostly angry at you. Don't get me wrong, I wanted to tear Neugent a new one, but I felt like I had to speak about someone else in front of all of those people from your work life. I felt like you'd left me behind. I suppose you did, in a way, but not because I wasn't good enough and that makes all the difference to me.

Knowing what you were doing makes all the difference too. When I think about you now I feel proud. I was married to someone brave who wanted to kick a giant in the ass and that's cool. It

*beats the hell out of grieving for someone I thought was a shallow
corporate sell-out, I can tell you that! Or, I would, if you were here.*

*You were brave, Lee. And I love you more for that now than I
did when we were messing it all up between us. But I can look back
at that and think, "She had a lot on her mind" and I can look back
at who I was back then and think, "He didn't have a fucking clue"
and then it's neither of our faults. See? Much better.*

*Now I'm crying. It's OK, no one can see me. I'm sitting with all
your boxes and, before I go, I'm going to pick one out at random
and I'm going to fix the first problem I find inside. I can do that
now. I wish you could see it. I don't believe you're watching from a
cloud. I think you're just dust now. Do you remember that thing on
Facebook I showed you? Probably not, you were stressed out at the
time. It was by that Carl Sagan bloke, I think. Something about us
all being starstuff. The bits that you were made of are now off doing
new things like making tree molecules and rainwater and I don't
know. Snow. Hopefully snow. You used to love that.*

*I love you, Lee. I'm going to try and fix all this shit you worked
your ass off to find out. I might take a while, but I will.*

Yours,

Sam
Mr Ferran
Lord Iron
Prince Fuckwit

He folded it over and kissed it and laid it on top of her
letters. He let himself sit and cry a while. It was supposed to
be healthy or something. It mostly felt like shit but when it
was over he felt like he'd done something important.

The first file he pulled out of the nearest box detailed the
terrible conditions endured by inhabitants of a village in

India located on top of a massive coal deposit. Leanne had painstakingly uncovered a series of secret payments from a subsidiary of CoFerrum Inc to incentivise the mining company to use open-cast techniques to up their production. In addition, she'd detailed overheard conversations about encouraging the company to leave underground fires burning in an effort to drive the villagers away.

It wasn't working; the people didn't have the financial means to move and were offered no help to do so. People were suffering from dozens of pollution-related illnesses and the average lifespan was over ten years lower than the national one. At first he couldn't see why Ferran was interested in the place, but then realised the cheap coal was used nearby in iron ore production.

Sam memorised the name of the village, the companies involved and the names mentioned in her report, then slid it back into place. He put his rucksack back on, kissed his fingers and pressed them to her lips in the photo and then left, locking his letter in with her legacy.

30

Cathy didn't dare sit down. If she did, she'd fall asleep. They'd brainstormed ideas, welcoming Will into the discussion after he'd snatched a couple of hours' sleep and agreeing on what should be announced at the Court that day. Occasionally she'd had to sit back and take a moment to realise it was actually happening. Miss Rainer was restored, Charlotte was free of the curse her husband had placed upon her, and Margritte and Will were working together. She felt exhausted and elated, excited and terrified all at once.

She looked at the clock. It was five to ten in the morning and Dame Iris would be arriving any moment. "Carter, could you check that Morgan has everything ready for the Dame's visit?"

He left and she began to pace. When she heard the sound of horses' hooves she went to the window and saw the Dame's carriage entering the driveway. Cathy smoothed down her dress, feeling sick. It wasn't one the Dame had commissioned on her behalf and it was bound to be the first thing she commented on, but being able to breathe easily was worth it.

"Everything is ready, your Grace," Carter said. "The Dame won't see anyone or anything out of the ordinary."

Managing a nervous smile, Cathy peeped from behind the curtain as the carriage stopped and the footman helped the Dame to step down. She still hadn't decided how she was going to start the conversation. As the clock struck ten the doorbell rang and Cathy fiddled nervously with her gloves as she heard Morgan escorting the Dame down the hallway.

"I won't let her do anything to you," Carter whispered.

There was a single knock on the door and Morgan entered. "Dame Iris," he announced and she entered in her usual haughty manner.

"Dame Iris," Cathy said and curtsied.

"Good morning, Catherine. I was heartened to receive your invitation, despite the inconvenience of the hour. It's quite refreshing to be invited rather than–" She stopped and frowned at Cathy's gown. "Oh, for goodness' sake, child, I thought we'd progressed past my having to select your outfits for the day. Do you intend to wear that to Court?"

"Yes, I do. Would you like tea?"

The Dame sniffed. "It is the height of laziness to receive a guest for morning tea in the same gown one intends to wear to Court. As you can see, I have taken the trouble to dress appropriately and will have the inconvenience of returning home to change before going to the Tower." When Cathy didn't reply, the Dame pursed her lips and said, "Well, inappropriate attire or no, to business." She reached into her reticule as Cathy watched, realising the Dame was going to drive the conversation whatever she said. She didn't seem to have noticed that Carter had remained inside the room and was standing by the door. Perhaps she had, and was simply demonstrating how expert she was at ignoring the servants.

"I understand Nathaniel is the Chancellor of Oxenford now."

"Yes." Dame Iris smiled as she pulled out a small pair of opera glasses. "He'll bring that archaic city into line in no time. I trust William is settled?"

"Yes," Cathy replied. "He's resting."

The Dame held the glasses up and looked through them at her. Her lips thinned into a disapproving line. "Still not pregnant, I see. Really Catherine, is it so difficult?" She folded the glasses closed and dropped them back into the reticule. "Perhaps I should be more sympathetic. After all, it must be a chore for William to have to do his duty with such a plain girl."

Cathy dug her nails into her palms, taking a breath to speak but the Dame was already fishing something else out of the bag.

"You need to drink this. You'll fall pregnant the next time he exercises his marital rights. As it's extraordinarily expensive and rather rare, I wish you to drink it in front of me. Then I can be certain you haven't failed to do that either."

"Dame Iris," Cathy said, taking the small glass bottle from her. "It may come as a surprise to you, but I didn't invite you here to belittle me."

"I beg your pardon?"

"Yes, I thought you'd find that difficult to understand." She raised the hand holding the glass bottle and then let it drop from her fingers. It smashed when it hit the edge of the table. "That's what I think of that."

For a few seconds the Dame just stared, open-mouthed, at the liquid dripping onto the rug below.

"*If* Will and I do decide to have a child it will be on *our* terms. I'm not going to let you make me feel inadequate any more. You're nothing but a bully, using your power to make all of the women in the Iris family terrified when you should be doing all you can to protect them from Lord Iris and this shitty Society we're forced to live in."

"How dare you!" The tip of Dame Iris' nose had turned an interesting shade of pink. "You insult me and make it clear you intend to disobey our Patron? I underestimated how irretrievably stupid you are."

"You did underestimate me, but don't feel bad – everyone else does. I'm not going to do anything you tell me to any more. I'm not going to thread another sodding embroidery needle. I'm not going to spend another minute of my life listening to you and your cronies keeping the pecking order with gossip and social cruelty."

"What gives you the right to speak to me like this?"

"Knowledge. I know what you did to get the power you have now."

The Dame's lips closed and she drew herself up to her full height. Her hand was swinging for Cathy's face before she'd even registered the movement, but Carter caught her wrist and turned her hand palm up. A tiny needle was poking from the inside of a gold ring.

"I saw her twist the ring, your Grace," Carter explained as the Dame cried out. "It could be poison or a curse."

"You're well-versed in curses, aren't you?" Cathy said. "You should know that I'm wearing a gift from my husband that will protect me from any Charms that you try to use on me, including the Fool's Charm. My bodyguard is also protected, as you might expect."

"This is unacceptable! Unhand me, you awful man!"

Cathy shook her head at Carter and he kept hold of her wrist. "You cursed the former Dame Iris to always speak the truth. It might seem harmless, but in the Londinium Court nothing could be more destructive."

"What nonsense is this?"

"But you only cursed her after you'd wheedled your way into her husband's affections and all but convinced him that his wife was going mad. It happens, after all. Some people can't cope with life in the Nether. I imagine you said something very like that to him."

"I... I did nothing of the sort."

"You put a thought in his head and then cursed her just before a critical soirée. You played the concerned friend, rushing to find him as the curse forced her to say things we all might think but would never say. You convinced him she had to be removed, that Lord Iris wouldn't stand for anything but perfection, after all."

She'd given up denying it and had started to look like she might faint. Cathy didn't put it past her to fake that, though, so she pressed on. "You might be wondering how I could know all this."

"I won't ask because it isn't true."

"Eleanor told me herself."

The Dame shuddered and her gasp was so sharp that Carter put his other hand on her shoulder, readying himself to catch her.

"She's still cursed, you see. She still can't help but tell the truth. I offered to lift it from her – yes, I could do that, if I wanted to – but she refused the offer. She's amazing. She said that being known as a truly honest person is remarkably liberating."

"She's dead," the Dame whispered. "You're lying."

"There was someone else you underestimated: your husband. He loved her and he couldn't bring himself to kill her, so he had her taken away to a secret asylum. You'll be finding out a lot more about that very soon – if you choose to come to Court now. You do look rather unwell."

"I will see to it that Lord Iris punishes you himself."

"No, you won't. Because if you do anything like that, or try to curse or Charm me ever again, I'll tell Sir Iris all that I know. And what's more, I'll reunite him with his first wife."

"I refuse to be treated with such disrespect! Call your dog off me! How dare you accuse me of something so preposterous!"

"You still don't believe me?" Cathy nodded. "We thought you'd find it hard after all these years of being queen bee." She went into the hallway and called for Eleanor, who came out of the room next door, her face flushed with excitement.

"Is it time for my dramatic entrance?"

"Yep."

Carter let Dame Iris turn, but still kept hold of her wrist. Eleanor came to the doorway, dressed in a fine black velvet gown, her white hair arranged in a luxurious loose bun of the Edwardian style.

"Rumours of my death–" Eleanor began but Dame Iris collapsed in a dead faint before she could finish the line. "Well, how irritating. I've always wanted to say that."

Carter laid Dame Iris on the sofa.

"Well, I think she's convinced now," Cathy said. "Eleanor, I really do think you should take up my friend's offer to stay with him. He'll be able to protect you better than anyone else."

"That smartly dressed young man everyone's been talking about? I may well do that. I imagine she'll be keen to do something despicable to keep me secret. You need to be careful too. You're making a lot of enemies in a very short period of time."

Cathy nodded. "I know. Carter, keep an eye on her. I'll send for her footman and they can take her home. If you'll excuse me, Eleanor, I need to get ready for the Court."

From her bedroom window she watched the Dame being carried into the carriage and reviewed the confrontation. She could get used to standing up for herself. But she wasn't going to gloat; both the Dame and the Agency would be seeking to have her removed now. Even though Sam had promised to protect her if Lord Iris summoned her, she knew it was only a short-term solution.

"How did it go?" Will asked from the doorway.

"Well, I think. She fainted anyway. I'll take that as a win. Carter was ace."

Will looked tired, but his injuries had been dealt with by a Charm – either glamoured or healed, she wasn't sure which one. "You look beautiful," he said. "Tackling Dames evidently suits you."

"So do you. Have you heard anything from Nathaniel?"

"No. I imagine he's too embarrassed to admit he's lost his first prisoner."

"He won't be too embarrassed to hunt for her though."

"No, but I've given Margritte a powerful Shadow Charm. She'll be safe until we think of a better long-term solution."

Cathy smiled as he came towards her. "You must have spent a small fortune on Charms in the last twenty-four hours."

"It's no trouble," he said and kissed her tenderly. "So how does it feel to be a force of chaos and destruction?"

She laughed. "Brilliant, actually. Is it time to leave?"

"Yes. Charlotte's already gone ahead. It's quite a team you've put together."

"Do you think we can do this, Will? Do you think we can actually change things?"

"We already have," he said, drawing her into his arms. "I don't know if we'll be able to do everything we want before Lord Iris intervenes or the Patroons mobilise against us, but we'll give it a good try. Are you ready?"

"No." Cathy rested her head against his chest, allowing herself a moment of comfort. "But I don't think I'll ever be."

They rode to the Tower in silence, sitting side by side, her fingers laced between his. She tried to think through what she was going to say and the possible responses and the ways she could handle each one, but it soon unravelled into nebulous fears. She thought of Sophia and whether to talk to Will about her theory about his uncle but decided it wasn't the right time. And what use would it serve him to know anyway?

She wondered how Josh was and whether he'd found happiness. She remembered when she'd thought she was in love with him, and knew now that it wasn't real. She squeezed Will's hand, felt him squeeze hers back, each comforted by knowing the other was there. He wasn't the man she'd wanted to marry but somehow they were making a life together. Did he really say that he loved her, the night before? Was that possible?

She thought of the third wish and what Poppy had said. What was her true potential? Could anyone really know before they'd fulfilled it? All she knew was that it felt like she was going in the right direction and no one had stopped her yet. She wondered if the magic had made Will so agreeable to her ideas and decided to put that from her mind. There was no way to know and she didn't want to destroy something wonderful with her neurotic doubts. He'd realised they had to move forward now and he was supporting her.

They arrived and went to the private antechamber. She picked a thread off his sleeve and he tucked a strand of hair behind her ear. He gave a nod to the page and the doors were opened onto the Court.

"The Duke and Duchess of Londinium."

They entered and walked past the residents of the city, each bowing and curtsying as they passed. They reached the gilded chairs and sat. Cathy sought out Charlotte in the crowd. She felt better when their eyes met and Charlotte gave her a look of absolute confidence.

"Many of you may have heard rumours that Oxenford has a new Chancellor," Will began. "I can confirm this is true." He paused as a murmur passed through the assembled. "As a new era begins for that city, so does a new era begin for Londinium. You know I'm a man of change. You know I'm not afraid to make promises and see them through. I've made the roads of this city safe and returned cherished jewels to many of you in this room. It's time to make more changes, some of which have never been seen in Albion. You have my word that these are not embarked upon lightly, nor will they be made without the interests of the people of this city at heart."

He looked at Cathy and she knew it was time for her to speak. "I know it isn't customary for the Duchess to address the Court, but, as William said, things are going to change." She stood as looks of surprise, indignation and doubt were exchanged in the crowd, and waited a moment for them to settle again.

Cathy felt a rush in her chest, a sure knowledge that everything had been building to this moment, this opportunity with boundless repercussions. There was no fear. There was no doubt. Only potential.

ACKNOWLEDGMENTS

It's inevitable that the same names will crop up here, seeing as this is the third in a series, but that doesn't mean those people shouldn't be mentioned again. As before, thanks to my editor Lee Harris and my agent Jennifer Udden for comments and encouragement about the book in its early forms. Thanks, always, to Peter for listening, commenting, checking the manuscript for stupidity and keeping me sane when the Fear was at its most horrible. Thanks to Kate for arranging the research trip to Lincoln College in Oxford on top of all the other support and general brilliance.

Speaking of that trip, I'd like to thank Laura Broadhurst who was kind enough to give us a tour of Lincoln College and answer all sorts of questions that might well have seemed odd at the time!

Thanks to my friends and family for supporting me through the new and... interesting territory of trying to finish a book whilst launching the first in the series.

And my last but not least goes to the fine people who have read the Split Worlds series, blogged about it, tweeted about it, said lovely things on Facebook and contacted me to say how much they've enjoyed it. Thank you, a thousand times, thank you. Knowing that I've made people love, worry about and shout at the characters who have been resident in my head for such a long time has given me the deepest pleasure.

About the Author

Emma Newman was born in a tiny coastal village in Cornwall during one of the hottest summers on record. Four years later she started to write stories and never stopped until she penned a short story that secured her a place at Oxford University to read Experimental Psychology.

In 2011 Emma embarked on an ambitious project to write and distribute one short story per week – all of them set in her Split Worlds milieu – completely free to her mailing list subscribers.

A debut short-story collection, *From Dark Places*, was published in 2011 and her debut post-apocalyptic novel for young adults, *20 Years Later*, was published just one year later – presumably Emma didn't want to wait another nineteen… Emma is also a professional audiobook narrator.

She now lives in Somerset with her husband, son and far too many books.

enewman.co.uk
twitter.com/EmApocalyptic

Read over fifty short stories by Emma based in the Split Worlds at

SplitWorlds.com